Long Walk Home

...a Civil War infantry soldier's love story

by James Funk

Dust Jacket Summary

Events spiral out of control for a young family just making ends meet on a small farm in rural Michigan. Civil War erupts. Reluctantly, Will Hodkins finds peer pressure and pride in country irresistible, causing him to volunteer as infantry foot soldier in the Union army. Answering an inner call to duty, he leaves behind wife Maria and two toddler sons. Can a simple brown leather-covered journal, a parting gift from Maria, become Will's lifeline? Or, tender exchange of letters between two lovers documenting travails?

Through brutal winter in army camp, Will and seven friends bond to become 'surrogate family' helping each other survive ...even as tragedy and loss strike. Meanwhile, back home Maria struggles to keep farm and children ...family loyalty ultimately tested by dramatic twists of irony.

Whether ambushed in Kentucky by regaled Confederate John Morgan's raiders, or awaiting epic battle alongside Chickamauga creek in Tennessee/Georgia, fear, bravery and heroics, honor and fortitude collide with weakness and treachery ...lives changed forever, even destroyed. Can Will Hodkins survive? After all, it is a promise made to Maria ...to get back home.

About the Author

James Funk draws on extensive education and diverse career to entertain readers with a refreshing, new and creative approach to storytelling. James Funk's career spans 35 years, since completing undergraduate education in electrical engineering at Northwestern University, and a master's degree in business at Stanford University. Experience includes executive in the automotive industry with Ford Motor Company, and builder and restorer of residential homes. He has been a golf course owner, builder, and operator.

Jim and wife, Marilyn, reside in Charleston, South Carolina.

See Author's Website: **www.james-funk.com**

Long Walk Home

...a Civil War infantry soldier's love story

A Novel

By: James Funk

This book is a work of fiction, although based upon historical events and situations which are true. Names and places, as well as detailed descriptions, have been changed to protect the privacy of all individuals.

ISBN: 978-0-615-52260-9 (e-book)

10-digit: 0615522602
13-digit: 9780615522609

Printed in the United States of America
Charleston, SC

Dedication

To Marilyn, wife and partner, friend and companion …for support, encouragement, and valuable assistance in writing the compelling love story based upon her great grandparents, Will and Maria. Will and Maria's nearly 150-year old journals are precious testimony to their life and their struggle.

Curiosity and research of Marilyn's cousins, Glenn and Marlene Hales, sparked first idea for this fictional story of a family torn apart by national tragedy …the story of Will and Maria, but mere thread in fuller fabric depicting Civil War's impact on lives of so many 'Americans' …both North and South. Their courage, sacrifice, and dedication shape our lives to this day.

Prologue

February 11th, 1861, dawned dank, gray, and windy in the South Carolina harbor of Charleston, where trapped and surrounded Federal soldiers awaited destiny within the island fortress of Fort Sumter. At that moment, in Springfield, Illinois, a special train belched smoke at the station, ready to carry beardless Abraham Lincoln on a journey to presidential inauguration in Washington. At 6'4" in height, with sleeves of black dress coat short by inches, and too-short trousers exposing large feet, Lincoln stood on train depot platform ready to board. He was about to be handed the problem in Charleston. The South was preparing for possible clash with soon-to-be inaugurated President Lincoln. States reacted similarly. Seven states followed South Carolina to secede, and vast numbers of weapons, ordinance, and property were seized by secessionists. Then, on March 6th, the South's President Jefferson Davis called for 100,000 volunteers to serve the Confederacy for twelve months …Confederates soon outnumbered U.S. Army by more than 3 to 1. Meanwhile, Lincoln was taking steps to get large feet firmly grounded.

Rain fell on Sunday, April 7th, in Charleston as churches filled with parishioners praying for God's continued blessing over their beloved city. In town, soldiers gathered weapons, awaiting a signal should bells of St. Michael's church toll …war imminent, but still no one really expecting it. Then, the city sprang into action. At midnight, April 8th, bells of St. Michael's sounded a call to action. Citadel cadets signaled with seven gun volley. Next several days, streets were bustling with messengers darting in all directions, on foot and on horseback. Uniformed soldiers were on

7

the move. Boats were launched to batteries at all points around Charleston harbor. Citizens watched, excitedly circulating rumors from street to street. Residents expected bombardment to begin anytime. Evening of April 11th, onlookers began drifting toward the Battery to form a growing crowd positioning for best view of the harbor. Suddenly cannons erupted with thunderous repetitive fury, their flash illuminating billowing traces of white smoke drifting upward into early morning darkness, while fiery projectiles arched overhead wending and hissing over water toward the hapless island target of Fort Sumter. Barrage continued.

Morning rose over Charleston on April 12th, with clouds and heavy mist hanging over harbor, concealing visibility of batteries on surrounding islands. By 6:30 AM, Fort Sumter still had not returned fire, although Confederate General Beauregard's guns fired about two hundred cannon shots ...island fortress taking a terrific beating. Then, Federal General Anderson's guns began to return fire. By mid-morning, rain started falling heavily, forcing citizen onlookers to disperse. It was as if sky were crying, tears falling as rainfall over doomed city ...foretelling horrific price and suffering sustained by both sides, throughout long and terrible 'un-Civil' war.

The South stood up to Lincoln, but Lincoln succeeded in goading the Confederacy into taking first artillery shots. The North exploded with anger at a flagrant affront to national honor, further uniting behind Lincoln. Lincoln acted by requesting Union states for a militia of 75,000 men to be called to duty for ninety days to counter Confederate threat and force secessionists to back down. But, the opposite occurred. The Confederacy viewed Lincoln's call-up of militia as a declaration of war, and responded by gearing defenses for the threat of invasion by the North. Four more southern states seceded. Now, eleven states comprised the Confederacy.

Distortion of passion and growing sense of hatred between North and South burst into gunfire at Fort Sumter in April 1861. Long years of sectional debate created deepening hostility. During the preceding decade, 'Americans' faced-off with growing feeling of hurt pride, distrust, and self-righteousness ...feelings eroded from spirited debate into shouting, and now into shooting. Across the land, public clamor developed to do battle …sooner rather than later. Each side prepared for combat to defend its homeland. Most Americans believed a single climatic battle, with decisive victory, would bring both sides to reason and persuade politicians to abandon war and settle conflict. Calls for volunteers sounded far and wide.

Michigan promptly met President Lincoln's initial national call for 75,000 volunteers to serve for three months. Enrollment of nearly 800 Michigan volunteers were equipped, uniformed and armed, departing Michigan in May 1861. All eyes turned to Manassas, Virginia, a scant twenty miles from Washington. Small town Oxford, Michigan, buzzed about the Michigan regiment's role at Manassas in July at the battle of Bull Run. Confederates won the first great battle. Yankees were whipped …North stunned. South's confidence soared.

Across America, public response to call to arms was contagious …citizens and community leaders in small towns and large cities reacted with unbelievable zeal. A new generation of Americans stepped forward enthusiastically, in proud tradition of their patriotic forefathers …an answer both spontaneous and exuberant. From farms and factories, schools and shops, tens of thousands answered the call …men and boys …all flocking to enlist with unknowing excitement, as if on the way to festive entertainment. Tiny Oxford, Michigan, was no different.

With military campaigns underway in both eastern and western theatres of war, President Lincoln issued a call on July 1st, 1862, for an additional 300,000 volunteers for the Union Army …Michigan's quota nearly 12,000 men. On July 15th, Governor Austin Blair of Michigan issued General Order No. 154, to raise regiments of volunteers, including a regiment to be known as the '22nd Michigan Infantry Volunteers' from the 5th Congressional District, which included the counties of Oakland, Livingston, Lapeer, Macomb, St. Clair, and Sanilac. The 22nd Michigan Infantry regiment was to rendezvous in Pontiac, Michigan.

No more shall the war-cry sever,
Or, the widening rivers be red;
Our anger is banished forever,
When are laurelled the graves of our dead!

Under the sod and the dew,
Waiting the judgment day;
Love and tears, for the Blue,
Tears and love, for the Gray!

****F.M. Finch

Chapter 1

He lay hunkered down in grassy ditch, aside steep mountain wagon trail, still rutted from torrential rains weeks ago that turned roadways into muddy quagmires ...but now roadway turned dustbowl from days of oppressive scorching heat. Back slumped forward, as if propped in place, knees drawn against chest. Arms encircled knees, clutching to steady weary body. Head bowed-down, leather brim of navy blue kepi cap bobbed against wooly sweat-stained pant legs. This forlorn figure dozed off and on, desperately capturing fleeting moments of sleep.

Will Hodkins was a down and dirty, foot-slogging infantry soldier, a private in the Union Army caught in a most 'un-Civil' war. Sleep was precious, after agonizing days marching across rugged mountainous countryside where lower Tennessee and northern Alabama and Georgia meet. Face unshaven, skin ruggedly tanned and weathered, he was caked with streaks of mud from roadway's ankle-deep dust and soot of campfire smoke, matted by perspiration from 90° heat. Jet-black hair, overly long, disheveled and dirty, sprang haphazardly from under cap. Blue greatcoat was grimy, its wool fabric much too heavy for unusually hot mid-September days ...boots worn and dusty. Feet ached. Overly tired leg muscles twitched sporadic from over-exertion after long days of endless marching. Alongside, knapsack and haversack lay on the ground, rifle propped against them ...nearly empty canteen nearby.

Eyes flicked open, rest too brief ...he gulped to clear parched throat, but no saliva ...only gritty dryness. Burning heat of mid-day sun baked sweating skin. Eyes squinted against sun's unrelenting rays …sunshine glistening and sparkling through branches of huge oak and cedar trees lining steep roadway. Massive trees stretched gigantic limbs skyward in majestic beauty, silhouetted against deep blue sky, broken only by wispy white clouds drifting ...cooler shade under tree's canopy so tantalizing, but not within grasp. Will Hodkins watched intently as a red-tailed hawk glided effortlessly, carefree across sky's backdrop. Glancing left beyond tree line, a series of limestone boulders and outcroppings wedged up steep mountain slope to its crest. Below in distance, the Tennessee River snaked serpentine-like through lush green valley ...all so beautiful …seemingly so peaceful.

Sporadic gentle breeze now and again moved treetop branches …grassy fields visible down valley wavered. Nearby clumps of black-eyed susans swayed in occasional breeze, golden yellow petals and black centers dancing ditch-side. Will Hodkins noted with pleasure a welcome symphony of modest movement …tree branches, grasses, and flowers …enjoying rare instance of cooling breeze on sweaty sun-baked skin. Dwarfed by grandeur of huge trees, grassy fields, and craggy mountainside thrusting skyward, Will felt utterly small and powerless gazing upward from resting place low in roadside ditch. Fatigue compounded helpless feeling, because morning's walk was brisk and arduous, like proceeding miles and days of unending march since leaving Nashville.

Will was not alone. Hundreds of fellow soldiers were roadside …each searching for rest in ditches on both sides of roadway. Meanwhile, sentries walked patrol in constant watch for enemy, marauding Rebels bent on disrupting Union supply lines. Horse-drawn supply wagons lined roadway, snaking a trail upward from river valley below. Will and Union comrades were somewhere near Chattanooga, in foothills of Lookout Mountain ….either in Georgia, Alabama, or Tennessee …three state borders meeting somewhere nearby. Will and enlisted friends were forced to guess exact locations and destinations, as officers of the Federal 'Army of the Cumberland' kept information under wraps. It was September 1863, and so much happened over twelve months, since 'Company A' of the '22nd Michigan Infantry Volunteers' mustered into service of the United States Union Army.

Right hand reaching to breast pocket of greatcoat, Will Hodkins clutched the trusty well-worn journal he kept dear. A little black hardcover journal with brown binding grew precious over the last year. Written within were innermost feelings, descriptions of suffering endured, fear and loss ...emptiness from being separated from home and family. On its pages, Will described soldier friends who shared this war ...friends who had become adopted 'family'.

Just touching the journal gave Will renewed sense of strength, security and purpose ...feelings often waning ...feelings he struggled to maintain through desperate times. The journal was a gift from Maria, sweetheart and bride, given the night before he left home. He remembered Maria's urging to write often, as they embraced and passionately kissed goodbye that last morning ...family left behind as he joined volunteer infantry rendezvousing in Pontiac, Michigan. Over the last year, Will scribbled words quickly onto lined page, capturing thoughts in brief moments ...other time, spending hours into lonely night, composing letters to Maria and family back home on their farm in Oxford, Michigan. The journal was his lifeline.

Looking sideway, Will plucked one black-eyed susan from a flower cluster growing in the ditch alongside. He stared longingly and lovingly at its golden yellow petals ...before murmuring softly so no one could hear, *"I miss you so very much, Maria. God, give me strength to get back home ...to you and our boys. Help me make them proud."*

He gently placed the single flower between pages of journal. When he posted a next letter to Maria, he would place the flower within folds of his letter. Will and Maria traded flowers via letters, a practice two lovers repeated time and again, linking romantically in a small and tender way though circumstance and distance separated them. Will looked down through misty eyes as a droplet of sweat from his brow landed on journal's cover ...as if a tear had fallen. He carefully brushed away its moisture, not wanting to soil the cover. Now, Will's thoughts drifted back to earlier days with Maria ...before military service ...while gripping tightly to worn cover of treasured journal.

Chapter 2

Will's thoughts raced back to just over a year earlier before enlistment. Life was good for Will and Maria on their small farm in tiny rural Oxford, Michigan, about fourteen miles north of Pontiac and northwest of Detroit. He mulled how quickly events occurred since meeting Maria six years ago, while visiting St. Louis. In determined manner, he followed Maria back to her home in the 'Finger Lakes' region of western New York State. In small town Penn Yan, he found odd jobs to make ends meet over two years as he courted Maria. It was torrid courtship, filled with unbridled romance, fired by passion of youth. Reverend BF Bradford married the young couple in a small family ceremony in Maria's Methodist church in nearby Jerusalem, Yates County, NY …four years ago on February 2nd, 1859 …such a happy four years.

After marriage, he moved Maria to Michigan to the family farm where he grew up. *"...farm means so much to me..."* he murmured, recalling his upbringing. Father came to America as a young man from Newcastle, England, and bravely started farming in what was uncharted wilderness. *"...Father toiled so hard"* …building a small 59-acre plot at town's edge into a successful farm and comfortable home. Mother died early with Will an only child, to be raised by Father. He left the farm as a young man shortly after Father's untimely death …loss and grieving too great. Travel offered escape …it was in traveling that he met Maria in St. Louis. The farm, left vacant and neglected, needed tending. So, with youth and enthusiasm of a newly married couple, they ventured west to start a new life on Will's farm, far from Maria's family …and her beloved Penn Yan.

14

Will was twenty-one years old ...three years younger than Maria. But age was not the only difference ...her background was so different ...a troubling difference despite best effort to dismiss lingering doubt. *"How can I be deserving of such a refined and beautiful lady?"* His education and upbringing were basic. Knowledge came from day-to-day first-hand teachings of Father, a hands-on farmer ...core values of hard work, dedication, and tenacity. Will remembered always trying to please Father. It was important that Father be proud. Often, Father said, *"Good job, Will ...do your best, and everything will work out"* ...advice Will took to heart. Father's compliment meant a great deal ...giving immense pleasure ...driving him to work even harder. Their relationship could not have been closer, and Will cherished memories.

Maria's upbringing was more polished and childhood more comfortable. Her father died early, when Maria was five years old. She was raised by her mother, in a household with two younger brothers, Joseph and Jared. Older sister, Louisa, died as a five month-old infant before Maria was born. Maria's mother was well-educated, and saw to it that Maria had similar opportunity. She read to Maria constantly. Aunts and uncles were nearby, and Maria cherished many hours and good times they shared ...Uncle Hixon and Aunt Rebecca, and Uncle Kelsey and Aunt Minerva. Aunts and uncles helped raise Maria and her brothers after their mother's death when Maria was nine years old.

Maria was well educated and loved to write. She was unabashed romantic...first capturing in a journal recollection of sermons from the Methodist church her family attended regularly. As she grew into young woman, she wrote extensively in her journal of romantic thoughts, including brief romances, and courtship with Will. She was given chance to travel widely, especially after completion of formal schooling. It was on such a trip to St. Louis for an extended stay that she met Will.

Maria, c. 24 years old in Penn Yan

Over four years of marriage, Will harbored agonizing thoughts of guilt and self-doubt …lingering worries he could not dispel …'thoughts' of causing Maria loss and loneliness from leaving extended family behind in Penn Yan. After all, he dragged her away …heading off to rugged unknown of Michigan and more difficult life. Anxiety gnawed away …operating below surface, deep within and unspoken. It was nothing voiced by Maria. *"She is always strong and positive …I am so proud of how she adapted to our new life …she never complains,"* he mused. Meanwhile, time passed quickly for them, both toiling hard on their small plot of ground, struggling to make ends meet. It did not take long to start a family …now, children kept them busy …William, Jr. born about nine months after marriage, and second-son, Walter, following eighteen months later.

Complicating matters, times in America were growing troublesome. Will and Maria, and a dear cousin, Robert, became entangled in a messy situation not of their making. Will's mind shifted to recall how circumstances occurred. Will's cousin, Robert Hodkins, emigrated years earlier with parents from England, to Charleston, South Carolina, and family lived nearly twenty years in the South. Robert visited Michigan with parents regularly as a young boy, and stayed with Will's family a number of times. So, Will and Robert became close. Their relationship was rekindled for Will when Robert began writing letters to Will and Maria, wrapped in emotion and describing events getting out of hand in Charleston. Robert was an adopted 'Southerner', and saw things different from Will and Maria.

Charleston was a bustling port city, and cotton changed people's lives ...it became 'King'. Robert was in his twenties, and working for a successful cotton merchant at a warehouse just off wharves on East Bay Street ...watching first-hand, how 'King Cotton' affected people's lives. Prosperity shone on antebellum Charleston's wealthy like nowhere else. But slavery was bedrock to the South's economic success, and its survival was becoming subject for growing debate. Southern planter with opulent lifestyle, and influential and wealthy merchants and professional people who profited and shared this lifestyle, had much to lose from threat to 'Southern way of life'.

Will visited Robert in Charleston only once, when Will was just twelve years old and Robert fifteen, but the city made lasting impression. Coincident with Will's visit, a great event occurred, spectacle indelible in Will's memory. South's highest ranking political statesman, John C. Calhoun, died in April 1850. Calhoun preached that slavery was 'good', and leaders of Charleston and throughout the South listened and believed. Then, a foremost political voice championing slavery in America fell silent. Calhoun's great funeral was held in Charleston, and Will and Robert happened to be witnesses, wide-eyed and impressionable. Will stood by Robert's side, awe and pageantry holding each silent. A funeral cortege assembled in Charleston's Marion Square, alongside the Citadel military academy's towering stucco walls and parapets, which reached skyward in majestic magnificence. With honor guards and distinguished pall bearers, including Jefferson Davis, the funeral cortege began its procession. A stillness and somber gloom filled air, as funeral procession moved through streets. The boys darted along blue slate sidewalks to follow, moving in and out through throngs of onlookers, lined several persons deep...all mourning and many weeping. The cortege moved down King Street with its string of shops, turned left onto Hasell Street to Meeting Street, and then moved down Meeting Street to a magnificent residential area overlooking Charleston harbor, known as 'the Battery' ...Atlantic ocean easily visible across Charleston harbor, merely a few miles onto horizon. Will never forgot splendid mansions lining the Battery, magnificent stately houses tucked pretentious beyond walled and gardened courtyard entries, so splendid ...beyond anything Will imagined.

Charleston, SC, c.1850

(Library of Congress)

Will remembered talking with Robert, late into night. Youthful exuberance caused them to bubble with excitement...back and forth they chatted and recalled details of awesome funeral spectacle. Will carried back to Michigan fond

18

memories of the grand city of Charleston ...its three rivers surrounding peninsula, emptying into harbor ...harbor reaching out to ocean, clear silhouette of Fort Sumter looming on horizon. Neither boy could ever anticipate events in Charleston harbor that would shape lives forever.

Chapter 3

For the decade following Will's visit to Charleston, newspapers across America touted growing debate over slavery, but Will paid little attention ...such a remote issue. He was too busy growing up and worrying about their farm, and most recently, Maria and two young boys. Life was not complicated, but that was about to change. Over the last year and a half, cousin Robert wrote several letters to Will and Maria, vividly describing events taking place in Charleston. Will recalled Maria's remark upon receiving one letter ..."*he writes with such flair, descriptive detail and passion ...he should be a journalist.*"

Robert wrote:

December 22nd, 1860

"....two days ago, I observed the most exciting of times. I went to the train station to see delegates arrive for the State Convention being held in Charleston. Because of fear of smallpox outbreak, the Convention adjourned from Columbia, SC, and reassembled here in Charleston. I wanted to be a part of all this, and went to watch.

Delegates arrived to such a wildly cheering crowd, and a 15-gun salute that seemed to rock the train platform. Everyone was in such frenzy. I could not help but be caught up in all excitement. At their meeting, delegates voted to secede from Lincoln's government, and form our own government.

Last night the city celebrated with parades, while bon fires blazed in our streets well into night. Cannons were fired at the Citadel. Church bells of St. Michael's rang out in celebration. Taverns were bursting with revelers, overflow tumbling onto streets. Firecrackers were booming, and rockets blazed across night sky. It was like 4th of July celebration. What an unbelievable sight! ...wish you could have been here to share our celebration with me..."

Best wishes for a wonderful Christmas,

Your cousin,
Robert

Another letter followed a few days later, further describing events unfolding:

21

December 28th, 1860

"....yesterday, the city was again scene of most remarkable of events. I walked to the Battery (Will, you remember this area from your visit), because word circulated that U.S. Federal soldiers had moved under cover of night from Fort Moultrie, just across harbor from the city, to island fort in our harbor, called Fort Sumter.

You can imagine our shock when soldiers on Fort Sumter raised the 'stars and stripes' flag, seen by crowds assembling rapidly along the Battery. Emotion of citizens erupted with anger and outrage at such act of defiance against our State of South Carolina. Governor Pickens ordered our militia to assemble post-haste, and they marched from Citadel parade ground on Boundary Street to a wharf on the Cooper River.

I was part of a growing crowd watching Fort Sumter in the distance. As militia approached, the crowd erupted into boisterous, noisy cheering for our men, slapping backs as they passed, and waving white handkerchiefs. We watched a small group board a boat, and push off wharf. In 30 minutes, the boat reached Castle Pinckney, a smaller island-fort in the harbor and closer to the city. Soon, the U.S. flag was lowered, and our glorious Palmetto flag flying proudly, as Federal troops could be seen boarding small boats in retreat to Fort Sumter. Not a shot was fired. How magnificent!

We are so proud of our brave citizen-soldiers of Charleston...."

Your cousin,
Robert

With snow blowing and cold wind howling outside, Will and Maria passed a stack of Robert's letters back and forth. Will, Jr. was tucked into bed and all was quiet as fire blazed giving warmth to their cozy home. Will and Maria sat side-by-side at the split plank kitchen table. Will reminded Maria, "Father made this table from a cedar tree fallen at creek's edge."

Maria answered, touching his hand gently, "I know. I know ...you have told me several times." Will nodded with sheepish frown, rubbing a hand lightly over table top ...fond memories returning. This evening was no different from many others. Will and Maria often ended each day seated and talking well into night ...fire turning to last glowing embers.

Will extended a hand slowly, placing it tenderly over Maria's ...recalling for Maria his experience during that brief stay with Robert in Charleston in their youth. Light from two candles flickered, causing shadows to dance against rough hewn walls of planking. Will became more and more emotional, haltingly telling his story, head bowed slightly and eyes staring at tabletop. Maria noticed eyes glisten in soft candlelight as moisture swelled from deep feeling. Maria listened quietly and intently.

He looked up with story concluded, and pushed Robert's last letter aside hastily with disgust. Will spoke in softest voice, "...does not look good." Will was a man of few words. Head moved side to side ...parsed lips giving emphasis to words. "Fort Sumter 'belongs' to the city ...symbol of pride to its citizens, and the State of South Carolina."

Maria answered, "I now understand why Fort Sumter's occupation, by Major Anderson and U.S. Federal soldiers, is such an emotional jolt to citizens of Charleston ...and Robert. I think I know some of the feeling Major Anderson and his men must have as they are virtual prisoners within their own fortress ...neither side is willing to consider the other 'enemy', it seems."

With smile of pride, Will answered, "How did you get to be so smart?" Maria shrugged coyly. Will continued, "You are my best friend ...I love you so much."

Maria moved a hand on top of Will's, patting his hand as she answered with tenderness, "You are a good man, Will Hodkins." Then, Maria reached to touch Will's head, running fingers through pitch-black flowing locks. "By the way, you need a haircut, my friend ...I must get shears out soon ...your hair grows as quickly as corn in your fields."

"Same fertile soil ...both places," Will added with a stab at humor bringing self-satisfying smile.

Maria laughed, returning loving smile, their eyes meeting with matching twinkle. "You appreciate humor ...it re-energizes you ...I wish you could find it more often ...sometimes you are far too serious ...most times."

Will winked and rose from his chair, walking across the room to blow out two candles ...then, arm-in-arm they adjourned to their bedroom for evening.

Over the next several weeks, Will and Maria read in newspapers and listened to neighborly gossip in Oxford ...news of a series of extraordinary events. A move to Fort Sumter by Federal troops was viewed across the North as an act of patriotism and bravery 'to enforce law and preserve the Union' ...though neither side was ready for war, or willing to accept inevitability. Robert wrote in one letter:

"...December 31st was a cold blustery winter day, as we stood on the Battery with crowds of curious onlookers, watching a bustle of activity on city wharves, as steamers moved in the harbor to and from Morris Island, ferrying soldiers, slaves, munitions, and supplies."

Rumors were circulating that Federal reinforcements were headed to Charleston. Another letter from Robert followed:

"Morning of January 9th 1861 dawned with glorious "Carolina blue" sky, as seabirds swooped overhead amid light breeze. Faint misty haze hung over the harbor, with promise of quickly burning away in glistening morning sun, driving temperature into the sixties. It was ideal weather for the SC militia's patrol boat to spot a large Federal ship on horizon. A sentry at Citadel cadets' camp on Morris Island spotted a signal rocket from the patrol boat indicating approach of the "Star". The cadet commander aimed canon at bow of the approaching "Star", and fired canon. "Star" hastily

retreated out of canon range, and beat a swift retreat back toward New York."

In the city, all became frenzy. With sound of first canon shot echoing, rumors passed from street to street. Occupants streamed from homes to see what was happening. People were running everywhere to gain a vantage point, women in cumbersome long skirts, and men on horseback galloping toward the harbor. Each strained to catch a glimpse of action some six miles off shore ...some with spyglass or opera glass. Then, quickly, it was over".

Robert's descriptions followed in snippets from further letters:

"...at 4:00 AM, morning of April 12ᵗʰ, bells began tolling from church spire at St. Michael's.

And, then at 4:30 AM, Beauregard opened fire on Fort Sumter. In night's sky, the first mortar shell, quite visible with its fuse glowing in darkness and bright streamers trailing in shell's wake, arched high overhead toward Fort Sumter. Crowds of onlookers in *the city saw it explode, and heard its loud boom, like a 4th of July fireworks display.*

Pandemonium broke out on rooftops and in streets of Charleston. Streets and wharves quickly filled with people, scurrying everywhere to gain best vantage point. Cheers went up for the Confederacy....then came brilliant flash of exploding shells from batteries all around the bay, while deep harsh tones of talking cannons echoed over waters, the scene sublimely grand...". Fort Sumter did not fire a shot."

Will and Maria followed these events …their main concern being safety and well-being of Robert, who seemed much too close to danger. On a pleasant spring evening, in quiet time, Will sat relaxing from hard day's work getting fields ready for planting. At kitchen table, legs outstretched, he fingered a coffee cup in hand. Maria sat across table shuffling letters from Robert. After reading and re-reading Robert's letters, Maria remarked pensively to Will, "I just do not understand what's to become of this. I worry about Robert, and wish he would leave Charleston. Who knows what's to happen."

Mind churning, Will raised his head slowly from distant gaze at half-filled coffee cup now cradled in both hands, looking squarely into Maria's questioning eyes. "It will all be over soon ...cannot last long ...people will come to their senses ...you will see."

Maria's head moved side to side in disagreement …unconvinced …parsed lips and continued. "It is much more difficult than that, Will. President Lincoln will not accept this

Union being torn apart by secessionists. And, Robert...I fear he is far too persuaded by their thinking. He seems to believe his State of South Carolina is more important than keeping the Union together. I worry that Lincoln will send soldiers to Charleston ...what will happen to Robert?"

"Robert is twenty-six years old ...can take care of himself," Will answered firmly. "Besides ...it's late and we need to turn-in. It's spring ...no telling what weather will be ...I have a lot to do to get our fields ready."

Weeks and months passed. Will and Maria found themselves caught up in growing fervor. They were not unlike many Americans ...simple folk ...farmers working hard, trying to make ends meet. They were busy getting family started. Will Jr. was only one and a half years old and needed constant attention like any toddler. Maria was now seven months pregnant ...expecting another child meant greater responsibility. Times were hard and economy depressed ...money and jobs scarce.

Will and Maria shared core values of their Oxford neighbors. 'Community' was all-important. Standards of community were respected, good opinion coveted, ideals embraced and interests defended ...even by going to war if needed. Soldiers were obligated to defend institutions and preserve hard-won liberty at all costs ...for family, and for community. Patriotic ideals were embedded deep within, taught from earliest years ...reinforced in home and schoolhouse ...shared by everyone, everyone feeling responsibility.

Every few weeks, Will hitched plough horses, 'Henry' and 'Jake', to buckboard and headed off. It was three miles into town for supplies, unless winter weather or spring rain made the regular trip impractical. After shopping in the general store, he looked forward to conversation with an assortment of town regulars. Locals congregated in town's pub, called 'Paddy's'...named for a rotund Irish immigrant ...friendly jocular proprietor of the popular establishment. On such a trip, Will entered the pub and glanced over the bar to see writing scribbled on a chalkboard in large script, impossible for anyone to miss:

Volunteer your cirveses...join now!"

Will pulled wood stool to bar and ordered a beer be drawn. He watched silent, as if removed ...taking in the entire scene. Paddy lifted a mug of frothy brew and boastfully toasted one young patron seated a few feet down bar. "Laddie ...we're not about to relinquish our dreams without a proper fight!" Paddy let out raucous belly shaking laughter, sending plentiful girth into convulsion, slamming beer mug onto bar top for emphasis, as gathered patrons hoisted mugs and glasses in unison to return a salute.

"No, sir! No, sir!" came the patron's cry, shouts loud and forceful ...its unanimity and spontaneity made great impression on Will. He would not forget. Will remained silent. He nursed his beer ...lost in thought, eyes glazed ...while jovial patrons milled about enjoying trivial conversation and trading rowdy gossip. Minutes passed before Paddy walked toward Will. Paddy dried a glass on soiled white apron and addressed Will, "Will, can I draw you another beer?"

"No thanks, Paddy. I have to be going home."

"Lad, I've known ya' long enough ...ya' don't seem yourself. Anything wrong, laddie?"

Will hesitated, fingering his wedding ring, twisting it nervously. Looking upward, pointing to the chalkboard sign over bar, Will answered softly, "This war's a messy thing."

"Sure enough is, laddie ...sure enough is." That said, Paddy turned and walked back to other patrons. Moments later, Will left change on the bar to pay for the beer and ambled out of the pub. It was the first time Will recalled feeling intense pressure. Forces were building within...irreconcilable forces, knotting the stomach. Life was no longer simple.

During winter and into spring of 1862 in Oxford, talk focused increasingly on war. In fair weather, town clan moved outdoors ...always there, easy to find, gathered in two's and three's ...men rocking or propped in chairs on elevated wood-slatted porches fronting shops. Some sat with cigarettes lit, coffee cup in-hand, precariously balancing on the rear two legs of a chair. Others sat with smoke circling from corncob pipes, whittling lazily at a piece of wood. Most were ready and eager to talk. On one trip to town, Will paused for a few moments in a rocking chair outside the General Store. Shopping was complete and items loaded on buckboard, but he lingered to enjoy crisp freshness of springtime air before heading home. Out of the blue, an old codger rocking next to Will leaned over and lectured for all to hear, "We need to show 'em we're 'true Blue' ...'Johnny Reb' will see the kind of metal us Yanks are made of."

Another doddering old-timer remarked, "Weeze-gotta stick this out ...manfully."

"Why ya' old fart, you're too old to git' up from that thar' chair!" a third man quipped.

"Easy nuff' for ya' to say now!"

The old man snorted, and spit a nasty wad of tobacco juice onto decking, "Old fart, ya' say ...well sir, this ol' dawg still hunts."

Laughing with others, Will left his chair and re-entered the General Store. Walking to the counter, he said, "Mrs. Dexter, I have one more request. Could I have two pieces of licorice candy for my boy, and a piece of chocolate for Maria?"

Mrs. Dexter reached into a wood barrel and retrieved candy, placing it in brown paper bag, handing it to Will. Smiling broadly, she said, "Give my regards to Maria."

"I will indeed. Have a good day, Mrs. Dexter." Will placed two coins in her hand, doffed his hat and left.

Often Maria accompanied Will into town. Their second son, Walter Graham Hodkins, was born June 4th, 1861 ...now nine months old. Will, Jr. turned two years old the previous October ...both he and baby Walter were being watched by the Bowles, a couple of good friends who lived on a farm down the dirt road. As Will and Maria entered town, they could not miss a rally underway on lawn fronting courthouse. Curious, they stopped to tether horses and wagon. Will and Maria edged to a rearmost fringe of the assembled crowd to listen, as a city councilman urged the crowd:

"...every man has to do his duty..."

He went on to talk about State pride, patriotism, and sense of duty ...an impassioned plea for citizens, and young men in particular, to come to the aid of their threatened country. "Soldiers," he said, "are 'fight-in' for their families, and their communities!"

Several women onlookers waved white handkerchiefs in support of the speaker's fiery and torrid oratory, while others hoisted and waved small U.S. flags overhead. One pert middle-aged lady, bedecked in deep blue crinoline dress and matching bonnet ...waving a flag ...hollered out, spectacles perched defiantly on bridge of nose, "I would go in a minute if I were a man!"

Crowd erupted in waves of raucous cheers, "Here! ...Here!" "Here! ...Here!"

The speaker ended remarks and a band struck notes to "The Bonnie Blue Flag" ...followed by roaring rendition of "Dixie". Its spectacle sent chills to all onlookers. Will and Maria eyed each other, deeply choked with emotion, expressions acknowledging the moment's powerful effect and crowd's reaction. They talked at length, a number of times over the last months, of growing pressure on young men around town to enlist ...and, most importantly about Will. "What's to become of us, Will?" Maria implored.

But, her question went unanswered. Will's thoughts and feelings were too deep and intense to vocalize ...even to Maria. Feelings were churning within ...building, deep down ...getting worse as months wore on. It was agonizing torment of uneasiness ...fear, because he did not want to bring shame to family ...or, people he knew so well in Oxford. He felt 'eyes' of community upon him ...guilt too, if he placed self-interest ahead of responsibility. Maria, the children, and their farm were dearest in life. "*...how could they do without him? What if he did not come back?*" He struggled to find answers ...it was tearing him apart.

Will celebrated a 24th birthday in February ...strong and muscular from upbringing on the farm ...considered tall at 5'10" and lanky compared to most other young men in town. With broad

31

shoulders, strong chiseled jaw, piercing hazel eyes, and deeply tanned olive complexion ...ample locks of dark black hair flowing out from under floppy slouch hat ...he cut a pretty imposing figure. He enjoyed turning heads of young girls in town...even more so when Maria caught the interplay and feigned chagrin. Ladies at church sewing circle would tease Maria about Will's good looks. Maria and Will enjoyed dancing at Town Hall and at the summer County Fair ...young girls giggled in envy as the handsome young couple spun about the dance floor. It was just innocent fun, because Maria and Will were known by townsfolk as a 'perfect couple' ...one with each other ...lover, friend, partner and companion. Theirs was a happy life ...and the children ...a young boy, and a baby. It was a wonderful family.

All this was being disrupted over many months. Will wrestled endlessly with a seemingly unanswerable question ..."*what to do?*" It was eating away at him ...destructive. He could not think of leaving Maria ...or the two boys. Besides, Will reasoned, *"what about the farm?"* ...they were working hard just to make ends meet, times were tough and prices depressed. *"How could Maria take care of the children ...and the farm ...hold it all together?"* But still, political persuasion and peer pressure were formidable. Speaker's words at the town rally kept coming back ...over and over ...haunting him:

"...every man has to do his duty!"

Will's friends were enlisting ...one after another. They were not married, like Will with family ...but Will knew most since boyhood, going through school together ...doing all things young boys do together. Will liked and respected them. His friend Josh's words kept coming back ...with boyish enthusiasm, Josh told Will, "I would be disgraced, if left behind." These words troubled Will deeply. But he kept pressure to himself, unable to free troubled feelings ...even to Maria.

He was certain Maria was fretting deeply as well. She was a smart young lady and very perceptive. He guessed she did not want him to volunteer...but he was sure she knew in her heart they were on a slippery slope. *"If war doesn't find some way to end, soon...,"* she mused off-handed, peeling potatoes for an evening meal.

Months wore on. Farm chores were completed each day ...young boys required attention of mother and father ...life simply went forward. Meanwhile, reports of valor and courage from first recruits in fields of battle, reported by newspapers and magazines like **Harper's Weekly**, fanned frenzy to enlist. Rallies, public meetings, exhortations in local flyers ...even sermons on Sunday from Reverend John Duckworthy ...all urged enlistment. Citizen-patriots were eager to join the fray and get their first taste of 'lickin' the 'Johnny Rebs' ...they wanted to enlist quickly before they missed action and peace could be re-established. In Oxford, Michigan, in small white clapboard three-room farmhouse, Will and Maria Hodkins reacted to news with growing fear and trepidation. Surrounding events were spiraling out of control. Pressure was building and choice dwindling. They managed to broach fears with each other in small snippets of conversation ...reluctant to face depth of anxiety head-on. Wartime was changing people's psyches ...simple folk from all walks of life were being asked to volunteer and become soldiers ...and killers. Young men, older men ...even family men ...were being asked to 'fight for the stars and stripes'.

On a late July 1862 evening, Will and Maria sat at kitchen table with good neighbors, the Bowles, from a farm just down roadway. Will and Maria invited Ezra and Nettie Bowles to share supper and visit with the children. Furthermore, they respected the Bowles' common sense outlook on life, and needed desperately to talk about their situation.

Supper was great. Maria cooked a tasty stew in the Dutch oven hanging over a fire in their fieldstone fireplace ...chunks of fresh cut pork purchased on a trip to town with Will the previous day, new potatoes, onions, carrots, and green beans grown in their garden outback ...all cooked slowly, with rich brown gravy made from residue of pork fat blended with flour. Maria baked fresh cornbread, perfect accompaniment for delicious stew. It was a simple meal, but Will and Maria enjoyed simple farm life. And, the Bowles' were simple country folk too, who became 'extended family' to the young Hodkins family soon after first arrival on the farm. Ezra and Nettie Bowles were older than Will and Maria …Will and Maria guessed they were in their late fifties. The Bowles had no children, so they befriended the young family …they "sorta became our child-in," as Ezra Bowles was wont to tell everyone.

After the meal, Will suggested, "Ezra, let's go out on the porch, while ladies clear the table …sunset should be splendid this evening."

"Good ide'r, Will," Ezra answered enthusiastically, spryly hoisting himself from the table, "Got some cof-fee weez kin' take with us?"

"Sure enough …pots a-boil-in' already," as Will reached for two white ceramic coffee mugs from an open shelf on the wall beside the table.

"Skee-dattle on out of here, fellers …we girls are fix-in' to git' these dishes a-soak-in'," Nettie chided, "we'll join ya' in no time …with some coffee a-brew-in' …and, we'll git' the young-ins' down for bed."

"Ain't argu-in' with dat," Ezra called, slapping a leg for exclamation, while reaching for broad-brimmed hat that hung draped on back of a nearby chair.

Neither Will nor Ezra were about to argue, so they hugged the two boys 'good night'. Will placed two coffee mugs on the table, before he and Ezra ambled out the front screen door onto the porch. "Let the ladies tend to chores."

Will gestured for Ezra to grab one of two white-painted wood rocking chairs. "Make yourself comfortable, Ezra," Will said, propping himself onto picketed white porch railing, leaning back against one whitewashed column supporting porch roof. Will surveyed his neighbor, and father-like good friend, as Ezra pulled trusty well-worn corncob pipe from pocket and tamped tobacco into bowl. Ezra was quite a character. New folks in town sometimes mistook Ezra for a 'Quaker' by first appearance …but hearty full-bellied laugh and ever-present good humor, charmed people early-on …dispelling any first notion of being stuffy or aloof. Ezra was about 5'8" in height, muscular and trim of build, supple of gait …attributes from constant labor on the farm, though he loved to eat. He dressed in Sunday-best worn earlier to church …black greatcoat with black wool trousers, spit-polished black high-top laced boots, and heavily starched high-neck muslin white shirt. He sported full gray free-flowing beard, bushy gray eyebrows, and penetrating dark eyes that peered intently over bulbous, rutted red nose. Large nose provided ample perch for rimless wire spectacles resting down front bridge of nose …glasses he peered over. A stiff, round brimmed black felt hat was placed squarely on long gray flowing locks, brushing slightly stooped strong shoulders. Ezra had little formal education, or 'school-in' as he would say …he was 'just a farmer' all his life. Yet, Will considered Ezra practical, and quick to grasp any thorny situation …'down home' way of thinking with ability to cut an issue to the chase …capabilities Will respected and trusted …traits Will remembered and admired about his father. *If only Father could speak with me now,"* Will thought to himself. *"I miss him so much, and could use his advice now. What would he tell me to do?"*

Will returned thought to Ezra. Smoke from Ezra's pipe drifted lazily upward …man seemingly lost in thought. Two men …good friends …sat silently, simply enjoying still fresh night air and pleasant aroma of burning tobacco. Quiet interlude was broken, as Maria led Nettie through squeaking front screen door and onto the porch, door left by Nettie to slam closed ...squeaking and slamming sounds shattering peaceful quiet. Mugs of coffee carried on a tray by Maria were served to Will and Ezra.

"I thanks 'ya, Mam."

"Thank you, ladies," Will responded.

"Perfectly lovely sunset," Nettie shouted, further breaking solitude …something Nettie did regularly. "Red and orange colors are amaz-in' …look at pink in dem' clouds." Nettie's shrill high-pitched voice sounded as if she considered everyone deaf.

"It is a beautiful sight," Maria agreed demurely …two ladies moving to share a two-person slatted swing at porch's end. Nettie, like Ezra, had little formal education. Though education and demeanor were worlds apart, Maria thought the world of Nettie. They talked easily, thoroughly enjoying time together.

"Have ya' made 'yer candles?" Nettie questioned Maria.

"Made some two days ago, but ran out of tallow."

"How 'bout 'yer knit-in'?"

"I made two pair of darling booties for Walter. But Will needs to shear more wool from our sheep before I can spin more yarn."

After minutes of small talk between ladies, mood changed abruptly as Will cleared his throat loudly. Everyone looked Will's way ...attention focused. Searching momentarily for words, his back and demeanor stiffened. He looked down, words finally coming. "War has Maria and I all tied-up in knots ...we can't decide what must be done. We were hoping to hear your thoughts, Ezra and Nettie," Will pleaded in serious somber tone. Previously they had talked about War and what was happening, but never more than casual. Now, everything turned deadly serious.

"Yes," Maria added, "we think so much of you both ...please let us know what you think." Maria and Will mimicked each other instinctively ...both crossing arms, leaning back ...pensively awaiting their friends' response. Each breathed visible sigh of relief, relaxing a little because the question was now out in the open ...both now bending forward, anticipating and focusing on Ezra and Nettie.

After moments of somber reflection, Ezra drew deeply on his pipe and exhaled a cloud of billowing smoke, intent on watching it drift lazily skyward. He sipped from coffee cup, and then in slow drawl said, "Yu-'ve got to do, what ya' hav-ta' do ...and, Nettie and I'll supports ya' ...with whatever ya' do ...it's as simple as that!"

Nettie added, "Will, if ya' gotta go, Ezra will help with farm-in', and I kin' make some meals ...and help with little-uns' ...yuz' can count on Ezra and me to help our dear Maria ...we'll all be alright, then. Yu'll see!"

Moments of abject silence followed ...no one daring to speak. Then, Will hoisted himself slowly off porch railing, rubbing fingers through thick black hair, thinking deeply ...hesitatingly. Drawing deep breath, he straightened shoulders, standing erect before them. "I have to go. It is my duty ...and, my responsibility!"

There, he said it. Words suddenly purged hidden agony that tore from deep within ...at least six months or more ...he breathed a huge sigh. Shoulders slumped forward, now relaxed ...world's weight suddenly removed.

"You are right, Will ...that is why I love you," Maria affirmed, strength of resolve and composure demonstrated again.

That was it ...decision made. Tension lifted instantly, four friends going to each other compulsively in heart-rending embrace. Then, Ezra broke seriousness of emotion by letting out the heartiest of belly laughs. He reached for coffee cup, raised both arms overhead, and toasted Will and Maria, "Here ...here!! Here ...here!!" he roared.

Everyone joined in laughter, all raising arms skyward ...then, arm-in-arm they spun like tops in a circle, celebrating and cheering together, "Here ...here!! Here ...here!!"

Over the next four weeks, Will and Maria stayed busy making preparation before Will left for enlistment in Pontiac, Michigan.

Chapter 4

An old and rickety wood-sided wagon was packed and ready, Will's carpet bag tossed into a corner, alongside winter coat and wool blanket. Volunteers were urged to pack light, but bring a blanket because the Army was in short supply. Will was sure he packed too much, but Maria insisted.

Wagon stood outside tidy white picket fence that enclosed front yard of Will and Maria's small white lap-sided farmhouse. Maria's pride and joy was a courtyard she tended with passion, working arduously to keep it neat and tidy, planting abundant perennials of assorted varieties, now ablaze with color ...especially a spectacular cluster of hydrangea sporting magnificent stately blooms of icy blue. A solitary crab tree stood in a corner of courtyard aside the fence, casting shade over wagon from first rising rays of morning sun. Perched atop wagon's driver bench, clutching leather reins to two old plough horses hitched to the wagon, was Ezra Bowles. Ezra Bowles was kind to offer transport for Will and two friends the fourteen miles or so to Pontiac, where the three volunteers were to rendezvous for induction into the Union Army.

In back of wagon, seated with legs outstretched on thick layer of fresh straw, and leaning against each corner behind driver's bench, were Will's longtime friends ...Johnny Predmore and Jerry Webb. Johnny was 'Johnny', but Jerry was known as 'Junior'. Both were watching anxiously, restless to get going, as Will stood on the porch saying 'goodbyes' to Maria, 3-year old Will Jr., and one-year old baby Walter fast asleep in mother's arms.

Johnny called out, with mocking hearty laugh, "C'mon, Will, ain't ya' gonna ever leave?"

Junior put hand to mouth, feigning embarrassment, but let out a belly laugh none the same. In top-spirits, the pair were revved up and excited about great adventure ...young and single, impulsive and eager. But, Will was slow to go ...more than a little reluctant. He was leaving family behind.

Last evening, Will and Maria shared best of 'last evenings' together. Maria surprised Will with a present, wrapped in white paper encircled by red ribbon and large red bow. Maria pulled the gift from behind her back, extending it toward Will in outstretched hands. "Will, I want you to keep this close to you, and think of me when you are away."

He took the wrapped package, and with both hands holding gift over head, he shook it back and forth teasingly ...with questioning look. "No rattle, no noise," he remarked joking, bringing smiles to both faces. He continued, "I also have a gift for you," and he went to retrieve his present from its hiding place.

Both stood facing each other, tears welling in eyes, choked with emotion. Maria began to unwrap the gift slowly ...trying to make a special moment last. She opened a small blue box containing a beautiful pearl white cameo brooch. She drew deeply to regain breath, tears flowing, while raising fingers to lips ...trying to recover composure. "Thank you, my dear. It is so lovely ...I will wear it always while you are away." She reached upward to Will's broad shoulders ...kissing him passionately, standing on tiptoe, hugging tightly.

Will removed ribbon and red bow from Maria's gift, and clowned placing the red bow on his head. Both laughed at a silly gesture. He turned serious, pulling wrapping paper away, revealing a bound hardcover journal with black cover and brown binding. He opened its cover. An inscription in Maria's hand read,

*"Sands of time pass so quickly thru
life's hourglass ...but with you, its gold
dust in my memory ...Maria."*

39

Will stood breathless. He flipped through lined pages of blank paper.

Maria offered, "I want you to write down what is happening ...every detail, so I can share it all ...the 'memories' ...when you return. And, perhaps you can post some of it to me, as often as you can."

"It is wonderful," Will answered. "I will write often ...I promise ...what beautiful thought." He embraced and kissed Maria passionately, lifting her off ground as if a feather, spinning her around.

"I have something else," Maria offered, pulling another surprise from dress pocket. "A white Impatient ...simple flower from our garden ...beautiful and pure white, like our pure love for each other. Press it between pages of your journal ...as a reminder of me ...and your home."

Will stood stunned. Maria was such a romantic ...caring and thoughtful friend ...and great lover. "Maria ...I could not love you more." They embraced again, holding each other tightly for the longest time, before moving off to bed and last night together.

They nestled snugly in bed, unable to get close enough ...talking long into night, wanting each precious moment to last. Each knew that 'memories' would have to 'make do' for some time. They were best friends ...steadfast partners, companions, and lovers. A lone candle burned at nightstand bedside ...candle flickered. Will's eye twinkled in candle's light, stealing a glance toward Maria ...her eye returned a look of passion and desire. Will was so very proud of 'his Maria'. He concentrated, as Maria lay resting ...wanting memory to capture a picture of *'his lady'* so he could recall each curve of body ...time and again after parting. He studied features, mind racing with loving thoughts ...passion growing.

She was much shorter than Will ...deliciously slight of build and fair in complexion, though strong ...certainly not frail. She carried herself erectly ...proudly ...countenance and demeanor 'determined' ...serious most times, but always enjoying good humor displayed by others. Silky white skin gave emphasis to piercing dark brown eyes ...strong chiseled chin and nose made all more remarkable. Full deep red lips and beautiful white teeth were displayed beautifully by wide smile. She turned heads entering a room ...beauty, coupled with persona of strength, depth of character, and strong resolve. Will was not sure he deserved her ...he treated her as *'his lady'* ...a striking young lady.

Maria's long and flowing dark brown hair was worn pulled back, parted down the middle, spread in light curling waves to either side of forehead. Often Will enjoyed watching Maria remove the comb from back of head, hair falling over delicate white shoulders, as she sat combing hair at the mirror before retiring. Will loved Maria's long free flowing hair and took great pleasure running fingers through it. Now, Will reached lovingly and gently toward her, caressing her locks with fingers of right hand, clenching her hand firmly in his left. Each peered longingly into the other's eyes. "Are you sure you will be alright?" he whispered. Thoughtful, Will continued, "I know this will not last more than a few months ...I worry about leaving you ...and, I worry about being strong enough."

Maria replied, with understanding and tenderness, "Will, I watch you working in farm fields ...laboring behind plow. I have watched you set that strong jaw of yours ...fierce determination on your face, as you set shoulders to the task. You are strong ...both in body and mind. You will succeed ...I know it!"

Will said nothing ...clenching jaw with a slight head nod.

Maria continued, "We will be just fine, Will ...besides, Mr. and Mrs. Bowles are just down the road, always willing to help."

Will sighed, "I just feel it my duty to go ...I have no choice ...my responsibility..."

Maria stopped him short, gently touching his cheek. "I know," she said. "You are right ...please never forget."

"With God's blessing," Will offered, "it will be over in a few months ...before fields need planting in spring ...I will be home again."

Maria whispered in Will's ear, "Yes ...yes you will. Promise me that you will. I love you so much, my Will...please use your journal and write often."

Will nodded, firmness and resolve to his voice, "I promise. I promise you!"

And then, young lovers rolled over, caressing each other's body ...tenderly exploring, each feeling pleasure ...passion mounting. Soon, rhythmic dance grew intense, bodies making love with lust and fire, forged in Will's mind forever ...memory warming heart and strengthening resolve whenever going became toughest. Love and devotion fueled inner strength ...strength he needed for uncertain time and events to come. Neither wanted night to end ...but end it must. Will hoisted himself upward, leaned over, and blew out the lonely candle.

Next day did arrive ...no stopping it ...time to say good-bye. Maria stood on front porch, holding sleeping baby Walter, extending a free arm around young Will Jr. standing alongside. Will looked tenderly into Maria's eyes, touching her forehead gently, saying sheepishly so others at the wagon could not hear, "I love you, Maria...so very much." Will backed away slowly, stepping down off porch into entry garden courtyard. He stooped, picking a single flower from its patch growing along walkway ...and returned to Maria. He spoke loving words softly, presenting Maria a single purple Coneflower held before her. "Purple," he said. "Purple ...for passion I have in my heart for you." He placed the flower gingerly in her apron pocket.

"I love you, my Will ...God speed. Return home ...soon."

"You know I will ...I promise." He looked down upon Will Jr. and urged, "Take care of your mother, and be good, young man." He hugged his son firmly. Then he turned, bent over and kissed baby Walter tenderly on forehead ...gently, not to wake him.

Nothing more could be said. Turning away with brown felt slouch hat in-hand, he stepped down off porch, and walked a few steps to fence and picket gate roadside. He pulled gate open, its creaking sound piercing eerie silence as if moaning. All were silent ...recognizing sadness in farewell. Will pulled himself up and onto the wagon, assuming a seat alongside Ezra Bowles on driver's bench. He looked back and nodded to Johnny and Junior. Will placed slouch hat on head, tugged lightly, and gestured for Mr. Bowles to go.

Ezra called, "Henry..., Jake..., giddy-up," laying reins to two sturdy horses whistling for response. Wagon lurched into motion. Horses and wagon moved slowly down dusty roadway. Will turned back waving to Maria and Will Jr. …they answered with waves and faint smiles. It was too much. Will turned away, unable to hide a small tear slipping slowly down the cheek. He missed them already.

Chapter 5

A rickety wagon bumped and lurched along dusty road. Four travelers knew their journey would be anything but pleasant. They left early, hoping to get a good start before the worst of mid-day heat and humidity. After all, late-August, and early morning sun beat down already. Late summer weather in this part of Michigan could be unbearably hot, humid and uncomfortable. It would be slow going.

Within an hour, narrow, weed and grass covered roadway fronting Hodkins' and Bowles' farms changed as they turned onto more traveled 'Old Lapeer Road' heading south ...main thoroughfare leading from northernmost Oakland County, and rural Oxford, south toward the county seat of Pontiac. Wider roadway surface, well worn from frequent travel, was deeply rutted from wagon and coach wheels traversing once muddy roadway following usual intermittent summer rains. Deep dry ruts nearly stalled the wagon at times, causing Mr. Bowles to put harness to the backs of Henry and Jake coaxing straining animals for more effort. Creaky wagon lumbered over grooved and furrowed ground, tossing occupants wildly, up and down, side-to-side.

The sky was clear blue ...just a trace of light, puffy cumulus clouds drifting lazily overhead. Occasional breeze yielded pleasant momentary bursts of fresh and clean early morning air ...urging travelers to draw deep and delightful breaths, before day's sticky humidity replaced freshness. Morning sun pierced thick forests roadside left, rays glistening on oak leaves

44

and branches overhead. Gently rolling hills lay covered by large stands of huge oak trees ...specimen trees, an abundance of which led to the county's name, 'Oakland'.

"Stop the wagon a minute," Johnny called out, leaping out of the wagon and running hell bent for nearest woods with a herky-jerky awkward gait. "I've gotta' water me a tree!"

Will shook his head sheepishly, glancing at Ezra, a mixture of disgust and embarrassment at his young friend's antics. "Ezra, he is 22 years old, but going on 15."

"Ya' got that right, my friend ...boys'll be boys."

"He's just a fat boy a-pee-'in," Junior volunteered.

Both Ezra and Will smiled. Will looked some forty paces toward Johnny standing at a tree ...relieving himself ...the back of Johnny's sandy blond hair falling helter-skelter onto slumping shoulders ...wide girth nearly blocking the huge tree. Will thought to himself, *"he has always been a little plump, and on the heavy side."* Johnny's response to nature's calling complete, he returned, jowls of his face flushing red from effort to hoist an overweight body up and into the wagon. Junior extended a hand to assist. "I'm a little lighter now," Johnny joked.

Ezra smiled, lightly cracked reins and called, "Giddy-up, Jake ...let's go Henry." Their journey resumed.

After a couple hours, sun's building heat made travel hot and sweaty, any trace of faint breeze long gone. Will and companions passed Long Lake, and then shortly, Canandaigna Lake just to the west. Sighting such beautiful, large expanses of fresh water, Will felt just a little cooler, as they rolled toward the small town of Orion. Two boys dozed carefree in back of the wagon, hats pulled down over faces. Ezra was silent, only occasionally uttering 'ur-gins' to his team of lumbering horses. Meanwhile, Will passed time watching and marveling at wildlife. He was fascinated by beauty of a Great Egret ...a long-legged wading bird, elegant with filmy white feathered plumes catching morning's sunlight, while foraging for crayfish in a marshy bog near its breeding ground. A Mallard Duck and her clutch of six fledgling ducklings feasted on pond weed nearby. He spotted a stunning Red-Shouldered Hawk, perched in the upper extremity of a huge oak tree ...overseeing its nest ...clear markings of reddish brown shoulder and white flecks visible on wing feathers. Further along, in a natural oak savanna of dead tree snags, a colorful Red-Headed Woodpecker, with brilliant red head and sharply contrasting black and white body, drew Will's attention with its harsh, rattling calls as it engaged as an avid fly catcher in territorial chase.

Will turned to Ezra, "With God's beauty all about us, how could there be such turmoil in God's plan?"

Ezra pondered momentarily, and then replied with wag of forefinger for emphasis, "Don't th-ee-nck we know 'da plan."

"You must be right, Ezra." Brief conversation ended. Will's thought drifted, pondering a simple brilliance to Ezra's remark.

Several miles down road, travelers approached the northern end of small town Orion. With one severe jolt from bouncing wagon, Junior awoke from slumber. "Let's git' us a lemonade," Junior shouted exuberantly, obviously self-pleased with a sudden good idea ...awakening Johnny as well with the outburst.

"Now, ya' know that's an idea-r," Johnny quickly agreed.

"You boys are alright," Ezra added with a wink to Will. "Mighty smart young fellers, don't ya' think, Will."

"Maybe so ...maybe so," Will answered with a skeptical smirk.

Here, four stopped to rest and take refreshment. And, Henry and Jake were grateful for time at the watering trough, deserving a little hard-earned rest, and good quantity of hay being offered by Junior from a bale stored back of wagon. Will reached into a straw basket behind wagon's seat. Inside, he reached for four sandwiches prepared by Maria, handing one to each man. Slices of salt pork and piece of cheese were topped by raw onion, sandwiched between two thick pieces of freshly baked homemade bread. Accompanying each sandwich was a large briny pickle. Eager hands reached out from hungry men, food being devoured in no time. "Maria's a thoughtful lady, Will," Ezra offered.

"That she is ...that she is."

After enjoying lemonade and resting briefly at the main street store, all four men boarded the wagon to resume their tedious journey. "Giddy-up, Henry ...let's go, Jake," Ezra called out again, snapping polished well-worn reins to prod reluctant beasts to action. They were off ...still another 10 miles or so to cover, and closing on noon. Sun beat down from directly overhead, its heat stifling. Will pulled a red handkerchief from a pocket, tying it as a bandana over forehead to stop sweat from running into eyes. He replaced his floppy hat, tugging it down over the eyes ...thoughts soon wandering. By the time wagon crossed Paint Creek, Johnny and Junior were curled up again ...fast asleep on straw bed in the rear. Johnny slept passively, at peace with the world. Junior started snoring loudly while deep in sleep. Will glanced rearward over shoulder, as Junior let out an especially loud snort. "They have not a care in the world," Will observed to Ezra. Ezra nodded agreement.

Time passed. Alone, just the two of them, Ezra remarked: "I admire ya', Will ...go-in' off like this ...volunteer-in' and such."

"Well, we have to defend against these contemptible traitors, trying to accomplish their hellish designs," Will answered stiffly. Relaxing somewhat, he continued, "I have to do what must be done."

"I mean will-in' to leave Maria ...and the little-ins," Ezra corrected.

"I feel a duty to my country ...it wears on me heavily," Will continued. "I have no other choice ...I have to leave and volunteer ...now, I just want to prove I can shoulder my share."

"Ya' all will be able to say ...ya' done what you could," Ezra said emphatically, head nodding resolutely for emphasis.

"I just want to do my duty, Ezra." Moments passed. Then, Will continued, "But, you know, Ezra, I am deeply afraid. I worry I will not succeed ...and I worry about Maria and the boys ...what will come of us, Ezra?"

"Ya'll make it, God will-in' ...ya'll see," Ezra reassured. "Will, yer' a strong man, ya' know ...mighty determined."

"I do not fear dying ...I do fear failing."

"Rest easy, my boy ...things have a way of work-in' out."

"I wish I could be as carefree as those two boys," Will replied, gesturing over shoulder. For the longest time, the two remained silent, lost in thought. It was somber time, as horse drawn wagon plodded down roadway.

47

Eight hours into their fourteen mile journey, road began to crowd with fellow travelers as outskirt of Pontiac drew near. People were pouring into the city, traffic funneling from feeder roads onto Old Lapeer Road, main entry from north. Farm wagons, carriages, and even fancy cabriolets comprised vehicular traffic heading into the city …even a few pedestrians making their way on foot. Fellow travelers were friendly enough, good-natured waves being exchanged upon passing. It was not long before Ezra and Will realized this event was going to be bigger than either imagined. As its magnitude became obvious, Will rubbed moist palms together, a signal of adrenalin surging and stomach knotting. When the bustle of activity awoke Johnny and Junior, all four men shared nervous excitement …unlike anything experienced before.

Northern outskirts of Pontiac were soon upon them. This was no small city. It was not as big as Detroit, 25 miles further to the southeast, but seemed large just the same to four 'country' boys …population of 20,000 residents many times larger than tiny rural and remote Oxford. Just northeast of the city, about one-half mile from downtown, the boys spotted Fair Grounds on the right side of Old Lapeer Road. This was camp ground and rallying point for the volunteers, and their families and friends accompanying them. Ezra veered the wagon onto the dirt entry road to the campsite. "Looks like we're here," Ezra called out.

Will pulled gold watch case from pant pocket, "Nearly 6 PM …almost twelve hours."

Wagon rolled under an overhead sign spanning roadbed and reading 'Fair Grounds'. To the side, the 'stars and stripes' flag hung limp with no late afternoon breeze. A uniformed guard raised an arm to halt the wagon, giving them information and directions, "Tents are available for your stay …town is overflowing …nearly 10,000 visitors and recruits expected …no rooms available in-town. Pull straight ahead to that large tent …you'll be assigned a tent for the night. Ladies are serving supper."

Ezra urged horses to plod forward with a flick of reins, and wagon creaked and groaned as if in agony …its passengers wide-eyed at spectacle before them …no one able to speak …too overwhelmed. Rows and rows of sparkling white tents glistened in muted early evening sunshine, all aligned neat and orderly as far as eye could see. Smoke curled lazily overhead, aroma filling air. A band could be heard playing in the distance. Camp was alive and bustling ...people gathered in groups, talking ...others strolling together, among pathways serving as avenues between rows of tents ...men and ladies, young and old ...even a few dogs roaming carefree, yelping playfully.

"All the feel-ins' of a festive affair," Johnny quipped, trying to break shock and awe shared by his companions.

At the large tent, the boys checked in with a lady ...one of many citizens of Pontiac who offered services 'for the cause'. They were assigned 'Tent #22, on Avenue J', and given directions. The lady suggested they get settled quickly, and proceed immediately to another large tent where meals were being served, because she said, "Food is a go-in' fast around here."

Boys and Ezra found their assigned tent without difficulty ...team tethered and given water and hay at a hitching rail not far away, and wagon unloaded. The tent was equipped for four persons ...no more ...four cots erected, pretty much covering available space within. Each boy selected a cot, after Mr. Bowles was given first-choice ...wisely he chose a cot near the tent's entry flap where any breeze could be felt, making intense heat inside a little more tolerable. Blankets were placed on cots ...belongings placed under cots.

"Mr. Bowles, you're now one of us boys," Johnny observed.

"Yes-sir-ee ...I be one of you 'boys' ...gol' darn," Ezra answered.

They were set ...though famished, hot and tired from a twelve-hour journey. Scrambling off eagerly and on foot to locate the mess tent, noses led them by unmistakable smell of 'good cook-in' permeating air. A line of ten to fifteen people stood waiting to be served. Long tables were aligned before them, with four ladies in aprons standing behind ...placing large portions of food on each plate. The four grew impatient, finally reaching the front table ...a courtly plump old lady greeted them with a most gracious smile ...handing each a tin plate and utensils. Then each plate was piled high with boiled chicken, dumplings, and fresh

green peas. A tin cup of coffee completed a scrumptious meal.
Moving from food line, four 'boys' found an open spot at one of
many wood tables under tent ...tearing into delicious food as if no
tomorrow. Junior boasted, "This army life ain't all bad!"

After the meal, the four ambled back toward their assigned
tent, taking a somewhat circuitous route because they wanted to
see what was happening. Men and women and children gathered
in groups around campfires, chatting and enjoying each other's
company. At one end of open space, a band was playing to a
rather large audience ...some audience standing, while others
sprawled on blankets on the ground in picnic fashion. As the three
young men and Ezra sidled up to join the crowd of onlookers, the
band struck notes to "Bonny Blue Flag", and then "Red, White and
Blue". The crowd was whipped to frenzy ...enjoying the moment
...fed on patriotic emotion.

After more music and torrid patriotic oratory by one of the
city's leading citizens, the four decided to turn in for the night
...exhausted. Besides, tomorrow will be a big day ...Will, Johnny,
and Junior will be signing enlistment papers ...before being issued
uniforms and equipment. As the boys sidled away, sunset was
gorgeous ...deep hues of scarlet and orange playing among
scattered clouds drifting in foreground and off on horizon. With
sunset approaching quickly, campfires became more visible
...glowing embers and dancing flames reaching skyward ...giving
illumination to a special evening ...eerily half-lighting faces
gathered, casting ghost-like dancing shadows on long rows of
canvas tents. The boys could hear the crackle of fires and pop of
dry wood as glowing orange sparks leapt upward highlighted by
growing darkness. And, last sounds of the band could be heard in
the distance playing "Battle Cry of Freedom".

Chapter 6

Dawn of Wednesday, August 27th, came quickly. Three farm boys from rural America arose energized and carried away by boyish enthusiasm. They were eager to get the day started, and Johnny tugged on Ezra to awaken the older man from deep slumber. "Git-up, Mister Bowles," Johnny implored. "We've got people to see, and places to go!"

Ezra Bowles cracked open a reluctant eye, knowing instantly there was no chance to gain a few extra nods. Boys were on the move, especially Johnny and Junior, and all he could do was join them. After pulling on boots and splashing faces with water from wood bucket outside their tent, the four headed toward the mess tent for breakfast. Hurriedly, they devoured a sizeable plate of scrambled eggs, country ham, and fresh baked biscuits, chasing it down with good stiff black coffee. They lingered little over coffee, before asking directions to the tent where enlistments were taking place. Arriving at the enlistment tent, they noticed others had similar ideas about early starts to the morning, so they took a place in line behind ten or fifteen other prospective enlistees. Little did they realize, once in the military 'hurry and wait' would become a familiar circumstance. Will shuffled weight from one foot to the other, fidgeted with hands moving in and out of trouser pockets, and glanced from time to time toward Ezra for reassurance. Ezra stood aside with family members of other enlistees, smoke drifting from pipe clenched tightly, thumbs tugging at suspenders, peering over rimless spectacles, enjoying the whole situation. Johnny and Junior engaged in silly banter, laughing and nudging each other playfully, making the event look anything but serious.

As men completed tasks, the line became shorter, and soon Will presented himself to the recruiting officer seated at the table. Ezra stood aside and watched, glowing with pride. A 'volunteer enlistment form' was pushed toward Will …he was asked to complete the form, committing to three years of service in the Union Army. Will, like other privates, would be receiving pay of $13 per month …good, reliable pay …particularly in these depression times with unemployment widespread throughout the land. Will decided to sign an 'Allotment Bill' which provided that $10 of his monthly pay would be sent home to the treasurer in Oxford, Michigan, who would make it available for Maria. This left Will with the balance of $3 per month for incidental expenses …to be paid at the army's convenience.

Seated next to the recruiting officer, was another uniformed officer …an army surgeon. The surgeon completed a portion of the form, stating he examined the recruit and opining the applicant 'free from all bodily defects and mental infirmity which might disqualify him from performing the duties of a soldier'. The 'exam' was conducted without the surgeon ever looking up from the paper before him. Anxious and nervous, Will fidgeted as the brief interrogation took place. Paperwork was passed back to the recruiting officer who attested on the form that he 'minutely examined' Will, finding him to be 'entirely sober when enlisted', of lawful age, and qualified to perform obligations of a soldier. The officer pushed the paperwork toward Will without a word or sign of emotion. Will's demeanor changed. He smiled, doffed his hat to the officer, rubbed fingers hastily through his hair, gulped, and bowed slightly to the officer. "Thank you, Sir," he said excitedly. Will signed the paperwork …and that was it. Will was a private in the Union Army. He turned to Ezra and gestured a 'thumbs up'. Ezra beamed and winked acknowledgment.

The same enlistment process occurred with Johnny and Junior, before the three moved away from the table smiling and excited. With arms locked around each other, they danced a little jig, clapping hands in celebration. They were friends who enlisted together ...they were 'true blue' and so very proud. "Now we're 'Billy Yanks'!" Junior shouted.

Next step was issue of uniforms and equipment. At the far end of the tent, boys lined up and were handed uniforms. Uniforms came in only four sizes, so the dispensing officer made a best guess as to fit ...a navy blue wool coat, wool trousers, 'kepi' field cap, and government-issue boots. Equipment for each man included: knapsack for personal belongings, haversack for rations, shelter tent, rubber tarp for the ground or use as a poncho, 3-pint metal canteen, tin cup, tin plate, knife, fork, and spoon. Sleeping blankets were to be provided by the soldier, as government supply was in shortage. Likewise, guns were not yet available for the soldiers ...they would arrive later.

With uniforms and equipment overflowing in their arms, Will, Johnny, and Junior headed back hurriedly toward their assigned tent, eager to try on uniforms and survey gear, while Ezra tried to keep pace at their rear. In the tent, three young men were exuberant and raucous ...each searching haphazardly through newly issued equipment, like boys opening Christmas presents. One could hardly imagine the pleasure garnered by strapping knapsack on back, fingering inside lining of the haversack, reading embossed lettering on the canteen, feigning drinks from the tin cup, unrolling the rubber ground cloth, and pretending to sword fight with the crude government-issued utensils ...all carried out with uproarious laughter, backslapping, and unbridled camaraderie. As the 'party' continued, Ezra played bystander ...standing to the side, content to watch the celebration ...knowing all too well that times were about to change ...far too quickly.

"Will, try on your uniform," urged Junior.

Will pulled off his trousers, stepped into new light blue kersey wool trousers, slipped on the uniform coat, and perched the field cap jauntily on his head. "How do I look?" Will asked with a broad grin. The two boys, and Ezra, agreed that Will cut a dashing figure in uniform.

Next to try on his uniform was Junior. Jerry Webb, or 'Junior' as he was known to everyone in Oxford, was 28 years old ...oldest of the three friends. He had always been known as 'Junior', because he was the youngest of a large family of six children, the oldest a brother, and four sisters. He was single, and still lived on the farm with his mother and father. As the last sibling, Junior was more than a little spoiled ...he readily admitted such ...enjoying his role and not eager to grasp maturity. Freckle-faced, with a good crop of red hair, thin features, and short of stature at 5'5", he presented a boyish image. Getting serious was not something he enjoyed ...Junior liked a good time ...often displaying a quick and sometimes crude sense of jocular humor.

Good humor was tested when Junior tried on the uniform. Will and Johnny tried to hold back a chuckle, as Junior slipped on uniform trousers ...pant legs too long, cuffs hiding feet. Worse yet, when Junior let go, the trousers fell to the ground ...the waist far too large for a wiry frame. His face contorted in disappointment.

"No worry-in', partner," Johnny offered, trying to be helpful, "we 'kin find some rope, an' tie it to y'er waist to hold up dem' pants." Will raised a hand to hide the smile on his face ...a few moments of silence passed ...then, Junior let out a belly laugh, breaking the tension ...all joining his laughter.

Johnny's turn came next. Sandy blond hair fell helter-skelter down his forehead ...jowls of his face flushed red ...contrasting against pale white freckled skin that never looked healthy. Johnny was plump for a medium height frame ...always on the heavy side, despite being only 22 years old. Uniform trousers fit pretty well, but he had to tug to get his coat to button. He said, "This wo-ol itches ma' skin ...it's a way too hot for summer."

"It will help you lose weight," Will offered. "Maybe we should forego dinner?"

"Noth-in' do-in', Will," Johnny answered.

And so it was. Will, Johnny, and Junior were now full-fledged members of the Union Army ...each equipped with new uniform and the paraphernalia needed by a soldier. Over the next several days their journey began.

Next day Ezra Bowles left for home. He would have liked to stay and see the boys off, but he needed to get back to Nettie and their farm ...and see what help he could be to Maria and the children. It was sad farewell, especially for Will. Ezra was like a father, and his being there meant a great deal. "Please describe everything to Maria. Tell her I miss her already ...and the boys. Let her know I will write often ...ask her to do the same," Will said in parting. "And, Ezra ...thank you for being our friend."

"God bless ...take good care, Will," Ezra called out, as he laid reins to Henry and Jake and the wagon moved away. "We'll take good care of Maria ...and the child-in' ...rest assured, my friend ...best of luck, boys." Three newly enlisted soldiers stood waving.

Wagon moved out of sight, Will gazing down at ground ...pensive ...sudden feeling of loneliness enveloping him, causing shoulders to sag ...stomach feeling great emptiness. Johnny and Junior moved away quietly, sensing their friend's loss ...wishing to give him time alone. Will was suddenly alone ...its realization striking like a huge hammer blow. He stood transfixed, lost in hollowness, emptiness and fear darting and flashing through subconscious. *"...I wish Father were here to give me advice ...I miss him so much. And, Maria ...our last night together ...the children ...our farm."* He felt anguish, heartsick, lonely ...and fearful ...for the first time.

Later that morning, three new recruits reported to the parade ground for first drills. Within a day their regiment had its full quota of officers and enlisted men mustered into service of the Union Army. Will learned quickly. They were part of the '22nd Michigan Infantry Volunteers', a regiment of 997 officers and enlisted men. It was soon apparent that most of the officers were ill-prepared and untrained in military ways. Military life was going to be a major learning experience for them, as well as Will and fellow raw recruits. The regiment's Colonel was Moses Wisner, 46 years old, from Pontiac, Michigan, and ex-Governor of the State. The Lieutenant Colonel was Heber Le Favour, 24 years old, from Detroit. Other staff included: Major William Sanborn, 27 years old, from Port Huron, as well as a Surgeon, Assistant Surgeon, Adjutant, Quartermaster, and Chaplin.

The '22nd Michigan' was infantry ...like 80% of the Union Army ...'foot soldiers' with no use for cavalry or artillery units. The 22nd Michigan Infantry Regiment, like other regiments in the Union Army, consisted of ten 'Companies' ...designated 'A' thru 'K'. Company A and Company B were assigned as right and left flank units, while Companies C thru K formed the interior of battle lines. Will, Johnny, and Junior were assigned to Company 'A' ...156 men ranging in age from 17 years to 45 years of age. Their Captain was Ezra Hatton, 43 years old, from Farmington, Michigan. The 1st Lieutenant was Edward Wisner, 19 years old, and the son of Colonel Wisner. The 2nd Lieutenant was William Albertson of Pontiac.

Marching drills took up the next several days on the grassy parade ground at the Fair Grounds campsite, as officers struggled to build discipline among raw recruits. It was a frustrating task ...even humorous at times. In many cases, these 'volunteers' were backwoods, untutored, farm boys ...and, the officers not experienced in teaching discipline. Even drill commands 'right face-left face' posed problems. Over and over, they struggled. Often, a command of 'right face' found several men in the company turned left, with sheepish looks on faces as they realized their mistake. Other times, men simply froze, not turning either direction as they sorted out their confusion. Mistakes brought giggles and snickers from the troops, compounding embarrassment to the confused soldier. Occasionally, one of the men let out a bellowing, country "hee-haw" shout, which sent men to raucous laughter.

Officers worked relentlessly to generate a semblance of discipline and order. It was drill, drill, drill ...and more drill ...then eat, sleep, and more drill. For the next five days, they worked. One innovative instructor came up with a creative solution to the problematic march cadence 'right foot-left foot-right foot'. He insisted that each man with a problem tie a wisp of hay to his right boot, and straw to his left boot. Then, the drill instructor called, "hay foot, straw foot, hay foot, straw foot." Amazing to Will, this not only entertained the men and broke monotony, but seemed to work. Improvement happened gradually, but there was a long way to go before these boys and men became soldiers.

After a sixth long day of drilling, and after evening meal, Will found time to write a first letter home. Johnny and Junior were out, wandering from campfire to campfire, meeting other soldiers and their families. This afforded quiet time for Will

…time to share thoughts with Maria. He located a wood barrel just outside the tent and turned it upside down to serve as writing desk. With nib pen and bottle of black ink, he sat on a log turned on end, and began to put pen and ink to paper.

He wrote:

Fair Grounds at Pontiac,
Michigan
Tuesday, Sept. 2, 1862

My dear Maria:

I am so pleased to be writing you. I have missed you, since the wagon pulled away. I must confess a tear came to my eye. My thoughts have been with you constant, since our arrival, and I think of the two boys. This is the earliest I could find to put pen to paper, because our officers keep us drilling, drilling, and more drilling.

My body is achy from the marching and standing, but I am fine. Our marching was awful rough to start, but all the men are getting much more accustomed to it. Food is good, though I miss your cooking. The ladies of

Pontiac serve our meals. Junior and Johnny enjoy the meals immensely.

I trust Mr. Bowles returned safely, and told you all about our trip, and the camp here. Please tell him I appreciate everything. Are you alright? And, Will Jr. and Walter? Please give them a kiss from Papa. What about the farm, and the animals? Remember to store some corn as you pick. The crib needs to be full for winter. Weed the squash.

I signed the allotment, so $10 per pay should be sent to Mr. Bloggs in Oxford. He will hold it for your use. On Thursday, the regiment marches into the city for a sendoff, and then we will leave by rail to Kentucky. Please write soon.

Your loving husband,
Will

The postmaster delivered letters in camp to soldiers each morning. The mail wagon arrived, and at break from drills, men gathered anxiously about the wagon as names were called for those fortunate to receive mail. Will joined the gathering on Wednesday morning, hoping enough time passed to receive a letter from Maria. But, disappointment showed, as he turned away with slightly hunched shoulders and bowed head when the last name was called.

Thursday morning, September 4th, dawned with a magnificent sunrise, as the bugler's call of 'reveille' broke early silence. This was the day of farewells for men who still had family in camp, and departure for the 22nd Michigan Infantry. The boys dressed with pride in newly-issued uniforms. After breakfast at the mess tent, Will, Johnny, and Junior returned to their tent to assemble belongings and pack knapsacks. They headed off to the parade ground, passing families hugging and tearfully saying 'goodbye' …loved ones about to go off to war …mothers clinging to their boys, weeping and sobbing, praying for their soldier's safe return. A gray haired father stood, tears trickling down cheeks, giving his beloved son words of comfort, urging him to be brave and do his duty. A sister wrapped arms around her brother's neck, reminding him of her love. Others were bravely shaking hands, fighting back emotion.

It was a sight and feeling Will could never forget. They paused briefly …awestruck. Three young friends glanced at each other …each knowing the other was also choked with emotion …thoughts of home, and loved ones, came to each …the serious nature of 'soldier' business struck minds with a chill thud. No turning back now …they were soldiers. Destiny was in God's hand …nothing need be said.

They arrived at the parade ground where nearly one thousand men were assembling. Hearts pounded at the sight of such power and spectacle …throats parched and dry, stomachs churning. No one was prepared for this. Officers on horseback pranced among enlisted men, as ten companies formed lines. Roll call was completed within each company. "Will Hodkins" was called by the officer, and Will called out, "Here". And so it went, on down the lines.

With companies formed, the regiment moved out by about 10:00 AM, displaying best hard-earned march discipline. As columns of men passed under the 'Fair Grounds' sign and left camp, columns veered right onto Old Lapeer Road. Already, throngs of bystanders lined roadway to show support and offer best wishes. It was about a one-half mile march southwest toward the city of Pontiac. From Old Lapeer Road, marching columns turned onto Saginaw Street, past crossing of 'Detroit & Milwaukee Railroad' railroad tracks, and into the city's hub at the junction of Huron Street and Orchard Lake Road. As soldiers drew near to the heart of the city, crowds grew even larger and more vocal and demonstrative. Roadways were lined four and five people deep.

Ten to fifteen thousand people were on hand. It was a farewell gathering, but also a town celebration. Fathers, mothers, brothers, sisters, wives, relatives, friends, and lovers were there, as well as ordinary city citizens who just wanted to be part of it all. No one wanted to miss seeing these future 'heroes' off on their journey. Flushed faces, wild eyes, and screaming mouths nearly drowned out a band playing 'Dixie', for 'Dixie' was a popular song in both the North and the South. Tears filled onlookers' eyes, as ladies waved white handkerchiefs, while others waved small flags of the 'stars and stripes'. Children were wide-eyed, smiling and waving. No soldier could help but feel exhilarated by this unfettered display of support. The new recruits basked in glory that only soldiers receive on their way to war.

In town, the regiment broke for a picnic just before noon. Will located Johnny and Junior who were separated in the march. They sat on the grass with food of all varieties provided by the ladies of Pontiac. A farmer brought a wagon load of delicious shiny red apples which were distributed to the soldiers. Johnny jumped up, scurrying to the wagon, and returned with three polished red Macintosh apples in hand, "I'm imagin-in' these are pretty tasty."

Junior chomped down, exclaiming, "Ya' bet-cha!"

After the picnic, men listened to patriotic speeches by several city dignitaries, which pumped the crowd to even higher fervor. The glorious occasion was disrupted for a few minutes when two dogs got into a fight and had to be separated. Johnny offered, "My dawg wud've wupped 'em." This brought laughter from the nearby crowd that overheard him, but did little to deter passion of the speakers. In between speeches, bands played the

'Battle Cry of Freedom', then 'Red, White and Blue'. A chorus joined in singing verses from 'Bonnie Blue Flag', and the crowd began singing as well:

"We're fighting for our Union,
We're fighting for our trust,
We're fighting for that happy land
Where sleeps our father dust.
It cannot be dissevered,
Though it cost us bloody wars,
We never can give up the land
Where floats the stripes and stars..."

Ceremony concluded with presentation of regiment's flag, sewn by ladies from the area. The flag was accepted by Colonel Moses Wisner, regiment's commander, and he offered a few remarks of appreciation and commitment ...the '22nd Michigan Infantry' would do admirable service to their country, the State of Michigan, and to the hometown of each man. With that, the ceremony concluded, and the regiment was ordered to form ranks to begin its march toward the rail station for loading and departure by 2:00 PM.

Chapter 7

March of the nearly 1,000-man regiment was impressive and awe inspiring. Will felt skin tingle and heart pound beneath uniform while gasping for breath, glancing side to side to absorb everything. All men were excited and enthusiastic with march-route lined by cheering throngs of well-wishers. First columns approached the rail depot after a one-half hour march. At first view of rail station and platform, Will could see the waiting train billowing smoke from its massive black locomotive. Visual spectacle of a long 20-car train, and large crowds poised to watch its departure, caused heart to pump even faster. He realized that for many rural backwoods boys, this was going to be a first trip by railroad. Will travelled via train before …first trip being St. Louis where he met Maria …but still new to Will as well. Advent of steam-powered railroads was recent, and burgeoning development of vast networks of railroads still occurring.

As more soldiers arrived, Will's studied the train. Its locomotive had four smaller leading wheels upfront, and four large drive wheels at its rear measuring four or five feet in diameter. An immense steam boiler sat atop locomotive's frame, steam climbing skyward from its chimney. Out front, a 'cow-catcher' iron structure was attached in the event of free-roaming livestock or to free the track of snow in winter. A wooden cab had a large bell and oil lantern at its side. Out of cab's windows, train's engineer and fireman were peering and waving at gathering soldiers. Locomotive featured extensive polished metal trim, highlighting gaudy red paint trim scheme.

Locomotive, steam-powered

(Library of Congress)

Behind locomotive came the 'tender' which carried stacked cords of firewood to fire the boiler, and a tank for water to provide steam. Steam-powered engine consumed vast quantities of both wood and water. Cordwood would be stacked at intervals along rail tracks by local landowners, who were under contract with the railroad company. Water tanks were placed at intervals of 5-10 miles, handy to source water from nearby springs, streams, or ponds.

Freight cars were of wood construction, rolling on cast iron wheels. Company A was assigned to the first three boxcars, and other companies were assigned in order down the line. Will and other men clambered aboard. 'Boxcars', or so-called 'house cars', were modified with benches added to transport enlisted troops. There were too few 'passenger cars', so these were reserved for officers. Will hurriedly moved to a seat on a bench at an outside wall of the second boxcar, fortunate to get such a seat because wooden walls were slatted with openings that provided some visibility outside, as well as source for fresh air.

Forty or fifty men packed each rail car allowing no room to move. Men scrunched together on narrow benches, while others sought comfort on rough sewn wood plank floor covered by straw three or four inches thick ...everyone close quarters, literally armto-arm, no room to move or stretch. Will had a different march position from Johnny or Junior. He looked around for them, but they were not on his rail car. Will turned to a soldier seated to his right, "I'm Will Hodkins ...from Oxford."

The young man looked to be about Will's age, "My name's Jeremiah Carpenter, and I live here in Pontiac. Glad to meet you, Will."

People liked Will ...he felt at ease talking with new acquaintances. A nice friendly nature ...unassuming, without pretense ...pretty much, what you saw and heard of Will was what there was ...nothing hidden, everything honest and straight-forward, no surprises. Will didn't say a lot, but when he spoke words meant something. Will turned left, to an even younger soldier. The soldier answered, "I'm Lucius ...Lucius Stickney ...from West Bloomfield. Pleased to meet ya', Will." Then, Lucius motioned to his left, "This is my friend, Jeptha Tucker."

Introductions and ensuing small talk were interrupted, drowned out by sudden and prolonged, shrill whistle of locomotive and sound bursts of steam belching from boiler. Screech of huge iron wheels of locomotive grabbing traction on shiny top surface of rails and sudden jerk, signaled train underway. Will reached for his pocket watch, a shiny gold cased treasure that was Father's ...it read 2:30 PM ...a little later than scheduled. Young recruits peered through slats in boxcar's sides to watch throngs of people waving 'goodbye', their cheers mixing with sound of a band striking up a marching tune. As a lengthy 20-car train gained momentum and began its steady roll, sounds of people and music faded. Men were suddenly isolated, sandwiched alone within a darkened crowded boxcar.

Late-Summer weather was hot and humid ...sun showing brightly all day ...throughout march from Fair Grounds into town, during ceremony, and then march to railway depot. Men sweated, new woolen uniforms making heat worse. Will felt fatigue ...body ached ...he knew others felt the same. Marching was new to Will. It was exhausting, compounded by emotion and energy maintained at high levels throughout an already long day. Many fell asleep quickly. Will fought the urge ...situation unpleasant. This was a well-used old rail car previously inhabited by livestock, and now co-habited by hot, smelly soldiers ...most deep in sleep and snoring loudly in a cacophony of sound reminiscent of cattle mewing. A sheepish smile crept onto Will's face as he realized its irony and humor ...he surveyed the scene, mind flashing, *"present occupants are not different from prior occupants."* He was embarrassed with himself, but rail car reeked with smell of cattle and traces of urine and excrement permeated wood flooring ...all more aromatic and obnoxious with buildup of afternoon heat and fifty sweating men, crowded close quarters with little air circulating ...hot, humid, and ripe with body odor of men with little room to wriggle ...unable to escape.

Trying to ignore unpleasantness, Will and Jeremiah spent time talking, while gazing at passing sights through openings of wood slats. The 'Detroit & Milwaukee Railroad' train moved 20 miles per hour top-speed through outskirts of Pontiac, southeast 23 miles toward Detroit. Will watched rolling hills of countryside, dotted by an array of small lakes, before train reached depot at Birmingham, Michigan. It was late afternoon when the train paused for a short time to take on more water, but men could not leave cars, making heat and unpleasantness more intense. Will was buoyed by small crowds of well wishers gathered alongside platform, some with young children in tow to memorialize the moment. All were waving, ladies hoisting white handkerchiefs. Shouts of encouragement were voiced toward cars of fresh recruits. And then, train whistle blew and cars began rolling.

Will asked Jeremiah about family. "I work with my father in his livery ...he is a blacksmith in Pontiac. I live with him, my mother, and two younger sisters in a small home in the city, a few blocks from the livery."

Will told Jeremiah of Maria back home, and the children. "It has been very difficult leaving ...my son Will Jr. is just 3 years old, and needs me. Walter is one, and just getting good at walking."

Jeremiah answered, "My sisters and I are very close ...they look up to me, to take care of them ...and, Daddy, he works long hours, even with me help-in' him."

Time passed and the train pulled alongside the next platform ...a sign overhead identifying the stop as 'Royal Oak'.

Another small gathering of well-wishers was on hand. The train took on water and cords of wood for the boiler's thirsty fire, but still no soldiers were allowed to leave the train. An officer explained, "It would take too much time for so many men to unload and reload. Schedules are tight and we are late ...hold onto yourselves, boys." But as the train rolled into countryside, one crusty long-haired youth nudged past everyone ...awkwardly bumping into crowded men, he hastily maneuvered toward rail car's slatted side. Will watched in disgust as the scrubby youth urinated through open slats ..."Oh, my ...oh my!" he sighed in relief, shaking himself before buttoning back up.

Will thought, "...*going to be a long, grueling trip ...all the way into Kentucky.*" He struck up conversation with Lucius and Jeptha, as Jeremiah nodded off and dozed. "Where are you boys from?" Will asked.

Jeptha answered, "Just down the way a-piece, from the 'Fairgrounds' ...on a small farm with my Ma and Pa, outside of Pontiac."

"I hail from West Bloomfield, a little south and west of Pontiac," Lucius offered.

"Do you have a family, or are you single, Lucius?" Will asked.

"I'm single ...just like Jeptha ...but I live with my aunt and uncle. My parents died when I was a young-un."

"You both look pretty young to me."

"I'm 18 years old," Jeptha answered.

"I'm just 19 years old," Lucius chided, "...but, we're ready and able to fight them Rebs!" He hesitated for a moment. "My aunt and uncle were against me joining-up," Lucius added, "...they've been like mother and father to me and my sisters ...but I finally convinced 'em!"

"I hope we git' there, before the fight-ins' over!" Jeptha exhorted with unabashed enthusiasm of youth.

"Heard ya' tell Jeremiah there ...that yuz' a married man, Will," Jeptha continued, "...but we're all 'boys' here!"

Will answered, "Oh, I'm married alright ...have a right nice family too ...but, I'm only 24 years old. You can call me a 'boy' too."

"All right, then!" Lucius snapped, slapping a knee and laughing. Will and Jeptha joined in laughter. Each seemed to enjoy the other's company. They continued small talk until the train pulled into the rail station in Detroit. Will reached for chain bob attached to his watch, and pulled the watch from pant pocket …nearly 5 PM …about 2 ½ hours from departure in Pontiac. Will nudged Jeremiah awake, "Jeremiah, we're here …in Detroit."

Will, Jeremiah, Lucius, and Jeptha scrambled off the rail car, bumping body-to-body with fifty other soldiers pushing hastily to boxcar doors that slid open …all anxious to stretch cramped legs and bodies, relieve themselves, and inhale deeply fresh outside air. The scene was repeated as men hurriedly piled out of twenty rail cars up and down the line ...all rushing pell-mell to depot's bathroom to urinate …quite a scene, humanity long overdue. With the regiment of nearly 1,000 men relieved and refreshed, recruits gathered in groups on the platform. Day's hot temperature subsided by late afternoon, and men found it pleasant to mill around and converse casually.

But, Will wanted to locate Johnny and Junior, and introduce them to three newly found friends. After dodging in and out, searching around soldiers on platform, Will and three friends spotted Johnny and Junior and moved quickly to join them. "Hey there, want you boys to meet my new friends," Will called excitedly to Johnny and Junior. After introductions and handshakes, six men exchanged small talk and groused about their grueling train ride and awful conditions within crowded rail cars. Before long, a bugle sounded and officers called for men to form ranks.

Ezra Hatton, Captain of 'Company A', barked orders for Will's company to assemble, but men were new to this and quite disorganized. Up and down the line, officers of ten companies struggled to organize men for march through the city toward docks on the Detroit River. Crowds of onlookers were assembled to wish troops 'bon voyage', so officers wanted to avoid embarrassment by turning chaos into disciplined marching columns ...but, to no avail. Will noted many onlookers enjoying such humorous dysfunction, particularly as patience of officers grew thin. Eventually, disarray was turned into semi-organized discipline, as columns of recruits began marching …'22nd Michigan Infantry Volunteers' on next leg of journey toward Union camp in Kentucky.

Word spread through ranks that next portion of travel was by riverboat steamer, departing from docks on city's eastern side, along the Detroit River which runs north-south emptying into Lake Erie. Will was excited, because paddle wheel steam boats were a 'way of life', but this would be a first experience …as for many men. Much transpired since Robert Fulton sailed riverboat *"Clermont"* up the Hudson River between New York and Albany in 1807. Steam power revolutionized water travel for merchandise, supplies, mail, and passengers. Steam power drove boats on all large rivers, like the Mississippi, Ohio, and Missouri, and across the Great Lakes. Now, it was employed to move troops. After thirty minutes marching, through city streets lined with cheering contingents, the regiment reached the docks. Men fell out to enjoy brief respite, while officers made final arrangements, before boarding an impressive steamship moored dockside.

Will stared wide-eyed, awestruck at immense size of the flat bottom sternwheeler. It appeared to be over 200 feet long …tall port and starboard smokestacks towering skyward …sun starting descent behind crewmen onboard, casting deep orange hue onto ship's black towers. Four decks were stacked upward, with engine exhaust and pilot house for its captain and crew on top deck. A deck was piled high with stacks of firewood to feed hungry boilers located deep within holds of its engine room. Elaborate markings and scroll work decorated ship's sides and railings …ornate gothic deck rail at its bow. Will stood transfixed …gazing upward at such a mammoth vessel …its aura of 'grandness' unmatched by anything witnessed before.

A bugle sounded, breaking Will's trance …time to form ranks prior to boarding. Men filed up steeply inclined gangplank to enter a breathtaking ship. Walking inside, Will gawked at grand staircases, carpeted lounges, and luxurious passenger cabins reserved for regiment officers. Meanwhile, he and other enlisted men were directed toward different decks, where they were to find space to store gear, and get as comfortable as possible for nighttime cruise to Cleveland, Ohio, on southern banks of Lake Erie.

By 8:00 PM, ship's whistle wailed into darkening night, as its huge paddle wheel began easing vessel away from dock. Men lined railings to catch best view. Sporadic cheers erupted, with good natured joking …an exciting first-time event for many ...as if departing on festive cruise ...a beautiful sight. Will watched docks and Detroit skyline grow more distant, silhouetted against brilliant colors of sunset now just receding on horizon. He stood at ship's rear railing, enamored by waters, churned into white frothy display, leaving a well defined trail in ship's wake. Gentle breeze blew Will's hair, and he removed his cap to get full enjoyment. Coolness felt good on skin, and he breathed deeply of clear fresh air out on water after a lengthy hot parched day.

Darkness overtook them quickly. As ship left waters of the Detroit River and entered massive dark waters of Lake Erie, all became pitch black, save for a few lanterns offering partial light on ship's decks. Crowds grew quiet ...thrashing of paddle wheel against water, and groan of steam engine the only sounds. Most men were exhausted from an exhilarating past twelve hours. They ambled off to find space on ship's deck to get much needed sleep. In short time, very few were moving. It was quiet time.

Will had one thing to do before he retired. He was feeling so good about the day, energized by newness of experience. He wanted to capture the feeling …share it with Maria. So, he found sitting room on deck, leaned back against a bulkhead under burning kerosene lantern, and took pen and ink from knapsack. He began to write:

Steamer on Lake Erie,
September 4th
Thursday night, 11:00 PM

My dear Maria:

I am writing from a steamer somewhere on Lake Erie, headed for Cleveland. My first trip on ship is most pleasant. I was reminded of your sailing to St. Louis. I miss you so much ...and the boys. I trust you are fine, and Mr. and Mrs. Bowles are of assistance. Please write, although I do not know when I will receive.

We left the Fairgrounds-Pontiac this morning, and marched into city. Had a most memorable ceremony, and picnic following. Crowds were cheering our every step as we marched to the rail. The rail trip to Detroit was most uncomfortable. It was very hot, and too many men in our car. I was separated from Johnny and Junior, but met three fine boys. I think we can be friends, and may be tent partners.

Ask Mr. Bowles to find help to bring in the corn, and dig potatoes. I hope tomatoes are still good, and beans coming nicely. I am very hungry *now, because we have not eaten since Pontiac. Must get some sleep. We have a long trip tomorrow to Kentucky. I promise to write as I can. I think of you always.*

Your loving husband,
Will

Will folded the letter precisely, gave it a kiss, and placed it in an envelope he addressed. It would be posted at first opportunity. He tucked the envelope in his journal. He sighed deeply, studying the white flower Maria had given him upon leaving home …flower now pressed securely between first pages of journal. Journal was returned to coat breast pocket for safekeeping. With that, Will pulled kepi cap down forehead over eyes, and fell fast asleep. Sleep came easily …awake nearly fifteen hours.

Chapter 8

Back home in Oxford, day-to-day life continued …best it could. Will was gone just a few days, but not same without him. Maria sat pensive at the kitchen table, shoulders slumped, hands folded limp, eyes transfixed but seeing nothing. Evening meal was complete, dishes done, and things tidy …two boys tucked in bed, fast asleep. She pushed aside a straw basket holding knitting …mittens and socks started for winter …but she could garner no interest for now. Darkness was approaching rapidly, a time of day when loneliness consumed her. She missed Will greatly …talkative he was not, particularly after hard day's work …but, his presence meant security and comfort …to an extent not realized before his absence.

She arose from the table and walked into the bedroom to pull her journal from its hideaway tucked hidden in rearmost portion of nightstand drawer. The journal was hers since childhood …she cherished that little book. As she explained to Will, *"…gives every moment memory."* She made intimate entries upon bursts of sporadic interest which came and went over years. More recently, it remained securely tucked away, pretty much untouched since marriage …and departure from Penn Yan. She returned to her seat at kitchen table, lightly fingering journal's worn hardbound brown leather cover, with a sigh of affection heard by no one. With soft flickering light of kerosene lamp giving visual warmth to empty room, Maria's thoughts turned to childhood years …and home in Penn Yan. *"I am so fortunate …a childhood of comfort and security,"* she mused. *"…so unlike life on this farm in Michigan …Will and I struggle so much making ends meet ...though our love and sharing make it worthwhile ...but now he is gone."* Suddenly chilled, she reached for an afghan recently knitted. Wrapping it about her shoulders, it did little good. She felt loneliness and lack of security like never before ...so unlike childhood, with warmth of love and security surrounding her.

Maria was raised in the so-called 'Finger Lakes' region of New York state, about 200 miles northwest of New York City. 'Finger Lakes' were eleven slim lakes of icy blue water, looking like finger marks pointing north ...gouges clawed by glaciers, from hilly heavily forested land. Seneca Lake was longest and deepest at 600 feet, extending 40 miles north-south, but only three miles across. Maria recalled vivid memories of its icy cold waters ...even in summer ...though it hardly ever froze over in winter. Penn Yan was a small town to the lake's west, named for the town's early mix of immigrants from Pennsylvania and New England. Nearest larger towns were about sixty miles away ...Rochester to the northwest, located on the southern shore of Lake Ontario ...Ithaca on the southern tip of Cayuga Lake, next lake east of Seneca Lake. The region was home to Seneca Indians, but Indians were driven away and white settlers moved in. Small farms developed, as oxen-pulled ploughs cleared forest land. Through early 1800's, farms thrived and became a prosperous breadbasket for the East Coast.

Rebecca 'Maria' Graham was born January 24th, 1835, to Joseph Graham and second-wife, Almira Benedict Graham. *"I cannot believe I am 27 years old ...it seems so old,"* Maria sighed. *"...and, Will three years younger ...how could I marry a younger man?"* Her father's first wife, Louisa, died three years before Maria was born, after twelve years of marriage and six children. Besides six step-brothers and sisters, Maria's two younger brothers are Joseph Stanley Graham and Jared Benedict Graham. An older sister, Louisa Maria, died as an infant of five months old. *"I cannot remember anyone calling me 'Rebecca' ...'Rebecca' is a name I dislike ...everyone calls me 'Maria' ...much warmer and more casual, I think."*

Maria lost her father when she was only five years old, and her mother died when she was nine. So, for a good portion of young years, she was raised by loving aunts and uncles in and around Penn Yan. She lived with Aunt Rebecca Graham Anderson, married to Uncle Hixon Anderson. Nearby were Uncle Kelsey Graham and Aunt Minerva. Maria's mother tutored her intensely ...until her death, when aunts and uncles saw to it that she was highly educated and well-traveled. *"So fortunate indeed ...an upbringing of comfort and love,"* she sighed, looking up from the table. She stared out the kitchen window into absolute darkness, mesmerized, lost in thought, curling nervously a strand of hair about a finger. Thoughts drifted again to childhood. The region around Penn Yan was isolated and thinly populated ...and gorgeous. *"Where nature had its sway,"* she told Will often. She grew nostalgic and sentimental, recalling her beloved Penn Yan.

It was a land of lake effect snowstorms, and bitter cold. In dead of winter, she recalled mornings with huge clouds of eerie mist rising from warmish surface of lake, into icy air glistening as sunlight passed through prisms of water vapor. Hard west winds sent gusts of snow chasing across fields and furrows of farm land. Cozy indoors as a child, she remembered spending endless time on comfy cushions of a bay window seat, peering at winter's majesty through windowpane ...nose pressed against icy glass, while holding book in hand. Visions returned of house roof gables fringed with hanging icicles ...charm of elegant homes of Victorian and Greek Revival architecture, sitting on ridges overlooking surrounding hills and valleys, enhanced by visual magic of winter wonderland ...a classical scene, bespeaking old-style European elegance and aristocracy. Peaceful quiet was interrupted occasionally by sudden boom of gunshot from a zealous hunter seeking deer, elk, or wild turkey. Maria remembered the fun of bundling in thick wool blankets, earmuffs and scarves for a skimming glide over snow covered roadways in horse-drawn sleigh. Only thing better was awaiting crackle of fire, returning to sit in its warmth at fireside hearth, with accompanying mug of tasty hot chocolate.

Signs of spring made lasting impression ...first flowers of April, bulbs popping from still snow covered ground ...crocus,

74

jonquil, tulip, and iris ...so lovely, before brief blooms faded with spring's arrival. Visions came back of beaver active in abundant meandering streams, red-winged blackbirds, and novel mating dances of pairs of cardinals. Pigeons and Blackbirds came and went in immense flocks that blackened sky, their roar of flapping migration sounding like an imagined tornado to ears of a young girl. Fond memories returned of fishing with Uncle Hixon for lake's cache of perch, northern pike, and lake trout ...prized targets for the many fishermen on Seneca Lake.

And, then came sultry summer evenings. Sights of expansive rolling cornfields were unforgettable, hues of green stalks with yellow and orange silk shimmering in setting sun, stalks nodding and swaying with wind's rhythm ...as well as dusky blue-green fields of cabbage, bordering undulating meadows accented by freshly mown row after row of rolled carpets of golden hay. Maria recalled fun she and cousin Rose enjoyed chasing flitting butterflies ...then as evening faded, entranced by off-and-on glow of fireflies captured and held in a glass jar ...and, lying on blanket on a warm evening, looking up to clear night sky to spy 'Big Dipper', bright red of Mars, and demurely to its right, Venus ...or, listening for chilling sound of an eastern coyote's wail, or unmistakable moaning sounds from a roaming pack of wolves.

Vivid pictures and recollections coursed through her mind ...poetic musings that touched her very soul ...visions of wonderful childhood and teenage years. Yet, she chose to leave home and loving family ...her beloved 'Penn Yan' ...all when she married Will and moved to Michigan. She paused. But, she loved Will dearly. This was her new life ...and, two young boys. She looked upward, clasped hands and sighed, voicing words quietly with no human to hear, *"I miss you, Penn Yan. And, Will ...I miss you so much! God, please protect them ...and give me strength."*

She rubbed fingers lightly, lovingly over trusty journal, before opening its cover. In April 1857, just over five years ago, Maria left Penn Yan for St. Louis, venturing down the Mississippi River via steamer, to visit and stay briefly with two other uncles and their families. It was in St. Louis that she met 'William

75

Hodkins'. She paged through the journal to find the location, and read from her entry:

September 27th, 1857, Sunday Eve

...I have fallen in love with a "German"
...he is very handsome, and so particular.
I saw him today peeking through the
windows of church at me...

Maria went on to write about 'William Hodkins', the 'German' she met a few days earlier:

October 8th, Thursday

...The "German" is as attentive as ever.
I do wish I could stop thinking about him.
(He is so perfect!)

Turning pages, she came to a section written after she returned from St. Louis, after meeting Will. She read aloud, in quiet whisper:

December 7th, 1857
It is Sabbath.

I am at Uncle Hixon's sitting in the parlor. Have been to church and heard an excellent sermon and am now writing in my dear little journal. Dear friend, you have been sadly neglected since I came home, but I will endeavor to make up for lost time now. I must retrospect a little. I left St. Louis in October, arrived safely at Rochester, saw all my friends there ...then came out here to brother's. Found them all well at brother's, and all so glad to see me after my long, long absence.

Maria kept reading and skimming ...pensive, and nostalgic:

December 17th

...Been reading the "Harps of Eden" and calling up old memories. It almost seemed to me that I was back again, in the happy past, and that one was in our midst. But alas the dream passed and I awoke to realize that he was far away, and that I might never see him again.

Oh, Will, where art thou tonight, and dost thou "give me one passing thought". One thought from your lips is more precious than all of life's gifts. But all is passed, and we may never meet again in this beautiful world. Oh! (if such should be) may we meet in that far off land where angels dwell, where our love will be unrestrained, and be our "whole existence".

Maria blushed and giggled in girlish fashion at such youthful romanticism. After all, she thought, *"I was a 22 year-old woman when this was written ...was I really that child-like, and foolish?"* She read on, memories of 'Penn Yan' streaming back:

Saturday Evening
December 19th, 1857

I am at John's. Sarah is mending the children's clothes and John is reading to Beatrice. I have a dear letter from "Rosebud" this week. Winter has barely begun his reign, yet for Friday it rained just as hard as it could. But today it is cold enough to forge the little brook in front of our house, but I think Crooked Lake is still unbound.

Sarah has made some of the best pumpkin pies today that I ever tasted. Nellie says that she has "left John's hat down to Didey's". Boliver Butler has been washing and ironing, and then set a little table for her and Nellie, and asked a blessing. Had a letter from Uncle Jarred. All are well. Well! Not withstanding the absence of Will and Rose and the noise of the children, this has been a very good week and enjoyed by me.

Oh! I forgot to say Boliver Butler has been breaking wind "to herself" to see how it sounds.

Maria broke out in laughter with the last sentence ..."*how could I talk like that in my diary? ...not very lady-like! ...what if*

79

someone reads this?" Embarrassed, but enjoying the moment, she read on:

Monday, December 28ᵗʰ

...Christmas ...I spent at home and a most miserable day it was too. And how shall I close with this year which has been one of the most eventful of my life. Commenced in New York happily, and joyfully from there to Missouri ...St. Louis, then to Illinois, and now back home again. I am yet single but happy and intend to remain so...

Happy to meet
Sad to part
And thrice happy to
Meet again.

She remembered longing ...heart broken ...for a letter from Will.   That last evening in St. Louis was so special ...Will promised to write, though he said, *"I'm not much for writ-in."* And, he promised to come to her in Penn Yan.

January 12th, Tuesday

Well, my Rosebud is with me today and she is blooming finely under the refreshing dews of James Taylor's love. (Rosa and James are to be married in the Spring and I think Rosa is deserving of a better husband. He is selfish, quick-tempered, licentious, and a little fond of a "drop" now and then.)

...Had a dream about Will last night. And my deep sad moments continue. I think of him and wonder on what strange skies those deep black eyes are looking. Should I never meet him again, I shall keep him in my memory as a kind of a beautiful dream ...too sacred and dear for the eyes of the world to gaze upon.

She paused, "*...there I go again ...what a hopeless romantic.*" Entranced, she could not stop reading.

81

February 6ᵗʰ, Saturday

John and Sarah went to Penn Yan today
and I stayed at home with the children.
They were very good and did not trouble me
much …We are all going up to Rochester
next week. I wish Will could be here to go
with us. The party will be incomplete and
sad without him. I wonder where is he.

February 12ᵗʰ, Friday

Arose quite early this morning …dressed and
then prepared to go down to Penn Yan.
After breakfast I walked down the hillside
to Chisholms and there waited for a chaise.
Rode with Mr. Brown to Penn Yan.
Went to Uncle Hixon's …found all well
and Rose looking like the "Old Harry".

Went down street in the evening …called
at Ms. Chisholm's …found that Sarah
Ann had gone to a party. Rose and I are

very indignant if the young people have gone there and left us. But we would not have them "get off their horses on our account" for worlds.

An awkward stab at half-hearted humor gave Maria pause for chuckle. Raising eyes locked onto pages, she realized more than an hour passed. She needed to get to bed because her boys would be up early, and she had many morning chores ...reading the journal was good. She felt better now ...somehow reunited with her 'Penn Yan'. She replaced a bookmark and closed journal's cover, tucking it back in its secure hiding place in the chest of drawers. Trusty journal was more than her friend ...she needed to get reacquainted. She vowed to read more another day ...but for now, tomorrow was another day.

Chapter 9

Blare of ship's horn pierced night's quiet, sun just beginning to rise with daybreak ...then another blast, followed by a third. With harsh jolt from deep slumber, Will awoke to see many soldiers awakening and milling around him ...steamship edging into dock at Cleveland. Will scrambled up from night's lowly perch on ship's hard deck. He wobbled from stiffness of unsteady legs, cramped from six hours sleep in contorted position far less comfortable than bed at home. Rubbing eyes to chase last remnants of sleep, he drew deep breaths of crisp clear morning air which refreshed and recharged him.

He sidled to ship's railing, watching the sternwheeler maneuver into port, scanning a panorama of Cleveland's wharf area. Three or four wharfs reached out from shore long distances into Lake Erie. To the east, a sprawling network of railroad tracks converged at a large red brick building, where he could make out large white painted words 'Union Passenger Depot' on its roof. Will overheard a fellow soldier tell a companion that the river off to their right and emptying into Lake Erie was the 'Cuyahoga River'. They pointed to a massive swinging bridge spanning 'Cuyahoga' near its mouth. A bustling avenue running alongside the river was called 'River Street' ...the fellow went on to say that 'Bank Street' and 'Water Street' merged at train station's entry.

Just then, up came Johnny and Junior, with the three new friends following close behind. Johnny called out, "Will, there ya' be!"

Junior added, "We thought we lost ya', Will."

Johnny turned and pointed to the three boys, "We'all spent the night together ...with Jeremiah, Lucius, and Jeptha ...down on second deck."

Looking toward shoreline, Junior exclaimed, "Ain't it beautiful ...never seen noth-in' like it!"

"She's a thing of beauty, alright!" Jeremiah agreed.

As six boys continued to admire scenery, paddle wheeler eased dockside and ropes were thrown to workers waiting to tie the vessel down. Officers called to men to gather equipment and prepare to disembark. The boys grabbed belongings, and followed other soldiers jostling toward stairways to first deck where the regiment was gathering to disembark. With gangplank in place, nudging and shoving humanity started to move single file down and off ship. The boys worked into line, finally trudging slowly down steeply inclined and narrow gangplank until they were off ship. "Feels good to get feet safely back on land," Jeremiah offered.

Johnny said, "I'm a starv-in'!"

Will agreed, "It's been nearly eighteen hours since we ate at the picnic."

Boys nodded heads in complete agreement. An officer overheard their interchange and answered, "Rations will be issued at the train station ...you'll have to wait a little longer ...takes some time to unload one thousand men from ship."

"Yes, Sir ...thank you, Sir," Will answered, saluting awkwardly. So, boys milled around on wharf with other soldiers, waiting and chatting. Within half an hour, officers began assembling men into companies and columns for march to nearby rail depot. Rest of journey to Kentucky would be via rail ...about 240 miles south, across the state of Ohio. Will pulled watch from pocket ...just after 7:00 AM. *"Friday morning, September 5th,"* he thought to himself. *"Must be about time Maria and boys are just getting up ...wonder what they will be doing today?"* Thought was broken when an officer shouted, "Attention!" Soon columns, four men abreast, were marching off wharf toward the train station.

At the station, first rations were issued and men directed to fill canteens with water. Will and the boys were famished ...even first experience with army rations seemed acceptable. Will moved through a line to receive an allotment of corn bread, hunk of salt pork, apple, and hardtack. At next station, Will extended tin cup for steaming hot coffee. "Thank you, 'mam …it smells so good." After Jeremiah, Lucius, Jeptha, Johnny, and Junior received rations, Will motioned for the boys to follow. Six boys found a spot to sit, leaned against brick wall of rail depot, and started to unwrap and investigate what they were given to eat. "Coffee tastes good …sure enough," Will said. "…smells even better."

Johnny held up salt pork and questioned, "What's this? …sure doesn't smell so good!"

A bite already in mouth, Junior answered, "Ain't so bad …once ya' git her past the nose."

Corn bread was readily devoured …apple as well …hardtack was a different matter. 'Hardtack' was a cracker about three inches square, half-inch thick, and very hard. "She gits' her name right justly, now …hard as a brick," Junior offered, struggling quizzically with cracker in hand. Jeremiah brushed off what looked like mold on his three pieces, before trying to break one with fingers. After several futile attempts, he exclaimed, "She can't be broken!"

Young Lucius and Jeptha watched silently …observing four older boys …wanting to learn. Johnny tried to bite down on one unyielding cracker, but winced and belted out, "I thinks I'm's in great danger of break-in' my teeths!" With infamous belly laugh, he added, "And she's a whole lot stale …she is." Others joined the laughter.

Will offered an idea for the stale, unsavory and tasteless crackers, "Dip them in your coffee …seems to work." As others made fun of the predicament, Will noticed a location to deposit mail on the platform near entry to the station. He got up and walked over to deposit his letter to Maria …he kissed the envelope, before dropping it gingerly into a hanging dinghy gray canvas mail bag. Having finished a first cup of coffee, he ambled over to a lady dispensing coffee. "Would be pleased to have a refill …if you'd be so kind," he said with coy wink to the lady. She returned a knowing smile, enjoying the flirtatious gesture of a good looking soldier. With full cup of coffee, Will returned to his friends

86

...before regiment's assembly in preparation for boarding a train just now inching into station along platform.

The train carried identification 'Cleveland Columbus & Cincinnati RR'. Soon she was poised and ready, smoke and steam spewing skyward from its locomotive. Once again, forward two passenger cars were reserved for officers, while enlisted men were directed to board boxcars to the rear. This time, Will and five friends scrambled aboard the same boxcar. They moved quickly to secure an area toward rear of car, with seating plank space and room to sleep against a corner near outer wall's open slats. The car was over crowded ...same as their rail trip from Pontiac to Detroit ...but this car was cleaner. Straw covering the floor was fresh, and car washed recently ...almost fit for human habitation. But, this was going to be a much longer, more tiring journey. With all men loaded, and boxcar doors slammed shut, train's whistle blew its shrill unmistakable wail, and train's cast iron wheels moved with a lurch. It was mere minutes after 8:00 AM, when the train rolled out of Cleveland's downtown area and headed southwest.

Will settled in for a long ride, mind drifting. He was alone ...others quickly napping. He traveled less extensively than Maria, but ventured away from Oxford several times. For others with no experience, the trip was both exciting and frightening ...new adventure into the unknown. Will was certain fellow recruits shared his helpless, scary feeling ...not knowing what a 'soldier's life' would be. He was apprehensive ...even scared. This was serious business. Hands became clammy ...he rubbed them on uniform sleeves, removed kepi cap and swiped sweat from forehead, nervously running moist fingers through straggling locks of hair before repositioning cap with brim in jaunty angular fashion. He sighed, searching for breath. At some point they were going to be facing the enemy ...putting lives in harm's way. He fretted over how he would respond. He said a little prayer to himself, *"God, give me the courage and strength to do myself proud."* He reached into breast pocket and removed his journal ...parting gift from Maria. He pulled nib pen and bottle of ink from knapsack, wiggled and squirmed to find elbow room, and opened the cover to small black hardcover book with brown binding ...beginning to write:

87

Friday, September 5ᵗʰ, 1862
On train out of Cleveland

I am thinking of you, Maria, as I write this first entry in this journal you gave me. We have made a good start to this soldier life, but I worry about leaving you, and the boys. You are new to the farm, and I took you from a much easier life in Penn Yan. I feel badly that you will be working so hard. It will not be easy, and yet I know how capable you are. You make me so proud.

I fret that I will be able to do my duty, and make you proud. I will try my very best to be diligent as a soldier, and prepare myself for whatever God has in store. I pray for his strength to assist me.

Maria was right. It felt good to write innermost thoughts on paper ...as if someone were there ...as if someone were listening. With small sigh, Will closed its cover, tucking journal safely away in breast pocket ...near the heart. More relaxed now, he was soon dozing comfortably ...like most men.

Train's wheels rolled with rhythmic groaning metallic cadence through Ohio countryside, rolling past towns of Grafton,

Shelby, Crestline, and Galion. Terrain was mostly flatlands so the train could make speeds of about 20 mph, stopping every two hours to take on water for its thirsty boiler, or load cords of firewood to stoke the insatiable appetite of its fire. At stops in the country, the scene was humorous mayhem ...train grinding to a halt, boxcar sliding doors being thrown open. Up and down the line, Will and fellow soldiers leaped out of boxcars, streaming pell-mell to nearby woods to answer nature's calling. "Scurry-in' like squirrels to a tree ...with a hound at their tails," observed Junior, all laughing heartily at clever insight.

"My. My. My. Isn't humanity amaz-in'!" Johnny exclaimed loudly.

"You've got that right, Johnny," Will added. "I feel lighter ...makes a far better trip."

"Lighter ...aim to git' me lighter," Johnny answered. "Sweat-in' so much in that car ...trouble breath-in' ...this here air outside feels so good."

"No chance of 'dat ...Johnny git-in' lighter, I mean ...even with army food," Junior chided.

"I'm a-gonna' lose some weight, now," Johnny answered, "...especially with no food here ...and all that walk-in' us soldiers gonna' do!"

At least these stops served to break monotony ...long hours passed ...nothing to do in cramped quarters, except sleep and get to know each other better. At one stop, the boys made arrangements for camp life. "How about being tent partners with Johnny, Junior, and I?" Will suggested to Jeremiah.

"Sure enough ...I'll be 'pards' with you boys," Jeremiah answered quickly. "Do you think we'll have enough room in the tent with Johnny?" All boys laughed ...even Johnny. "But ...but ...what about Lucius and Jeptha?"

Will raised hand to face, standing perplexed, pondering a dilemma. "We'll have to find tent partners for them." Will surveyed the scene ...men mingling and engaged outside boxcars ...most in small groups of numerous men. But a few paces away, Will spotted two outliers standing silently off by themselves ...two characters, clearly unlike most other recruits. Will walked over to them, introduced himself, and began to chat. It worked out well, because Lucius and Jeptha were soon hooked-up with tent mates …Ira Goodrich and Nathan Soper, both from Pontiac, Michigan. These 'boys' were not so young …Nathan was 29 years old, and Ira …well, Ira was the oldest in Company A at 45 years. Will led Ira and Nathan back to introduce them to Lucius and Jeptha, and the three other friends.

Will stepped back and away, while the group were getting acquainted with the two new 'pards' of Lucius and Jeptha ...he made a mental image of Nathan and Ira. Nathan Soper was tall, thin, and lanky ...brown hair cut short ...features chiseled, skin stretched over high bony cheeks. Appearance was quite ordinary, like a precursor farmer's version of 'Ichabod Crane'. Army trousers were issued small to fit his thin frame, but too short to traverse fully his long frame ...he wore the 'flood runners' with white stockings and white bony legs showing above boots. He said little …speaking only when required.

Ira Goodrich seemed a likeable character …much more outgoing than Nathan. Ira was medium height, but robust paunch required issue of the largest of four sizes available for uniform trousers …to circumvent a spacious waist. Bright red canvas 'poor boy' suspenders, attached by two buttons at front and two buttons at rear, kept pants from falling …each button showing strain from its load. Because pant size was large, pants were too long …but Ira wore cuffs rolled up over ankles. He valued appearance of little importance ...hair unkempt graying and long, flowing out from under forage cap, bushy at the temples, its length onto his shoulders. Thick gray eye brows and puffy deep red cheeks framed dark sunken eyes. Rimless wire spectacles perched precariously on a bulbous red nose. A simple clay pipe jutted from the mouth, tobacco stained teeth and mouth mostly concealed by scruffy salt and pepper gray beard. All in all, he appeared to be a jolly old fellow …hardly image of proper soldier.

"You look a little long in the tooth, Ira," Junior threw out without considering diplomacy or propriety.

Everyone laughed, including Ira …he didn't mind …all good fun. "It will be good for Lucius and Jeptha to be tent mates with older fellows …both are young and can learn from Ira and Nathan's experience," Will said.

"Sounds good by me," Lucius answered. Jeptha nodded agreement. Eight men got along nicely, and decided to take meals together. They would be 'mess mates' ...'soldier talk' for enlistees that cook and eat meals together in camp.

After nearly ten hours travel from Cleveland, the train arrived at Columbus, Ohio. Here the regiment switched trains ...a nearly 1,000-man regiment unloaded, and then climbed aboard a waiting train identified as the 'Columbus & Xenia RR'. It was nearly 6:00 PM. Sun was beginning to set ...another 100 miles to go before reaching Cincinnati. Within a half-hour the train began to roll out of Columbus. Men were issued additional rations, but nothing of substance ...uncomfortable, hungry men quickly learning army life to be less than pleasant. The train continued south ...its droning metallic sound of iron wheels rolling on iron tracks, pitching and swaying of boxcar becoming all too monotonous to overcrowded men. Now pitch black outside, depot sign at 'London' barely discernible, their train continued through small town without stopping.

Further down seemingly endless track, about two hours out of Columbus, train's brakes were applied and it squealed to a stop at 'Xenia' Ohio. Again, the regiment switched to another train identified as the 'Little Miami RR' ...disembark and re-board becoming routine, each switch taking less time. At 8:30 PM, they were rolling again. Train chugged its way, belching sooty gray smoke through small towns of Morrow and then Loveland. Most men slept in various contorted positions, in darkness, illuminated only by two flickering kerosene lanterns hung on either end of boxcar. At midnight, train neared journey's end, approaching outskirts of Cincinnati, after an exhausting 16-hour rail trip from Cleveland covering about 240 miles.

Chapter 10

An overloaded train began chugging hard, laboring heavily as it approached steep hills surrounding river basin nestling Cincinnati. Lumbering up and down city district hillsides, it wended past numerous homes and businesses perched precariously, clinging to uneven terrain. Obvious to boys now awakening, peering through slatted boxcar, this was an immense city ...larger even than Detroit or Cleveland. Founded at the confluence of three major tributaries to the Ohio River, giving river access to many northern cities, Cincinnati became a regional center of river trade ...population swelling to over 150,000 citizens.

Cincinnati was a leading center for meat packing, giving rise to derivative industries of leather, lard, candle, and soap. Surrounding hills trapped pollution from foul odors of rotting pig and cattle blood, horse manure, and lingering smoke from cooking, heating, and manufacturing. Stench was noticeable, especially within confined boxcar, causing men to hold noses and rub eyes as they awoke to screeching groans of straining locomotive.

"What a God awful smell," Jeremiah observed, fingers pinching nose.

"Wouldn't want to be a 'hawg or a 'dawg in this here town," Johnny quipped.

"Looks like we're almost here," Will said, offering some hope for end to unpleasantness.

"None too soon, either ...my body is a-ach-in' now," Junior answered, "...and I'm right hungry too!"

"I could even eat that thar' 'har-tack' …with all dem' critters on it …even a smell-in' like she does," Johnny continued, while all boys winced and groaned at the thought.

"It's been a long trip, don't ya' reckon?" Jeptha added.

Slowly, their train descended into a basin at river's edge and crept into 'Union Depot', just a few blocks up river. It came to a halt, long train ride over. Boxcar doors slid open up and down the line in a screeching cacophony of sound …a regiment of enlisted men tumbling out on wobbly legs, empty stomachs, and full bladders. A usual rush to depot's urinals ensued, before relieved men returned to gather on platform. Half an hour passed with men mingling and chatting, while officers jockeyed to get organized. Eventually, orders were given to form columns, and midnight march began over several blocks toward upper market area, or 'Fifth Street Market'. As marching columns of the '22nd Michigan' drew nearer to market, unmistakable aroma of cooking bacon and ham pervaded air, even masking partially unpleasant odors of area's pollution. Boys eyed each other, broad smiles coming in recognition, eagerly anticipating a much needed meal. Johnny winked to Junior. Junior returned a 'thumbs up'. "She smells mighty good," Johnny gushed to Will, marching alongside.

Will tipped his head and feigned a 'salute' in recognition of Johnny's remark …too exhausted to continue conversation. He glanced down several blocks toward a market area now coming visible …though middle of night, kerosene lights illuminated the building. Will could see a block-long 'A'-framed roof structure filling area between two streets. Its roof was corrugated metal and sides open. Long lines of tables were aligned beneath the structure. Will surmised this to be a bustling market …come morning, he presumed, stalls would be filled with vendors displaying goods for sale on tables …throngs of citizens milling about and shopping for fresh meats, fish, vegetables, and fruit.

As men marched past, Will noticed a horse-drawn trolley car rolling on rail tracks. The conveyance crossed the intersection of Fifth and Vine streets before marching columns of soldiers crossed. The trolley had a roof covering rows of benches upon which two passengers were seated …signage on car's side read

'Vine Street Trolley'. "I do think she's a funny kind of railroad," Junior quipped.

"Never saw that before," Will answered, "…strange to see a 'wagon' rolling on tracks."

Looming over the market structure in the background, Will noticed a huge red brick building with large white lettering painted on its side designating 'A & H Strauss Company'. When regiment arrived at Fifth Street Market, located between Vine and Walnut streets, officers informed men that early 'breakfast' was being served by appreciative citizens of Cincinnati …immediately, spontaneous cheers of "Here! Here!" erupted and grew in waves from a famished 1,000-man contingent. Regiment broke ranks haphazardly, quickly jostling and shoving to form lines to be served. Will waved and called to be sure Ira and Nathan joined their group. All assembled, eight 'boys' hurried to a place in one line …Will at the head, followed by Johnny, Junior, Jeremiah, Ira, Nathan, Lucius, and Jeptha. Their line advanced too slowly for empty stomachs waiting to devour anything placed on plates. After what felt like endless agony, they reached a serving area and were given tin plates and utensils …told to retrieve tin cups from knapsacks for steaming fresh brewed coffee. "Nothing can match the aroma of fresh brewed coffee …along with bacon and ham frying …aromas can't be beat," Will observed.

A stout lady server, dressed in muslin black long dress and white apron, reached out toward Will. She placed a golden brown stack of three flapjacks on his plate. With broad smile and nod, she acknowledged Will's bug-eyed appreciation for food being served. Will tipped his cap. Next station offered a huge helping of scrambled eggs …and next, fresh apple slices baked with brown sugar. Finally, a combination of crisp bacon and fried ham completed pre-dawn 'breakfast'. Will led eight new 'friends' hurriedly toward an open table where one famished group clamored onto wood plank benches on either side of a sturdy plank table. No one wasted time devouring their tasty meal …a little slice of heaven. In no time plates were clean, and they settled back with coffee cups in hand to chat. Will remarked, "Wonder what the story is on this Fifth Street Market?"

An old-timer ...a citizen volunteer who helped prepare and serve meals, was resting casually on a bench nearby ...pudgy legs outstretched, huge meaty hands crossed and resting upon soiled white canvas cooking apron, partially concealing pronounced paunch. Disheveled hair was long and snow-white, strands darting haphazardly at all angles ...flowing beard of white showing brown stains of tobacco spittle. Overhearing Will's question, he turned toward the boys, peering over rimless spectacles perched jauntily at nose's end. "Hear ya' have an interest in the market," he said. "She's been here for some thirty years, I reckon." He went on, "One of nine public markets in the city ... primary source of perishable food for residents ...houses butchers, fish mongers, farmers, and produce vendors." Pointing across the street, he said, "Abe Lincoln gave a speech here ...in 1859 ...from dat' thar' balcony, in dat' hotel over yonder." After some interchange back and forth with the boys, the old man added, "Yup, she's a muster point now ...fer' troops a-go-in' south ...on's the way toward Kentucky and Tennessee. We try to support ya' men by feed-in' ya' right proper now."

Will answered, "You prepared a right tasty meal, Sir."

"You betcha ...a mighty tasty meal ...we thanks ya', Sir," Junior added.

"Here! Here!" ...all eight boys cheering in unison ...raising coffee cups to salute the old codger.

"You're a welcome now," the Cincinnati senior citizen volunteer acknowledged with a stiff salute. "God speed," he said as he ambled back slowly to his duty spot in the serving line.

After the man was gone, Jeptha pointed toward the corner of Fifth and Vine Streets, toward a three-story brick building ...shiny metal roof, wide brick chimneys on either side. Windows lined second and third floors ...one building side painted white over brickwork, while the other half was painted bright red. At street level, two canvas canopies denoted entrances to two adjacent saloons ...one sign read 'Henry Saloon', and the other 'Hoffman's Saloon'. Johnny said, "Wish I could git' me some ale there ...would be a fitt-in' end-in' to these fine eat-ins', don't ya' think!"

"You young-ins' are up too late already," Ira scoffed with a teasing chuckle. "Past yer' bedtime now ...too late for carouz-in', ya' know."

"Yes, Papa," Jeptha shot back.

"Papa, ya' say ...well now," Ira replied. "I ain't as old as ya' thinks ...jest 45 years, now!" Everyone laughed heartily, enjoying themselves immensely. But, a nickname for Ira was cast in stone ...'Ira Goodrich' became simply 'Papa' to everyone in Company A.

In fact, saloons were clearly closed for evening ...no real temptation. It was hours past midnight and 'breakfast' drew to a close. Before leaving tables, the regiment was 'ordered' to fill haversacks with apples, pears, salt pork wrapped in brown paper, dried beans, and hardtack ...an 'order' never repeated ...no one needed to tell these new soldiers to stock up on food when available.

Officers began calling out to assemble men in companies. Captain Ezra Hatton called out to 'Company A', assisted by two Lieutenants, 1st Lieutenant Edward Wisner and 2nd Lieutenant William Albertson. Company A was directed to assemble in one corner of the market area ...other nine companies of the 22nd Michigan Volunteer Infantry doing likewise in other areas. It was time to be issued weapons. Will and the boys huddled, moving close to Lieutenant Albertson so they could hear. Lieutenant Albertson explained, "When war broke out, neither North nor South was prepared or equipped ...stockpiles of rifles and handguns and other weapons are limited ...both sides are using antiquated weapons, some dating back to the War of 1812." He continued, "High technology new weapons are cherished ...from American rifle and gun manufacturers like Sharps, Colt, Remington, and the United States armory at Springfield, Massachusetts." He went into detail, educating his men, "...recent invention in 1855 of the 'rifled' barrel, which has a spinning-grooved track enabling the bullet to spin as it fires thru the barrel, makes all older 'smoothbore' rifles obsolete. Spinning bullet, combined with long length of barrel, improves both accuracy and range. American-made 'Springfield' rifle musket is the most desired rifle in the Union army ...as well as most desired by

Confederate soldiers, although the South's limited manufacturing capability means that most 'Springfield' rifles in Confederate hands are obtained via capture on battlefields."

Lieutenant Albertson reached for one new weapon, holding it aloft to demonstrate. "Springfield rifle musket is a single-shot, muzzle-loading gun detonated with percussion cap. It is the first rifle to fire a .58 caliber 'minie ball' ...an inch-long bullet-shaped projectile, rather than a round ball used in older muskets. A long 39-inch rifle-grooved barrel makes it possible to hit a target with 'minie ball' at a range up to 500 yards." Numerous murmurs and gasps grew audible among recruits ...Will listened intently, impressed with weapon's capability. Lieutenant Albertson ended by saying, "New 'Springfield' rifles are the finest equipment available ...we are very fortunate to be issued such weapons ...as such, it is every man's duty to maintain his rifle in top-working order ...important for your well-being ...and besides, each rifle costs nearly $15 apiece." Men of Company A broke into laughter at their lieutenant's humor.

Everything turned deadly serious ...men grew silent. Company A fell into order for roll call. One-by-one each man's name was called, he stepped forward one pace, and an officer presented the new recruit with rifle, bayonet and scabbard, and cartridge box ...moments charged and highly emotional. Will felt shivers course the body and stomach knot, as the name "Will Hodkins" was called. After presentation of arms, Company A fell out ...allowed to mingle, most men staying to themselves ...studying their new weapon. Will Hodkins moved off and found an unoccupied spot ...leaning against brick wall of market building. He wanted to be alone, away from the boys a few moments. New, shiny rifle meant so much to Will ...like a diamond in the night ...sparkling from flickering muted light cast by burning kerosene lanterns. Will considered himself an accomplished hunter, first learning early from Father on the farm, and later hunting regularly ...but always for food ...deer, wild turkey, partridge and quail, and occasionally a few rabbits. Killing gave him no pleasure. Rather, hunting had purpose ...a basic need to obtain food for family. He was accustomed to guns, but this was the finest weapon ever hoisted. He smiled with pride, *"What a beauty she is!"*

Fingers chased lightly, brushing surfaces of the gleaming new .58-cal. Springfield rifled musket …across oiled blued metal barrel, and polished walnut stock with three shiny metal bands along the 39-inch barrel. He stood weapon on end …overall, the rifle measured nearly five feet in length …almost eye-height. He hefted the rifle …it weighed about 9 pounds. A ramrod was engaged underside of barrel. A designation '1861' for M1861 model was stamped on lock and barrel. Will raised rifle to eye down barrel, through its 3-leaf long range site. Rear sight was graduated to 900 yards. With weapon raised, he fingered lock, hammer, and trigger guard in mock gesture of firing. He gleamed.

He paused momentarily to reflect …realization struck coldly …chills running down back, hair rising on forearms. He grew uneasy. Purpose for a gun changed. Now, rifle was a weapon …being asked to *"shoot, and kill, the enemy"* …before enemy killed him. Realty of becoming a 'soldier' struck head-on, like a thunderbolt …chilling panic, as if looking directly into enemy's barrel of loaded rifle. He felt torn by inconsistency …emotion striking …almost overwhelming. First, he felt pride …pride in doing what was right for country …*"doing his duty"*. At the same time, he felt fear …cold stark fear of killing …or being killed. He would have to find a way to deal with fear …it would not be easy.

Composure regained, Will leaned rifle against building, and eyed the black-dyed saddle leather scabbard that contained bayonet. Two brass rivets made a pattern on scabbard's side. At scabbard's end was a small brass tip, held in place with brass brads that pierced leather. Will figured brass tip served as safety protection from pointed end of bayonet stored within. Will drew bayonet from scabbard slowly and carefully. Shiny, carbon steel bayonet glistened, even in dull lighting thrown off from lanterns burning and hanging from brick wall of market building. Bayonet was about 18 inches long, with triangular-shaped blade, and deep grooves designed to permit drainage of victim's blood …very thought sending shivers again up Will's spine. He looked carefully, studying locking ring, eyeing letters "US" stamped into metal. The weapon was very sharp.

Next, Will explored black leather M1861 cartridge box which stored ammunition. Cartridge box came with a 55-inch long sling with two narrow 5"-6" long billets and brass eagle breastplate. Breastplate was attached to strap by loops of metal bent over inside of strap. Cartridge box had a brass plate reading "US", attached with leather wedge in center of box flap. Inside cartridge box were tins to contain cartridges, 'minie ball' and charge of powder wrapped together in paper. But no cartridges were in the box. Officers explained earlier that ammunition was scarce and late in arriving ...ammunition to be dispensed when it arrived. Will parsed lips, shaking head side to side, thinking, *"We are soldiers ...with weapons ...marching off to war, without ammunition!"*

Then call to march was issued. Columns formed, and Will and regiment marched off into night. South onto Vine Street, and then two blocks to 3rd Street heading west, columns moved in step ...newly issued rifle on shoulder, bayonet and scabbard at waist belt, cartridge box slung from shoulder across chest. Together with knapsack, canteen, and fully loaded haversack, Will was feeling the 'weight' of a marching infantry soldier. At Central Street, columns turned toward the Ohio River, past Front Street, then Water Street, and River Street. Despite darkness, waters of the mighty Ohio River became visible, muffled sound of water lapping at Cincinnati shore. Pontoon bridge reached into water, seemingly leading nowhere, darkness concealing destination and Kentucky shore on the other side. It was eerie as columns marched onto bridge's swaying wood surface, anchored to pontoons afloat on water ...river's waves slapping against pontoon's sides, all glimmering from a spectrum of light cast from bobbing lanterns carried by some men to light the way.

Will marched onward, unknowing ...queasiness filling stomach from unsettling swaying of bridge's motion. No one spoke ...silence broken only by regular cadence of marching boots meeting planks, bridging moat. After what seemed like endless march, but in reality only minutes, first soldiers reached shore. Will stepped gingerly onto Kentucky soil ...town of Covington,

Kentucky, before him. He checked pocket watch. *"...4:00 AM, Saturday, September 6th ...an exhausting 40-hour journey from Pontiac Fairgrounds on Thursday morning,"* he calculated. Regiment reached its destination, but in very early morning hours, a small town was not prepared. Nearly 1,000 tired men had no place to sleep. So, hard cobblestone-paved streets of Covington became their bed.

Will stowed gear about him, and arranged knapsack to serve as pillow. He glanced over toward Johnny, Lucius, and Jeptha. The three youngest of Will's new friends were wrestling awkwardly with equipment, looking a great deal uneasy at prospects of what little remained of night. Will sought to soothe them, "I'm afraid we'll all be fight-in' a soldier's first battle ...we'll be spend-in' our first night on the cold, cold ground."

'Papa' was already down on ground, looking almost comfortable ...45 years teaching him to take things as they come ...make best of a poor situation. Hearing Will's words, Papa chuckled and added, "Boys, she's not yer' soft bed at home, but she'll do in a pinch!"

"Easy 'nuff for you to say, Papa, you got's a lot of cushion there," Lucius snapped back, three young boys breaking into uneasy childish laughter.

"Nuth-in' kin' keep me awake," Johnny injected, rolling over on side assuming fetal position.

Will and Papa just smiled, nodding heads ...both knowing a lot of learning was needed. Hard was bed ...sweet the sleep, for eight new friends ...exhausted men of the '22nd Michigan Infantry' ...lying in search of much needed rest from arduous journey.

Chapter 11

Bugle sounded to rouse men still in slumber ...fitful rest interrupted brusquely at midday by alarming news of approaching Rebel forces. Word spread quickly, "... *'enemy' is on the doorstep*" ...immediate chaos and panic spread among raw recruits. Men realized they had no ammunition and many did not know how to load and fire weapons anyway. "Not the kind of soldier-in' I had in mind," Junior said in understatement, boys reacting in helter-skelter motion.

"What do we do, poke 'em in the eye with a stick?" Nathan asked ...sudden horror gripping all ...distress evident on young faces of Lucius and Jeptha.

"Beats me," Will answered with a shrug toward Nathan, as men all about them scrambled to gather equipment, adjust uniform, toss haversack and knapsack over shoulder, grab musket and move to assemble in companies. Papa returned unknowing shrug toward Will, while motioning boys to gather equipment. Captain Ezra Hatton informed hastily assembled men of Company A that the regiment was going to march toward outskirts of town where a reported attack was about to be made by Confederate forces under command of Major General Edmund Kirby Smith ...Rebs pushing deep into Kentucky from south, occupying Lexington, and now threatening towns as far north as Cincinnati.

Under threat, raw recruits of the '22nd' regiment moved out at double time. Nervous clumsy execution of military maneuvers appeared comical to a scattering of curious citizen onlookers. Pell-mell 'march' in mayhem ended about two miles out of Covington in open farm countryside with the regiment awkwardly positioned

101

in semblance of battle lines. Here on a knoll, amid a field of leafy cabbage, the '22nd' took its first stand ...fear-laden, ill-prepared to meet an enemy ...fixed bayonets their only measure of defense.

Lieutenant Colonel Heber Le Favour ordered Company H forward as skirmishers to 'feel the enemy'. Plowing clumsily through expansive fields of unpicked blue-green cabbage, trepid skirmishers advanced. Will and the rest of Company A watched from afar. But, the enemy did not engage. Confederates apparently caught a glint of bayonets flashing in bright noonday sun, thought better and fled ...not knowing Union troops were without ammunition. A situation dead serious while 'battle was on', men now realized the enemy was in retreat and laughter broke out. Junior found humor, "Boys, I think she'll be known as the 'Cabbage Hill Fight' ...she was a tough skirmish ...we just managed to slaughter a good field of southern cabbage."

Will joked, "You've got that right, Junior ...slaughter she was." Word spread ...men affectionately dubbed their first 'soldier-in' engagement the 'Cabbage Hill Fight'.

Through early evening, the regiment made its way toward Covington Heights to join an established fortified camp. As men trudged in marching columns along dusty dirt road, toting cumbersome knapsacks overloaded with 30-50 pounds of items, Johnny looked over to Will marching alongside. "What a way to spend Saturday night, hey Will."

"Not my idea of a good party," Will replied.

"My feets ah' hurt-in', and my backs ah' ach-in', Will," Johnny added.

"Young branch of a tree ...takes all bends one gives it, Johnny," Junior chided.

"Ya' don't know diddly squat," Johnny answered. Just then, they crested a small hill at a bend in roadway that appeared endless. Before them, in expansive valley below, appeared spectacle that took everyone's breath. "Looks like ah' smok-in' city of white canvas," Johnny observed with tremor of excitement. A massive encampment lay before them, with perhaps two hundred large tents resembling Indian tepees arranged in precise orderly rows, each with white canvas catching last rays of setting sun ...westerly blue horizon painted with brilliant floating colorings of orange and pink ...all contrasting against lush green of Kentucky blue grass hills rolling in foreground. Billows of smoke curled lazily skyward from burning orange embers of a hundred campsite fires ...dark shadowy silhouettes of soldiers huddled about fires, adding mystical aura to expansive panorama. Instinctively, without order being given, columns of marching men drew to abrupt stop ...such beauty and power. Regiment resumed its march ...down roadway, into valley, toward the huge tent-city of Camp Wallace. Here, men were assigned tents ...Camp Wallace would be 'home' for uncertain time ...regiment assigned to the Union Army of Kentucky.

Will and seven friends were fortunate to stay together in one tent. Will opened the tent flap at one end and they entered, peering inside. 'Sibley' tents were eighteen feet in diameter, each housing 12-18 men. An upright 8-foot pole in center bridged another pole across tent's top. Canvas stretched over sides pegged to ground. Pot-belly stove stood in center, piped to tent's top ...soldiers slept encircling stove for warmth.

Will tossed haversack to ground, and reached into knapsack for gum blanket ...a waxed cloth groundsheet which he placed on straw covering tent's floor. This and blanket from home would be his bed. Boys watched Will, all following his lead. Papa said, "Let's get us a fire go-in' ...make us some coffee." Nathan was quickly outside in search of firewood. Will searched knapsack for wood matches. Will and Papa took the lead instinctively. Nathan returned with an armful of firewood from a stack nearby, and Will began to arrange logs. A fire of hickory logs was soon crackling outside tent. Papa was busy grinding coffee beans, using bayonet to crush illusive beans into powder. He roasted the powder in a fry pan over fire, careful not to scorch ...aroma already wonderful. From everyone's canteen, water was collected in an iron pot left on the stove. In no time, scent of coffee brewing over campfire was wafting into crisp night air. Boys extended tin cups eagerly, Papa pouring welcome brew into each cup. Even hardtack and salt pork from haversack rations tasted fine, chased down by freshly brewed black coffee ...nearly eighteen hours since 'breakfast' at Cincinnati's market. "This here har'-tack is begin-in' to be ma' friend," Johnny quipped.

"Not much of a recommendation ...boy will eat anything," Will added.

"Hand knows where da' mouth is," Johnny responded, unwilling to yield last word.

Sun set completely ...in darkness about dancing campfire, they relaxed, told stories and joked into night ...smirking, self-satisfied and reveling in afternoon's 'victory' at the 'Cabbage Hill Fight'. "We'll never again be able to look a cabbage in the eye," Will joked. "Let's get some shut-eye." Tight knit bond was developing.

Dawn came as eastern sky grew pink, rolling lush green hilly countryside revealed through parting moist gray mist. Shrill incessant cries of ravens pierced morning's quiet ...hundreds of large birds gliding through mist, swooping to tops of chestnut, hickory and maple trees encircling camp. Throngs of immense, glossy black-winged birds thrashed heavy early morning air, lurching crazily, settling precariously on slender swaying uppermost tree branches. From lofty perches, ravens surveyed sprawling city of white canvas.

Reveille sounded all too soon at 5:00 AM. Junior turned over, chilled from cold ground seeping moisture through now dewy blanket. Awakened from imperfect and all-too-short slumber, he shook away cobwebs. "Ain't that the most un-human sound possible from a bugle!" he exclaimed loudly. "And those birds are just a-mock-in' us down here." Then came resonant roll of not-so-distant drum, calling peaceful camp city to life with thumping rattle. Will stepped outside tent hurriedly. Canvas tent flaps flew open up and down the line, languid soldiers pouring out ...bleary-eyed and disheveled, uniforms in disarray ...facing cold morning chill. He observed mayhem ...now reluctant 'volunteers' emerging between rows of tents ...all milling in disorganization. Officers moved among them, gently pushing, prodding and gesturing to generate semblance of discipline.

Eventually, Will and boys joined a ragtag group forming a hasty line ...men rubbing backs of hands to get 'sticks' out, stretching, trying to get limber. With quizzical forlorn look standing in line, hair on head went in all directions ...standing on end like quills of a porcupine. They were a conglomeration from all walk of life ...carpenters, coopers, blacksmiths, lumbermen, clerks, teachers, lawyers, farmers, and laborers. Education and age varied. They shared little in common, except now being soldiers. Following roll call, 2nd Lieutenant William Albertson informed Company A that ammunition would be issued, followed by drill on loading and firing muskets. "Go now and prepare breakfast," Albertson ordered. "Return at 9:00 AM."

Will and boys hurried back to tent. "Lucius, you, Johnny, and Junior, go to the Quartermaster's tent to get rations," Will directed. "Nathan, Jeptha and Jeremiah can scout for more firewood, while Papa and I get a fire started and coffee brewing."

"First, I've gotta' find da' 'sink' down by da' creek," Johnny called, turning back and moving quickly in search of latrine ...a disgusting, hastily dug trench, and filthy repository for contamination ...left open, baking in sun and wind ...breeding ground for sickness and disease. But, sanitation and cleanliness were not army priority. "Me, too," Junior added, as Lucius hurried to catch up to quick-stepping Johnny and Junior.

Will and Papa shrugged and turned to prepare campfire, and get breakfast started. Will and Papa worked well together. Papa had knack for cooking and began to ply magic to simple rations on hand, while Will got coffee brewing. Papa placed slices of raw briny pork in government-issue eight-inch stamped steel fry pan with steel handle, and began frying. He soaked hardtack in water, added a little sugar, and then fried three-inch square crackers in pork grease residue. Lucius, Johnny and Junior returned from Quartermaster's tent with apples. Papa cut up apples, added sugar and water, and fried the mixture into delicious applesauce. Boys ate off tin plates, with Federal-issue flatware stamped and hot-tin-dipped, forks having four long tines. Jeremiah opined, mouth half-full of scrumptious vittles, "I think Papa should do all cook-in' ...and Will be assistant." "Here! Here!" the group called out in unison ...all raising tin cups of coffee in salute. And, so it was that duties began to be parceled out among eight friends and 'mess mates'.

At 9:00 AM sharp, call to drill came ...at parade ground, men were issued ammunition ...cartridges passed out, about fifty per man, consisting of 'minie' ball and charge of powder wrapped together in paper. Each man stored cartridges in tins within black leather M1861 cartridge box with leather sling. Next came instruction on loading musket. Each soldier was told to remove cartridge from cartridge box, tear open paper with teeth, empty powder down barrel of musket, and insert 'ball' pointed up. Draw ramrod from beneath gun barrel, tamp ball and powder, before returning ramrod to its place. Next, half-cock the hammer and place a firing cap atop the little protrusion at back end of barrel. Take position, cock hammer fully, aim musket and pull trigger. It was complicated procedure …even in quiet and peaceful surroundings …let alone deadly nervous conditions of battle.

Recruits nervously began practicing step-by-step procedure of loading muskets. Will was adept with a musket, but many men were not. He watched men fumble and wondered, *"…could be a deadly proceeding in face of battle …not sure I want to follow these foxes into a foxhole."* Captain Ezra Hatton gave an order that became so familiar, "Load in nine times—load!" With humor he added, "If you can do it, go ahead …I can't!" Men laughed, quieting anxiety. Drill proceeded awkwardly …over and over again through morning hours.

"Musket weighs a ton," Johnny implored to Will.

"She won't get lighter," Will answered, dashing Johnny's hope. Time came to fire. Men raised nine-pound weapon to shoulder, holding rifle in aiming position, while drill sergeant walked slowly up and down the line …raising muzzle of one gun, depressing height of another, correcting positions as he went, until arms and shoulders of men ached.

"She feels like a team of horses be tugg-in' at my shoulders," Junior quipped loud enough for many to hear.

"What a wretch he is!" Johnny cursed, referring to the drill sergeant. Command came to fire. Most raw recruits cringed …some shut eyes, turned away head, and pulled trigger. "I fear result of service to be performed by one of these 'howitzers'!" Nathan said. Fear was realized when he pulled trigger …explosion knocking him backward to ground, skinny legs kicking skyward. Company A broke into gut-wrenching, back-slapping laughter. Nathan picked himself off turf, brushing away dust …trying to look impervious to howling laughter. Another rookie instinctively turned head to the left as he cringed, but musket spun left with him ...immediately men hit the ground, ducking in horror.

Eventually, morning drill ended. Will and exhausted boys ambled back to tent for rest and dinner call at 12:00 noon. Following noon meal, they drilled for two hours on march maneuvers, before being dismissed for late afternoon rest. Will took the opportunity to move outside for quiet time, while others napped in tent. He moved a hickory log to a cooler spot under shade of nearby hickory tree, and sat down to enjoy what little breeze blew. He reflected, realizing it was Sunday afternoon ...a moment to write Maria. He retrieved pen and ink from knapsack within tent, returning to shady spot under hickory. With journal in hand, he took gold nib to ink and began to write:

> *Covington Heights, Kentucky*
> *Camp Wallace, September 7th*
>
> *My dearest Maria:*
>
> *Just three days since writing last, and less than two weeks from leaving you and boys, but it seems an eternity. I am hoping postmaster will arrive anytime soon with your first letter, as I miss you greatly.*
>
> *It was exhausting travel by rail from Cleveland to Cincinnati. I arrived to find a great breakfast served by citizens. Marched across the Ohio River in early morning, and arrived*

Covington, Ky. We were greatly surprised, and fearful, when awakened to hear Rebels were nearby. We marched to outside of town, but enemy turned tail and ran. We succeeded in trampling a perfectly good field of cabbage. Junior called it the 'Cabbage Hill Fight', and name seems to stick. Met new friends, and now eight of us are 'pards' sharing a tent and cooking our meals.

I thought of you going to church today with William and Walter. Hope you extended my best wishes to everyone. My thoughts are always with you, the boys, and the farm. Squash is probably just right for picking. Have you been started at canning? I trust Ezra and Nettie are a help. Please write.

Your loving husband,
Will

Chapter 12

Monotony of camp life became apparent to Will and boys over the next ten days at Camp Wallace ...bugle calls, drumbeats, and drills. Junior summed it up, "First thing in morn-in' is drill, then drill, then drill again ...in between, its drill, drill, and a little more drill. Sometimes we stop to eat a little, and have roll call." If not drill, they were fortifying Covington by digging trenches ...or, policing camp, extending latrine pits, gathering firewood, repairing equipment, and cleaning weapons ...manual labor and menial work quickly gave Will and boys a taste of 'fatigue duty' ...fatigued they were. After a full day of drill and work, dress parade occurred around 6 PM ...then, drum or bugle call of 'tattoo' sounded 'retreat' and men returned to quarters to prepare supper. Free time prevailed until 9 PM, when 'taps' sounded calling for lights out.

Monotony was broken the first morning mail arrived in camp. With buzz of great excitement, Will stood among men watching mail wagon arrive. Will called out, "Mail wagon's here." Drawn by two large white horses, wood-spoke wheels tossing wagon side-to-side and up-and-down, it traversed rutted terrain, smaller wheels in front and larger wheels in rear. Canvas cover extended from over driver to the rear, with inscription 'U.S. Mail' on canvas sides. Mail systems were amazingly reliable ...postage costing 3¢ per letter. Mail arrived by rail as near camp as possible. Division's mail carrier met the train, picked up sacks plainly marked with name of division commander, and took sacks to division headquarters. Mail was sorted and put into brigade sacks, delivered by wagon to respective brigades, distributed into regimental sacks, sorted by company and distributed to each soldier.

Mail Wagon 'call' lights up faces

(Library of Congress)

Everyone rushed to gather about Captain's tent. Names were called …heartwarming to Will to see soldier's face light up as name was called …stepping forward with bounce to step to receive a letter or package from loved ones up north in 'God's country' …disappointment showing for men not called. Will beamed as "Will Hodkins" was called and he stepped forward to receive the first two letters from Maria. Jeremiah received a letter from two sisters, and Lucius from aunt and uncle ...but, that was it ...five other friends walked away dejected. "You're a lucky man, Will," Nathan sulked.

"I know that I am," Will answered, hurrying back to quarters to open letters from Maria. From his tent, Will grabbed knapsack and moved to wooded area nearby …where he could be alone. Opening first letter and beginning to read, a beaming smile appeared.

Maria wrote:

7 September 1862
Sunday Eve

My dearest Will:

I wore the beautiful cameo brooch to church today . . . ladies commented on how lovely it is . . . a gift so dear to me. It will always remind me of your tenderness.

Nettie and I are busy canning vegetables from our gardens. We also made jam from apple and cherry trees out back . . . they are 'yummy' and William cannot get enough . . . Nettie and I baked bread, but William could not wait for it to cool out of cook stove . . . jam was everywhere on his face! Walter is walking everywhere, and getting into everything . . . he wears me out with his bundle of energy . . . but, those smiles are wonderful!

I went into town with Ezra . . . bought yarn at General Store and will have plenty to keep me busy this winter. Nettie and I promised to do quilting with

the church group of ladies. Ezra located a
young man, named Ned, who has a bad leg
and walks with crutch. Ned needs work, so
Ezra arranged for him to come by and help
me with chores. I will give him meals and
some pay.

We miss you, Will ...but we are
doing our best until you come back home.

All my love...Maria

Will broke into loud chuckle with the second letter from
Maria:

...William is helping me. He
enjoys throwing corn over fence to chickens
in enclosed pen beside the coop, watching
them flap wings wildly and scrap for feed.
But yesterday, he and I went into the coop
to gather eggs. I was reaching under hens
in nests to get eggs, so William reached out
toward one of the Bonnies ...she pecked
his hand. He jumped back, started to cry,
but remembered he was to be brave

...whimpered a little, and left the coop.
I'm not sure if I'll be able to get him back
to the coop soon!

In her second letter, Maria related that she enjoyed looking back through her journal from Penn Yan, childhood and courtship with Will. A tear came to Will's eye as he read that Maria voiced a sigh aloud, *"Will, I miss you so much!"* Will completed reading letters, reread them, and vowed to save each and every letter from home. At night he reread letters following supper, before rejoining the boys in their nightly routine. Typically, relaxation came each day as boys gathered with coffee in hand around campfire. Papa would light clay pipe for leisurely smoke, someone would start spinning tall tale or gossip, and others would follow with tales of their own. Most nights the sound of a fiddler playing 'foot-stomp-in' tunes provided backdrop for conversation. This night, Will suggested they drift down to fiddler's campfire to take-in festivities. Will felt down and withdrawn ...a bit sorry for himself and homesick after reading Maria's letters. *"Perhaps the fiddler will perk me up a bit,"* he thought.

Boys moved out following 'stomp-in' sounds to locate fiddler's campfire ...fast-moving, resounding beats to "Sally Ann" and then "Bonaparte's Retreat". Fifty-some soldiers crowded two or three deep encircling campfire, its crackling hickory embers spitting glowing chards into air, as if fire itself were dancing to mystical music. Each man strained to get better view of the lone fiddler's showman-like antics ...a local 'citizen' who came to camp to entertain soldiers with his musical skill. The fiddler performed trance-like, lost within frantic strains pouring forth from dancing instrument played so vigorously. Working in and out among the crowd to gain best vantage point, Will eyed the old codger making trusty fiddle come alive with "Green Eyed Girl". With long gray beard stained with tobacco spittle, he wore large-brimmed floppy brown slouch hat, large white goose feather tucked in its band. Bib overalls and high-top boots concealed a tall lanky frame. Head darted to and fro with rhythmic cadence of tune, while dirty boot tapped beat. Eyes squinted half-shut, lost and mesmerized by music. Johnny and Junior started singing aloud "The Girl I Left Behind Me" ...other boys and boisterous crowd of fellow soldiers picking up on words.

"I'm lonesome since I crossed the hill,
And o'er the moor and valley,
Such heavy thoughts my heart do fill,
Since parting with my Sally.

While friends sang loudly, Will mouthed words silently ...too embarrassed when he tried to sing, though appreciating music greatly. He had no musical ability ..."*could not carry a tune with a shovel,*" he would say often to Maria, apologizing for not singing along in church. So, mimicking song and mouthing words was what he did ...eyes growing moist, stomach knotting, words striking note of sorrow.

I'll seek no more the fine and gay,
For each but does remind me,
How swift the hours did pass away,
With the girl I left behind me.

Sound reverberated through valley, while campfire's glow cast eerie shadow on faces of raucous gathering. Fiddler went on tirelessly into night ...crowd rollicking, dancing jigs, back-slapping and knee-slapping ...much like chickens prancing, wings flapping. Night ended with strains of "Hell Broke Loose in Georgia". Boys gathered to walk back to tent ...along the way Johnny complained, "I ain't get-in' ah' proper sleep ...those damned mules set up an infernal chorus."

114

"Your gol'-darn snor-in' drowns out mules," Junior replied under breath.

"Whad' ya'say? ...Junior, ya'all mumble likes' a treed coon," Johnny shot back ...everyone brought to laughter.

"Ya' looks' to be snug as a bug in rug," Junior answered, "...sleep-in' hard ... in dat' dar' tent of ours."

"Hush yer' mouth, friend," Johnny shot back.

"Ain't it something," Nathan observed, "...we're learn-in' mysteries and miseries of a soldier by day ...and 'tom-fool-in' at night."

September 18th, Thursday, regiment was ordered to travel 'in light marching order' ...meaning no tents ...around countryside in search of Rebels ...Confederate John Morgan's cavalry threatening attack. Company A's 2nd Lieutenant, William Albertson, told men to reduce gear carried to only essentials. "...haversack is to carry grub ...it'll be best friend you'll find in the army," Albertson coached. The boys marched eleven miles southwest to Florence, Kentucky, and camped over night beneath stars at the Fair Grounds. Next day, they marched south of Florence nine miles, and the following day another eight miles further south. Then, on the fourth day, they reversed, retracing steps over same route to within twelve miles of Covington.

"Nothing to do except 'bout face and git' home again," Jeremiah lamented.

Lucius remained boyishly enthusiastic, "I keep look-in' for Rebels show-in' their teeth."

"They're just play-in' possum, I reckon," Jeremiah offered.

March was grueling. Johnny turned sullen ...young, but overweight ...and Papa too. Papa's forty-five years showed ...stout paunch not "best for march-in'." It was tough on everyone, but especially Johnny and Papa ...red-faced, huffing and puffing, they strained under weight of knapsack, gun and equipment ...woolen uniforms veritable ovens in heat and dust.

"I'm plumb tuckered out," Papa admitted.

"Drink plenty of water," Will cautioned, "...use your canteens, boys."

Boys fidgeted during long delays in march. Junior drifted away, returning with a handful of fresh blackberries stowed in handkerchief. "Blackberries are good for us …keeps diarrhea and 'itch' away ...have some, boys," Junior said, offering to share with others.

For the next three weeks, Camp Walton was 'home'. Personal baggage left behind as they departed Michigan …it had not arrived in camp, so no one could bathe or change clothes. "I'm a gonna stay upwind of Johnny," Junior complained. "He smells so bad even skeeters won't touch him."

Making matters worse, over the last ten days their only water came from a green, stagnant duck pond. Even that ended. One morning, Lucius came back from filling canteens at the pond, a horrified look on face. "Ya' ain't gonna believe this," Lucius reported, "…there's the carcass of a dead mule ly-in' in weeds, just into water, at edge of pond over yonder."

"Nothin' do-in!" Johnny protested, face contorting in squeamish anguish.

Junior snapped back, "Can you believe? …Papa, yer' secret's out! …that's why yer' coffee's bin' tast-in' so rich in flavor!"

"Guess it's a good thing we've been boiling water real good, Papa," Will added. With that thought, Nathan raised hand to mouth, face turning ghostly white …turned back to the group and headed off in haste toward woods …about to be sick, not able to stomach the thought.

"I'm beginning to greatly dislike Kentucky," Jeremiah added, capturing everyone's feeling …each man filthy, dusty, irritated and homesick. Compounding unpleasantness was lack of sleep ...disrupted by bugle calls up to five times a night …to form lines of battle to meet threatened attacks by Confederate John Morgan. Around campfires, men traded stories and gossiped about the man they were chasing. Lore of John Morgan …'Rebel Raider' …grew within the Army of Kentucky as it did throughout the South. Cavalier and romantic, he was for the South what Francis Marion 'Swamp Fox' was to colonists during Revolution. Adopting tactics of guerilla warfare, he terrorized Federal forces …destroying railroad trestles, telegraph lines, and stealing Union supplies. His marauders carried unconventional shotguns, striking unexpected, sometimes even masquerading as Union officers

...they fled utilizing hit-and-run tactics before Federal soldiers could regroup.

Confederate John Morgan, swashbuckling marauder

(Library of Congress)

Will and boys heard frightening stories that Morgan's men strike out of nowhere, from concealed positions within dense Kentucky oak or hickory forest. Papa sat at evening campfire, teeth clenching clay pipe ...removing pipe slowly, he began telling a story. Younger boys sat entranced, teeth chattering, cowering on every word. He went on, "...a sudden flash and roar of shotguns, followed by bloodcurdling curses and commands filling air ...then moans from wounded hitting ground writhing. Within seconds it is over ...Morgan and men running to waiting horses, galloping away in clouds of dust ...like phantoms." In hushed voice, Papa continued, "Union pickets imagine Morgan lurking in every grove of trees. Lonely soldiers stand in fear and panic, imagination 'seeing' phantom Morgan riding through mist, along shrouded hillside valley in murky distance. Or, sudden owl's hoot or rustle of cattle in underbrush startle them to fear unknown." Myth grew …Union soldiers terrorized by mere notion of John Morgan's presence in the area …Will and boys were no different.

With no actual sightings of the illusive John Morgan, regiment received orders to march south. Marching through night, weary soldiers arrived in Cynthiana, on the Licking River, the following evening at 9:00 PM after grueling twenty-two hour march covering nearly forty miles. Three days 'rest' guarding railroad line came as welcome relief to Will and boys ...rest did not last long. Early morning October 18th, Will and boys watched with other soldiers as a railroad handcar rolled toward camp from the south, three Negroes pumping furiously to provide motive power. They leapt off handcar and were ushered hastily to Colonel Wisner with information from Lexington. Report was that John Morgan was planning to attack nearby Paris, Kentucky, with 2,000 cavalry next morning. Colonel Wisner moved out …regiment marching with utmost urgency ...order given to march in 'route step' to cover long distance quickly, with neither precision of march in-step or in-silence required. They traversed eighteen miles in a mere five hours …unusually quick.

Apparently upon learning that Paris was reinforced, John Morgan called-off attack and moved to vacate Kentucky. Another set of orders reversed course, and the '22nd' regiment proceeded to Lexington and a large Union winter encampment, arriving October 26th, a Sunday ...last seventeen days and nights, Will and boys learning a tent was 'soldier's luxury' …instead sleeping under stars …on cold hard ground.

Chapter 13

Back in Oxford, Michigan, first Sunday in November found Maria rising early at rooster's first crow to prepare breakfast and get William and Walter dressed and ready for church. The Bowles stopped to pick up Maria and boys on their way to church. Church was in-town ...small, white clapboard structure ...simple and unpretentious. Maria was warmly accepted by its small tight-knit congregation ...pastor was friendly enough, though Maria found Reverend John Duckworthy's sermons less than inspiring. In introducing himself to newcomers, Reverend would usually say, "Name's John Duckworthy ...but you can call me 'Jack' if you know what a duck is worth." It was catchy hearing first time, but grew old quickly upon hearing over and over ...much like Reverend Jack's sermons. She missed church in Penn Yan, but this would do. Maria, children, and Ezra and Nettie always sat together in third pew from front, left side ...but church was not the same each Sunday without Will alongside. Sunday's were toughest for Maria ...often she sat during sermon, thought drifting, missing Will and praying silently for his speedy safe return.

On a typical Sunday after Will left home, Ezra and Nettie stayed after church to help with whatever needed tending on the farm ...most often the Bowles stayed for supper. They were such comfort and children loved them dearly ...'Grandpop' and 'Grammie'. But this Sunday was different ...something terribly wrong over the last weeks, though Maria remained silent. She considered herself intelligent, good Mother and highly capable of dealing with difficult situations ...self-assured and strong-minded. But, this situation was totally unexpected ...far different from anything she and Will contemplated. It was causing great anguish, shaking self-confidence and lingering without answer. She decided to talk with Ezra and Nettie today ...waiting uneasily for just the right moment.

Maria took pride in how she handled everything in Will's absence. With Ezra and Nettie helping and Ned's part-time assistance, she managed to take care of farm chores. She maintained the garden, harvested fall vegetables, tended to chickens and rooster, two cows and two plough horses. Potatoes and squash were in cellar for winter ...cucumbers made into pickles, beets and green beans pickled. With Nettie, she spent two days stewing tomatoes and canning in glass jars. Ezra and Ned worked hard assembling needed firewood. All was ready for approach of winter ...maybe not perfect, but a great deal accomplished with much hard work.

She even managed to slaughter a chicken yesterday ...a task Will tended regularly, but first-time experience and challenge she was uncertain could be handled. She plucked a chicken from its nest, grabbed tightly by its legs and whisked it away ...wings flapping violently in protest. She smiled ...recognizing the same bird that pecked William a few weeks earlier when he tried to gather eggs. Unlucky bird's head was placed on stump of tree Will used as chopping block. With queasy stomach, Maria winced bringing ax down on doomed bird's neck ...instinctively releasing it from grasp, gasping for breath as she recoiled backward. Headless chicken fell to ground, still violently flapping wings, darting about backyard for what seemed endless moments ...until it keeled over dead. Meanwhile, young Walter awakened from nap, coming on a run out of farmhouse upon hearing clucking protestation ...he pulled up frozen, watching wide-eyed the surreal last moments of bird's frenzy. Maria hoped to keep butchery from young eyes, but everyone on a farm had to learn early ...she was sure this moment would never leave Walter's memory. Maria put carcass of limp bird in tub of hot water to soak and soften feathers, while Walter stood alongside wide-eyed with curiosity. One-by-one, she plucked feathers, struggling mightily with some that refused, and then cleaned and dressed the bird ...nasty task complete and bird ready for next-day Sunday's supper with the Bowles.

Following Sunday church service, everyone returned home for leisure afternoon and supper. Maria checked chicken simmering nicely on pot belly stove. Carrots and onions were added. Flour batter for dumplings was being kneaded. Nettie was putting finishing touches on piecrust ...pumpkins harvested from the garden would make delicious pumpkin pie ...a perfect end to chicken and dumplings supper. Ezra was outdoor repairing a front gate not closing properly and creaking, while children were with him playing and spending time with 'Grandpop'. Maria thought, "...*right time to broach my dilemma with Nettie.*" She proceeded slowly with uneasiness, searching awkwardly for right words. "Nettie ...I do not know how to say this ...I have a big problem."

"Go right ahead darl-in', ya' know words ain't a problem for me," Nettie answered.

"For last several weeks, I have been so worried, Nettie," Maria continued. "I just do not know what we're going to do."

"Go on child," Nettie urged, "...what is it?"

"William just had a third birthday last week ...such a good boy, since Will left ...trying to help me as much as he can ...but he still requires so much. And Walter ...he's not yet one and one-half years old, but just getting to be a devil ...into everything ...needs constant attention," Maria hesitated as she spoke.

"Yes, Maria," Nettie replied, sensing Maria's emotion about to overwhelm.

With tears coming, Maria burst out, "Nettie, I'm pregnant!"

"I'll be gol' darned!" Nettie screeched, throwing arms into air. Regaining composure, Nettie pushed bowl aside, reaching compassionately with outstretched arms for Maria. Two friends hugged tightly, Maria sobbing uncontrollably, "What am I going to do? ...How can I manage?"

Just then front door burst open, Ezra barging forward carrying armful of freshly cut firewood. Caught off-guard, surprised to see two women embracing and Maria crying, Ezra opened his mouth with first thought coming to mind. "Well, da' gate ...she's fixed, gol'darned thing ...just a loose hinge, ya' know.

Ya'all kin' always use more firewood, so I used ax and maul," he said sheepishly. "What's da' matter here?"

"Maria's pregnant, Ezra," Nettie blurted.

"I'll be damned! ...I mean ...I mean ...I'll be jiggered." Ezra tried to extricate himself ...for 'church-goer', nothing should be 'damned' ...especially spoken in Maria's presence.

Nettie tried to reassure Maria, "Maria, it'll be alright, ya' know ...we'll all work on this together ...yu'll see!"

"She be right now, Maria," Ezra added. "Sit yer'-self down and let's talk about this."

Maria regained a degree of composure as Ezra and she sat at table. Nettie finished putting pumpkin pie together and placed it to bake, before drawing a chair at table. Maria explained that conception probably happened the night before Will left for Pontiac. Will did not know about her pregnancy ...she wrote four letters over the last several weeks, but could not tell him. At first she hoped she was wrong about pregnancy, but now it was certain. Maria said, "I do not know how I can tell Will. This war has everything upside down ...we should be so happy with the news. But, I know he will worry so much. He has enough to worry about, just keeping himself safe, so he can come home soon." Ezra and Nettie did their best to soothe Maria, saying again they would all be working together. "What would I do without you both?" Maria sighed, standing to give each a grateful kiss and loving hug. "You are family to us ...you know."

"Good enough, then," Ezra said, "Let's have us our supper ...I'm a starv-in' just now." Ezra brought everything quickly back to basics ...nothing more could be said. After supper, Ezra and Nettie spent time with Maria and boys ...enjoying each other immensely. Ezra and Nettie left for home at twilight.

Maria went off to bathe the children, before tucking them into bed early. She needed to get close to Will ...she was lonely ...lost in loneliness. If only Will were here to share excitement ...and help her. It was not to be. Instead, she turned to her journal ...to feel closer to Will. Retrieving worn hardbound book from nightstand, she opened to a red ribbon marking last page read. She tried to relax, slumping into a chair, untying and brushing flowing hair back and over shoulders. She removed the ribbon slowly. Sighing heavily, she began to read:

February 14th, 1858
Valentine's Day, Sunday

Rose and I did not go to church today, but stayed at home and read "Bride of An Evening". Snowed all day. At night we sat in the parlor and had a good chat such as we have had in days of yore by 'our window'. Oh, these friendly communings, how many happy associations are connected with them. We delved deeply into the mine of memory, and found there many a hidden gem, cherished only too sacredly. "I would not give my heart the brief joy, the long sorrow, of those who love and part".

She reread her last line again *"...those who love and part"*. Her heart felt emptiness ...loving Will, yet uncertain she would ever see him again. She eyed the floor with distant glassy gaze ...emptiness ...thought and emotion rushing back. She regained semblance of self control and resumed reading:

February 17th

In evening, Rose and I went to a surprise party at Mr. Morse's. Danced all night until 5 o'clock in the morn. Had the pleasure of Mr. Ready's company home, and Rose that of Mr. Briggs. Northern lights shone very bright through the forepart of evening, but disappeared about three. All things considered, we had a most delightful time.

Maria laughed at what seemed now to be foolish youthful romanticism ...how much life changed. She glanced to next entry ...the day *'her Will'* came back ...*her 'love', forever!*

February 21st Sunday

"At home"

Came from Uncle Joshua's, and who do you think I found. Who else should it be but 'Will. I will not write what I think, for words cannot express my joy. He has not changed a particular, but has to me the same old look.

Happy to meet,

Sad to part,
And, thrice happy to meet again.

She recalled vividly Will's look that day ...just twenty years old, but acting older ...she never thought of him as three years younger. He had confident air, not cocky but self-assured ...quiet, not boastful ...tall and strong, with big shoulders ...someone *'you could count upon'*. *"But, oh those eyes!"* she thought. Piercing deep hazel eyes saw right through her ...they weakened her ...no different now, after marriage and children. *"I love you deeply, my Will!"*

Friday, February 26th, 1858

I have often wondered if there was ever a true 'heart book' written. I do not believe there was. I do not believe true feelings of the heart can be expressed by words. None are powerful enough to express the great joys, or sorrow, of a heart. There is one continual theme in my heart, and a joy newly found. I wonder if his feelings will change at this distance. They always have in every other. I hope not, for if they do, I will guard my heart forever from the attack of 'Cupid'. He is a

dangerous friend, and will not accept a part
of the heart, but demands the whole.

"...*words ring true today*," she sighed. She gave her heart
to Will, and he gave his to her ...she missed him so much, longing
desperately for his safe return. *'Helpless'* was the feeling ...unable
to change their situation. She was always good at getting her way
...but now, everything out of control ...powerless ...and alone.

March 1ˢᵗ Monday

...now I am at 'dear old home', and have
seen Will. He is at Milo today, but
expect him back tonight or tomorrow. Last
night winter of 1858 took leave of us. He
gave us farewell tears in form of a snow
storm, but this morn spring sun is shining
'with splendor untold'. In a few short
weeks, Nature will awake from long sleep,
cast aside snowy counterpane, arise and put
on mantle of green, and deck herself with
flowers—Nature's beauteous gems. Soon
we shall hear 'songster's cheerful cry' in
every grove, and then to me will be the
happiest season of the year.

Sunday March 7th

It is the twilight hour, and I am at home. Sarah and Will are sitting by the fire, John is doing his chores, and the children are in all kinds of Devilment. Was at Penn Yan yesterday, and while away, Will came. John, Sarah, and Clara went to church today. I stayed home, for I preferred a 'communion' of the heart, to a 'communion of the Methodist Church'!

Sheepishly, Maria giggled at irreverent impish words of self gratification. Beloved journal was working magic once again ...feeling better already ...today's troubles moving back into shadow. She read further, entranced by her story of courtship.

Monday, March 8th

Will and I went down to Penn Yan to spend the evening. Expected the Milo people down, but were disappointed. However, we had a pleasant time.

Wednesday, March 10th

Arose quite early. After breakfast, we let
fire go out, and then moved the stove into
the South room. Will and I moved the
bedstead. We made a fire, mopped the
floor, arranged the bed, had supper at four,
and now we are domiciled in the pleasantest
room in the house. Pleasant to me from
dear past associations... Now, no more
sighs, no more "blues" for me!

Maria could feel heat from her blush. *What a 'naughty'
girl!* She vowed to keep her little book hidden from snoopy eyes
of young boys.

Sunday March 14th

Did not go to church today. Had a good
race with Will upstairs. I won the bet.
After tea, went out on the North porch to
listen to church bells, and who should come
after me, but Will, the chivalrous one!

Had a most obsequious and excruciating time!

Next entry reminded her of their spat ...now, it seemed childlike.

August 10th

Received a letter from Will requesting to address me with a warmer feeling than friendship. Never, no never! We can never be anything but friends, and hardly that. I would sooner cast myself into the sea than become his wife. I shall answer it kindly and friendly, as my heart prompts, but there can never be any love...

Fortunately, they overcame that little skirmish. She announced their engagement.

November 28th, 1858

Made an engagement with William Hodkins today. Happy day—happy day!

How glad I am to be so fortunate. God bless his dear soul!

With broad smile, Maria replaced the red ribbon bookmark, closing journal's worn cover ...treasured lifeline working magic once again ...Will was closer. She placed the purple coneflower between journal's pages ...purple 'passion' flower he gave her. She uttered silent prayer, *"God, bring Will home again."* She turned to light kerosene lantern ...daylight slipping away ...she needed to write. In flickering light, she labored carefully to draft her letter informing Will of unexpected news.

Chapter 14

Camp Ella Bishop was a large Union camp in Lexington, Kentucky, where Will and boys spent four months of winter ...performing guard and picket duty, while protecting camp and city of Lexington. It soon became a miserable winter ...weather causing army life to lose any glamour. Six inches of snow occurred first day of arrival in camp, but snow did not last. Weather conditions were changing. Mist and rain lasted for days making camp a veritable mud swamp, before making way for dust that became stifling. During drills, dust clouds suffocated, sifting into eyes, nose and mouth ...perspiration matting dust to skin and clothing. Junior complained during drill, "My mouth's so full of dust, I don't want my teeth to touch one another!"

Papa replied with a grin, "Now that's what I call a 'dry sense of humor', ya' know." Initial excitement with army life turned to disenchantment. Foul weather combined with homesickness, filth, disease, lack of privacy, stern discipline and general discomfort operated on minds and bodies of Will and fellow soldiers. If all not enough, sheer monotony and dullness of camp life added to misery. Will's journal became 'trusted friend' ...within its pages, he poured innermost feeling and emotion ...it became a lifeline like Maria's journal for her.

Bayonet drill is regular routine,
but boys laugh at the scene of
awkward thrusts and lunges ...like a

dance made equally by frog, sand-hill
crane, sentinel crab, and grass-hopper
...all jumping, swinging, thrusting,
and striking every which way, all gone
stark mad.

Today we drilled with bayonets.
Nothing disgusts or sickens me more
than the thought of ramming that
instrument into a Reb. Bayonet serves
far better purpose as a candle holder,
or spit to cook rations. Major made
us nauseous, saying, "...when they
come, catch Johnny on your bayonet,
and pitch him over your head".

...we were lined up waiting for
drills to begin. Major caught one of
the men with hands in trouser pocket to
keep warm. Major called for all to
hear, "Son, what are you nursing?"
Company broke into such laughter as I
have ever seen.

Guard and picket duty were demanding. Will was assigned
sentry duty with the two youngest boys, Lucius and Jeptha. It was
raining, cold chilling and blowing rain ...conditions making
drudgery of their twenty-four hour shift. Jeptha and Will talked
while reclining at the base of a craggy oak, fending off elements

under ponchos, while Lucius patrolled a nearby break of woods bordering grassy open field. Each carried loaded weapons with bayonets fixed. "Keeps on rain-in', Will," Jeptha said, "...so much mud ...seems ya' take one step forward, and two steps back ...gets to be so depress-in' for me."

"Soldiering ...not what you thought it would be?"

"My Aunt Bess and Uncle Tom would say 'told ya' so' ...dead set against me volunteer-in', ya' know," Jeptha answered.

"I remember," Will replied, sensing Jeptha needed to talk.

"Aunt and uncle and Ma and Pa are good people ...just simple folk ...no one was itch-in' for this war," Jeptha went on. "What's gonna' happen to us, Will, and where do ya' think we're headed?"

"Looks like we'll be in camp for winter ...War seems to be 'on hold' ...then we'll probably head south ...maybe Tennessee in spring, is my guess," Will offered. "Depends on where Johnny Reb takes us."

"Ya' know Will, Kentucky weather and mud get men to cuss-in' ...vexes chaplain much with their swear-in'. Tent next to us annoys me no end with the dirtiest talk I ever heard in my life ...those fellows had no rais-in', Will."

"Old Tom Barker fairly blues air about him with vocal brimstone," Will agreed. "...a most accomplished, full-lunged blasphemer."

"I laughed heartily when Captain sent him out on picket 'to swear at trees until manners return'...remember, Will?"

"Nothing to deter trashy talk but a man's own scruples ...and the chaplain," Will offered.

"Ya' know, I've really come to enjoy chaplain's prayer meet-in's," Jeptha added, "...kinda' interest-in' how all us come together ...Presbyterians, Methodists, Catholics, and Jews ...like Papa and Nathan ...and 'nuth-ins' like me."

"We're all in this together," Will agreed, "...trusting to higher powers."

Conversation was broken abruptly when Lucius called out from sentry, "Who comes here?" Will and Jeptha scrambled to feet ...adrenalin pumping, rifles poised.

Answer came from a figure emerging from woods, "Friend, with the countersign."

"Advance, friend with the countersign," Lucius replied. All three slumped and relaxed with relief ...'countersign', or password code, was issued daily from headquarters allowing officers or couriers to pass sentry.

Hours later, the three returned to camp chilled and soaked to the bone. Will remarked, "Hope Papa has hot coffee ready ...long stand in wet and cold takes its toll on a man's health." They arrived in camp to find Papa waiting with coffee ready, and a letter for Will that arrived earlier. Excited, Will thanked Papa for coffee, and hurried off anxious to read Maria's letter. Firewood chopping block handy, Will sat down, hastily tearing open envelope and beginning to read:

> 2nd November 1862
> Sunday Eve
>
> My dearest Will,
>
> Went to church today with boys and Ezra and Nettie. Enjoyed service, but had constant thoughts of empty pew beside me. I miss you a great deal. After church, returned to our house for chicken and dumpling supper and Nettie and I made pumpkin pie. I know you would have wanted to be here.
>
> Received a letter from cousin Robert ...made me so angry. In June, Federals

tried to enter Charleston by land and battle ensued. Though Confederates drove them back to Port Royal, Robert feels his beloved Charleston threatened, so he enlisted in the Confederate army to defend the city. I am sickened to no end to think of Robert as a 'Rebel'. What has hideous war done to our family?

I fear I have no good way to tell you of next unexpected news. It should be happiest of times, but war changes all. Please be happy with this news, though I know it will cause you added worry ... Lord knows you already have such burden. Will, tenderness and love of our last night together has been consummated by my becoming pregnant. As you gather yourself, I ask that you please be happy for us, and not worry unduly for me, or William and Walter. We will be alright, and Ezra and Nettie will be here for us. I do not know what we would do without them ...they are 'family' to us.

Your loving and grateful wife,
Maria

Emotion overtook Will. Folding letter, he lowered head, putting both hands to face, beginning to sob uncontrollably. Papa noticed and moved slowly toward Will, uneasy with what to do for his friend. In kind and caring gentle voice, Papa asked, "Will, what is it?"

Slowly, Will's head lifted, hand moving to wipe away tears streaming down cheeks of mud-caked soot-stained face, moisture welling in reddened eyes ...looking forlorn and beaten. He looked up, struggling awkwardly to regain composure. "Every bird loves its nest," Papa observed compassionately.

"Papa, I should be such a happy man, but I feel I'm letting my family down. I should be with them ...instead of running off to be a soldier ...so far away, not able to help. My wife, Maria, is pregnant!"

"Ah, I see," Papa answered, immediately deciding to be upbeat and supportive, "...but that's wonderful! Ya'll see ...it'll work out for the best." Papa moved toward Will with open arms to embrace his friend.

Will nodded, acknowledging their friendship, bear-hugging Papa. "Papa, you and boys are like 'family' to me ...I thank you so much." That said, Will moved away to be alone ...conflicting thoughts troubling deeply ...*reluctant to volunteer because 'family' is so important ...deciding to 'do my duty' and leaving home so difficult* ...all in question again ...conflicting thoughts. Maria needed him even more, yet choice was gone ...he was a soldier. He could only hope War ended soon ...so he could go home to Maria and boys ...before the baby arrived in spring. *I must stay strong ...weakness will not help Maria. I must be 'happy' ...as Maria requested.* He resolved, *"I will be the best soldier I can be, and get home quickly."* He trusted God would find a way.

Will moved back to the tent to get pen and ink. His letter told Maria how pleased he was with her news, *"Perhaps it will be a baby girl, as you want ...if we keep our faith, good things will*

136

happen." With letter complete, Will hurried away to place it in mailbag before mail courier left for Brigade Headquarters. He was feeling better already. Walking back from mail drop, he focused on beauty and majesty of gray smoke curling upward from chimneys of hundreds of white canvas tents lined precisely in rows, rows rolling gently over lush green countryside ...glorious sun setting, diving toward far horizon, silhouetted against timbered ridge of hillside to the west ...setting sun moving each day further southward with days becoming shorter. Nature's grandeur inspiring ...he felt presence of a higher power ...he murmured, *"Give me strength to get through this."* Campfires were dancing as messmates huddled to prepare evening meal. Will smiled, recalling Junior's saying, *"...boys will huddle round cook's fire like a lot of half-grown chickens under an old hen".* Junior's humor put things in perspective ...Will envied Junior's carefree humor ...wishing humor came easier.

Will approached the tent, seeing Papa and boys gathered around campfire busily preparing the meal. Papa called out, "Glad you're back, Will ...we're all gonna' have ourselves a party ...da' boys here decided to celebrate yer' good news ...expect-in' a new little-un."

Nathan jumped to add, "Papa's fix-in' a special meal, Will."

Lucius added excitedly, "...plenty of 'toddy' for the party!" It seems Johnny and Junior ventured away from camp and purchased whiskey from a local named Rufus, who came down from a makeshift still operating in the hills ...doing booming business with soldiers in camp. Nathan purchased sardines from a Sutler. Jeremiah grabbed maul and wedge to split firewood for campfire. Everyone pitched in to help.

Papa was preparing special accompaniments to 'red eye' whiskey and sardines ...hardtack 'sheet-iron crackers' ...grinding 'teeth-dullers' into fine powder, adding wheat flour, making stiff dough. "Good thing Papa's doctor-in' those crackers ...if ironclads be eaten raw, could scarcely be broken by teeth," Johnny offered.

Junior agreed, "Ya' gotts-ta' bite steady, as there is great danger of break-in' teeth."

Lucius added, "If we could load our guns with them, we could kill 'seceshs' in a hurry."

Nathan joined the discussion, "Water makes very little impression on it."

"And, those 'squirmers'," Jeptha commented, referring to worms densely populating moldy crackers, "...if we eat crackers in the dark, cannot tell which ones are untenanted."

Papa worked onward oblivious to boy's chatter. He rolled out dough on a cracker box lid like pie crust, covering it with dried apples and a few raisins. Walnuts were shucked from pulpy husks and added. Mixture was then rolled in cloth and boiled in water. "In no time we'll have us some 'hardtack pudding' ...she'll taste right good, I reckon," Papa said. In addition, he fixed a dish of baked beans, prepared in an iron three-legged skillet called a 'spider'. Small beans were white and round, like soup beans ...pork fat covering the top of par boiled beans ...mixture placed to bake on top of campfire's red coals.

Boys extended tin cups, and Johnny poured 'red eye' ...party underway. Soon, mood became festive and jocular, especially following second and third rounds of red eye. Papa offered a salute, "Let's give three cheers for Will and Maria." Boys raised cups toward Will and let out with "Here! Here! Here!"

Joking continued well into night. Even Jeremiah, most serious of all, retold a joke making rounds in camp, "What's the difference between a good soldier and a fashionable lady?" he asked. No one answered, waiting for punch line. "One faces the powder, the other powders the face." Everyone laughed ...good time had by all.

At Camp Ella Bishop 'blue jackets' in 'Billy Yank's' army learned to cope as weeks passed. Camp excitement reached fever pitch with announcement of paymaster's arrival. Eyes watched roadway anxiously for the man who carried the panacea for all ills. Will and boys gathered, as Junior observed, "Paymaster's arrival produces more joy than sinner's repentance in heaven."

Pay-time was an early Christmas present ...Will's first receipt of wages earned since departure from Pontiac in early September. Will stood in line, and stepped forward as 'Will Hodkins' was called ...he watched intently as the paymaster counted $8.50 for service since September, assured that a balance of $28.33 was being deposited in Oxford for Maria. One soldier remarked to Will as he left line, "...tis' wonderful how money affects us ...we walk straighter, look happier, and act more independent."

"You've got that right, my friend," Will answered.

Jeremiah quipped, "Our children's children will never have it in their hearts to say we were governed entirely by mercenary motives."

"No question about it, Jeremiah," Will replied. "I'm going to camp barber to shave my beard and get hair trimmed ...before money runs out."

Days passed, weather remaining miserable and getting colder ...sheer drudgery. Will wrote in the journal:

Camp Ella Bishop, Lexington, Ky
December 5, 1862

Nature has been angry. Bugle sounds, we are roused at dawn, crawl out of tents, stand half-dressed for company roll call, then return to damp blankets. Faces are black from soot of campfires, eyes red and smarting, and faces burn from fire while our backsides are drenched and chilled. I went to camp barber to shave my beard and trim hair ...he nearly wore out heavy leather strap as he stropped razor often to cut through unruly

growth ...my hair resisting course
bristles of hemp brush.

I am making the most of it.
Have lost 15 pounds, and have
persistent cough, and soreness of lungs,
but regiment's doctor has prescribed
quinine. Conditions are rough.
Overbearing stench fills camp from
poor attention to garbage pits and
latrines. Water is scarce, and seldom
good ...warm and muddy, often filled
with wiggle tales and tad poles ...or
sand rattles down the throat. We have
to be sure to boil water before drinking
or cooking.

Men try to bathe in the nearby
stream ...imagine a hundred naked men
frolicking in water. Sometimes draws
a crowd of Lexington citizens who
stand on the banks, young girls
giggling to watch the men. But it is
not of much use, odor of unwashed feet
fills our tent making a most
unpleasant experience. I spend
sleepless nights listening to snoring,
coughs and labored breathing.

Idle time is getting to wear on me. I find myself sitting by campfire with coffee cup, amused by watching black flecks of coffee grounds swirl and sink to cup's bottom ...and then I do it over and over again. When not writing, I amble off to do some reading. 'Harper's Weekly' and 'Frank Leslie's Illustrated Newspaper' are passed among the boys, and I keep up with War's progress.

I have been attending nightly prayer meetings when held. But, I must confess, I have taken to chewing tobacco, as it helps pass time. Most men either chew or smoke, and swear habitually, so I figured chewing was lesser of evils. Five soldiers are playing hearts in the grove, and I am hurrying to join them.

Will closed the journal. Junior walked up, bushy red hair springing in all directions from beneath kepi cap, sheepish look on freckled face. Hesitatingly, Junior asked, "Will, yer' so good at writ-in' letters ...will ya' write home for me? I'm not so good at writ-in', ya' know."

"Sure will, if you like."

Junior continued, "My Ma and Pa will be a worry-in' ...my four sisters too."

Will reached into knapsack for a piece of paper, gold nib pen, and new bottle of ink purchased from the Sutler. "What would you like to say?"

"Tell 'em I'm enjoy-in' myself finely," Junior answered. "Give my respects to all who may ask about me. Tell 'em I've made some good friends, and we sleep under the same blanket, and drink from the same canteen." With coaxing, more was added, and Will completed the letter for Junior. A few days later Johnny asked Will to write to his sweetheart.

Other boys used wages from the paymaster in different ways. From a Sutler, Jeremiah and Jeptha bought clay pipes and tobacco bags. Arriving back at tent, Papa took the boys under wing, eagerly training two novices on subtle aspects of tamping tobacco, lighting and drawing down on newly acquired treasures. Hours were idled away around many campfires, as Papa and new recruits puffed away on pipes and spun tall tales.

Nathan was an introvert. He purchased best seller books, like Victor Hugo's *'Les Misérables'*, Edward Bulwer's *'A Strange Story'*, and Timothy Shay Arthur's *'The Withered Heart'*. It was not uncommon to see Nathan's tall thin and lanky frame ambling away from camp, 'flood runners' lost in wavering grass, seeking serene meadow, returning only after hours of solitary reading.

Johnny and Junior were far different. Newly acquired wages burned holes in uniform trousers. The precocious pair purchased Kentucky bourbon 'pocket ticklers' from a moonshiner and acquired a ravenous penchant for gambling. Gambling was endemic in camp, and the two boys found no trouble locating poker, 'chuck-a-luck', or 'old sledge' card games. Gambling, drinking, swearing and whoring were rampant, though strictly against army rules. Will and Papa cautioned Johnny and Junior, but they would have none of it ...until a day in late December. A group of six soldiers became far too intoxicated, gambled openly, and were loud and boisterous ...Johnny and Junior among them. Officers had no option but to discipline the soldiers. After a quick and perfunctory trial before Colonel Moses Wisner, the six received punishment, both humiliating and degrading.

Will and five friends watched aghast as Johnny and two others were ordered to "march a circle with a rail on yer' back." A heavy split log rail was tied with hemp to arms and positioned on shoulders of Johnny and two fellow transgressors. Three marched in circles carrying their burdensome load to boisterous jeers of many watching. Johnny's paunchy out-of-shape frame was no match for the ordeal, straining greatly under awful load. Perspiration matted sandy blond hair, running down fleshy jowls of plump beet-red face, salt burning eyes. Friends could do nothing, watching helplessly. Still intoxicated, three men stumbled and fell repeatedly, soldiers dragging them back to feet to march onward.

Junior's punishment was just as bad. He and two accomplices were 'tied by the thumbs' to a tree limb overhead. Hemp rope was tightened taught so only relief came from standing on tiptoe, becoming more and more excruciating over seemingly endless time. Mockery and laughter from soldiers watching added insult to pain. And then it was over. Johnny and Junior survived their punishment …hopefully, bitter lesson learned.

Time passed slowly in camp. Pranks and practical jokes were played on friends …'tom fool-in' going on as 'bluebellies' searched for ways to kill time. Jeremiah placed hot coals close to bare stinking feet of Nathan as he slept, until he awoke from heat, cursing at laughing buddies. "He struts like a rooster," Jeremiah chortled, as Nathan jumped around doing a quick-step to stay off hot feet.

"Ya'll won't hear the end of this," Nathan warned. All knew it was just having fun.

But the best pastime of all was music. Guitars, fiddles, banjos, and accordions supplied music. Songs were played, like 'Yankee Doodle', 'Annie Laurie', 'Mockingbird', 'Dearest Spot on Earth', and 'Be Kind to the Loved Ones at Home'. Ladies were not available so 'stag dances' took place. Will and boys were standing by sidelines as the lead musician called for 'lady volunteers' …band striking notes to 'Peas in the Pot'. Junior was pushed into center of circle. Aghast, Junior hollered, "I ain't gonna' be no lady," hurriedly retreating back into crowd safety with onlookers hooting and laughing wildly. With that, Papa and Nathan stepped forward to 'volunteer'. They were given white

handkerchiefs to be worn on left arms designating them 'ladies'.
As partners moved toward them, the band swung into the 'Virginia
Reel', while Papa and Nathan and other dancers began to whirl,
twirl and quickstep to lively music. Crowd cheers, clapping, and
good-natured chiding erupted as dancers moved in a blur. Men
'danced the juber', popular rollicking dance with men clapping
hands and stomping feet to the jig. Other dances followed …'My
Old Kentucky Home' and 'When Johnny Comes Marching Home'.
Night's festivities ended with everyone singing 'Home, Sweet
Home'. At last refrain, Johnny called out loudly in melancholy
moan, "I want to go home". Spontaneously, men joined in chants,
"I want to go home …I want to go home," before the gathering
turned to walk away.

Days later, Will jotted thoughts in journal:

> …boys are like wild colts.
> Junior gets furlough to go into
> Lexington for 'horizontal
> entertainment'. Many women
> congregate about camp in guise of
> launderess …dressed to fits, with hoops
> and shakers, they tempt men in no
> uncertain way.
>
> There are a good many sick now,
> caused by imprudence. One soldier,
> who I shall not name, has been caught
> in bad company, and is so bad off that
> he has not made duty for weeks, and
> may be discharged and sent home. I
> worry about Junior catching the disease
> because medications of poke root with

> *whiskey, mercury, sarsaparilla, and sassafras seem to be of little good.*

After Christmas, weather turned unusually cold …ice formed on nearby stream …snow and rain frequently turning to sleet and freezing rain, wind gusts driving freezing rain through tent flaps into faces. Frost formed in mornings on canvas tents …boys huddling on oil cloths, seeking desperately to avoid damp chill that penetrated bones. Everyone suffered. Aching muscles and joints, accompanied by shivers, kept everyone from precious rest. When they rolled over, ice cracked on ground below. Time wore on, while patience wore out.

Lucius, Johnny, and Junior returned to camp one morning from picket duty, soaked after enduring hours in a mixture of rain and snow. Lucius walked up to Will and Papa at the campfire, saying, "Last night at midnight, I thought I would drop down. I felt all numbed, but I danced around lively, and got to feeling warm. I knew you two would have hot coffee when we returned."

In impolite manner, Junior added, "My snot runs and I'm shiver-in' like a dawg! Where's the coffee?"

"You got that right, pards," Papa answered offering tin cups of freshly brewed coffee, "Coffee keeps this gol'darned army operat-in', ya know."

In January, Will wrote in journal at night in flickering light of candle speared at point of bayonet:

> *…my appearance disgraces a beggar. Pant cuffs in tatters, and uniform stained with mud and ashes. I write under great weariness of body. I cannot get over the difficulty of my bowels. Diarrhea and dysentery spread through camp, brought on by foul weather. Respiratory ailments are*

commonplace. My cough comes and
goes, and I often have trouble breathing
...sweating one moment from hard labor
or drilling, shivering the next. Men
sleep together 'spooning' for warmth by
lying on one's side in a circle with
shoes near fire as a wagon's wheel,
belly against back and back against
another pard's belly, like spoons in a
stack. I have burned my shoes trying
to warm my feet at campfire.

Coughing, wheezing, and snoring
make it difficult to sleep. Sixteen
hours a day, and then no rest, in
Uncle Samuel's pigpen ...becomes
more and more difficult to bear.

On another occasion Will took pen to ink to describe
menacing critters ...particularly lice which men labeled
'graybacks':

Chiggers, wood ticks, sand fleas,
mosquitoes and gnats give us pleasure
enjoying a good scratch. But worst of
the creatures are graybacks. Everyman
seems to have the itch. We shun visitors
to our tent for fear of unwelcome
creatures accompanying our guests, and

146

*leaving their calling cards. Yet,
despite all caution, our blankets are
infested with graybacks. Our sweat
stained woolen uniforms are a haven
for the creatures. They are impossible
to avoid. We spend time, sitting cross-
legged, taking fun by watching each
other skirmish for graybacks, pinching
critters between thumb and forefinger.
We take pleasure from holding clothes
over campfire to smoke them out and
listening to critters pop like popcorn
from the heat.*

For months they heard nothing of the enemy. "…seems War has been put on hold for this gol'-darn winter," Junior groused. "Anything would be better than deteriorate-in' in this hell-hole of a camp." Disease grew more widespread, plaguing camp.

*…so many men suffer from
illness. My cough lingers, although it
seems to improve with weather. Nearly
everyone in our tent suffers from the
itch and has bowel complaint. The
runs continue to plague us. I have
taken so much quinine that I fear I
will not master hardtack with loosened*

teeth, or will ruin my constitution for
life. Boys call the doctor 'Old
Quinine'.

Malaria, like a nightmare, has
settled in camp and many suffer
shakes and fever. Many are lost for
duty, some discharged or dying. A
man died in hospital ...some said the
smallpox ...raised an awful excitement
and very near caused general mutiny.
Colonel LeFavour marched us all in
line, with bared arms, before the
surgeon. Surgeon made three or four
passes with his knife, cutting skin,
before punching vaccination matter into
the wound, and then each of us ambled
off to stop the bleeding. We were
well nigh disabled for service for ten
days. Such a wholesale slashing and
cutting of arms I never witnessed.

Winter's agony cast its pall over Will and boys, dealing a
crushing blow. Will wrote with heavy heart:

Johnny has fallen ill. Violent
congestion of the stomach. Painful
siege for three hours. Has suffered all

it is possible. Dr. Strong and
Chaplain do all they can for Johnny.
Castor oil prescribed, while the Doc
tried to be cheerful, urging Johnny,
"down with it, my boy, the more you
take, the less I carry".

Kept hot bricks to his feet, and
hot cloths on the stomach, but cold
clammy sweat runs out of every pore,
cold as death. A concoction of ground
mustard seed and hickory leaves, laced
with whiskey, was tried to no avail.
He receives opium and ether as pain
killers. But, such hours of suffering,
praise the Lord his holy name.

Will tried to shield Maria and family back home from their
bleak situation …he tried to be upbeat:

Camp Ella Bishop
January 10, 1863

My Maria:

My dear, I hope this letter will
be legible as I await purchase of ink
from a Sutler, so I write by nub of
pencil. I am plumb straight this
evening. I have just returned from the

149

creek where I took a good wash and put on a clean shirt for the first time in three weeks. I wrote you most of the news last, but trust this letter will reach you by your birthday the 24th this month ...28th year, I do believe! Enclosed is a ring that I whittled, and trust it will fit, so it can be worn as a reminder of me, and our fourth anniversary year of blessed marriage. I miss you so very much. No greater desire exists but to return home to you. My journal is well used as I make entries most days.

Johnny continues to be very ill. We struggle to do what can be done, but it is of no comfort. I fear for his life. Several of our Company are sick. Indeed, our Company only mustered today half of the men for duty, the rest being too ill.

Kiss the children for me. Give my respects to Mr. and Mrs. Bowles, and all who inquire of me. Tell them I am all right.

Yours with most affection,
Will

Meanwhile, Will and friends were lost in dealing with Johnny's worsening condition. It was insidious sickness. At first, Johnny and boys thought it was just 'bowel problems'. Johnny complained of headache, discomfort and sleeplessness. Tossing and turning and thrashing at night kept Will, Jeremiah, and Junior awake. "Johnny, quit yer' gol'-darned toss-in' and turn-in', will ya' please," Junior chastised, "...we can't get no sleep."

Sickness grew progressively worse. Fever grew excessive ...cheeks became flushed. Abdominal pain increased with difficult breathing. Papa asked Johnny, "Stick out yer' tongue, boy." Papa and Will glanced at each other with fear ...Johnny's tongue dry, brown and glazed, redness at tip and edges ...inside mouth, sores about lips and teeth. Johnny complained constantly of being thirsty. He vomited often, boys taking turns regularly helping him from his blanket to leave hurriedly ...tending also to frequent bouts of diarrhea.

January moved into February ...more than three weeks passing since Johnny's first sign of illness. Papa and Will spent much free time 'nursing' Johnny. Nathan helped whenever needed. Junior fell apart. Junior and Johnny were best friends back home, before dreadful war began and they volunteered for 'soldier-in' together. Junior's abundant humor disappeared. He moped, seemingly adrift ...thoughts elsewhere. He was of no help in offering care. Will and Papa worried that Junior might be drinking excessively again, as he wandered off from time to time. Jeremiah, and the younger boys, Lucius and Jeptha, just seemed stunned.

By early February, Johnny became prostrate, unable to get up from bed ...pulse quickened and he began to experience tremors and jerking muscles. Johnny was placed on a stretcher by medical staff and carried to waiting ambulance wagon for transport to the overloaded hospital in Lexington ...gravity of situation apparent. During the next week, a couple boys at a time received passes to visit Johnny at the hospital. Despite a brief rally, Johnny's condition rapidly sank. He was day-to-day. Then, cold clammy skin signaled a fall in temperature, and he was gone. Death occurred from exhaustion.

A brief funeral ceremony was held two days later. Bugler's notes pierced crisp morning air in fitting lament. Then, a small group of hastily recruited 'musicians' flailed away at "When Johnny Comes Marching Home."

When Johnny comes marching home
again,
Hurrah! Hurrah!
We'll give him a hearty welcome then
Hurrah! Hurrah!
The men will cheer and the boys will
shout
The ladies they will all turn out
And we'll all feel gay when Johnny
comes marching home.

The old church bell will peal with joy
Hurrah! Hurrah!
To welcome home our darling boy,
Hurrah! Hurrah!
The village lads and lassies say
With roses they will strew the way,
And we'll all feel gay when Johnny
comes marching home.

After a few words from Colonel Le Favour and regiment's chaplain, ceremony was over. Johnny's remains in wood casket were lifted onto horse-drawn wagon for transport to the rail station, and final trip home to Oxford. Junior requested furlough to accompany his friend's body home, and it was granted.

Train's locomotive belched gray smoke into clear blue early afternoon sky, sounds of steam belching from boiler …shrill whistle of engineer's signal piercing otherwise somber quiet. Train's huge iron wheels screeched and lurched, hesitated and lurched forward again. Inching away from depot, the train seemed reluctant to start Johnny's last journey home. All six boys stood respectfully in line peering from the platform, misty-eyed. Each waved to Junior, hanging precariously out railcar window to catch last glimpse of friends, while waving back. Then, the train was out of sight and Johnny was gone. "Here I am," Jeremiah observed, "…lame, blind, crippled, and whatever else you can think of …but I am still kicking."

"Started this thing a boy …now I'm a man," Lucius added.

Papa spoke a last word before they returned to camp, "We must move on from here, boys."

Chapter 15

Home in Oxford, Maria was doing her best to keep family and farm going. She kept saying, "*If I can just make it through this day ...tomorrow will be another day.*" Beside farm chores, Maria prepared meals and kept children in tow. During night's quiet time ...with boys tucked into bed fast asleep ...she turned to other tasks, such as mending clothes and socks and ironing. Ezra and Nettie were of huge assistance, coming as often as possible to help, or just providing good company ...'family' she could talk with easily ...simple folk, always listening thoughtfully to anxieties and giving reassurance. She and Nettie were a team ...Nettie helped with the garden, weeding and harvesting into fall, and then pickling and canning vegetables for winter. She assisted often with meal preparation ...regularly bringing prepared food with each visit ...and she did laundry and ironing. Ezra was a workhorse, doing farm chores and tending the animals. Both Ezra and Nettie made sure that Maria could get into town regularly to get supplies and attend church functions ...on Sundays, Ezra and Nettie picked up Maria and two boys for church service. Trips into town were important, a release from day-to-day farm drudgery ...providing social outlet to talk with other people.

Ezra also made arrangement for part-time help of Ned Hales ...it was working out well ...Ned was a young man with lame leg who walked with a crutch. He was strong and muscular, but bad leg kept him from military service ...he needed work, and helping Maria gave satisfaction that he was contributing to war effort. He was youngest son of Isaac Hales, elder patriarch of a family who lived nearby down the road. Isaac was also a post rider who delivered Maria's mail. Ned was extremely handy, grew up on a farm, and quickly began helping Maria with numerous farm chores. In return, Maria and boys shared meals with Ned when he was working ...Ned was good with the young boys and they liked him a great deal. Maria paid Ned what she could spare each week ...it proved a good arrangement for both Maria and Ned. Maria considered herself blessed and fortunate to have Ned, Ezra and Nettie's friendship and assistance ...they made everything possible.

Despite help, each day was exhausting for Maria ...getting more difficult as pregnancy entered its fifth month. She was weary ...boys a handful, particularly with Walter reaching nineteen months of age. More than a toddler, he wandered everywhere, inquisitive and wanting to explore. Will, Jr. was three years old, celebrating a birthday three months earlier in late October. Young Will was old enough to miss his Father, frequently inquiring of Maria, *"Where is Papa? When will he come home?"* Sensing the void, he wanted to help Mother constantly ...trying in a child-like way to be 'little man' of the family.

Bundling with heavy coats, scarves, knit caps and gloves ...bracing against ferocity of Michigan's winter ...Will, Jr. followed Maria outside. Across open unprotected farm yard they trudged through knee deep snow, steeling against fierce bitter-cold northerly wind howling ...leaning into storm, shielding faces from icy arctic air ...blowing, swirling snow pelting skin, making visibility difficult. Young Will stumbled, getting a mouthful of snow and sputtering. Maria hoisted him back onto feet from a drifted snow bank. They reached the chicken coop ...she knew young Will disliked walking through the chicken yard with its disgusting droppings and smells, but now disguised by snow cover. Maria took Will, Jr. on chores to gather eggs from the coop. He winced while reaching under straw bins for illusive eggs, amid fierce cackling from objecting chickens. Maria smiled. *"I just know he remembers the hen's pecking,"* she mused, *"...though he does his best to show bravery and hide feelings."*

The barn was more to young Will's liking. He enjoyed barn smells ...rolling playfully in hay. He was fascinated by harnesses hanging on rough hewn walls ...putting nose up to harnesses and sniffing …he liked smell of leather. He fingered melons that Maria stored in oat bins for winter. And, he loved to watch cats lurking and stalking in search of barn mice. He reminded often, "Mother, we need a dish of milk …for the cats." …especially because baby brother Walter's curiosity overturned dishes, spilling milk on more than one occasion.

Two cows needed milking twice each day, once at 5:00 AM and again in late afternoon. Most time Ned would arrive on horseback each morning, early enough to handle pre-dawn milking …but sometimes the task fell to Maria. *"I could never imagine milking cows one day …pulling on cow's teats …but I am pretty good at it,"* recalling now distant upbringing in Penn Yan. Often young Will accompanied her for afternoon milking. 'Brownie' was his favorite cow because she was so friendly, except when she swished a tail across his face. Maria chuckled as she recalled first time this happened …young Will jumped backward in fright knocking over a pail of freshly drawn milk. Fresh milk was stored in large cans in water trough near the house to keep fresh and cold, unless it was freezing weather.

Mother and young son pumped water together from their backyard well for drinking and cooking …filling troughs for milk cans and animals. Young Will strained with all might to move the cast iron pump handle, but needed help from Mother. On their way back to the house, they brought firewood inside for the pot belly stove, young Will struggling to balance two bulky pieces of wood in arms.

Inside their cozy home, Maria stoked fire while storm continued to rage outside …she seated herself at kitchen table to gain a moment's rest, glancing lovingly toward young Will and Walter playing with wood blocks on rough sewn plank floor. Walter swiped at the blocks violently, sending them flying across the floor to consternation of young Will. Will, Jr. was a typical three-year old needing attention …but, Walter was another challenge entirely …an energetic toddler wont to wander off at slightest inattention. Maria recalled an episode a few weeks earlier …before bad storms of winter.

She was seated at the table, lost in uninspiring task of peeling potatoes for evening meal …she let thought drift for unguarded moments ...fanciful memories of Will and courtship in Penn Yan before the children. After mere seconds adrift, she regained the moment, realizing young Walter was nowhere near. Rising from kitchen table hurriedly ...pushing bowl of potatoes aside, she turned anxiously and called out, "Walter, come here. Walter, where are you?" No response. She moved toward two small bedrooms at the rear of their cozy bungalow, but no Walter. Turning on heels, she noticed house door slightly ajar. She moved quickly, frantic now, reacting to rushing mixed feeling of guilt and fear ...she neglected Walter, allowing him to wander outside. Walter was nowhere to be seen. She called out again ...over and over ...excitement building, voice rising with each plea. She heard no response.

Hitching long skirt up from ankles, she hurried to the chicken coop. No Walter. At a run now, she tugged hard to pull open the large half-open wood sliding barn door. She glanced inside ...breathless, fear and panic mounting ...no trace of her toddler. Thought flashed to the stream behind the barn. At that instant, Will Jr. appeared. Recognizing Mother's fear and sensing panic, he mirrored her fear immediately. She grabbed his hand and tugged ...half-pulling Will Jr. along as she darted for the stream. Awful visions of Walter falling into the water caused heart to pound. Up and down stream's banks she scrambled, with Will Jr. in tow ...frantic, too frightened to speak. Mere minutes searching, but anguish suffocating ...self-anger surged for not protecting young Walter.

Then, she retraced steps, moving back toward the barn. Inside, she peered around a corner of stall and heart stopped. In stall's corner ...on straw covering rough wooden barn flooring ...Walter sat entranced and carefree, watching a barn cat licking fur from her litter of just-born kittens. Walter loved cats prowling barnyard. He chased one cat into the barn and discovered the mother cat with litter just moments old. Mesmerized, Walter watched trance-like ...Maria's frantic calls passing unnoticed. Maria rushed to embrace Walter, crying in happiness for his safety ...dear and tender moment. Will Jr. tugged at Mother's skirt, saying, "Mommy, don't be angry at Walter ...he just loves cats."

Maria smiled, regaining composure, hugging both boys tightly. "Mommy's not angry ...just worried to death that's all," she answered. "I just love you boys so much." Bending to kiss each boy's cheek, she bear-hugged Walter, spinning him off ground. "Come, Walter," she admonished, "...let's leave mommy cat with her new kittens." The three turned away, walking hand-in-hand toward their house.

Later that afternoon, Ezra stopped and Maria excitedly told her story. He came to shovel manure from stalls in the barn. Manure piled and stored just outside barn doors had grown nearly to Maria's height ...it would freeze over winter ...its smell not offensive until thaw with spring's approach. After finishing a nasty chore, Ezra took Will, Jr. in-hand and walked to a fenced area where plough horses 'Jake' and 'Henry' were feeding on a bale of hay. He hoisted young Will bare back onto 'Jake' for a brief ride into the barn.

Will, Jr. was getting so big Maria observed ...Ezra making him duck head before horse and grinning young rider walked through barn doors ...guided by beaming and proud Ezra. "Mercy ...mercy me," Ezra gushed, "...will ya' look at this young man."

Maria's recollection of that scary day weeks earlier ended ...she reconnected with Walter and Will, Jr. playing on the floor ...she needed to get supper started. That evening following supper, boys in bed and alone hours into winter's darkness, raging snowstorm and high winds still swirling, Maria sank down weary at kitchen table. In flickering light of burning lone candle at elbow, glowing red embers casting warmth from nearby fieldstone fireplace, she wrote:

Sunday, 18 January, 1863

My dearest Will,

In utter darkness, a fierce snowstorm is howling ...as it can in Michigan. I do worry for you, and hope winter is not as cruel in Lexington, with only a tent to protect. We are doing fine, and boys seem to be growing inches every day. My belly is showing, and I feel first kicks of our baby fluttering like a butterfly inside. Everything goes well, although each day I am more exhausted.

Will, I miss you so much. Next Saturday the Bowles' have planned a birthday gathering for me . . . but I feel so much older than my twenty-eight years . . . it will not be a 'party' without you! Ezra has taken a package to post in town. For your birthday in two weeks, and our 4th anniversary next day, we are sending a Bible and an ambrotype of me . . . I do so wish it looked better.

I have read of President Lincoln's declaration freeing all slaves in areas in rebellion. I pray that God will let the blows fall heavy and fast . . . until last

159

vestige of this awful secession is expunged.
Please come home to us safe and fast.

Your loving wife,
Maria

Chapter 16

Saturday February 21st, 1863, could not come soon enough. Bugle sounded and men of the 22nd Michigan Infantry scurried to line up, at least those fit enough to report for duty. Only a little over six hundred men of nearly one thousand that left Pontiac took positions ...now a haggard lot ...standing slouched, dirty worn tattered uniforms. Tired, drawn and thin faces gazed hollow-eyed at officers. Still they were there, unlike forty percent of brethren who died, fell ill, or simply 'skeedaddled' back home unable to weather fierce winter conditions at Camp Ella Bishop. Will and six friends listened intently as Colonel Le Favour addressed the regiment, "Boys, we have marching orders," colonel shouted. "We will move out immediately to answer threats from John Morgan's raiders ...Confederate forces have crossed the Cumberland River from Tennessee." Spontaneous cheer erupted ...men thrusting arms skyward, back-slapping everywhere ...calls of 'Hip-hip-hooray!' 'Hip-hip-hooray!' 'Hip-hip-hooray!' resounded with thunder, echoing through the valley. "Let's get on with it, boys," Colonel Le Favour answered, "...seems War has resumed." It was news Will and friends needed ...still mourning loss of Johnny two weeks earlier. Junior returned one night earlier, reeling from arduous train ride to Michigan and back ...happy to rejoin friends.

Columns moved out, walking south through four inches of freshly fallen snow. Late evening they completed a twenty-mile march to Hickman Bridge, a covered wood bridge crossing the Kentucky River. Hickman Bridge's single span of poplar and pine planking provided two twelve-foot wide lanes ...good access for supply wagons, artillery and troops ...its defense strategically important because a break in high cliffs or palisades at river's edge gave access to ford the mouth of Hickman Creek. Following day they marched further south fourteen miles to Danville, Kentucky, only to retrace steps next afternoon back to Hickman Bridge ...arriving at midnight, tired and foot-sore, lying on bare ground without tents. Scarcely had they rolled into blankets and closed eyelids, when officers urged exhausted men to get up. By 1:00 AM, in pitch black darkness, they were moving again. By daybreak, the straggling caravan reached Nicholasville, marching fifteen miles over night. Junior sidled up alongside Will, "I should-uv' stayed longer in Meech-igan ...miss-in' this gol-darn trip ...ya' think anyone in this here army knows what their-a-do-in', Will?"

Before Will could answer, Papa interjected, "We've bin' scurry-in' about da' country ...dat's for sure ...like a 'dawg' with fleas, chas-in' its tail round and round ...I'm too old fer' dis' nonsense."

Will answered, "I sure hope someone up the chain has answers ...I'm frustrated ...but too tired to object."

"Object?" Junior shot back, "...ain't gonna' do no good ...would be like that 'dawg' of yours, Papa, bark-in' at two coons up a tree ...do-in' no good, no sir-ee!" No shots fired, no enemy sighted ...just bodies aching, feet blistering ...pus and blood marking snow through frayed holes in boots and socks ...still devastated by their loss of Johnny.

Next morning was like every other ...nothing special. Bugler's shrill notes of reveille pierced dismal cloud cover. Even mules nearby brayed discordantly. Tent flaps were thrown aside as soldiers tumbled out groggy, went to toilet, and assembled to answer roll call and receive orders. This morning, Will and boys were moving out in haste to join forces with another infantry regiment, one of mounted infantry, one of cavalry, and an artillery battery ...entire detachment to march south, cross the Kentucky River at Hickman's Bridge, and proceed further south to Danville.

Columns moved out four abreast, like a flowing river of human creatures. Army wagons, drawn by six mules, jerked to start ...some loaded with gun-beds and heavy rope screens for embrasures. A wagon of eight or ten mortars was drawn by a team of twenty horses. Wagons carried forage for horses and mules ...others carried spare rounds of ammunition, company mess equipage, and officer's baggage ...and then the hospital wagon. First hour was orderly, men preserving ranks and marching in solid column. Then, a lively fellow cat-whistles in the air, somebody starts a song, and whole columns break out in laughter. Disciplined order is replaced by singing, laughing, talking and joking. A young officer on horseback canters by Will's position ...officer jauntily sporting new bright red hat with huge brim, plume of large white feather jutting from hat band. Good-natured calls and jeers erupt from enlistees. With look of chagrin, Will turned and looked over shoulder as Junior called derisively to the officer, "Come out of that thar' hat ...ya' can't hide in thar."

"How do ya' do!" Lucius added. The young officer stared ahead sheepishly and kept riding.

One man starts singing *"John Brown's Body"*, and others take up the chorus, including Junior, Lucius and Jeptha:

"He's gone to be a soldier in the Army of the Lord;
He's gone to be a soldier in the Army of the Lord,
His soul goes marching on.

Glory, glory, hallelujah,
Glory, glory, hallelujah,
His soul goes marching on.

John Brown's knapsack is strapped upon his back;
John Brown's knapsack is strapped upon his back,
His soul goes marching on."

Hours passed ...endless march cadence broken occasionally by the order "Halt" for men to take to ditches for relief. Snow cover vanished with warming of first spring-like days ...winds of March drying ground. A caravan of nearly two thousand marching soldiers, accompanied by endless string of wagons with horses and mules straining under load, turned pike into dust bowl. Will's nostrils filled with dust, 'grit' ground between teeth and eyes blurred ...heavy wool clothes great annoyance. Will dug deep, quietly occupied within himself, calling upon all strength and endurance. "Close up, men ...close up," called an officer. Not everyone held up to the grueling walk ...stragglers fell by wayside or drifted back rearward until overcome from exhaustion. Officers prodded, coaxed and cajoled weary foot-soldiers. At a stone well of a dilapidated farmyard, three men bolted from ranks, sprinting with canteens toward promise of fresh cool water at the well. Throngs of thirsty soldiers swarmed around the well anxiously awaiting turn to fill canteens. An old white-haired tobacco farmer in tattered bib overhauls and floppy hat emerged, hobbling through farmhouse's rickety screen door onto shed roof porch. A white-haired robust lady followed in long checkered dress with soiled white apron about her waist. They stood defiant, side-by-side checking the commotion. With a smile, the farmer spit a hefty wad of tobacco, cocked head and raised an arm in gesture of approval. "Glad ta' have you 'Yanks' in this here neck of woods," words rolling in lazy cadence. "Drink til ya' be filled ...there's a trough over yonder for animals." An officer on horseback saluted the farmer, wheeled his horse and sauntered off.

Papa's age and paunch wore on him as hours passed. Will walked alongside Papa, continually offering encouragement, "Keep drinking water, Papa." "You can make it, my friend." "Just look at that ridge on horizon, and keep walking toward it." Will kept a brave front as example for the boys as he pushed relentlessly, but found head spinning lightly, consciousness drifting in and out. Irony struck him, *"...from above ...it must appear surreal ... string-like mass of human form nearly a mile long, wending along winding dirt pike, enveloped in swirling dust cloud ...obscuring lush Kentucky vista of green hillsides, marching through valleys and plateaus of wavering bluegrass."*

After eight hours marching, weather changed drastically ...quickly, clouds darkened and storm developed. Wind shifted, blowing strongly from the north ...rain started. Rain was welcome relief ...cheers went up as first cool droplets of moisture hit parched skin. But, rain became heavy ...sheets of rain in steady downpour. Northerly wind grew chilling, blowing cold rain down men's necks ...men hunched over, droplets dripping from brim of

164

kepi caps. Wool uniforms, shoes, and blankets strapped to knapsacks became soaked increasing weight of load. As they neared the Kentucky River, numerous creeks were forded, creeks now suddenly swollen by rushing runoff of torrential downpour. Roadway became a muddy quagmire for horses, mules, and wagons ...ruts developed causing wagons to jerk violently or slip from side to side, animals straining, slipping and stumbling to make progress. For each foot-soldier, every step required extra effort to pull squishy shoes and boots from mud's suction. With red hair matted from rain, wetness making freckles more evident, Junior quipped to Nathan, "Seems those 'flood runners' are good for someth-in' ...keeps those trousers out of this here mud." Nathan saw little in Junior's humor ...he grumbled under breath, lowered head and forced sore feet to keep walking.

Terrain grew more difficult near the Kentucky River, which serpentines between cliffs and palisades rising nearly five hundred feet above its waters. In impending darkness, eleven hours and twenty-two miles out of Lexington, weary convoy crossed the Kentucky River ...still another fourteen miles to go before reaching Danville. Soon roadway became pitch black. Lucius stumbled from unevenness of road surface, sprawling face-first into roadside ditch. Junior showed no sympathy, "Does your mother know you're out?" Just as words left mouth, an overhanging tree branch from hidden protruding limb smacked Junior across the face. He uttered a stream of profanity. Papa answered, "If ya' want to keep yer' head, don't wag yer' tongue!"

Following close-up with a soldier just ahead, Will inched too close and stepped on the man's heel. Stumbling, the man called over shoulder, "Let me walk on em' ...all by myself ...will ya', Sir."

They arrived in Danville at 3:00 AM Sunday morning ...trek of nearly forty miles, traversed in eighteen hours ...exhausted beyond description. Sanctuary was offered by a minister within a church on outskirt of town ...simple, white clapboard structure offering warmth and shelter. Boys slept on hard wood pews, propped against one another. Will thought, *"...seems proper to spend early morning hours of Sunday in church."* They rested for two days.

Wednesday morning, March 25th, dawned bright and sunny with gentle breeze ...a sky with no clouds. Will and friends were marching again, but north this time at tail end of a huge wagon supply train. As he walked, Will listened with delight to plaintive, mournful tone of a turtle-dove in nearby woods. Further up pike, on a dead twisted oak limb, a woodpecker sounded a 'long roll' call ...reminiscent of times he paused to hear woodpecker's pecking on deadwood at his farm in Oxford ...mind drifting as he lumbered along. Jeremiah said, "Visibility must be a mile ...but can never see lead wagons beyond horizon."

Jeptha answered, "Train must be nearly a mile long ...awesome sight, sure enough." Supply wagons inched along, creaking and lurching on rutted pike, climbing through a pass between low mountains to either side. Will and boys walked with Company A guarding supply train's end. Officers on horseback sauntered up and down keeping foot-soldiers moving ...watching, ever alert for sign of the enemy. Skirmishers worked dense clusters of woods flanking roadside ...wooded savannahs interspersed among open fields of tall grass wavering peacefully in wispy breeze.

It came before they knew it ...late morning ...a 'pop-pop' sound could be heard. Will and Papa turned eyeing each other with quizzical looks. "What was that?" Papa asked. Before reply could be uttered, both men gasped noting a puff of smoke ...and then another ...cloud-like cottony puffballs of smoke rising white in stark contrast against deep green tree covered hillside to their left. Mere moments passed ...then repeating sound of 'pop-pop' ...then crashing report of artillery from mountain side. Look of horror crossed faces upon recognition ...they were under enemy fire.

Will and Papa stood dazed at first shattering notion of danger ... momentarily frozen, yet reacting. Instinctively, men threw themselves to ground at first exploding shells from Rebel batteries upon the slope. Rookie officers caught off guard and stunned, regained composure. Officers rallied, shouting orders to form defensive lines ...pandemonium and panic. Junior quipped, "...thar' jump-in' up and down like bob-tailed dawgs' in high oats." No one took it funny. Cannonading artillery grew deafening as Union gunners wheeled into position and began to return fire toward the hills. Union battery's first shot was directed with splendid accuracy, its shell striking near Rebel gunners …enemy gunners streaming for cover to cheers of Union infantry soldiers. Junior spouted, "Damn! …they're a runn-in' like ants from an ant hill!"

'Green' soldiers looked about for swarms of bees, before realizing buzzing and zipping sounds were minie balls in flight. New recruits like Lucius clenched teeth and cheeks paled with first recognition of screech of bullets. Lucius, who was so eager to get to battle *'before fight-in's over'*, lay prone and muttering with hands covering head, frightened beyond control. "Wha'd ya' say?" Jeptha asked, touching Lucius with pat of reassurance on elbow, "…you're mumble-in' like a treed coon …get a hold of yerself!"

Union skirmishers make initial contact with enemy within woods off roadway …now Federals burst into the open through tangle of trees and briar, backpedaling in disarray out of woods and across pike …forced by intensity of Confederate musket fire to take to heels and seek safety of Union lines organized haphazardly around wagons. Rebels emerge from dappled shadow of forest, furiously firing volleys as they advance …yelling with a fury making hairs stand on end. "Yelling like savages …swearing like demons," Jeremiah shouted.

Will and boys were under direct fire, air filled suddenly with objects flying like birds …soft whispers in their ears, flying over heads on ghastly missions of death. Will heard Papa say, "Wish I'd be a ground squirrel or possum so I could get to a hole." Adrenaline surged through Will's body …feeling both fear and resolute concentration for task at hand. Quiet prevailed among fellow soldiers. With pallor on every face, rifles are brought to full cock …arms tremble, as guns rise. All eyes are on advancing Confederates some six hundred yards distant, bedecked in various uniform configurations of 'butternut' dyed from hulls of walnuts. Union officers give the order, "Fire!" Springfield .58 caliber muskets belch with explosive fury that delivers a staggering blow to Rebels, curtailing their advance. Smoke clears for Will to see Rebels regroup. Battle is on.

First shot fired took fear away for Will. He looked down line to 'his' boys ...they seemed to be alright ...even younger Lucius and Jeptha. Nathan was holding his own. Jeremiah was a tough one. Nothing bothered Junior. Papa and Will nodded approvingly ...seeing their boys reload more calmly and fire muskets again and again, up to two to three rounds each minute. They were holding their own. Will dropped down on one knee, reached for a new cartridge, tore open paper with teeth, emptied powder down barrel and inserted minie ball. Drawing ramrod, he tamped ball and powder. Hammer was half-cocked, firing cap seated. Hammer was cocked fully, musket aimed and trigger squeezed. Load and fire, fast as possible ...that's the task.

Lieutenant Colonel Sanborn galloped wildly along lines, checked and whirled on all-white horse, calling to the boys. 'Green' Union soldiers flinched, and sometimes cowered as gunfight raged ...but held ground, forcing Rebels to retreat to cover of woods. Will and Papa urged instructions. "Crouch over, stay low!" "Stay down!" "Fire quickly!"

First two hours of battle passed ...deafening sound of artillery, muzzle blast of cannon and shriek of large projectiles overhead, contrasting with crackling of musketry. Twelve pound shells hummed and cracked overhead, dotting deep blue sky with little globs of white smoke marking explosions, sending buzzing fragments in all directions. Soldiers ducked and jumped instinctively as huge projectiles hit ground and exploded, fragments of shells, dirt and tree limbs hurtling through air. Musketry gave off continual 'zip-zip' sound as bullets hissed through air. Ping or tearing sound "...like popping corn," Jeremiah muttered. Bullets passed so close that Will felt pressure as if skin were brushed. He felt no need to dodge, recalling a veteran's advice *"no one hears the whistle of the ball that hits him."* "...cutting air like a knife," Will observed to Papa, while firing from deep crouch behind a stone wall.

"...like striking a cabbage leaf with a whip's lash," Nathan added.

"Screeched, she did ...like tread-in' on ah' cat's tail," Junior observed.

Bullets slapped against trees with force as if struck by sledge hammer ...tree limbs torn and splintered. "Sounds like throw-in' stones against sides of a wood barn," Papa remarked. Clouds of powder smoke obstructed vision and cloaked senses ...acrid smell of sulfurous air, combined with heat from explosions and surging adrenaline, made breathing quick and difficult. Will choked, and peered down line at Lucius and Jeptha gasping for breath. Smoke burned Will's nose, throat, and eyes ...almost like fire. Concentration became more difficult.

"Keep cool and aim deliberate," Will called to Jeremiah.

Junior said, "Cool? ...why Jeremiah's so cool, water will freeze in his canteen!" Heads turned, as a mounted Rebel officer on horseback galloped from cover of woods and drew rein within six hundred yards of Union lines. Ignoring raking fire, with cool aloofness he raised field glasses and surveyed the scene calmly as if on Sunday picnic. Union sharpshooters drew bead, but he bowed gracefully, whirled horse sharply and galloped unscathed back to cover. Will looked in opposite direction, sensing approaching 'butternut' in gray slouch hat ...took aim and fired, but missed. Defiantly the Reb scoffed at Will by thrusting an arm, giving Will a sarcastic one-finger salute before retreating to safety of woods.

Mid-afternoon, Union officers decided to make a run for Hickman Bridge and crossing of the Kentucky River. If wagons could make it across, pursuit by Rebs would be foolhardy because natural defenses of mountain pass were nearly impregnable. Supply wagons began to move. Will and boys joined other soldiers moving out at 'double-quick', scrambling down the lane at right angles to the stone wall. Beyond a stream, over intervening split rail fence, and into heavily wooded section they moved. They exited wooded cover through beaten stalks of cornfield at the base of a gulley.

Then the unthinkable occurred. Will glanced at last supply wagon safely crossing Hickman Bridge. Just then, he felt and heard a hard 'thump' on left hip bone ...as if struck by blunt object ...first reaction to turn and look if he bumped into something. But he collapsed to ground, striking right wrist on a sharply pointed tree stump ...hand opened and rifle dropped. "Oh, Lord!" Will cried out. He knew he was hit. Instinctively, he attempted to get up but could only raise his head ...hips and lower limbs like lead. He could see blood soiling the left pant leg. He grimaced, mustering every bit of strength, probing the wound with fingers ...gash deep and blood pooling on ground about limp leg. He fumbled for white handkerchief stored inside band of cap, placing it firmly against the wound.

Will looked up to see Papa, Jeremiah, and Jeptha standing over him in utter disbelief ...paralyzed by shock, gawking with open mouths ...frozen, unable to move ...sheer horror on faces. Papa was first to regain composure, shouting for Jeremiah to run for assistance. "Jeptha, fetch your canteen ...hurry!" he shouted. Jeremiah and Jeptha bolted away. Papa kneeled, grasping Will's hand firmly ...reassuringly. Papa's rimless spectacles slid down nose from perspiration flowing profusely down forehead. Leaning close to Will's ear, he whispered, "Yer' gonna' be alright, my friend ...she's not so bad ...helps a com-in' now." Will's breathing became hard and labored ...gasping for breath.

Junior came rushing, all serious kneeling alongside Will, "We're with you, friend ...your boys need you ...hang in there, partner." Jeptha returned with canteen offering water to parched lips. Lucius and Nathan joined the huddle over Will ...all oblivious to danger from enemy fire. Jeremiah returned directing two stretcher bearers accompanied by an Assistant Surgeon. Papa and boys stepped back. The surgeon offered Will a stout drink of whisky, as he cut pant leg away revealing a nasty wound ...he dusted and rubbed morphine into open wound. To staunch bleeding, lint was packed into the wound, before wet cloth bandage was tied in place. More whisky was offered, while a splint was prepared by stretcher bearers. Will was hoisted onto stretcher in obvious great pain. As stretcher bearers carted him off, Will looked forlornly at stunned friends, voicing softly, "Bid everyone 'goodbye' ...go whip the Rebs."

Hospital ambulance was a four-wheeled wagon with bed suspended by crude leaf springs to cushion ride. Staples on sides secured white oak bows, covered with heavy cotton duck cloth painted with letters 'U-S-A'. Rear end-gate opened via hinges and Will was transferred gingerly from stretcher to cot inside.

Ambulance's driver turned backward from a seat on wagon's bench, "My name's 'Throgmorton' ...my bays are spirited and good steppers ...hang on, soldier ...we'll get you to hospital soon as can be." Throgmorton put reins to the bays, and two well-groomed horses responded.

Wrapped in coarse-fiber army blanket, Will suffered a bumpy, jostling ride, cold and shivering from shock ...writhing in pain. He fought to stay conscious ...thoughts darted through foggy mind ...desperate panic regarding extent of injury, despite reassurances from medical attendants. "You'll be alright, soldier," they kept voicing close to his ear. An excruciating twenty-mile journey north took forever. Early morning but still in darkness, hospital ambulance arrived at U.S. General Hospital #2 in Lexington ...large and sprawling single story building of wood construction. He was transported inside to wait for a Surgeon ...never losing consciousness. He glanced about a small hospital room ...candles lit, making its scene macabre. A male nurse assembled instruments from the Surgeon's kit nearby. From well-polished walnut case, glimmering precision instruments were removed ...one-by-one, each ravaging instrument placed in ready position on a table aside the gurney. Fear and trepidation raced through Will's veins, causing violent shivers ...almost oblivious to throbbing pain ...frantic from awful fear of pending 'amputation'.

A Surgeon ambled into the dimly lit room with no apparent urgency ...a burly figure with unkempt flowing white hair ...peering over smudged rimless spectacles perched precariously on nose's end. He looked exhausted, endurance over-taxed. Will strained to focus eyes on the name 'R. Peter' stenciled on a label pinned to blood and puss-stained soiled white frock. "How do you feel, young man?" Surgeon Peter inquired, rubbing hair wildly as if shaking cobwebs from preoccupied mind. "Awful," Will mumbled, barely audible. With gesture from the Surgeon, a male nurse offered Will a hearty swig of whiskey ...Will gulped it down without objection. "That will make it feel better," Surgeon Peter quipped. "Think I will join you," he added, grabbing the bottle out of nurse's hand, taking a good size gulp. "Ah, now I'm ready!"

Without washing hands or instruments, the doctor grabbed an instrument, holding it between clenched teeth ...as one hand opened Will's wound, while index finger of the other hand probed the injury. Nurse held lantern aloft over table. The doctor searched for bits of cloth, bone or bullet fragment. Painful probing complete, Surgeon Peter wiped bloody hands on a soiled rag. He reached for a sponge, fumbling and dropping it onto the floor ...he retrieved it, rinsing sponge in cold dirty water from a basin, before mopping Will's wound. Will grimaced with excruciating pain at each step of rough exploration. "I think you'll be alright, young man," the doctor observed. "We'll take good care of you ...when you awake, repairs will be complete." Will nodded semi-recognition, only half-hearing. With that, Surgeon Peter applied liquid anesthetic chloroform to a cloth, holding it firmly over Will's mouth and nose ...Will lost consciousness.

Will awoke to sunlight streaming from a window across narrow hallway of hospital ward ...sunlight too bright for squinting eyes, brightness making aching groggy head swirl. Blurry vision noted cots lined-up three rows wide stretching long distance in both directions. He was lying on a cot, army blanket atop clean sheets, head resting on straw-filled pillow. Thirsty and in pain, sick to the stomach with throbbing headache, he shivered with fever ...*"certainly not 'heaven' ... 'good news' ...I am alive ...made it through."* Will struggled to reach down and touch wounded left leg ...he breathed deeply with huge sigh of relief ...*"leg intact ...no amputation."* Will turned to a young lad on a cot to his right, and slowly uttered words, "What day is it, friend?"

A blond-haired youth, who looked no older than eighteen, was watching Will awaken. "It's Friday, middle of the day, March 27th ...welcome to Lexington Hospital #2."

Before further conversation, Surgeon Peter walked up to Will's cot, "I'm Surgeon-in-Charge, Robert Peter ...no time for introductions when I last saw you, soldier ...how you feeling?" Will's head moved slowly, side-to-side without speaking, effectively answering *'not so good'*. Surgeon Peter wasted no time. He explained medical judgment, "Minie ball is made of soft lead weighing an ounce or more ...strikes human tissue and creates a ragged ugly wound ...struck center of your left hip socket ...split apart, half exiting thigh ...other half passed down thigh bone fracturing it and lodging above knee." He continued, "Bullet fragments were removed, arteries tied with silk thread, and morphine dusted into wound ...repaired damaged bone through resection, or excision, to save the leg ...prognosis is good because they treated your wound within first twenty-four hours, before infection showed itself."   Meanwhile, the doctor continued, "Bandages should be kept wet ...remain quiet as possible ...frequent doses of whiskey will be offered, as you please ...nurses will be along shortly with quinine for your fever."   With that, Surgeon Peter moved toward next patient.

Chapter 17

Boys were eager to play outdoors after returning from church. It was one of the first nice days in Oxford ...pleasant blush of spring in air after long cold winter. They would be alone but Maria relented, while she completed housecleaning chores inside. Will, Jr. came running into the house, screen door slamming loudly in his wake, breathlessly informing Mother that young Walter tripped while running. Walter followed behind older brother, crying at top of lungs, more scared than hurt ...torn pant leg evidence of skinned knee. Maria finished calming Walter, inspecting and cleaning a scraped knee ...putting a fresh pair of trousers on the boy, when she heard sound of a visitor approaching her door. A 'knock-knock' sounded. Maria patted Walter on behind, a gentle pat of affection, and left the small bedroom to greet the visitor. "*I am not expecting anyone ...visitors are few and far between out here ...Ezra and Nettie would not be knocking,*" she wondered.

Front door stood open to let fresh air inside ...screen door all that separated her from a man waiting anxiously on the porch ...fidgeting and tapping nervously a booted toe on wood porch slats. Her heart sank deep within a hefty protruding belly ...he was in uniform. An uneasy soldier pivoted as he sensed her approach. He was tall ...dark olive-skinned complexion, with jet-black hair ...swarthy full black mustache curled up at ends. He cut a dashing figure in full uniform, complete with sword and scabbard at his side. Broad-brimmed black felt hat was accompanied by feathered red plume projecting from red hatband. He doffed hat brim in gentlemanly acknowledgment of a lady, "Mam, are you Mrs. Hodkins?"

"Yes," Maria answered swallowing hard for breath, trying desperately to conceal fright.

"Regretfully …Mam, I must inform you that your husband …Private William Hodkins …has been wounded near Danville, Kentucky. He is alive and recuperating at a hospital in Lexington."

Maria stood stunned. She gasped, stepped backward, funneling hands over mouth. Regaining composure, she asked the young staff officer, "I am sorry …please step inside, Sir." Hat removed, he pulled screen door open and stepped through doorway. "Could I offer you a cup of water?"

"No thank you, Mam."

"Well, I do believe I need a cup of water myself," Maria said, moving toward the sink. "Please give me more information." This he did, although he did not know much more of what happened.

Moments later, he bid farewell, "Best wishes, Mam." Doffing hat brim in deference, he turned and strode off the porch to a horse tethered to picket fence gate. Maria stood in shock on the porch …frozen, unable to move …watching him ride away until no longer visible, beyond dappled afternoon shade of tree-lined roadway.

Walking back inside, she slammed screen door a frightful jolt, venting some anger. Releasing anger helped, but she was panting …difficult to breath, light-headed, feeling faint. She reached for another gulp of water. She must gather herself. Maria called for Will, Jr. and Walter, ushering them outdoors to play …she could not deal with them now. She tried to organize thoughts, *"What can I do? I must write to Will … all I can do …something to feel better."* Alone, she sank down at kitchen table, slumped forward and with quivering arm took pen to paper.

Sunday, March 29, 1863

My dearest Will,

I am reeling from news delivered by a young Army officer who knocked on our door just moments ago. He told me of your wound in battle, and that you are now recovering in a Lexington hospital. I am stunned, but can do nothing ...I must write these words so I can feel nearer to you. My love for you could not be deeper than I feel at this moment. I need you, and the boys need you. Your strength, and God's grace, will see you through your pain and suffering. Please get better, and come home to us! As I worry of you, I know you will worry of us. Be assured that boys and I will see this through. We are doing fine.

Will, my prayers are with you, but I must confess I am angry ...angry over this War that seems to have no end

...War that tears our family apart. And yet, we have no choice, but to struggle on with faith and strength. I want you to know how proud I am of you, and your bravery. Get well soon, my dearest.

Your loving wife,
Maria

Letter complete, she folded the page ...but something was needed. Arising from the table, she walked outside to courtyard garden ...spotted a particularly vibrant colorful flower, reached down and plucked it by its stem, before returning. Inside letter's folded page, she placed the purple pansy. *"Purple ...color of passion ...one of first flowers signifying coming of spring and nature's renewal,"* she thought, fitting for the situation. She pressed the delicate flower within folded page, giving it a last tender kiss before placing letter and flower carefully in an envelope. She must get it posted immediately. She was thinking clearer now. Writing brought Will closer. Now, she must tell the children and gather them quickly for a trip to Nettie and Ezra.

Within ten minutes, Will, Jr. and Walter were standing quiet ...intently watching Mother struggle to get horse to take the bit. Maria was not accustomed to harnessing Jake and wagon. Ezra handled that chore with Will away. Jake shook its head, unwilling to cooperate as Maria fumbled to get unruly animal harnessed. Jake whinnied in protest, sudden twisting head movement bumping against Maria's belly, knocking her off balance. Boys eyed each other sheepishly and fearfully. Being seven months pregnant, the boys took great interest in her belly, amazed as it protruded more and more. Maria talked to them regularly, letting each touch her belly and ask questions as she prepared them for new baby's coming. "Boys, my belly just keeps getting in my way," she said, smiling to assure she was unhurt by Jake.

With persistence, she succeeded in readying horse and wagon. Both boys scrambled up and into wagon's bed ...more difficult for Maria. She walked Jake alongside a tree stump that served as barnyard chopping block, and used it as stepping block to hoist herself awkwardly onto wagon's driver's bench ...not easy getting things done these days ...creativity needed. Grabbing reins, she called, "Giddy-up, Jake."

Jake cooperated and wagon started moving. They headed toward the farm of Ezra and Nettie, not quite a mile down bumpy dirt road. Within thirty minutes, they arrived. Ezra and Nettie were relaxing in white wood rocking chairs on front porch ...rocking without care, enjoying Sunday afternoon's spring-like weather. Surprised, they rose abruptly worried to see Maria and boys ...guessing something wrong. Maria dismissed the boys quickly, telling them to run out back and play.

Out of breath and speaking fast, fumbling for words, Maria explained news of Will's injury and hospitalization. She proceeded to tell what little she knew as Ezra and Nettie stood dumb-founded, eyes glazed. As words ended, they stumbled backward in unison, nearly collapsing ...unable to fathom her news. Maria guided them with outstretched arms toward chairs. Maria leaned against porch railing to steady herself, trying to catch breath. "What can we do?" Ezra asked.

"Only one thing I can do ...I must go to be with Will."

"But ...but ...ya' be in no condition to travel, ma' dear ...why ya're seven months pregnant," Nettie screeched. "T'is too risky for ya' ...and the baby ...ma' dear, we'll have none of dat!"

Two women argued back and forth, passionately. Ezra listened and watched, choosing not to enter the fray. Noting steely glint of sheer determination in Maria's eye, he said finally, "Nettie ...she's determined as an Irishman in a pub eyeing his last draught of beer."

"Say-in' ain't necessarily do-in," Nettie responded, wagging a finger in Ezra's face.

"Wow' now, ladies ...she be a strong woman, Nettie ...she can do it. I will accompany her to help," Ezra continued.

"I'm as tough as any woman …you know that, Ezra Bowles," Maria interjected.

"Ya'ar indeed …yes sir-ee."

Silence lasted several moments. Then, Nettie offered, "I kin' keep da' yung-ins' …it'll all work out." Ezra reached into pocket and pulled out his pipe without speaking, slowly tamped tobacco in bowl and struck wood match …holding match over bowl, he drew deeply …giving wink of eye toward Maria.

"Yes sir-ee …yes sir-ee," he said with a twinkle, blowing circles of smoke to emphasize accomplishment. Maria and Nettie shrugged and smiled. It was decided …rather, it was accepted. Trip preparation began immediately …all agreeing Maria and Ezra would depart on Wednesday. Ezra needed to make arrangements over the next two days for work to be done on the farms while they were away. With stern urging of Ezra and Nettie, Maria agreed reluctantly to make several overnight stays to ease burden of an arduous four hundred-mile trip to Lexington.

Isaac Hales, neighbor and friend, lived on a small farm nearby but further down road. He offered to take Maria and Ezra fourteen miles by wagon into Pontiac to catch a train. Early Wednesday morning, Ezra helped Maria board Isaac's waiting wagon with a push to hoist her backside. Ezra boarded last with Maria sitting between the two men. Alongside the wagon, Nettie stood with arms around shoulders of Will, Jr. and Walter. Both young boys stood stiffly, eyes welling with moisture. "I will give Daddy a hug for you …boys, be good for Grammie." Last instructions for young sons complete, Isaac called 'giddy-up'. Lightly flicking reins, he set two horses to action and wagon rolling. Maria threw a kiss to her boys and waved …boys and Nettie waved in return, until wagon passed a bend in road and moved out-of-sight.

Wagon headed east toward Oxford, turned south onto Old Lapeer Road, taking them past the town of Orion, crossing Paint Creek, to northern outskirts of Pontiac. Maria thought along the way of Will and his journey along the same route just seven months earlier. Pace was slow …Isaac trying to avoid bumps and ruts of well-traveled thoroughfare. After nearly seven hours of jostling journey, sign for 'Fairgrounds' appeared. She recalled that first letter received from Will ...describing initial experience of military life in camp at this very spot. *"Such short time ago ...yet feels like eternity, so much happening ...now he needs me by his side."* Thought drifted as wagon veered onto Saginaw Street. In another half-mile, they arrived at the corner of Huron Street and Orchard Lake Road at city's hub ...not far from the train depot. Here they found a hotel for the evening, warm meal and much needed rest.

Next morning Isaac saw Maria and Ezra to the train depot, where they boarded a passenger rail car with words 'Detroit & Milwaukee RR' painted in white on its side. Isaac said 'goodbyes', doffed cap and walked back to the wagon for the all-day trip back home to Oxford. Maria and Ezra settled down for a tedious rail journey to Lexington, Kentucky. After twenty-five miles from Pontiac into Detroit, Maria and Ezra changed trains, boarding the 'Monroe & Toledo RR' for next leg south toward Toledo, Ohio. Train was rolling by mid-day, as Maria stared blankly out a window lost in thought ... through towns of Wyandotte, Trenton, and Monroe. After nearly three hours, the train completed its forty-two-mile trip, arriving at the depot in Toledo. Next leg of the trip was two hundred miles further south to Cincinnati, so Maria and Ezra spent the second evening in Toledo. On Friday morning, they breakfasted in the hotel before returning to railroad depot, boarding the 'Dayton & Michigan RR' for twelve-hour trip south to Cincinnati. Later, the train rolled across Blanchard's Fork River at Ottawa, and then into Lima and Wapakonetta.

Along seemingly endless ride through flatlands of Ohio, Maria read intently from 'The Atlantic Monthly', magazine of literature, art and politics. Maria was reading the 'March 1863' issue when she came to page 288 ...a poem written by Oliver Wendell Holmes, Sr., entitled *"Choose You This Day Whom Ye Will Serve"* ...its fourth stanza struck deeply:

...."No sides in this quarrel," your statesmen may urge,
Of school-house and wages with slave-pen and scourge!
No sides in the quarrel! Proclaim it as well

To the angels that fight with the legions of hell!

They kneel in God's temple, the North and the South,
With blood on each weapon and prayers in each mouth.
Whose cry shall be answered? Ye Heavens, attend
The lords of the lash as their voices ascend!"...

Thought raced ..."*awful aspects of awful War ...bitter conflict, Will now wounded ...brother against brother, family against family.*" She thought of cousin Robert somewhere in Charleston, at danger and fighting against the very cause that she and Will held dear. "*When will it end? ...how will it end? ....how much bloodshed will it take?*"

Meanwhile, Ezra passed most hours dozing and lightly snoring. She marveled how a person could spend so much unproductive time in sleep. She returned to reading ..."*A Call to My Country-Women*" by Gail Hamilton, then a poem "*Lyrics of the Street*" by Julia Ward Howe, whose lyrics "*Battle Hymn of the Republic*" was first-published by 'The Atlantic Monthly' in February a year earlier ...now being sung with increasing popularity. About 8:00 PM in growing darkness, she could just make out Mill Creek running alongside tracks to the east. Beyond Plank Road, tracks crossed over Mill Creek at Whitewater Canal, minutes before their train arrived at Fifth Street train depot in Cincinnati. An exhausted couple disembarked ...both exhausted despite Ezra's long hours napping. Ezra signaled for transportation three short blocks to a hotel at Fifth and Central Avenue. Here they enjoyed a late meal and retired for the evening.

Hardest part of their journey over, Saturday would be much shorter ...only about ninety miles to Lexington. In early morning, Maria and Ezra took wagon transportation from their hotel, across Ohio River to Covington, Kentucky, and train depot where they caught the 'Kentucky Central RR'. Their train departed the station about 10:00 AM, across Bank Lick Creek. Then, it rolled along and across the Licking River beyond Falmouth, into Cynthiana, and further to the town of Paris in Bourbon County. Onward they moved, Maria becoming more and more anxious as miles of lush Kentucky bluegrass countryside passed before them. About six hours later, 4:00 PM Saturday afternoon, after nearly four hundred-mile journey over the better part of four days, Maria and Ezra stepped off train in Lexington, exhausting journey's end.

'Kentucky Central RR' depot was at the east end of Short Street. An agent in the train station directed Maria and Ezra to a small hotel on the corner of Mill Street and Maxwell Street, just a block west of Broadway. Ezra hailed a wagon which transported the couple a block north, where it turned onto Main Street heading west. Four or five blocks and a couple turns later, it pulled up to a two-story white clapboard hotel. Registering in the hotel, they were told 'Market House' is just a few blocks away, between Main Street and Vine Streets. "It is the major area of attraction," the hotel clerk opined. "City visitors should not miss it ...throngs flock farmer's market area on weekends." But Maria was interested only in getting to the hospital to see Will, though it was late-afternoon. She inquired directions to Lexington General Hospital #2. "It is not far north on Mill Street," the clerk answered. With hotel rooms secure and luggage checked, Maria and Ezra rushed away to obtain transportation to the hospital.

Chapter 18

Only in the last two or three days did Will feel well enough to begin reading. A nurse brought a copy of 'Harper's New Monthly Magazine', March 1863. Will was lying on his cot reading page 557 of the 'Monthly Record of Current Events'. He sensed someone approaching. Putting reading material aside, he looked up ...jaw dropping in shock, stunned and speechless. He saw Maria smiling widely as she strode briskly toward him. Ezra followed just behind, awkwardly trying to keep pace with Maria's rapid gait. "My poor dear, are you surprised to see us?" Maria gushed, feigning understatement.

"Will, ya' sure nuff' gave us good fright, now," Ezra chirped.

Will nodded, head moving side to side ...gesture of utter disbelief, finally gathering composure to speak. "You should not have come, Maria ...simply too far and too risky ...and the little ones," he said. "But it is sure enough God's gift to me." Pointing to Maria's belly, Will laughed and added, "And ...sure enough ...you have gained some weight, my dear."

Maria laughed and bent over hugging and kissing Will. "I have missed you so much," she whispered. "...never ceased worrying ...how are you doing, my dear?"

At Maria's persistent urging, Will explained circumstance of battle and how he received the wound, trip by ambulance wagon to hospital, surgery and last week of recovery. He said first five days were worst ...severe pain, but given morphine. "Surgeon tells me I am fortunate," he continued. "Feeling is beginning to return on my left side ...some nervous twitching in the leg." He paused ...emotion choking words. "I wrote to you on Thursday ...as soon as strength permitted," he told Maria softly. "...assured you I was alright ...told you not to even think of making this trip, because I know how stubborn you can be if you set mind to coming."

"She be one strong and determined lady, now," Ezra offered. "She'd have none of our convince-in' ...not to come, ya' know."

"I know. I know," Will agreed, sensing Ezra uneasy about allowing their trip. "I can always see it in her eyes ...when mind's made up ...sets her jaw so strongly."

"Ya' got that right, yung-un!" Ezra agreed, slapping a knee, thoroughly enjoying his own hearty laughter.

Maria glanced to the side noticing the birthday gift of a Bible sent to Will. It lay alongside hardcover black journal with brown binding ...both placed on bed stand beside Will's cot. Catching Maria's longing look at Bible and journal, Will related how much each gift meant. "Lying wounded on the field, I requested to not be carried away, until Junior fetched my knapsack with Bible and journal ...could not be parted from either."

Over the next several days Maria and Ezra spent a great deal of time at the hospital ...hours at a time bedside with Will ...but also making rounds about the hospital, talking with visitors, nurses and surgeons. Maria learned the hospital was a hotel before being thrust into its present role ...a sprawling 3-story complex, built of red brick, but retrofitted to accommodate present usage. Several wings extended from the central building, accommodating fourteen hospital wards connected by wood walkways. At its hub, operating rooms, pharmacy, kitchen, ice house, offices and supply room were centrally located. Patients numbered from 150-200 soldiers, mostly bed-ridden, but a small number in convalescence. Presently, the hospital was filled to quota.

Each day she summoned latent courage to cross hospital's threshold. Flies circled constantly ...air filled with vile stench of festering wounds and loose bowels. Toilets were wood seats over sloping tin trough ...with water in short supply, trough was flushed only after many occupants. "Disgust-in' ...worse than a bare foot step-in' on a fresh cow pie," Ezra complained to Maria after answering nature's call. Still, Maria was drawn to walk lengths of unpainted board-wall hallways partitioning wards. Pity and caring forced her to walk among patients, traversing long narrow rows of iron bedsteads furnished with layer of straw, straw pillow, two sheets and one coarse army blanket …or simple wood and canvas cots thrust into duty as overflow beds. Three rows of beds extended the length of each ward, between which surgeons, nurses, and visitors made rounds.

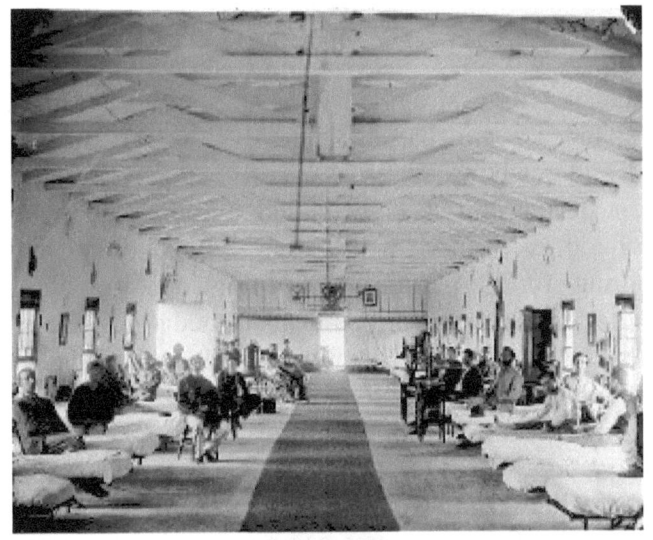

Typical Hospital Ward

(Library of Congress)

Sense of horror chilled her heart …beds filled with distressed soldiers …hard cold realty of imminent death pervasive. Gaping wounds and feverish thirsting lips conveyed ghastly agony and torment. Groans of suffering articulated sharpest anguish, while highlighting abundant courage demonstrated by so many. Eerily, sounds of woe comingled with sounds of boisterous laughter …stark contrast, as patients sought ways to separate from their adversity. All too often Maria observed hospital staff

185

shuffling past an open door, litter bearers carrying stiffening corpse from amid barely living souls to so-called 'dead-house' outback ...a low wood building with crude benches aligned to lay cold white corpses ... soldiers never to return to waiting wives, children and families ...fearful testament to utter destruction waged by brother pitted against brother.

Maria watched local women visitors come and go, kept busy making bandages, scraping lint to pack wounds, and toting culinary delicacies. Society women deserted card games and teacups, opting instead to knit socks or do whatever to ease burden of suffering heroes. She marveled at generosity and self-sacrifice of surgeons and nurses. Nurses, being mostly volunteers, cast aside timidity and squeamish feelings, summoning courage via silent prayer as they struggled against tugging dread pervading hearts. Nurses were hardy women, from all walks of life, dedicated and ready to sacrifice comfort and well-being to ease pain and suffering of sick or wounded soldiers. They went about customary duties armed with wash bowls, soap and towels ...distributing food to patients, keeping bedding and clothing clean, and administering various drinks, medicines and stimulants as ordered by surgeons. Beyond this, they served as soldier's friend, source of calm relief ...like mother, wife or sister standing bedside ...smoothing pillows, moistening parched lips, or whispering tender words of encouragement.

Maria thought it wonderful to see soldiers react child-like to sympathies bestowed ...nurse or volunteer lady citizen applying wet towel, with soft deft touch of hand to face, bronzed and bearded man too feverish to express depth of gratitude ...nurse tenderly parting and combing hair over a forehead hot as a barrel of overworked cannon. Maria watched one wounded man as a nurse offered food, but he shook his head. "Thank you, mam," he said. "...don't think I'll ever eat again, for I'm shot in the stomach ...but, I'd like a drink of water, if you ain't too busy." She felt sick emptiness as one poor fellow received attention ...eyes shot away, head badly shattered. A nurse bathed him. He lay silent, with no reaction ...as if both speech and sight were lost in untold terror. But, as the nurse completed his bath, he uttered a simple phrase in low voice, "Thank you." It meant so much.

On their way back to the hotel on Monday evening, Maria said to Ezra, "We must do something to help these poor men, while we are here."

"I darn well agree, but what's ya' got in mind?" Ezra answered.

"Do not yet know, Ezra. Let's think about it and do something in the morning."

Next morning Maria was rested and eager to pursue her idea. "I want to visit with as many men as I can," Maria offered. "Let us stop on the way to the hospital, so I can purchase cookies and candy, and writing paper and stamped envelopes."

Ezra said, "Good! ...bin' a-think-in' about it a good bit myself ...I'll buy me some brandy for ones who kin' partake."

Maria was not sure about wisdom of Ezra's brandy idea. *"...not sure if acceptable to Methodists in Penn Yan,"* she thought. But she decided to go along anyway. *"...anything to ease burden of tormented souls,"* she thought. "Alright Ezra," she replied, "I think we have a plan."

Out of their hotel they went ...to 'Market House' to do their shopping. Upon arriving at hospital, Maria and Ezra went hurriedly to Will to share excitement of giving to patients. After hearing her idea, Will said, "Maria, you are a caring person ...I am so proud ...and love you dearly." Looking toward Ezra, Will smiled and winked, "...and you too, Ezra."

Next two days, Maria and Ezra alternated between long visits with Will, and time spent going bed-to-bed, cot-to cot ...visiting sick or wounded. On one bed lay an Indiana man wounded in action ...next to him a patient from Illinois suffering with tuberculosis. Some were too ill to speak. In other areas, men talked loudly over War news, while others related 'back home' stories of mothers, wives or family left behind. Men read newspapers or magazines ...'Harper's Weekly', 'Frank Leslie's Illustrated Newspaper', 'American Review', or 'Atlantic Monthly', or their Bible or letters from home. Convalescents were paired playing chess or checkers, whist, or dominoes. Still others were opening and inspecting care packages from home. One man smoked a pipe carved from briar root. Maria alone, or accompanied by Ezra, spent time talking with patients ...offering a cookie from the tin or piece of stick candy. She found many eager for her to pen a few words 'to anxious souls back home' ...so she tirelessly wrote letters dictated by ailing soldiers. Ezra found numerous takers for his brandy ...no problem.

Most gravely ill patients bore bravely their throes of pain ...each bore a look of hero. In Ward D a soldier from Ohio just returned from another operation to remove more loose splinters of bone ...brown-skinned face lit by eyes full of determination. In another area, a young wife sat bedside with her husband fighting typhoid fever. Further down aisle, a mother with white muslin cap and dressed 'country' sat bedside with her son. She told Maria she had seven children, and "this one is my youngest." Maria stood for moments in Ward E watching a nurse help a poor fellow who began hemorrhaging ...nurse gently assisted him, holding cloth to mouth as he coughed blood ...so weak he could barely turn head on pillow.

One young Indiana man with bright handsome face lay several months in agony from a nasty belly wound ...bullet striking through bladder low in stomach area before exiting his backside. He suffered much ...watery fluid oozing unchecked ...disagreeable puddle wetting his bed. "I am right comfortable at the moment, mam," he answered Maria's inquiry, "...but my throat's feel-in' bad." He was delighted when Maria offered a stick of horehound candy to soothe raspy throat.

Maria vowed she would never forget a soldier who said, "Soldier-in' is certainly not beneficial to the mind ...and by look of it, does not appear to do much for body health either."

While Ezra dispensed brandy and visited patients, talking freely to all who listened, Maria spent hours of quiet time with Will. It was time to catch up ...mere seven months since leaving home ...seemed so much longer. Maria told Will everything about Will, Jr. and Walter ...they missed him in so many ways. Maria related the incident with Will, Jr. in the chicken coop, and Will chuckled ...fear and panic she felt when she thought Walter was lost. She simply could not make it without Ezra and Nettie ...how helpful and supportive they were ...like 'family'.

Maria and Will talked about the coming baby. She was doing well, but baby was so active ...kicking off and on, more and more. She asked Will to feel her tummy for baby's movement …a tender moment. She related how Will, Jr. and Walter enjoyed and marveled at touching her belly. Maria and Will talked of hopes …and worries for baby's health. They spoke of added responsibility. They wondered whether it was boy or girl …and enjoyed teasing with funny possible names for the baby.

Will relished telling Maria in great detail of experiences over the seven months since he left home. He told of new friends …how close they were. "Why, they are like family to me," Will said. "…I hope you can understand." With sadness, Will related details of Johnny's illness and passing. Maria and Ezra attended Johnny's funeral ceremony in Oxford, while Nettie tended children back home. Junior, Will said, grew a bit from the tragedy …more mature …even becoming a leader among the boys.

Maria and Will talked about the War, and speculated on what was to come. Not only did she fear for Will, Maria said, "I fear as well for cousin Robert in Charleston. It is 'tragedy' that Robert is fighting for the Confederacy …I am angry with his choice, but I blame the War …it is awful that family members are fighting each other."

"That it is. That it is," he replied. He told her he would be sent back to the regiment following recovery, *"…because every man is needed."* Will sighed deeply, with hesitation, "I feel torn, Maria, because I want so much to be back home with you and our boys …and yet …I know this does not make sense …and yet, I believe I must get back to my 'boys' in the regiment ...my six friends …I feel strong duty to them, as well. Can you understand?"

"But I do understand, my dearest," Maria answered. "You see …you are strong and resolute …and hold 'duty' in such high honor …it is what I love about you, Will Hodkins! Of course, I understand ...though your tenacity perplexes me at times," she said smiling, a quizzical teasing look coming with last phrase.

Will nodded, thinking silently, *"how fortunate I am to share life with such a smart and strong-willed woman."*

Time passed quickly ...five days at the hospital. Ezra had duties on both farms …Nettie's hands were full with chores and two young boys. And Maria needed to return home, before an arduous trip became even more difficult and dangerous. A melancholy farewell came too quickly. "I love you so dearly, Will Hodkins," Maria pleaded, tears welling. "Please promise to come home to me …and our boys …we need you. I need my 'German' home!"

"I promise …my word …I will come home!" Will answered with stout determination, fighting overwhelming urge to shed tears …moisture in eyes …lone teardrop trickling down cheek.

"God speed, my friend …keep'er safe, now," Ezra offered.

Chapter 19

Locomotive belched smoke and bells clanged, wheels spinning on shiny rail tracks glistening in early afternoon sun. The train started its herky-jerky pull-away from depot platform in Lexington on Saturday, April 18th. Locomotive was painted vivid scarlet which shimmered with sun's bright rays ...equipped with string of three red lanterns at its front which burned at night ...all coloration signaling a hospital train ...never to be bothered by Confederate cavalrymen. In nine days since Maria and Ezra left Lexington, Will's recovery progress continued. He walked a little, but always with nurse's assistance and aid of crutches. Surgeon and hospital staff determined Will's condition satisfactory for transfer north and further therapy and recuperation, as Lexington's hospital was overloaded and beds needed for dire cases.

Will was among patients loaded onto hospital train for a tedious ninety-mile journey north to Cincinnati and Marine General Hospital. 'Medical cars' were converted passenger cars, equipped with two tiers of bunks for patients, bunks being suspended on hard-rubber lugs. As boxcars rolled without springs for suspension, jerky jarring motion was sheer agony for many suffering patients. But Will was a happy man. Wounded left side was better each day ...aching from time-to-time, for sure ...but he could live with that ...severe pain gone. He worried constantly about Maria's dangerous trip home in her seventh month of pregnancy. Being carried by stretcher out of the hospital, he was handed a letter written hastily upon Maria's return to Michigan. As hospital train departed, Will smiled with content while lying on a bunk in the second hospital car, reading and re-reading Maria's letter.

My dearest Will,

I arrived safely today, Sunday, April 12th, after nearly four long days travel. All is well. Both Ezra and I are exhausted, but our journey was timely. It meant so much to see you, and be assured you were going to be alright.

Will, Jr. and Walter are fine, and I kissed and hugged them for you. Nettie has been so wonderful with our boys …what would we do without Nettie and Ezra to help? You are in my prayers always …I hurry to post this note, as I know you worry.

Your loving wife,
Maria

Will refolded a precious letter, tucking it between pages of journal for safekeeping …this time, shedding a tear of happiness.

Typical Hospital Train

(Library of Congress)

Train rolled leisurely from station to station across Kentucky countryside. Will recalled his original rail trip to Cincinnati, among a group of naïve recruits …men and boys of the 22nd Michigan. In less than eight months since departing Pontiac, they tromped all over Kentucky, in all types of weather, making it through horrible winter in camp ...all but Johnny. Through all, they bonded …good relationships ...six best friends …'boys' he left on battlefield along the Kentucky River. *"I must get back to them quickly."*

At each train station along the way, throngs of citizens assembled, offering cheers and clapping hands to salute heroes for their sacrifice. Will looked out a window as the train pulled into Cynthiana. A dapper silver-haired old man doffed stove-pipe top hat in tribute to soldiers peering from hospital car windows. Citizens brought baskets of provisions and gifts. Ladies came onto the train bearing wines, strawberries, jellies, cakes and flowers for poor suffering wretches. One man offered whiskey, saying, "It's new and fiery, rough and nasty." Another rich old man went cot to cot handing out $5 bills, saying over and over, "Make yourself comfortable …make yourself comfortable, my good fellow." Eventually the train reached its destination in Cincinnati.

Next three weeks, Will worked hard on recuperation in Marine General Hospital, doing extensive therapy and pushing himself to walk. He knew once he rejoined the regiment long marches would resume. He had no choice but to regain best conditioning he could muster. Likewise, as Will became stronger, hospital staff expected him to assist in nursing, cleaning, and feeding other patients, as well as seeing to disposal of bedpans and urinals. Between therapy, long walks, and hospital support duties, Will spent time reading, writing letters to Maria, and jotting innermost thoughts in the journal. He wrote letters to Papa to share with the boys. Papa wrote a letter …Will read and reread his letter.

April 5th, Sunday 1863

Will, my friend

We be much pleased to hear from Lieutenant Albertson that you are recovering nicely. You gave us all a fright.

All wagons reached Hickman Bridge safely, and boys laid down late that night, tired, wet and hungry in the mud and rain to get some sleep. Next morning, we was ordered out on Danville Road and posted ourselves a picket line, with some firing going on. Next days, we marched to Nicholasville, then Camp Robinson, Lancaster, and Crab Orchard. On March 31st, we moved toward Somerset in pursuit of Rebs.

*Camped in snow without tents at
Buck Horn Creek.*

*On April 1st, we was ordered to
Nashville. Marching now toward
Lebanon Junction to catch rail.*

*Best regards,
Ira ('Papa')*

Will also read and talked with soldiers about War heating up …now that winter was over. In early April, Union naval forces bombarded Fort Sumter, but with little impact on Confederate defenses of Charleston's harbor. In the North, a growing movement developed for capture of Charleston. Fort Sumter's loss embarrassing, people in the North were eager to wreak vengeance ...public opinion spurred on by newspapers. Lincoln viewed capture of Charleston a necessary moral, political, and symbolic victory because Charleston was 'Cradle of Secession' …rebellion's birthplace.

In early May, Will read from **Harper's New Monthly Magazine,** Volume 26, Issue 155, April 1863, of military action around Nashville:

"...Another unfavorable encounter occurred on the 6th of March at Springfield, Tennessee, in the neighborhood of Nashville. Colonel Coburn, with about five regiments, advanced from Franklin, and after some slight skirmishing with the enemy on the 3rd and 4th, was, on the 5th, assailed by a superior force of the enemy under Van Dorn, and lost by capture a considerable part of three regiments..."

Will lay magazine aside and grew pensive ...gazing with blank stare out a window across aisle from his hospital bed ...lost in thought. "...*action is heating up ... the 22nd Michigan is headed toward Nashville.*" Within days another letter arrived from Papa:

April 27th, Nashville

Will,

Letters are mighty pleasing to us all. Boys are itching for you to join us again. They say my cooking's not same without you, friend.

We arrived Lebanon Junction, Ky, April 9th, and waited beside rail cars behind stacked arms for near two days, before orders to board. Junior and other boys found some whiskey and indulged heavy now. Weather so hot, men rode on top of train cars. Junior, and others, so drunk they were tied to cars to keep from falling off.

Arrived Sunday evening, 13th, Nashville, and assigned to Reserve Corps, Army of the Cumberland, General Gordon Granger. Last two weeks, regiment posted to guard duty at depot, market, and town jail. Some picket duty at roads into

196

town. Will, you will see 'rough folk' here in Nashville.

Yours, Papa

It was not long before Will was on his way to rejoin their group. On Friday May 9th, Will was pronounced fit for duty and boarded train for a two hundred eighty-mile trip from Cincinnati to Nashville. He looked forward eagerly to joyous reunion and celebration with the '22nd' and good friends.

Chapter 20

He was unaware of time lapsed after collapsing into grassy ditch roadside, following agonizing days marching across rugged mountainous countryside since leaving Nashville. Hundreds of fellow soldiers shared ditches, recouping on both side of roadway. Will regained thought ...fallen deep asleep, mind reliving events of his last twelve months. Drifting in and out of consciousness, aided by dream-like visions, clear images in vivid detail appeared so real ...enlistment in Pontiac, Maria pregnant, winter camp and Johnny's death, being wounded and recovery following Maria's visit, rejoining regiment and friends in Nashville. He struggled to shake cobwebs ...eyes focusing on flower clump of black-eyed susans swaying alongside ...exhaustion all he knew. Left leg throbbed and ached from injury six months ago. He checked himself ...now in foothills of Lookout Mountain near Chattanooga ...Sunday September 13th. Hands clutched journal. He brushed aside perspiration beading on brow, and read the journal entry written last evening.

*I have no blanket, and little to eat.
Wrapped myself in overcoat about
9:00 o'clock, and lay down on ground
to sleep ...upon a bed of stony soil boys
call 'Alabama feathers'. Aches
possess me constantly, but a terrible*

toothache has taken hold, and J was compelled to get up and find what relief possible by walking the road. Moon shines brightly, and many campfires still glimmer aside the mountain.

Now he reached into pocket for stub of pencil to scribble.

J am a little lame, but not much. Feel older than my years. J must look the same.

It made little sense …writing took all energy, but so worthwhile. He closed journal's cover making certain the solitary black-eyed susan for Maria was ensconced safely within its pages. He sighed noticeably, flicked a drop of sweat from its black cover, and returned precious journal to breast pocket.

Will glanced left. Papa was hunched over, fumbling with top of canteen …fingers awkwardly trying to manipulate its cap …too tired to perform simplest function. On Papa's other side, Jeremiah was cleaning rifle, red handkerchief polishing barrel after wiping sweat from brow. Further down, Junior, Lucius, and Jeptha were dozing …Junior snoring loudly. Will turned right, where Nathan lay absorbed in thought, reading from the *'Old Testament'*. With everyone accounted, Will's eyelids closed again, but no sleep …mind racing over last four months' events, since discharge from Cincinnati hospital and return to regiment mid-May in Nashville.

Foothills of Lookout Mountain, near Chattanooga

(Library of Congress)

Smile crossed his face, thinking of Maria and everyone in Oxford. In mid-June he received a letter from Maria ...baby daughter was born in late-May. All was fine ...baby and Maria doing nicely. Maria and Will spoke at length of the coming baby during Maria's visit in Lexington. Will was convinced the baby would be a girl ...they agreed its name would be 'Minnetta', in honor of Nettie. Minnetta it was. Maria wrote that baby Minnetta resembled Will, but Ezra and Nettie saw much of Maria's likeness. He ventured a guess ...*perhaps Maria took baby Minnetta to church that very day* ...Maria would be so anxious and proud to show the baby at church. Will tried to envision baby Minnetta ...*how wonderful it will be to hold her ...another reason to make it home!* Eyes closed again, and he fell deep asleep.

So much was happening in all theatres of War. General Hooker crossed the Rappahannock River to attack General Lee's army. Lee split his army, attacking a surprised Union army in three places, resulting in huge Union defeat as Hooker was forced to withdraw across the river. Victory at Chancellorsville was costly to the Confederacy ...its biggest loss, General Stonewall Jackson died from pneumonia following amputation of an arm. In June, General Lee took War north to Pennsylvania, where Union

200

and Confederate forces clashed at Gettysburg, forcing Lee to retreat to Virginia.

In July, Union artillery from a fleet of ironclads opened fire on Charleston's defenders at Morris Island. Federal assault of Battery Wagner on Morris Island resulted in heavy casualties after brutal hand-to-hand combat. Confederates held, but this signaled start of Union bombardment and siege of Charleston.

In the West, Union General Grant put Vicksburg under siege to regain control of the Mississippi River. In July, Confederates surrendered the city and 30,000 men.

Focus of War in central Tennessee shifted through Summer and into Fall 1863 to a small frontier town of 2,500 people, nestled in a valley at the neck of a bend in the Tennessee River …called 'Moccasin Bend' …town being Chattanooga. Cherokee Indians gave its name …meaning 'eagles' nest' for a towering rampart known as Lookout Mountain which overlooks river and town below.

View from Lookout Mountain below to Tennessee River

(Library of Congress)

Chattanooga stands strategic as 'door to the South'. Union forces can block future invasion into middle Tennessee or Kentucky, and obtain open gateway into Alabama and Georgia. Even more, Chattanooga is vital to control of railroads, being hub for three important Confederate rail lifelines ...'Nashville & Chattanooga RR' running north-south, 'East Tennessee & Georgia RR' running northeast along Blue Ridge Mountains to Knoxville and into Virginia, and 'Western & Atlantic RR' which provides access south to Atlanta and the 'Memphis & Charleston RR' running east-west. Railroads carry a large share of the Confederacy's arms, munitions, food and other supplies. Aside from Richmond or Atlanta, Chattanooga is the Confederacy's most important rail hub.

In Tennessee, two great armies jockey for position, making chess-like moves, each seeking strategic advantage. Union 'Army of the Cumberland' is under command of Major-General William S. Rosecrans. Confederate 'Army of Tennessee' is led by General Braxton Bragg. Both armies fought six months earlier at Stone's River, near Murfreesboro, southeast of Nashville and eighty-five miles northwest of Chattanooga. The Union declared victory after three days of intense though inconclusive fighting, when Confederates withdrew thirty-five miles south to defensive positions along the Duck River around Tullahoma and Shelbyville.

For six months, through the balance of muddy and frigid Tennessee winter and into spring, two armies regrouped, re-supplied and reinforced on opposing sides of the Duck River separated only by a range of foothills. Meanwhile, Confederate cavalry raiders under the daring Nathan Bedford Forrest, Joseph Wheeler, and John Hunt Morgan harassed Union supply lines along the Cumberland River and Nashville, firing on transports, attacking wagon supply trains, and demolishing railroad bridges, trestles, depots, and freight cars and locomotives.

Union Major-General William Rosecrans

(Library of Congress)

In late June, Rosecrans began to move, executing a series of crafty flanking maneuvers that compelled Bragg's army to abandon Tullahoma defenses, flee south over Cumberland Mountains, and cross the Tennessee River into Chattanooga. Six weeks passed, as Rosecrans reorganized and planned for next stage of the campaign south. Despite intense prodding from Washington to get moving, Rosecrans was deliberate, knowing he had to advance through rough country, needing to stockpile supplies, worrying that Bragg might be reinforced with troops coming from East or West. In mid-August, Rosecrans was underway, moving swiftly, succeeding in catching Confederates by surprise again. On August 21st, a battery of Federal guns began lobbing shells into Chattanooga, causing melee everywhere. Federals staged such clever show of force that Bragg thought the entire Federal army about to attack from north or northeast.

Confederate General Braxton Bragg

(Library of Congress)

Instead, Rosecrans marched a main force of 50,000 infantry and 9,000 cavalry toward crossings of the Tennessee River twenty miles west of Chattanooga. By September 4th, they crossed the river unseen, intent on making a sweeping left wheel from the southwest toward Chattanooga and Bragg's army.

It was a bold maneuver, and risky. The Great Valley of the Appalachians lay as a natural trough at the western foot of the Blue Ridge. Looming over the Great Valley on the northwest runs the eastern rim of the Cumberland Plateau. Rising at points one thousand feet above the Tennessee Valley, Cumberland Mountains pose a formidable barrier. Terrain between Tullahoma and the Tennessee River, just thirty miles by crow flight, is difficult for men on foot, wagons and artillery. It requires crossing rugged Cumberland Mountains …barren, devoid of forage, sparsely populated, and offering little drinking water. Endless desolate oak ridges, cedar thickets, and dark gorges are home to a handful of crude log cabins inhabited by simple mountain folk, farming small parcels with corn or wheat. Only rutted, narrow wagon trails zigzag through gaps in mountains, along rough stony steep precipices. Wagons with supplies traverse nearly impassable trails with straining mules. Any route through the mountains poses a nightmarish supply problem, and presents dangerous positions where enemy army can be hiding in ambush. An army can find itself fighting with its back to a towering escarpment, with questionable lines of retreat. It was daunting as soldiers gazed up at the lofty Cumberland range, warm rain falling and lightning dancing over mountain peaks. Across a sixty-mile front, long columns of blue uniforms began snaking up wet muddy mountain trails.

Caught unaware, Bragg realized a massive river crossing threatened his left flank. He vacillated, uncertain what to do. By September 7th and with supply lines in immediate danger, Bragg ordered his army south ...abandoning Chattanooga without resistance. Rosecrans telegraphed Washington triumphantly, *"Chattanooga is ours without a struggle."*

Chattanooga, Tennessee, c. 1863

(Library of Congress)

Confident now, Rosecrans ordered his army to pursue at full tilt Bragg's fleeing Confederates ...convinced Bragg was in complete panic and retreat. He was wrong. Bragg was reorganizing, twenty-five miles south of Chattanooga in Lafayette, Georgia. Hefty reinforcements were beginning to arrive from east Tennessee, Mississippi, and Virginia in the form of Lieutenant General James Longstreet's three-division corps dispatched from

Lee's Army of Northern Virginia. Bragg's plan is to turn back to face unsuspecting Federal columns …setting a trap, hoping to smash the enemy as they pour through gaps in mountains …"*like rats coming from their holes.*"

Will Hodkins and fellow enlisted soldiers were not privy to any of this. All Will knew was that on September 5th the 22nd Michigan regiment received orders to strike tents and head for northern Georgia or Alabama. The trip was one hundred thirty-five miles from Nashville, part of their journey via train on the 'Nashville & Chattanooga RR'. Will and regiment arrived in Bridgeport, Alabama, on Friday evening late and camped on Seven Mile Island. With trestles and track destroyed by marauding Rebel cavalry, their last two days were spent in arduous march through rugged Cumberland Mountains.

Their trek began by marching east to Shellmound and into Georgia, then through and over Sand Mountain, with its fifteen-mile wide plateau of barren oak ridge brushed with course weedy grass. They marched through a gap at Raccoon Mountain at Sand Mountain's northern extremity …to crossroads of Wauhatchie, where a crescent of high bluffs tower over the south bank of Tennessee River. Trail was so narrow and tortuous that two wagons could not pass, and no place existed for wagons to turnaround. Once past Sand and Raccoon Mountains, marching columns reached the western foot at the north end of Lookout Mountain …a majestic and beautiful escarpment towering fourteen hundred feet above valley …dizzying bluffs capped by magnificent fifty-foot sheer rock face.

Chattanooga lies on the south bank of the Tennessee River at the foot of Cumberland Mountains, near the southern boundary of Tennessee, near the place where Georgia, Alabama, and Tennessee join. Here, the river turns from southwest to west as it leaves the Great Valley, and breaks halfway through the Cumberlands in a scenic, winding gorge, before turning southwest again and flowing into Alabama. Just west of Chattanooga, the Tennessee River gorge separates Walden Ridge on the north from Lookout Mountain on the south. Southeast of Chattanooga, the long straight line of Missionary Ridge bisects the Great Valley, rising six hundred feet above the town. East of Missionary Ridge, Chickamauga Creek flows north to join the Tennessee River.

It is here that Will and friends seek rest and refuge in grassy ditch, with backs against Lookout Mountain's magnificent escarpment ...aside dusty mountain wagon trail ...overlooking the Great Valley of the Cumberland and Tennessee River with 'Moccasin Bend' snaking its way below. Will's eyes open, startled from dream-like semi-slumber, as officers ride up on horseback calling out to soldiers resting roadside. "Everyone up! Everyone up!" they call brusquely, cantering along, kicking up dust as they pass.

Will and fellow soldiers begin to move, prodding aching bodies for more marching. The 22nd Michigan regiment is part of Major-General Gordon Granger's Reserve Corps, in the First Division consisting of two Brigades under command of Brigadier-General James Steedman. Steedman pushes men relentlessly over rocky mountain terrain ...hooves, boots, and iron capped wheels of caissons and gun carriages churning roadbed into suffocating clouds of dust. Will looked over as Jeremiah whined, 'I'm ach-in', and it's so damn hot!"

Junior answered quickly, "It'll be even hotter if we catch up with them Rebs."

Papa added, "They be a skee-daddl-in', I reckon ...don't seem to want a good fight."

"Let's hope you're right, Papa," Will replied, as boys scrambled up ditch bank to fall into four loosely formed columns for continuation of unrelenting toil ...amid blazing heat and ankle-deep dust ...ironically, set against backdrop of profound natural beauty. Majesty of mountains awed Midwesterners. Papa exclaimed, "She be prettiest view I ever saw."

"That it is. That it is," Will answered as they trudged along making small talk. Will rubbed stinging sweat from eyes, "I hope to show it to Maria and our boys ...and baby Minnetta ...some day." The two men looked back to survey long slow moving columns of 'bluecoats', shining rifle barrels glistening in glaring hot sun ...white-topped army wagons dotting dusty roadway, serpentining behind and below ...river wending like silver thread reflecting warm sun's rays. They crossed Lookout Creek, where canteens were refilled, parched throats quenched, and water splashed childishly as each man savored brief moments of refreshing respite. But it was too brief ...officers chided men onward, warning, "Yesterday a wagon team slipped and tumbled down rocky slope, killing mules and scattering supplies." Now, teams are doubled on artillery limbers, at times taking twelve horses or mules to pull a single gun up slope. Sections of trail have to be widened, underbrush cleared, to get wagons through.

Will and boys stopped abruptly when the 22nd Michigan was called to halt ...several boys being called out and issued picks and shovels. Junior motioned, and Jeremiah, Lucius, and Jeptha, and a few others slung guns over shoulders, stalked up mountain trail twenty paces and stacked arms. Junior hollered at top of lungs, "Charge!" Others mimicked with wild cheers of "Charge!" With picks and shovels outthrust, they surged down mountainside to 'attack' trees, rock and debris blocking roadway ...bringing laughter to everyone watching, even officers. Will, Papa, and Nathan stood aside laughing ...shaking heads in mock disbelief. Trees were felled, boulders moved, and grade leveled ...even officers and staff shared contagious good spirit, dismounting to assist enlisted men push cannons and caissons over a ridge.

In hottest part of afternoon, Jeptha glanced over to see Jeremiah slowly slump to ground, fainting from heat exhaustion. Jeptha called for help, and Papa and Will rushed over to revive Jeremiah with water from Papa's canteen. With troops continuing their march past, the three helped Jeremiah to roadside and cooler shadow of tree's shade. Will stayed with Jeremiah, mopping neck with wet handkerchief, offering sips of water. Papa and Jeptha scrambled away to regain position within marching columns of comrades. After sufficient recovery time, Jeremiah and Will walked double-time back to forward position.

Relentlessly, men were driven ...now at a pace that outstripped progress of wagons, leaving caravan ever growing distance behind and hidden by dust cloud. Wagon roadway snaked around the foot of Lookout Mountain, weary marching columns of slumping staggering men following its course into night. Major-General Granger's orders were to get Reserve Corps into defensive position near Rossville, just into Georgia and directly six miles south of Chattanooga. As darkness of Sunday night fell, eerie glow of distant fence rail bonfires burned across panorama of mountainside. But around Will and boys, all was pitch black. Onward they trudged, stumbling along in darkness ...so exhausted. Jeremiah began to fall asleep marching, head bobbing down upon chest until Junior nudged him awake. Junior began singing *"John Brown's Body"*, and soon everyone joined in singing:

John Brown's body lies a-mouldering in the grave,
John Brown's body lies a-mouldering in the grave,
But his soul goes marching on.

Glory, glory, hallelujah,
Glory, glory, hallelujah,
His soul goes marching on.

He's gone to be a soldier in the Army of the Lord,
He's gone to be a soldier in the Army of the Lord,
His soul goes marching on.

Refrain drifted from mountainside mysteriously echoing into dark night. By early Monday morning, September 14th, after a march of more than forty miles, Will and friends stumbled into Rossville ...order given "stack arms", and all retired for much needed rest.

Chapter 21

Poised just south of Chattanooga are two great armies. Federal forces under Major-General William Rosecrans total 60,500 men, plus Granger's Reserve Corps of 5,400 men including Will Hodkins and friends in Rossville. Rosecrans' intelligence pegs Confederate forces under General Braxton Bragg at 28-30,000 men ...maybe more. Braxton Bragg's Army of Tennessee is all that stands between the Union Army and its 'entrance to the sea'. Bragg's plan is to cut Rosecrans off from Chattanooga as 'Yanks' come through the mountains. East of Lookout Mountain runs a north-south narrow spur called Pigeon Mountain, and tucked between Pigeon Mountain and Lookout Mountain is a fertile valley known as McLemore's Cove. The cove is just six miles wide where it spawns Chickamauga Creek ...a sometimes sluggish, sometimes rushing stream that flows north and empties into the Tennessee River. Bragg needs to cross Chickamauga Creek rapidly to close two roads between the creek and Missionary Ridge, both escape routes for Rosecrans back into Chattanooga.

Roadway nearest Chickamauga Creek to the east is known locally as La Fayette Road, which crosses the creek and runs north eight miles to Rossville Gap. Here it turns west through the gap and past the town of Rossville, before continuing another four miles into Chattanooga. A second escape road further west is Dry Valley Road ...more a crude trail than true wagon road. Dry Valley Road bumps up against Missionary Ridge, following the ridge two miles before passing through McFarland's Gap, then running north to Rossville where it joins La Fayette Road heading into Chattanooga.

Waters of Chickamauga Creek are neither clear or swift or especially deep, rising to no more than ten-foot depth during heavy rainstorm. Yet, Chickamauga Creek is formidable barrier to crossings …its banks steep and rocky at points, or low and swampy. Translated from Cherokee, Chickamauga Creek means 'River of Blood' …an ominous name.

Will Hodkins and soldiers of the 22nd Michigan are in bivouac as part of three infantry brigades and two cavalry divisions of Granger's Reserve Corps, posted to guard approaches to Chattanooga through Missionary Ridge. They are camped in open field in vicinity of Rossville Gap just off Ringgold Road, one-half mile east of where it joins La Fayette Road. A small white clapboard structure known as McAfee's Church stands nearby aside roadway.

In their rapid two-day march east around rugged Lookout Mountain, Brigadier-General Steedman pushed Will and infantry soldiers of his First Division relentlessly, far outrunning supply wagons. So men are in camp without rations or prospect of any arriving soon. Granger issues strict orders against foraging …unreasonable orders under their circumstances, so Granger's officers quietly ignore them. "Get to the woods, and keep out of sight," Colonel Daniel McCook tells men from his Second Division, as he watches them move off in search of needed food. Other officers likewise turn blind eye to foraging.

Papa and Will talk with the boys before deciding that Junior, Lucius, and Jeptha should go scouting for food. Jeremiah needs rest to recover from heat exhaustion of just hours earlier. Papa, Will, and Nathan will stay behind to set up camp. "Watch out for Reb pickets …they must be somewhere close," Will called to the three as they moved cautiously through cornfield toward forest. "God speed."

Terrain within the valley is mostly untouched from when Cherokee Indians hunted the land and called it home. White settlers made few improvements, carving crude homesteads from cedar glade and pin oak and blackjack oak forests, living off land best they could. One or two-bedroom log cabins sit scattered …remnants of tree stumps checker simple farmland. Haphazard and poorly cleared fields show corn planted carelessly, with cattle

211

and hogs roaming loose …fending for themselves, wandering into nearby forest. Crude split rail fences mark haphazard boundaries. La Fayette Road separates rolling farmland nestled west against the base of Missionary Ridge from low-lying heavily forested land to the south and nearer Chickamauga Creek. Where cattle graze and hogs root in timberland east of La Fayette Road, visibility can exceed one hundred yards …in other areas of briar-laced underbrush and thicket, visibility is nonexistent.

After one-half hour trudging through dense forest and thicket with nothing found, Lucius hears a voice call. "Quiet!" he called to Junior and Jeptha walking just ahead. "What's that?" As the three turned to look backward over left shoulders, a figure lurking behind a tree stepped abruptly into view …each boy's hair stands on end.

Startled and frightened, they eyed a stranger …an old mountain man with long flowing white beard, shoulder length locks of snow-white hair under floppy wide-brim brown felt hat, crudely-fashioned walking stick in hand. He beckoned to them in soft friendly voice, "It's alright …no harm by me …follow me."

Junior answered, alarm and caution in voice, "We're hungry and look-in' for food."

"I reckon …follow me," the old man urged, turning and walking away. Three boys eyed each other with questioning looks, then shrugged acquiescence and followed. They stumbled to keep up with a spry old codger, trundling through thick undergrowth snarling their path under dense canopy of cedar and oak. A short distance ahead, the old man emerged into a tiny clearing. He walked toward a small chinked log cabin, gray smoke curling lazily skyward from river rock chimney. A portly woman dressed in long gray muslin dress with stained apron, came through its front screen door. Two young boys trailed, tugging at her skirt with fear on faces as they peered at three blue-uniformed soldiers following their father.

Junior, Jeptha, and Lucius were invited into the cabin by the woman with warm welcome. "Come-on-in …ya' boys look to be a-starv-in' …don't be a-fear-in' now …my name is Gertie."

"I'm Franklin," the old man said. "Them be our boys …Jed and Josh."

Three soldiers were seated at a rough hewn wood table which centered one-room cabin. Gertie went to the springhouse, returning with water, butter, and fresh milk. Gertie placed newly baked biscuits and honey on the table ...all delicacies not tasted in some time by trail worn soldiers. The three wasted no time in devouring the scrumptious offerings ...mouths stuffed quickly with food, rather indelicately. Young Jed and Josh watched in amazement at the three gulping food ...then scurried outside at their parent's urging. Franklin and Gertie pulled chairs to the table ...Franklin resting walking stick carefully atop the table before removing his hat and seating himself. A tin cup or two of homemade applejack brandy followed ...boys thoroughly enjoying warm hospitality as they talked with their hosts. "I sure fancy that walk-in' stick ya' have there," Junior mentioned, pointing to the knotted and knurled, hewn and honed wood cane, obviously fashioned by Franklin's knife.

"She's ma' friend, alright ...keep's her rubbed and polished," Franklin answered, patting it with pride. "She be with me always ...when I goes out yonder ...wouldn't go without her, no Sir."

"She's a beauty," Junior added.

With that, Franklin and Gertie related their situation. "We be poor mountain folk ...suffer-in' at da' hands of da' Rebs," Franklin said. Men are forced to hide for months in woods or caves nearby to evade Confederate conscription officers bent on adding them to ranks of Rebel army. Unsuccessful evasion carries a stiff price ...sometimes grizzly execution as families watch helpless. Despite hardship and poverty, Gertie and Franklin look upon the three Union soldiers as liberators, openly bestowing generosity.

"Sir, have you seen any Rebs?" Jeptha asked.

"Word has it dey' be jest' down da' way apiece," Franklin answered. "...big group, I hear."

"We're a-chas-in' em' ...sure enough," Junior added. Conversation continued for thirty minutes or so ...pleasant experience for all. They left Gertie and Franklin with warm hugs of affection and best wishes for family. "Many thanks ...for be-in' so generous," Junior said. Waving 'goodbye' with broad smiles, they departed with gifts of food for friends back at camp.

With spring to their step and good feelings bubbling through conversation, congratulating each other on good fortune, they strode back to camp. The unsuspecting threesome sauntered into camp carefree, passing the tent of Major-General Gordon Granger ...the General leaning back balanced on two legs of campstool in front of tent, hat pulled down shielding eyes, half-drowsing in afternoon's heat.

Union Major-General Gordon Granger

(Library of Congress)

Granger is a forty year-old career Regular Army officer, grizzled veteran tested in battle and graduate of West Point ...but his own worst enemy. He talks little, commands gruff and brisk ...hardcore military attitude and strict disciplinarian, enforcing everything 'by the book'. He is quick to criticize, language course, opinion voiced without regard to impact on either fellow officers or enlisted men. Fellow officers cotton to him no more than enlisted men.

Sensing movement, aroused from semi-slumber, he rocked forward on his stool, pushing hat up from eyes. Granger caught sight of Junior, Lucius, and Jeptha …privates loaded down with fresh food. He corners them …discovering sweet potatoes in a burlap bag, other fresh vegetables, crock of honey, loaf of bread, and freshly butchered chicken. Irate, he berates them for disobeying his order against foraging. The boys stammer, trying unsuccessfully and in panic, to explain to their Major-General that items are gifts …not stolen. Granger accepts none of it, commotion drawing staff and other officers, all embarrassed by Granger's temper tantrum. After confrontation, the officers convince a reluctant Granger to listen and be sympathetic …no harm done. Besides, Junior relayed Franklin's report of enemy nearby …information giving Granger reason to relent. The Major-General sulked and walked away.

Sheepishly, three boys made it back to Will, Papa, Nathan, and Jeremiah, trying not to feel sullied by their ugly confrontation. Instead, they eagerly related their story of the friendly mountain family who so generously shared what little they had. Meanwhile Papa and Will worked to prepare a most welcome meal, as Nathan and Jeremiah saw to a campfire.

Tuesday and Wednesday passed with men recuperating and resting in camp …ordered to "lie upon your arms" ready for instant action …each man now issued three days rations and sixty rounds of ammunition. The 22nd Michigan regiment was down to around five hundred enlisted men and officers fit for duty …only half of nearly one thousand men who rendezvoused to serve the Union cause just over a year ago in Pontiac. They melded together as a 'band of brothers' …forged like blacksmith's steel from hot fire of adversity …long marches, endless drilling, miseries and diversions of camp life, and loss of comrades through sickness and death.

They were not alone. Other regiments of infantry and cavalry and artillery totaling about 5,400 men shared a matted cornfield aside McAfee's Church. White canvas shelter tents dotted trampled cornstalk field making an awesome sight. Papa and Will shared a pup tent, buttoning halves together to create the tent, muskets serving as ridge poles …sleeping at close quarters with only rubber ground cloths between them and stubble of

215

cornfield. Jeremiah and Junior, Jeptha and Lucius paired together. Nathan enjoyed a tent to himself. "Keep your canteens full," Will advised. "We're going to need 'em ready."

Junior added, "Rebs are nearby …whole slew of 'em …Franklin said."

"Figure we'll meet 'em soon …if they don't high-tail it," Papa offered.

Waiting was difficult and tension filled the air. All sensed momentous conflict about to take place. Nights were most difficult. Wednesday came and went. Sun sank slowly …little by little …beyond peaks of Missionary Ridge. Will sat mesmerized by a quarter moon's movement breaking through distant tree branches now and again, clouds drifting to blur its image …stomach churning …palms of hands clammy with perspiration. By campfire's flickering light, Will studied faces of men around him. A few veterans were calm, puffing on cigars or pipes, cleaning weapons or even dozing …content to let destiny take over. A majority of the '22nd' were green recruits with little battle experience …many spooked and fearful. Night's chill from cold mountain air sent shivers through taut nerves. Night sounds added to tension and jumpiness …rustling tree branches and bushes, cicada's call or owl's shriek, braying of mules, cursing or coughing men. Jeremiah turned to Will and Papa, all sitting together gazing blankly at dying orange embers of campfire. "I have great fear of 'showing the white feather' when fight-in' starts," he lamented sheepishly.

Papa answered, "…'white feather' means a 'coward' …you're certainly not a coward."

Will boosted Jeremiah's spirits, saying, "You love your country …you're a brave man …you'll do just fine, and make your family proud."

"…throat and mouth are dry as desert …can't catch my breath," Jeremiah said.

Papa tugged at suspenders, pushing spectacles up bridge of red nose, pulling pipe from mouth …clearing throat, he said slowly and carefully, "Whatever's meant to happen, will happen …I reckon." He paused. "For me …I believe by God, no bullet is meant for me." Papa was not being totally honest with Jeremiah or

Will. "…just in case, I've scribbled my name on a small scrap of paper, and pinned it inside my shirt …want'em to know who they got."

Will and Jeremiah smiled at Papa's awkward stab at humor. It seemed to relax everyone. Papa was pleased …he stood and crumpled a last letter received from home, having just reread it one last time …he reached into campfire and lit the paper as a torch to relight his pipe. He and Jeremiah turned and walked away, leaving Will alone. Will gathered himself, rubbed sweaty palms together, and pulled trusty journal from breast pocket. He removed Maria's ambrotype from between journal pages, and studied her countenance longingly. Nub of pencil in hand, he began to write:

September 16ᵗʰ, 1863
Wednesday, outside Chattanooga

My dearest Maria:

I am obliged to write with pencil, and trust this legible. We are on picket …and waiting. I fear a terrible clash about to erupt. Johnny Rebs are very near, and seem to be in great numbers. Three days prior we passed over and around Lookout Mountain, a most beautiful sight, which I hope to show you one day. You will be pleased to know I am camped close to God's presence …at the foot of 'Missionary' Ridge aside

McAfee's Church ...viewing signal lights swinging in mountain tops.

Have lost some weight and had occurrence of toothache on our march, otherwise I am well. Left leg is doing well, though it twitches at night after marching. With six days growth of beard, caked with dust and sorely in need of bath, you would not know me. I look at your ambrotype often ...and longingly.

I trust approaching battle may serve to end this abominable War. If ever I get out of this War, I'll bet I not get in another. May I meet my duty with honor. Give regards to Nettie and Ezra, and anyone who inquires of me. Kiss and hug our children.

May God bless,

Will

Next morning Will placed letter and single black-eyed susan flower in envelope and posted it for six-mile trip by horseback into Chattanooga. Then, everything began to change quickly ...even the weather.

Chapter 22

Cold north wind began to blow Friday evening and temperature plummeted to near freezing. Will and boys scrambled for wool blankets, shivering from cold, uniforms still damp from perspiring in unusually warm 90° heat over their last two weeks ...weather change an ill omen. Two huge armies faced each other within rifle shot, along a four-mile stretch running north-south, separated only by Chickamauga Creek ...Federals with backs against Missionary Ridge. Light skirmishing occurred over the last several days, as Rosecrans and Bragg jockeyed for position and Bragg waited for reinforcements. By nightfall, Bragg managed to move only 9,000 men across the Chickamauga, but the bulk of his army crossed the creek at various fording points during the night.

Saturday, September 19th, dawned cold, bright and clear. Fighting broke out almost by accident. A brigade of Federal infantry, ordered to make reconnaissance of reported Rebel crossings of the creek, encountered some of Nathan Bedford Forrest's cavalry and opened fire. A fierce melee erupted ...soon the battle exploded. Other brigades were called, and confrontations mushroomed with furious fighting in heavy woods west of the Chickamauga. Seesaw battle grew ever more intense through morning with neither side able to gain advantage. More divisions entered the fray, as battle became a gigantic vicious brawl. Through afternoon, two armies surged back and forth. On the ground, ghastly mangled dead and horribly wounded soldiers lay strewn along banks of the Chickamauga ...a creek living up to its Cherokee name, its water running 'red with blood'.

Will Hodkins and boys of the 22nd Michigan infantry, along with Granger's other reserve forces, could do nothing but wait. Will watched and listened with trepidation, huddled with friends behind lines some three miles away. Clouds of increasingly heavy smoke rose skyward above treetops, first from intense musket and artillery fire ...then woods catching fire from exploding shells. Sound of battle echoed ominously off mountainside. Sheer horror painted faces of Will and boys ...as if their world were ending. Regiment's chaplain rode up to Will and friends huddled quietly in abject fear. "Boys, it is but little I can do for you in hour of battle, but there is one thing I can do ...I will pray for you." Will and others uncovered heads and bowed in reverence, arms clasped tightly on rifles, bayonets glistening in afternoon sun. The chaplain raised himself in the saddle, waving hat back and forth, "God bless you ...God bless you, boys ...Amen!" Will and others murmured in unison.

Junior looked toward Will, "In ma' stomach ...butterflies are a danc-in' like a warm spring day."

Overhearing, Papa replied, "Ya' got that right, pard-ner."

Late afternoon, Brigadier-General Steedman ordered Colonel Le Favour to report with the '22nd' and 89th Ohio to Brigadier-General Whitaker, who was under attack near McAfee Church. Colonel Le Favour positioned the '22nd' on roadway left, with the '89th' to the right and 18th Ohio Battery at the rear. Will and Papa crouched together nervously, watching as Rebel sharpshooters emerged from thicket of woods below roadway, several hundred yards away. They moved through open field to a nearby log house. From open chinks of old log, Reb sharpshooters opened fire when they spotted Will's comrades on roadway above. They went scurrying back to cover of woods and thick underbrush when the 18th Ohio Battery crashed several shells at the log cabin, sending fragments of wood flying. Following that limited action, Le Favour directed Will and others back to camp for evening.

By nightfall, main armies were deadlocked despite hellish slaughter and desperate frenzy, fighting nightmarish struggle only several miles away ...heavy casualties suffered by both sides on this first day of battle. Confederate losses totaled 6,000-9,000 men, while Union losses were about 7,000 men. Fighting front stabilized along country track known as Brotherton Road, through woods to Brock's field and thicker woods that opened onto La Fayette Road. Federal lines backed the vital La Fayette Road, Rosecrans' main connection to Rossville and escape beyond to Chattanooga.

Nighttime temperature in northwest Georgia hill country plunged again toward freezing, cold north wind whistling shrill through woods. Dense fog arose from creek bottomland, mixing devilishly with overhanging clouds of smoke from gunfire and burning forestland and field grass. With armies close together in darkness, no campfires were allowed, night being lit only by thin moonbeams knifing through small gaps in haze and cloud cover. Only sounds were occasional faint moans and wails of wounded, gloomy symphony echoing mercilessly against distant valley walls ...constant clatter of axes reverberating through dense cedar glade and oak forest, soldiers working feverishly through night constructing crude protective breastworks from fence rails, rocks and fallen trees. Eerie, macabre feelings filled the mind as Will retired desperate ...body chilled to bone ...both from nature's cold and gravity of fear unshakeable.

On Sabbath Day, September 20th, Will awoke with little sleep mustered. Papa awoke also and rubbed smoky dry eyes, "...ma' teeth are a-chatter-in', Will."

"Mine too," Will replied. "I am freezing." Will pulled back tent flap, gazing out, "Papa, look at this." Frost blanketed ground white, dense fog lingering low in distant forest bottomland ...still smoldering brush fires causing smoke to hang in suspended stillness ...sight beautiful though ill-boding. Fifty-four hundred soldiers of Reserve Corps awoke to calm quiet Sunday morning at McAfee Church, answered roll call and prepared breakfast. Junior, Jeremiah, and Lucius started campfire, while Jeptha and Nathan went off to fill canteens. Will and Papa prepared breakfast of fried bacon with fried hardtack rations ...and of course, boiled coffee. Breakfast commenced unusually quiet and solemn ...everyone mentally preparing for their day.

After breakfast, boys cleaned weapons and each received an additional eighty rounds of ammunition. At 9:30 AM, all hell broke loose ...fighting erupted three miles away with deafening violence same as day before. Two brigades of First Division under Brigadier-General James Steedman fell into ranks around the church and waited. Second Division's brigade under Colonel Daniel McCook would remain behind to guard Major-General Granger's headquarters and the important escape route through Rossville Gap. No orders came, and men rested in ranks, lounging in crumpled cornstalk meadow. "This is hardest ...waiting," Will said to Papa. "I just pray I will not blink when we 'see the elephant' this day." Will hesitated before going further, "I did some powerful thinking last night, Papa ...came to me all of a sudden ...crystal clear it was." Will gathered himself, took deep breath, continuing choked with emotion, "It is not about me or my life ...instead, it's about my family, and God's plan for me ...whatever is meant to happen will ...I just need to reach for God's guidance, and do my duty."

"Powerful good think-in', Will," Papa answered nodding. "...you're a good man, and I be pleased to call ya' ma' friend."

"You know, Papa ...I think of all you boys as my 'family' ...we've become more than friends."

"...couldn't agree more, my son," Papa exclaimed, pushing spectacles back, tobacco stained teeth clenching hard on pipe, turning away to walk toward Lucius and Jeptha mere steps away ...two youngest boys huddled together, anxious and frightened. Papa moved toward them to settle nerves. Will glanced to Nathan on his right, off by himself reading from the Bible, trying to gather courage. To the left, Jeremiah and Junior were elbow to elbow, talking quietly. Jeremiah was writing a letter as he talked ...Will speculated, "*probably to blacksmith father, mother, and two younger sisters at home in Pontiac.*" Junior, habitual card player, tossed a cherished deck of cards high into the air, watching them float haphazardly scattering onto ground. Will thought, "*...he must fear the worst ...not want evidence of misspent time sent back home to mother and father on the farm in Oxford.*"

Will stared entranced into campfire's dying embers, lost in thought ...about Maria and early days of romance and courtship in the beautiful 'Finger Lakes' region of Penn Yan ...and about his boys, Will, Jr. and Walter, and now baby Minnetta whom he never laid eyes upon "*...if only I can make it back home!*" Thought drifted. Then Will glanced upward, stood and walked shoulders slumped toward nearby McAfee Church. He plucked a white and lavender wildflower growing amid a clump against church wall …hopefully, to go with next letter to Maria. Just in case, he pulled trusty journal from breast pocket and penciled a note before placing the flower between pages.

Please give this flower to Maria …my last thought is of her.

Morning wore on. Will stared southwest, gazing trance-like toward huge clouds of white powdery smoke continuously drifting skyward, accompanying intense thunder of musket and canon. Amid ferocious clatter of gunfire, Will glanced over as Granger fretted and paced outside his tent, nervously pulling at bushy dark beard …in full view of the men. He spoke frequently with staff, unable to reconcile whether to jump into the fray or stay put to cover the Rossville escape route. Will and other soldiers watched as Granger sent three staff officers riding in different directions in hope of intercepting messengers who might be bringing orders from Rosecrans or Major-General George Thomas. By 11:30 AM, all three staff officers returned empty handed.

Granger and Steedman conferred before sulking away to respective tents located about three hundred yards apart. Not long after, Granger emerged from tent, visible concern and worry etched on face. He climbed atop a haystack to gain visibility, frustrated and with field glasses shaking in hand, trying to make sense of dust clouds rising on horizon and sweeping sound of battle deafening. Will overheard one officer's offhand remark, "Thomas is having a hell of a fight over there."

That was enough …Granger stopped nervous pacing, "I can't stand this any longer. We are needed over there, and if we don't hurry it will be too late. Bragg is piling his whole army on Thomas. I am going to his assistance."

Steedman agreed. He ordered men to their feet, ready to march within minutes. Will and boys jumped to the ready

...adrenaline surging through Will's body ...knowing time near. By noon, their march began ...Granger and staff rode to the head of columns arrayed four men abreast. Brigadier-General Walter Whitaker's brigade took the lead, including Will and the 22nd Michigan.

They were heading into a fray with Confederate Lieutenant-General James Longstreet, dispatched by General Lee in Virginia to assist Bragg's Army of Tennessee ...arriving late the night before after a circuitous nearly eight hundred mile rail journey. Longstreet launched an all-out thrust of 16,000 men. A gap in Union lines resulted as Rosecrans shifted units, and Confederates came streaming through, resulting in collapse of the Federal right flank. As Federal troops began streaming to the rear, Thomas formed a defensive line on Snodgrass Hill.

Here, one-half mile of interconnected craggy peaks form an easternmost fragmented spur of Missionary Ridge. George Snodgrass and family moved from Virginia fifteen years earlier to farm this most unpromising tract of land. Snodgrass raised a log cabin one-half mile west of La Fayette Road, on northern slope of wooded knoll, now known by locals as 'Snodgrass Hill'. A simple cabin, only 18' by 20' in size, is home to the sixty-year-old farmer, wife, and seven of nine children, youngest being four years old.

Snodgrass Hill and Snodgrass Farm

(Library of Congress)

A heavily timbered range of peaks rise from lower grounds of Snodgrass fields, and angle west to form four major heights separated by ravines. To the west some three hundred yards, and fifty feet higher at its summit than the cabin, 'Horseshoe Ridge' terminates at its western extreme in a sharp drop to Dry Valley Road.

By 1:00 PM, Major-General George Thomas arrives to assume command of deployed Union defensive lines of Harker and Brannan, and establish headquarters at a crest of ridge just north of the Snodgrass cabin. Later in the afternoon, Rosecrans and the other two corps commanders depart in haste for Chattanooga, leaving Thomas the ranking officer on the field.

Will and boys trudged off at 'double-quick' with the contingent of Granger's and Steedman's Reserves to come to Thomas's assistance. Day grew warm, sun now beating down unmercifully upon marching men. Moving with closed ranks, over narrow road covered ankle-deep with dust, nearly 5,000 marching men of two brigades and officers on horseback kick up huge clouds of dust sweeping along like desert sandstorm. "I am suffocate-in' and I can't see a damned thing," Junior complained to Will at his elbow.

"Stop complain-in' now ...shut yer' filthy mouth, or ya'll git' yur-self a mouthful," Papa advised.

Two miles into their march, Rebel skirmishers and artillery opened fire on Granger's men, from a position in woods three-quarter mile off roadway to the left. Granger halted briefly to 'feel' the situation, green soldiers instinctively ducking and throwing themselves to ground at the spitting of cannon fire. "Not very friendly of those boys," Will offered from prone position.

Granger uttered a string of curses but would not be distracted. "To your feet men ...Forward ...Forward, men!" he urged at top of lungs. Men responded and moved onward, at even quicker pace as skirmishers held off outnumbered but pesky Rebels. Drawing closer to the northern fringe of fighting, signs were less than encouraging to Will and boys as they gazed first-time at scene of battle. Discarded cartridge boxes, muskets, knapsacks and other equipment lay strewn and littering roadway. Stragglers and wounded limped past ...making their way to the rear …greeting Granger's men with lurid expression of terror witnessed. After an hour and nearly four miles marching, vista opened of McDonald cornfield spreading three-quarter mile running north-south. Gray haze lay across landscape from burning fire of fences, woods, haystacks and houses. "…whole dang' country is on fire!" Junior gasped.

Clouds of powder smoke hung over cornfield, masking all visibility. Sulfurous odor of burned powder comingled with a stench of death …cornfield strewn with grotesquely contorted bodies. Will peered over shoulder to ashen faces of Jeptha, Lucius, and Jeremiah …Jeremiah sobbing uncontrollably. Just then, Jeptha bolted from ranks and doubled over to the ground, wrenching and gagging with dry heaves. Will could do nothing but trudge onward …lost in his own struggle, an old saying flashing to mind …*a hero dies once, a coward a hundred times*. Spitting last remnants of sickness, Jeptha regained control and came jogging back to resume position within marching columns. Will glanced down row …beyond Papa and Junior to Nathan on the far side. Nathan was mumbling, head bowed …*probably reciting the 23rd Psalm*. Will's chest heaved, desperately gulping air, chest pounding …fear overwhelming. They were now in range of Confederates on the northern end of Polk's wing. Will and boys began to take additional incoming fire.

"Double quick!" came the command, as Will tugged cap brim down tighter over forehead, crouched and leaned forward, breaking into a trot across grisly field …remnants of cornstalk stained with blood. They moved in unison, offering bizarre image of men steeling themselves, leaning into fury, as if against raging wind and rainstorm. Will touched inside of breast pocket, reassured precious journal safe …thought flashed briefly to Maria. Feeling crushed …feeling impending loss …tears welled in eyes. Regaining composure and concentration, he brushed tears aside, picking up pace amid renewed volley of enemy fire.

In the distance Union Major-General George Thomas raised field glasses to survey a large column of troops approaching at double-quick, dust cloud masking whether friend or foe. Thomas was on horseback, peering northward from headquarters now stationed on a northern slope of Snodgrass Hill.

Union Major-General George Thomas

(Library of Congress)

Thomas was easy to spot in saddle, a large man of six foot height weighing over two hundred pounds. He sat rigidly upright and rode slowly because an old injury caused great pain on horseback. Troops lovingly dubbed him 'Old Slow Trot' for his riding pace, or simply 'Old Pap Thomas'.

Thomas fidgeted with brown, gray-streaked beard, fingers stroking beard nervously. Horse became skittish, so Thomas could not hold field glasses steady to see through clouds of dust and shimmer of sunlight on metal ...though he thought he could make out the 'Stars and Stripes' flag. Thomas sent staff officer Lieutenant Ambrose Bierce galloping off down slope and across cornfield to confirm. A few minutes later he came back furiously spurring horse to speed good news ...it was Granger and Reserve Corps. Relief marked faces among officers, while Thomas remained taciturn, mumbling something unheard.

It was about 1:30 PM. By this time, numerous astonished and terrified Federals were fleeing in panic as Confederates raced through a gap in exposed right flank of the Union Army. Most of McCook's corps and Crittenden's were in headlong flight, making hasty retreat to the nearest escape route through Missionary Ridge, either McFarland's Gap or the Rossville Gap ...foot soldiers

227

unscathed and walking wounded, wagons, guns, and officers on horseback ...all fleeing hellish inferno. With roughly half of the Union Army in full retreat, Thomas organized a last ditch defensive line to cover the backside of Rosecrans' fleeing army and prevent total rout.

Here on Snodgrass Hill and Horseshoe Ridge, on a desolate series of little-known spurs aptly-named Missionary Ridge, with the 'River of Blood' called Chickamauga Creek nearby to the west, stood Major-General George Thomas, calm and massive as a bear ...'standing like a rock' while urging his men to hold on a while longer. At this critical moment, with Federals nearly out of ammunition, Granger's troops arrived to report to Thomas ...5,000 men of two brigades ...most importantly, 95,000 rounds of ammunition desperately needed.

Chapter 23

Will stood awestruck by an imposing figure of Major-General Thomas sitting on horseback, back rigid and shoulders squared, emphasizing full stature of large frame. He projected an aura of command and confidence, horse prancing with energy not twenty paces from Will. Granger and Steedman sauntered horses to Thomas and saluted. Thomas returned a salute. Three officers traded firm handshakes before beginning to confer. Will Hodkins and other foot soldiers collapsed to ground nearby, amid cover of log and rail breastworks, totally exhausted from their rapid march. Will gasped out of breath, unable to control breathing, sweating profusely, dusty and overheated. He wiped perspiration from brow and lifted canteen to lips, savoring the water ...welcome relief to parched lips and dry throat, though lukewarm. Left leg was aching ...too much exertion for a recent injury. He rubbed the leg for more circulation. Glancing sideways, he saw Papa panting and gasping, chubby cheeks and jowls nearly crimson. "...you alright, Papa?" Will inquired, worried look mirroring concern.

"This ol' body sure's not lik-in' this fast walk-in', son," Papa answered, coughing to clear dusty throat and regain breath.

"We're like so many dawgs' ...lapp-in' our tongues and pant-in' for air ...tired from the chase," Junior quipped.

"Papa, take some water ...not too fast, now," Will said, passing canteen to Papa.

Will turned back to watch animated discussion underway among the generals. Thomas was gesturing firmly as he talked, pointing southwest up the steep fifty-foot rise to a crest of main ridge that comprised the 'horseshoe' of three hills. Will strained to hear as Thomas spoke loudly allowing as many as possible to hear. "Those men must be driven back," he exclaimed, pointing again emphatically to the distant ridge. "Can you do it?" he questioned Granger.

Granger replied, pointing toward his troops, "Yes, my men are fresh, and they are just the fellows for that work." With that, Steedman wheeled his horse toward the men, shouting orders as he raised great girth to stand in saddle while waving hat. "We must save the Union Army, boys!"

"Here! Here!" men answered spontaneously in unison, thrusting arms and rifles skyward. Despite rest too short, Will and others scrambled to their feet, stiff muscles reacting slowly to Steedman's order ...again moving off on the double-quick ...each man digging deep to muster energy. They deployed on the run, half a mile or so, moving north and then west to gain access to the ridge. Direct access from the west was up a steep hill thickly treed and dense with thicket and briar. Slowed here and there by fallen trees, uniformity of marching columns disappeared ...everyone scrambling ...across a series of ravines, then back into the double-quick. Will and men of the 22nd Michigan were in the lead, with Colonel Le Favour and Lieutenant-Colonel Sanborn spurring them onward, quite literally 'into jaws of death'.

Steedman's two brigades were split, with Colonel Le Favour and two infantry regiments drawing the daunting task of relieving a thin line of bluecoats guarding the Union upper right flank, farthest west on the ridge. They were assigned to Brigadier-General John Brannan, whose 21st Ohio regiment was fighting valiantly on the far right ...taking a licking from onslaught after onslaught of Rebel rushes. The 89th Ohio and 22nd Michigan regiments ascended long ridge from its northernmost slope, with forty rounds in cartridge box and the balance in pockets of each man ...bayonets fixed. Will stole a look anxiously to Papa straining to keep up, "Good luck ...and God bless, Papa," Will gasped out of breath and panting.

"And, you ...you the same, ma' friend," Papa replied solemnly, winded and stammering, gulping for breath.

Image of Maria darted through Will's mind ...*no time for that now.* Will heard first pattering of gunshot ...'pitter-patter'

...like first drops of refreshing spring rain. Ragged tearing report from skirmisher's volley followed ...then awful deafening roar of deadly musketry. This changed everything for Will ...instantly 'fear' disappeared ...calm resolution and concentration took over. Will relaxed ...thinking becoming sharp and lucid ...reactions quick. It was peaceful calm ...'destiny' replaced fear. "*...whatever will be will be,*" he thought. It was about 2:30 PM, mid-afternoon.

Will could see uniformed men fighting at close range, some hand-to-hand ...but only Confederates atop the ridge. Colonel Le Favour urged men onward, waving hat and shouting like a madman.

Union Colonel Le Favour, 22nd Michigan Infantry

(Library of Congress)

Will and the '22nd' under Sanborn led the way, with the 89th Ohio closely behind, as they climbed yet another ravine onto Hill #3. Over its crest bluecoats surged, raising piercing yells to the heavens, scurrying through and around stunned and exhausted soldiers of the 21st Ohio, straight into Anderson's astonished Mississippi Rebels of Hindman's Division. Confederates reeled and skedaddled downhill, Will and others following in headlong spontaneous pursuit, despite Sanborn yelling himself hoarse. "Stop! Stop, boys! Pull back! Pull back! Boys, pull back!" he screamed.

William Sanborn galloped forward throwing himself into harm's way, shouting and gesturing wildly to save his men …finally succeeding in getting them to halt in a hollow at foot of hill. Will's pulse surged from frenzy, heart thumping wildly from adrenaline rush, managing blindly to fire a shot at scurrying Rebels. He stooped and hunched to reload …stomach wrenched and sickened, watching Sanborn fall from saddle upon a bullet's strike. Then blistering grape and canister fire raked Michiganders from a battery on ridge to their right.

Amid melee and confusion, Will managed a second shot but could not tell if it found its mark …then momentary lull in firing. "*I am still breathing,*" he thought. He looked around to see a hundred comrades down, either dead or writhing wounded. "*…just a few minutes fighting.*" He lost track of friends. It was pandemonium …every man for himself …guerilla warfare …one army 'bushwhacking' the other …farm boy against farm boy.

Unimaginable Sacrifice and Suffering

(Library of Congress)

Within moments, Kershaw launched Confederate counterattack against Hills #2 and #3 to cover Anderson's retreat.

Kershaw's 2nd South Carolina struck the '22nd', giving ferocious Rebel yells as they advanced. Colonel Le Favour remained on horseback atop the ridge with the 89th Ohio, watching helplessly as slaughter of his regiment unfolded below hill's crest. Captain A.M. Keeler, who replaced wounded William Sanborn in command, ordered the '22nd' back up the hill. Will backpedaled, crouching, stumbling over bullet-riddled bodies ...men crying out in anguish ...as he made it back safely to the crest. He breathed sigh of relief spotting Papa moving rearward.

At top of ridge, Colonel Le Favour galloped up and down haphazard lines of bedraggled men, rallying Michiganders best he could. Pursuing Confederate 2nd South Carolina regiment nearly reached the crest of Hill #3, but fell back to a hollow unsupported and under fire from the 89th Ohio. Le Favour ordered the decimated '22nd' to move back from the crest and turn fighting over to the 89th Ohio and 21st Ohio. Will and Papa joined other men scrambling to ground for cover ...moving away from the deadly crest, seeking momentary relief more out of harm's way ...trying to catch breath, trying to calm frazzled nerves ...knowing Rebels would keep coming. Junior, Jeremiah, and Nathan found their way by crawling on all fours to Will and Papa. "Anyone see Lucius and Jeptha?" Will pleaded. All three could only shrug, looking back and forth apprehensively ...questioning looks ...panting and breathless, unable to speak.

"We got separated," Jeremiah finally offered. "You haven't seen them?" The unthinkable crossed minds at the same moment. In unison, heads bowed. No one said a word. Will's hands covered face, grief shaken ...dreadful images ...two youngest boys missing on that bloody hillside. "Maybe they are with another group ...got lost from us?" Will ventured. "If wounded, hope they made it to the rear for help." No one knew. A brief twenty minutes of deadly horror decimated their '22nd' regiment ...one hundred to two hundred men killed, wounded or missing ...no choice but to regroup.

It was mid-afternoon, about 3:00 PM. Reckless seesaw fighting became a pattern as afternoon wore on along Horseshoe Ridge ...raging back and forth at close quarters ...back Rebels came, again and again, attack and counterattack. Confederates of

Kershaw's brigade joined divisions of Hindman, Bushrod Johnson, and finally Preston's reserve division …all hurled into the fight on Horseshoe Ridge. Making matters worse, Bushrod Johnson's division wedged its way into rear of fighting on Hill #3, cutting-off the 22nd Michigan and 89th Ohio from the rest of Steedman's division, though Le Favour and Carlton did not know they were isolated. At hill's crest, Will, Papa, Junior, Jeremiah, and Nathan scrambled furiously between Rebel charges to move anything available to build breastwork for better cover to impede relentless advances. Will and Junior strained to lift and roll two logs into position. "Horseshoe Ridge …what a name …she does not appear to be a lucky 'horseshoe'," Junior quipped.

"You got that right, partner," Will answered. "Let's roll that log to the side." Jeremiah and Nathan hustled to find large stones or small boulders. "Stay low. Stay low," Will called. Papa gathered loose tree limbs downed by ferocious shelling. He returned, crawling and dragging tree limbs …from behind improvised breastwork, five boys rested …hunkered down, trying to regain breath.

Then two brigades of Preston's came out of dark woods shrouded in smoke …up the slope of Horseshoe Ridge they came, directly against the center of Brannan's bedraggled line. Bravely and steadily forward, they picked their way among and over fallen comrades and Union fallen encumbering the slope. Rebels came yelling like demons, valiantly in do-or-die charges, bravely marching with heads held high, muskets in hand …defying Yankees to stop them. Will and boys crouched low to ground behind their improvised breastwork, rising only to fire directly down on the Southerners. Shot after shot found its mark, doing great damage, but Rebels kept coming. Will spotted a butternut-clad Reb advancing gingerly, almost on tiptoe …slouching low, moving forward timid, as if trying to dodge inescapable hail of bullets. Will raised rifle, eyed the hapless Reb through gun sight, placed finger slowly on trigger and squeezed. Gun belched fire. Will watched the fainthearted man fall, knowing first time his bullet did damage …it devastated Will …horror of killing evident. Will froze momentarily, stomach knotting …dryness in throat. "Oh, my God," he called. Sickened, he fought dry heaves. Mind raced, "*...he has family like mine ...this War is so wrong.*" About eighty yards short of hill's crest, Rebels stopped amid flaming yellow bursts and deafening thunder from Federal volleys.

"Now we've got 'em ...see 'em wobble," Junior shouted.

"We'll not be moved by lead bullets, or demon-like yells!" Jeremiah answered, adding gusto to resolve ...trying to cast a brave front.

Smoke hung like thick blanket making longer range visibility nearly impossible, compounding helpless fear ...gunpowder's acrid sulfurous smell permeating air, burning nostrils. Will and boys choked and gasped for air, chests heaving. With powder-streaked faces, they peered into half-empty cartridge boxes. Will looked toward Junior and shrugged ...Junior shook his head acknowledging their dire situation ...ammunition dwindling fast. Rebs paused only briefly, then raised muskets and returned fire. Union soldiers and Confederates stood frozen, firing at close range into each other's ashen face ...no one flinching. Rebels tried to dig boots into hillside, Federal musket fire and heavy artillery guns firing directly into them ...they staggered and fell back downhill. It happened time and again over the next hour.

During one close encounter, a long lanky 'Johnnie' in butternut threw down his gun, raised hands over head, and came uphill running and yelling toward Will and the boy's breastwork. "I surrender! Don't shoot! I surrender!" Will stayed low peering through a small gap in knotty tangled twist of cedar limbs, eyeing warily the Reb's panicked advance. As he crossed lines, Will heard Papa say, "...he's a Mississippian." The dark swarthy-looking Rebel turned to Will with surprised look after surveying Union lines, saying, "Good God! whar's all yor' men?"

"Look for yer' self," Junior answered.

Astounded, the Reb replied, "If dey' knew how few ya' be, ya'all wouldn't last five minutes ...dey' thinks thar's a whole division massed on dis' here line." A staff officer hustled the captured Reb to the rear.

Rebels reformed at foot of slope, moving back up again in all-out desperate surge, trying to break through Federal lines. It was bloodiest of fights ...back and forth across cedar thickets close and dense. Wounded lay everywhere, crying out in anguish, with no one able to aid …corpses strewn over ground, lying in ghastly contortion. Then woods and grasses caught fire …inferno, echoing with thunderous explosion of artillery fire and incessant salvo of musket volley. Will's ears were ringing …he could not hear. Guns grew too hot to touch, some jamming with overuse. He watched a gun explode in a soldier's face ..."Oh, my God! Oh, my God!" Will screamed in bloodcurdling horror, wanting to vomit, seeing a headless soldier fall limply to ground. He observed cartridge boxes being pitched aside …empty.

Will rose to his feet alongside a young sapling, using a tree branch to steady rifle's aim, thinking he could get off a better shot. But a musket ball screamed, cutting the string of his canteen …canteen careening to the ground. Then, a ball pierced haversack …he heard and felt its thud. He dove back to ground, newly convinced to stay behind cover of breastwork. A brief lull occurred in fighting. Will struggled to regain breath and calm himself from adrenaline rush following near misses. He felt welcome refreshing gentle breeze on perspiring skin, noticing wind blowing through tall tree branches gnarled within a stand of nearby oaks, vivid yellow and red leaves sailing through hazy smoke, settling lazily and limply on ground. "…*leaves falling, like men falling about me*," he thought. "*…young Lucius and Jeptha missing …out there somewhere.*"

Desperate fighting wore on …acts of untold bravery multiplied. By 4:30 PM, lack of ammunition was becoming critical. Cartridge boxes were brought up, but rounds were wrong caliber. Unit integrity evaporated with regiments intermingling. Will recognized dire straights of the 21st Ohio regiment on the left, because few Ohioans had cartridges to fill any of five chambers of their Colt repeating rifles. Will motioned to Junior and Jeremiah to follow. Keeping low, the three crawled rearward …going from body to body, pawing over dead and wounded, frantically scavenging for unspent cartridges. Seeing this, other soldiers followed. Confederates were doing the same down slope. As Will surveyed the rearmost field for precious ammunition, he noticed woods alive with 'skulkers' hiding behind trees and brush …laggards concerned only about personal safety, even officers, all quivering in fear of fusillades of deadly missiles hissing in air about them ...concealing themselves from view, only their cowardice showing clearly. It stood in stark contrast to bravery exhibited, but sickened Will, strengthening resolve, "*...it is best to die with honor, than to live without.*"

Gunfire resumed as Will, Junior, and Jeremiah scurried back to cover of breastwork, distributing what little ammunition they garnered. Will looked to the right at Papa and Nathan huddled elbow to elbow. Papa reacted to a next burst of gunfire, head jerking abruptly to the side as he rose to fire a shot ...glasses flying off his nose, bouncing off top log of breastwork, before lodging halfway down on a piece of exposed rail. Instinctively and without thinking, Papa rose and reached over breastwork to retrieve needed spectacles. Same moment a minie ball tore into flesh of Papa's protruding stomach, causing a visible wince, as he grasped illusive spectacles tight in hand. "Papa, you wounded?" Will called out.

"Yes ...sons o' bitches!" Papa answered.

"Where?" Will asked, noting shock and horror on faces of Junior, Jeremiah, and Nathan, all lying frozen by the moment. Will reached for Papa ...blood already soiling shirt. "Let's get you out of here," Will offered. "Can you walk?"

"Don't know ...I'll try," Papa responded. Now minie balls were coming thick and fast. Papa crawled back from the ridge on hands and knees, Will steadying him along the way. An old tree stump positioned near a base of large oak offered protection. Will propped Papa against the stump, as Papa coughed and sputtered unable to catch breath ...blood oozing from Papa's shirt and pant legs, around cuffs rolled up above ankles. Will slipped suspenders down from Papa's limp shoulders, handed him a handkerchief to stanch bleeding, positioned haversack between back and stump for comfort, and placed canteen in his free hand. "Go after them Rebs, Will," Papa said. "...you've done all ya' can for me. Let me rest a spell here. Take my cartridges and go."

Will moved away reluctantly ...back to the others. By now nearly one-third of Union defenders were down. Western height of Missionary Ridge cast deep dark shadow shrouding forested slopes, sun setting behind mountain only partially visible through hovering dense smoke and haze. Fighting abated. Federals picked over cartridge pouches, coming up empty. They pleaded with officers to get more ammunition. Colonel Le Favour dispatched adjutant, Lieutenant Drake, on a perilous ride rearward and west across Hill #2 to the Snodgrass cabin where he requested ammunition from General Granger. Drake was fired upon by both sides as he galloped back to Le Favour with Granger's reply. Will Hodkins was within forty feet of Le Favour as Drake returned, saying "Granger says …tell Carlton and Le Favour they must use bayonet and hold positions at all hazards."

This was the last order received from Granger …Granger left the field to meet General Thomas on the escape road to Rossville …without notifying Le Favour or Carlton that withdrawal was ordered. Thomas received orders for complete withdrawal from Rosecrans, who retreated earlier to Chattanooga. Last remnants of Federal army continued withdrawal …Harker withdrew at 5:00 PM, Steedman at 5:30 PM, and Brannan at 6:00 PM. These officers 'stealthily' abandoned their three regiments, leaving them behind and surrounded on Horseshoe Ridge …the 21st and 89th Ohio, and 22nd Michigan regiments …abandoned to 'stand firm and use cold steel' with no ammunition.

Nearly an hour lapsed since last flurry of intense fighting. Morbid hush fell over Horseshoe Ridge as darkness enveloped Will and boys isolated at its crest. Gunpowder smoke hung in air comingled with smoke of burning brush and leaves …growing darkness making it virtually impossible to distinguish anything more than six to eight paces away. Only a muted outline of bright moon could be seen piercing haze, adding to a ghostly surreal spectacle being played out in deadly drama on Horseshoe Ridge. Uncounted wounded suffered, left unattended because no one could get to them in woods and fields …agonizing groans and cries heard reverberating through chilling mountain darkness …heart-rending sounds of anguish. "Oh, water, water!" they cried. "Oh, for God's sake come and help me!"

"We've got to get help for Papa," Will said to Junior, Jeremiah, and Nathan …all huddled together helpless, shivering in fright.

"One of us needs to go see to Papa," Junior said, all heads nodding.

"Nathan, you should go," Will directed. Both Junior and Jeremiah shook their heads in agreement. "Go now!" Will said forcefully, both arms motioning Nathan to move rearward. Nathan crouched low and moved away.

In eerie deepening darkness, Will, Junior, and Jeremiah hunkered down, with empty cartridge boxes, praying they had seen the last Confederates. Le Favour sensed trouble. A terrific burst of musketry broke out in woods to their right, while all remained quiet at ridge's front. Then a roar from the south sounded like advancing troops only two hundred to three hundred yards away, though invisible through brush and smoke. Will and boys waited anxiously ...darkness and murky haze accentuating taut nerves already frayed beyond comprehension. "Jeremiah, you can be proud ...your family can be proud ...no 'white feather' for you," Will whispered.

"Will and Junior ...you can be proud too," Jeremiah added. They nodded silently.

In cool mountain air, teeth chattered and hair stood on end ...they shivered and cowered helpless, unable to do anything but await fate. In moments, ghostly blurred images of Rebels on the right could be seen hurrying north through woods and to their rear, like spooky apparitions. Down the line from Will, shooters with a few cartridges remaining took shots at scurrying Rebs. Their movement on open right flank convinced Colonel Le Favour to hightail it out of there. Without orders, he motioned silently for men to move rearward, thinking they could rejoin Steedman's division.

Will and others faced about and scurried three hundred yards backward downhill. Will, Junior, and Jeremiah looked side to side in search of Papa or Nathan ...or any sign of Lucius or Jeptha ...all missing, seven friends down to three. As men reached a hollow, they were halted by a Federal officer on horseback who saluted Colonel Le Favour. The officer was a large man, dark and swarthy, with black hair and beard. Will was no more than twenty feet away, and heard an agitated officer say emphatically, "Colonel, orders are to hold the hill at all hazards ...use cold steel if necessary ...reinforcements and ammunition will be here soon."

"But my ammunition is completely exhausted," implored Le Favour.

"Then orders are to hold at point of bayonet," he answered, wheeling horse and galloping away. Le Favour made a contemptuous salute toward fleeing rider's backside ...shrugging shoulders, with no answer. He faced men about, marching them back up hill to the very spot occupied just ten minutes earlier. What remained of the 22nd Michigan faced south at crest of ridge, while the 89th Ohio held position in its rear obliquely facing southwest, straddled by parts of the 21st Ohio on right and left flanks ...less than three hundred grim-faced men waiting ...virtually defenseless. After less than twenty minutes in darkness lying on damp ground at the ridge, Will heard soldiers filing through depths of great ravine to their right. "Maybe it's Steedman's brigade," Will whispered to Junior. Hushed murmurs filtered through Union ranks ...men calmly, curiously and almost listlessly wondering who approached. Wrapped in smoky fog, hapless Union soldiers strained to see more clearly ...a mass of humanity facing front, moving slowly uphill with orderly precision of a grand parade ...like so many phantoms. Shivers coursed Will's spine.

Colonel Le Favour dismounted, standing aside horse bridle in hand, only a few feet from Will. Marchers closed to within twenty to thirty paces, when someone called out "Rebs!" Instinctively, Will and fellow 'Yanks' sprang to their feet, raised guns to shoulders, and pressed fingers to trigger at the ready. Rebel brigade did likewise. Face to face they squared off. Then came most deadly, menacing sound ...sound Will would never forget ...'click' of locks cocking in unison on trigger of each gun. "Surrender, boys, we've got you!" their officer called.

Without ammunition, men in blue were without hope. Union soldiers began lowering guns slowly. Just then, a treacherous Confederate wheeled his musket toward Colonel Le Favour. Without hesitation and on impulse, Will Hodkins sprang from his feet, hurling himself toward Colonel Le Favour to shield and protect as fiery flash of gunshot lit murky night. Treacherous assailant was immediately pummeled by Rebel brethren, aghast at cruelty and stupidity of an unnecessary act. Will Hodkins lay on ground …writhing in discomfort and shock …minie ball striking Will in his left shoulder. Colonel Le Favour, untouched by gunshot but greatly shaken, knelt over Will as Junior and Jeremiah rushed to his side. Will was bleeding profusely. Colonel Le Favour said, "Son, you may have saved my life. Your bravery is an example to us all."

Soldiers stood awestruck, both Union and Confederate …marveling at such heroic act of common soldier ...down and dirty, foot-slogging infantry private …man willing to give his life for an officer. They huddled together in small groups …talking in hushed voice, anxious look on faces …while Confederate medical personnel tended to Will's wound. It was the last shot fired on Horseshoe Ridge ...two hundred forty-nine Federals captured by the Confederate 54th Virginia and 6th and 7th Florida regiments of Colonel Robert Trigg's Brigade. Colonel Trigg faced captured Colonel Le Favour, as enlisted Union prisoners were shuttled rear under guard. Le Favour turned over horse, bridle and saddle to Colonel Trigg. He handed Trigg a pair of large-size Smith and Wesson pistols and then his sword, saying, "Take good care of them, as I hope to get them back some of these days."

Trigg replied with courtesy of a Southern gentleman, "I will certainly take good care of them, and make good use of them, Sir." He saluted Le Favour. Le Favour returned the salute.

"I request one more thing of you, Sir," Le Favour added.

"And kindly, what is that, Sir?" Trigg asked.

"That young soldier, who showed such valor in protecting me," Le Favour explained, "…he is a member of my staff, and I request that he be allowed to accompany me."

Trigg winked knowingly to Colonel Le Favour. With great compassion, he said, "Your wish is granted …of course, Colonel."

A two-day 'Battle of Chickamauga' ended. General Bragg's Confederate Army of Tennessee was victorious, wrecking the Georgia offensive thrust of Rosecrans' Union Army, forcing demoralized Union fragments to flee to safety in Chattanooga. Cost to both armies was staggering ...Union losses totaled 16,000 killed, wounded or captured ...Confederate losses totaled 18,000. This 'barren victory' sealed fate of the Confederacy, because Union army escaped annihilation, slinking away to lick wounds and regroup to fight another day. Its escape stands as a testament to bravery and valor of a small group of Ohioans and Michiganders …abandoned …left isolated on Horseshoe Ridge to cover retreat.

Chapter 24

Junior and Jeremiah watched silent and stunned …anguish in eyes, greatly frightened as Confederate medical men worked over Will. A minie ball struck Will from the rear as he leaped to throw himself in front of Colonel Le Favour, but fortunately ball exited shoulder from the front. Morphine was administered and cloth bandages wrapped tightly about the shoulder to stem bleeding. Will's breathing became labored …he spoke to medical men with croup-like sound, dazed and half alert, grimacing with pain increasing as they lifted him onto a stretcher. Will looked up at Junior and Jeremiah, saying softly, "Take care, boys. I will see you soon."

"We'll do it," Junior answered. "…yer' a good friend, Will."

"We need you, Will," Jeremiah added with tears welling. "Come back to us."

Will nodded. With that, he was lifted and carried off the 'Horseshoe' and downhill, while Junior and Jeremiah were herded away to join other captured Union bluecoats destined for Libby or Andersonville prisons. Stretcher bearers moved downhill slowly toward the Snodgrass cabin …now confiscated by Confederates and being utilized as field hospital. They exited smoke-filled forest onto open hillside somewhat visible by moonlight. High on Horseshoe Ridge brush fires still burned. He was placed on ground within fifty feet of the Snodgrass cabin to await a surgeon. Pain and shock coupled with cool crisp nighttime mountain air caused Will to shiver and tremble. He fought drowsiness trying to stay alert …not lose consciousness …awful stench pervasive from dead bodies already decomposing after two days of killing. All about him were blackened swollen corpses, discarded equipment, and shattered trees ...ground strewn with debris, tree branches and tops of trees as if felled by giant storm. On ghastly scene, moon's rays cast ghostly silhouette in hollows of trampled Snodgrass fields below ...Confederate and Federal dead, wounded and dying everywhere, scattered in grotesque contortion. Soldiers ventured out with dimly lit lanterns, lantern lights bobbing and weaving in eerie moonlit darkness, searching faces of wounded comrades ...dancing lights casting unreal aura to ghoulish scene. Groans and moans of wounded added pitiful cacophony of sound ...Will heard boyish voices calling, "Mother! Mother!" Poor souls still alive were being carried back to hastily established field hospitals ...dead left for burial later, where they fell. It was as if Will entered hell, viewing work of the devil firsthand.

Snodgrass Cabin, utilized as field hospital

(Library of Congress)

Will began to hallucinate ...involuntary thought darting. He thought of Maria and children, "...*will I ever see them again?*" Eerie God-forsaken Rebel yells replayed over and over, echoing loudly in his mind, confusing and muddling thought. Worries of Lucius and Jeptha, and Papa and Nathan flashed before him ...four friends out there somewhere ...fate unknown. "*What about captured Junior and Jeremiah?"* He lay frightened and alone ...chilled, lips dry, throat parched.

He hailed a passing Reb for a drink. "Ya'all wants some spider juice?" the Reb asked, stopping and standing before Will dressed in coarse homespun cloth of butternut color.

"Just water would do me fine." Kindly Reb obliged, reaching for canteen. "Battle's a horrible thing ...like a bad dream, it seems," Will said, savoring lukewarm water.

"Ya'all got that right! Terrible thing! Terrible thing she be!" Johnny Reb answered before turning away.

Moments later Will heard someone from open door of cabin say, "We haven't facilities for our own men, much less prisoners." A Confederate officer standing aside the surgeon answered, "Colonel Trigg wants you to take good care of him." Surgeon shrugged, motioning reluctantly for Will to be moved inside cabin. The Confederate surgeon examined Will's wound roughly, saying brusquely without Will's comprehension, "Axillary nerves seriously injured ...artery does not seem to have escaped ...though no hemorrhage ...impulse in radial artery very slight." That said, he motioned for an assistant to redress wounded shoulder and moved to next patient. Will muttered, "Old 'sawbones' is none too friendly." Assistant shrugged.

With wound re-dressed, stretcher bearers carried Will further down hillside to a hollow southeast of Snodgrass cabin. They moved past campfires where groups of wounded huddled, pathetically suffering ...some praying, some dying ...faces blackened by powder and smoke. Will noticed a figure squatted by side of tree, rifle still propped on tree branch and aimed at breastwork fifty yards uphill ...head leaning forward limp, shot through the heart. Another corpse faced down, one hand on musket's muzzle, other hand clutching rammer. A Confederate shot in the mouth, lay with both hands clinched at long black whiskers still oozing blood ...next to him, a headless Federal soldier no more than five feet away ....grizzly scenes unending.

Will turned head away gagging, stomach squeamish and wanting to vomit, unable to swallow phlegm sticking in throat ...unable to give further witness to such pathos. He shivered with chill, anger all consuming ...anger at vast destruction of life

…*"each man's family suffering."* Anger intensified watching marauding stragglers search haversacks and bodies of dead and wounded for plunder …Yankee coffee, hardtack, ham and sugar …others stripping boots and shoes from carcasses of fallen Federal soldiers or confiscating new rifles.

Horrific Death Everywhere

(Library of Congress)

Not far past the hollow, stretcher bearers arrived at a dilapidated old log cabin. They opened rough hewn wood plank door, hinges screeching, and carried Will inside. A blanket was spread on dirt floor. Will was rolled onto the blanket …wincing with excruciating pain. Cold shakes overtook him, sending spastic shivers coursing through body. "Good luck, soldier," one medic said as they departed. A one-room cabin was lit by single candle burning on lone center table, room's only furnishing. Will turned slowly, agonizingly onto right side to see a wounded Confederate lying next to him …unable to speak. Soon after, another wounded man was brought into the dimly lit cabin and placed directly on dirt floor to Will's left …a Federal shot through the groin and in pretty bad shape. Hinges groaned again …as if in audible heartrending witness to immense suffering. A portly woman entered, dressed in coarse homespun cloth. Her gait was of a young woman, but countenance drawn and tired. Full length dark gray dress appeared freshly laundered, white apron clean ...auburn hair pulled back tight in a bun. She eyed Will, cautious smile brightening face, visage conveying warmth and tenderness. "I'm Clara ...Clara Cowper ...my husband, Benjamin Cowper, is a Confederate soldier ...and away, I do not know where."

"I'm ...I'm ...Will Hodkins, 'mam," Will answered softly ...stuttering, teeth chattering.

She pointed to one dark corner behind Will at far end of her twenty by fifteen-foot cabin. "Those are my two children ...and my mother who lives with me." Will looked over shoulder at two small children cowering ...an old woman standing with arms protective around children. "A widow lives here as well ...with her two boys ...they are out looking for food." She paused hanging head, dejected and resigned, "We have not a mouthful of food in our home ...children have been crying for something to eat."

"Mam, ...pieces of hardtack and some coffee in my haversack ...I'd be pleased if you took them." The Federal lying next to Will, severely wounded and delusional, moaned quietly calling for water. Will asked if she had water. She brought a ladle of water, carefully placing it to hapless soldier's lips, urging him to sip. It seemed to quiet him.

She went to a bucket for fresh ladle, "You must be mighty thirsty yourself, Will."

"Thank you, 'mam." That was all Will remembered of Sunday evening ...he lost consciousness, sleep quickly overtaking him.

Monday morning dawned cold and clear. Will awoke with first stream of daylight pouring through a solitary small four-pane window ...cabin's only daylight, except for several unkempt open gaps in mud chinking between logs. A splitting headache, but he was awake. He thought, "*...I am lucky to be alive.*" He turned, horrified ...locking eyeball-to-eyeball in frightful deadly gaze with cold white corpse staring back, eyes fixed and glassy ...Federal next to him dying in the night. No Cowper's were in the cabin, apparently all out foraging. Will struggled to get to feet, wanting to lift himself to the window. With every ounce of effort expended and in extreme pain, he hoisted himself just enough to peer over window sill. Frost formed during night, painting corpses strewn over nearby ground with ghost-like shroud. He could see no activity about the cabin. Pain overtaking him, he removed shoes and lowered himself back to the floor. He fell asleep.

Mid-morning, Will awakened, startled by a Reb straggler bursting through cranky creaky cabin door. Inside, he spotted Will's Federal uniform and spied Will's shoes placed on ground bedside. Surly Reb wore well-worn boots, remarking with haughty snarly guffaw, "Hey, Yank ...how's about trad-in' these here boots for yer' shoes thar?"

In weak voice Will answered, "Not interested, Sir, I intend wearing them."

Reb turned dead serious, "Ya'all never wear 'em agin' ...Yank!" He picked up the shoes. "See ya', Yank," he taunted, doffing brim of floppy gray felt hat, walking out abruptly without removing dilapidated boots. Will was too weak to make a fuss.

Not long after, another defiant Confederate plowed through the door, brandishing gun in hand, swearing a terrible oath. "Where ya' wounded, Yank?" Will pointed listlessly to left shoulder. Reb raised his gun at Will's head, saying, "Guess I'll knock your brains out then!" Gun cocked and Will flinched, just as Mrs. Cowper rushed through the door, pushing Reb's arm away, spinning him around with fury.

"Can't abuse these men," she said, fearlessly wagging a menacing finger toward the man's eye. "They are wounded ...he is a prisoner." Reb threw hands into air, grudgingly and disgustingly, bolting from cabin cursing a blue streak, slamming groaning door in his wake.

"Thank you, 'mam ...much obliged." Will gasped, breathing deeply with visible sigh of relief. He reached to breast pocket ...in frenzy of fighting and being shot, he gave no thought to the journal. He felt journal safely lodged within breast pocket, "*...I can lose my shoes alright ...I cannot lose my journal.*"

Will spent the next three days recuperating under attentive care of Mrs. Cowper, family nursing wounded Confederate soldier as well. It was very cold and Will suffered without blanket, just wool overcoat from dead Federal used as cover, and without shoes. Food was scarce. First two days, Confederates brought each person a half-pint of gruel ...on Wednesday, some hardtack and two pounds of bacon. Famished, Will ate his portion of bacon raw ...most welcome at that. A portion of pickled beef or 'salt horse' stunted appetite being so foul smelling and rancid.

On Thursday, weather warmed but rained steady. Mrs. Cowper dressed Will's wounds with fresh moist cloth. "Entry and exit wounds are closed nicely by clotted blood ...seems to be mending." Will's physical pain eased with three days healing, but so much troubled him. He wanted to talk. Mrs. Cowper proved an ardent listener and eager conversationalist. "Mrs. Cowper, tell me more about your husband Benjamin."

"Will, please call me Clara."

"I will indeed ...thank you, 'mam," Will answered.

"Benjamin had no choice ...did not want to fight ...did not want to leave us alone, but Confederates gave no choice," she said. "It's been nearly six months since hearing from him ...he's not very good at writing."

"Where did you meet, and how did you get here?" Will questioned.

"Benjamin and I met in Atlanta, where I was teaching school ...he was raised a farm boy, and we came out here, where land was available to start our farm ...but, it has been a struggle, and now War has changed everything."

"It is remarkable how similar your story is to mine and my wife's ...her name is Maria." Will related his story of coming to Michigan with Maria to farm his father's land. "Maria is such a smart and determined lady ...like you, Clara," Will continued. "But now I am sick with worry about her ...what will happen to our family when she learns I am wounded again ...and a prisoner."

"I am certain she will find the strength to survive ...that is all any of us can do."

Will choked with emotion, sadness and tone of defeat coming to voice. "Last year has been a disaster, since I enlisted ...lost my friend, Johnny, to sickness in winter camp. Four other friends are out there somewhere, lost in battle. Now Junior and Jeremiah are captured and gone. I feel like a failure, not being able to protect them ...and Maria, I have failed her as well."

"You have lost a great deal, Will. But, you are certainly not a failure."

"My seven friends helped me survive …we were 'family' …now I am alone and don't know if I have the strength to survive."

"You must find the strength …Maria can survive if you give her hope …you must do this for Maria," Clara implored.

"You are right, of course," he lamented. "Talking with you, Clara, has helped so much …given me clearer thinking …cannot worry about me …I must do this for Maria, and our children."

In afternoon, three Confederates came to remove Will and other wounded fellow. Will expressed deep appreciation to Clara Cowper and family for kindness and compassion extended a 'Yank' …he was lifted and carried to a government wagon waiting at doorstep. "Thank you kindly, Mrs. Cowper …I wish you and family the best …God-speed for Mr. Cowper's safe return …stay strong."

"I will, and you do the same, Will …I would like to meet Maria some day." Will managed a feeble wave to a humble family, all gathered arm-in-arm, waving 'goodbye' to wounded guests.

With lurch and jerk, two-wheeled 'avalanche' wagon moved away, beginning a three mile journey south. Here, Rebs assembled wounded soldiers, including what looked to be about five hundred captured Federals. As he waited, Will tried to scan the gathering to see Papa or Nathan …or Lucius or Jeptha …maybe they were among the wounded. But he recognized no one. A Rebel officer circulated among wounded taking name, commander, and outfit from each man. "William Hodkins, Colonel Le Favour, 22nd Michigan Infantry," Will responded. Then, a Rebel surgeon examined Will's wound. Hospital wagons were loaded, moving out in continuous stream to haul wounded another twelve miles further south to the Georgia town of Ringgold. Will was hoisted at rear of four-wheel hospital wagon. He was tossed onto rough lumber boards of wagon bed along with eight or ten suffering men …all packed elbow-to-elbow, body-to-body, no room to wiggle. Wagon began moving and soon pulled onto one of the roughest roads imaginable. Wagon bounced, swayed and jostled, bringing further agony to injured occupants. Next to Will, a man's wound began bleeding profusely, reopened by tossing jarring motion …Will watched unable to help, as blood puddled on wagon floor boards. Their wagon joined a caravan of one hundred or more wagons, all loaded with sufferers, all wending toward Ringgold. Beside wagon caravan, one hundred of lesser wounded filed along on foot, slowly hobbling and trudging in the same direction.

Rain became heavier. Will and others were soon soaking wet, drenched by rain coming through leaky canvas cover. Torrential rain was soon washing rivulets of blood, draining off wagon's tailgate. "…*like melting water dripping from an ice wagon*," Will mused. Despite ordeal, several poor fellows joked and bantered as their wagon tossed about roughly. One fellow, who lost the bridge of his nose to a bullet, looked over at Will and said, "Hallo, Son …tried to git' yer' arm off did they?"

"Yes," Will answered, "…but they did not make it. I see they came pretty close to getting into your head."

"Yes …came damn close to missing me too," the craggy veteran answered smiling.

Hearing this, another soldier rolled to his side, patting where a bullet put a hole in the buttock. "Them Rebs shot ass off of me this time," he offered with toothless grin. Banter broke up a miserable four to five hour ordeal before their wagon arrived at a place called 'Burnt Shed', some fifteen to twenty miles from battlefield. Here wounded waited at 'Bragg Hospital' for rail transportation, using a spur of torn-up railroad track to Ringgold hastily re-laid to transport men. Will was carried by stretcher from wagon into dreary building …scene of horrific suffering …hundreds of patients, lying cramped on beds of straw, pine needles and brush strewn on dirt floor. In darkness with no lighting, nurses stumbled among wounded, kept busy rolling and replacing bandages. Stretcher bearers carried Will up a flight of stairs to second floor balcony where he was placed among wounded not requiring immediate attention …all waiting to be loaded onto rail cars. Will waited and watched, wrapped in wet wool blanket, lying on rain soaked balcony floor. Ambulances kept coming …bearing precious cargo …injured men covered with soot and grime, blackened faces distorted, grimacing in pain.

Ladies of Ringgold toted baskets of freshly baked biscuits, distributing a treat among men that could eat.   A makeshift Confederate band struck notes of 'Dixie' …braying discordantly in soggy late-afternoon drizzle.   Will could only watch tortured, steeling amid sorrowful scene.   Men with lesser wounds stood shivering below in cold rain, cooking around campfire.   He thought, "…*what perfect war between elements …fire and water …nature is shedding tears …nation weeping as well*."   He vowed aloud, "I must survive …whatever Libby Prison offers. I owe this to Maria and our children …I must find a way back home."

Chapter 25

Maria sat in rocking chair aside their front window, anxiously squinting against bright early October afternoon sun for signs down country dirt road of approaching post rider. She gazed longingly through streaked panes of glass. *"I must clean these windows,"* she thought. Eyes moved to knitting basket in her lap, mind returning reluctantly to menial task at hand …knitting socks for the boys and hat for Minnetta for approaching winter …fumbling nervously with knitting needles. Stomach churned constantly with worry over the last five days …since receiving Will's letter written 16th September from outside Chattanooga. He wrote of impending battle, tone leading her to believe he would be engaged. Words haunted her day and night … *"if ever I get out of this War …may I meet my duty with honor"* …words he wrote ringing 'final' and so ominous.

'Not knowing' proved most difficult. Farm chores and mother's duties were difficult without Will …but she could do something about these tasks …they were in front of her everyday, more under her control. 'Not knowing' was entirely different. Without assurance of Will's safety, she could not shake devastating empty feelings …she was helpless. Intuition nagged and tugged constantly from within …intuition of danger and trouble.

Concern grew deeper yesterday when Ezra stopped with reports circulating in Oxford of a great battle occurring on the 19th and 20th of September with the Federal army withdrawing less than victorious. Will, Jr. and Walter stayed overnight with Ezra and Nettie, so they were away. Four month old baby Minnetta was fast

asleep napping in her crib in the bedroom. Maria sat alone ...
frantic emotion all consuming, last twenty-four hours a nightmare.
*"...if something happens ...I must sell the farm ...move children
back to Penn Yan. No. No. That is wrong ...I must stay positive."*

Amid foreboding thought racing and darting sporadic, she
looked up to notice clouds of dust from distant rider sauntering on
horseback down roadway. Breathing quickened when she
recognized Isaac Hales approaching in saddle ...friend and farm
neighbor who doubled as post rider. Isaac wheeled his horse at her
gate as Maria scurried outside, dropping knitting basket abruptly
...knitting needles and yarn balls bouncing and rolling across
wood plank flooring in her wake. "Good afternoon, Isaac ...I have
been so anxious for you to arrive, hoping you have a letter," she
blurted breathless. He did have a letter, and handed it to Maria
...it was from Will. She tried to engage Isaac nonchalantly,
politely masking excitement and impatience. Isaac was wont to
babble-on, rambling with small talk and gossip. She did not want
to be rude, but cutting him short proved impossible. He talked
about weather, neighbors down the road, even an aching back.
Chatter seemed unending, despite her uneasiness.

"I hope Ned has been a help," Isaac inquired.

"Ned has been wonderful," she answered, fidgeting and
nervously tugging at her dress. "Without Ned's help with chores,
and all that Ezra and Nettie do to help and support me ...why, I
simply could not make it without their help and support."

"Have you heard recently from Will?"

"Yes, he writes often ...but I am so worried ...I pray this
letter tells me he is safe."

"I can see you are eager to read it ...trust it will be good
news ...forgive me for taking so much of your time. Please let me
know if I can be of service in any way."

"Thank you, Isaac." Finally conversation ended. She bid
him adieu and best wishes as he rode off. Wasting no time, Maria
bolted for the house, heart pounding as she sat down at kitchen
table and tore open envelope. Inside, she removed a single solitary
white and lavender wildflower. Maria stared wistful at her
wildflower, eyes growing misty. "Will, you are so good at
remembering ...wish I were that good," she voiced aloud. She

kissed the wildflower, sighing, "Will Hodkins, you are a kind, thoughtful and sensitive man …I love you dearly." She unfolded the letter and read:

Ringgold, Georgia
Friday, 25th September

Dearest Maria:

Through amazing mercy of God I am alive, though barely. I just passed through terrible ordeal of hard battle. No time to give particulars, but will write at length. God forbid I should ever witness such scene again. Carnage was awful. A thousand thunderstorms turned loose could not equal its noise and fury. I managed to lift my heart to God in prayer and place trust in him, knowing loving wife and others were praying for me. I felt calm and secure, never losing my wits. I trust you will be proud.

I fear Lucius and Jeptha were lost. Papa was wounded badly, and Nathan went to his aid. Junior, Jeremiah, and I were captured by Rebs, though I was shot in the left shoulder, but believe I shall recover.

255

Rebs treat me well ...Colonel Le Favour arranged for my good treatment, as I may have saved his life. I do not know disposition of Junior and Jeremiah, as I am recovering here in field hospital. I am alone, and miss my friends greatly. I believe I will be sent by rail to Richmond. My trust is in God. I will be home! Comfort and hug our children.

I love you always, Will

Maria's eyes filled with tears, chest heaving with uncontrolled sobbing. She reread the letter and placed it on the table. She raised hands to face, tears streaming ...gulping for breath, fighting to regain composure ...trying to think clearly. Just then Ezra appeared at the screen door. He came to see if Will, Jr. and Walter could stay another night. He heard Maria wailing, slumped over kitchen table, "Maria, it's Ezra ...what's da' matter in 'thar?"

"Ezra ...oh, my God! ...come in." Ezra rushed to her with open arms. Putting arms around her shoulders, he tried to give comfort, but she continued weeping convulsively. Moments later, she blurted, "Oh, my God! ...Ezra, Will's been wounded again ...and captured!" Maria gathered a degree of composure and related letter's contents to Ezra.

"Let's do some talk-in' ...talk-in' kin' do some good, now," Ezra offered.

"Will is alive, that is good news ...but wounded again," she stammered with tears pouring down cheeks. "I fear it more serious than he wants me to believe ...he is trying to spare me."

"Will's a strong fella, ya' know ...got better before, kin' do it again."

256

"This is much worse than the wound at Danville. We could go to him then. He is captured now ...a prisoner! I feel helpless ...can do nothing to help. I feel weak and defeated ...do not know how I go on."

"Wez' gotta stay strong ...dat's all ya'all can do fer' Will ...me and Nettie will be here fer' ya'all."

"What and how can I tell the boys?"

"We'll find us a way ...you'll see," Ezra offered. "Wez' gotta trust in God's plan ...keep faith, ya' know."

"This is nightmare beyond proportion," she sputtered. "I am so angry ...will this calamity ever end?" No answer existed. It was all too much. She lowered forehead upon table, sobbing and chest pounding, struggling again for breath ...anguish unbearable.

Chapter 26

Tuesday September 29th turned momentous and solemn for Will and fellow prisoners. Weather grew threatening, skies rumbling, darkening clouds and gloomy overcast lingering …threatening as if portending things to come. Prisoners were drawn into line, counted off and marched away …those that could walk. They shuffled away with sullen face, slumped shoulder, sadness in eyes, as if marching toward their own funeral. Enlisted men were loaded into overcrowded railroad cattle cars, where blankets, overcoats and new boots were removed …without these men suffered from damp bitter cold. Will was more fortunate, being carried by stretcher to a hospital car equipped with hard tiered wood bunks …some heat given off by a solitary cast iron stove burning firewood at one end of rail car. A nearly six hundred-mile rail trip proved dreadful, overloaded cars inching north over three grueling days …bound for prisons in the Confederate capital in Richmond.

Arriving in Richmond, prisoners in boxcars were ordered out and into line, counted off and herded to Belle Isle Prison, already legendary as a prison of untold horror …located on an island in the James River covering ten or twelve acres across from the city. Will watched and waited among wounded prisoners. Across the 'long bridge' near lower part of island, serpentine-like line of captured Union soldiers moved slowly, heads hanging down, shoulders hunched …pathos of their situation hanging heavy. Dejected, forlorn and scared, they marched toward captivity on a cold bleak piece of ground, where winter winds swept freely upriver. Will eyed a forsaken moving mass of humanity, squinting and hopeful to catch a glimpse of one of the boys. Thoughts flashed before Will ..."*Jeremiah and Junior at Belle Isle? ...Jeptha and Lucius alive and captured? ...fate of Papa and Nathan?*" Will waited just across one half-mile expanse of river, but so very far away. "*I am alone and abandoned ...no one available for support.*"

Will and other wounded, as well as Federal officers, were sent to 'Libby Prison' ...an old tobacco warehouse converted into makeshift prison and hospital. Will's recovery was progressing over nine days since capture ...wounds beginning to heal, severe pain less frequent. He could walk a few steps, still too weak to go further. Psyche remained with far greater damage. Carried via stretcher, Will glanced up at an imposing, dark and frowning three-story brick and wood structure, its white-washed exterior tired, moldy and in dire need of maintenance. From its corner hung an old weather-beaten sign, reading 'Libby & Son, Ship-chandlers'. Upon entering the prison, officers were separated from enlisted men. Will and others were asked to give name, rank, company and regiment. "William Hodkins, Private, Company A of the 22nd Michigan," Will responded, before being carried forward to a next Reb officer. Confederate sergeant said, "Give up yer' Yankee script, now ...20¢ Yankee be worth $2 Confederate, ya' see ...if ya' give 'er up easy, we'll keep it for ya' ...may get er' back some day ...then again, maybe not." Will gave up his money without further coaxing.

A lower first floor east room served as prison hospital. Sashes from windows had been removed, replaced by grates fashioned from one-inch vertical iron rods intersecting three cross-bars firmly imbedded in brick foundation walls. Will was placed on a grimy stained canvas cot. "This place'll be yer' quarters for present," he was told.

Will asked the Reb sergeant, "Could we have some rations, as it had been thirty-six hours since last eating?"

Sergeant answered politely, "She's after prison ration hours, and ya'all hav-ta' wait till next day, now."

And so began Will's first day *'alone in all my glory'* ...alone and isolated from friends and family ...captured and wounded prisoner, knowing no one. In the hospital area, no stoves meant bone jarring cold dampness, especially through desolate never-ending long nights ...made hideous by agonizing moan of suffering wretches.   It did not much matter if stoves were unavailable, because extreme short supply of firewood existed everywhere in Richmond.   Wounded coexisted with those suffering diarrhea, dysentery, fever, ulcers, gangrene, and scurvy ...all lying side by side, all struggling to survive.

For first thirty days at 'Libby', Will stayed anchored to cot in hospital ward. Recuperation progressed, though he needed to stay prone and resting most time.   Blood clots seemed to be dissolving ...no sign of pus emanating from either of two surface wounds ...though he suffered pain through entire left side and occasional nervous twitching in arm and shoulder. After another month, wounds healed sufficiently though strength and motion of left side remained impaired. He began to walk, exercise rebuilding some stamina.   Despite dismal existence within Libby, Will's plight continued better than most.   Colonel Le Favour struck a 'gentleman's agreement' upon capture on the 'Horseshoe' which probably saved Will's life, and Confederates were honoring that agreement. They treated him as if he were a staff officer.

Through early weeks of incarceration, Will received numerous letters from Maria.   Her very first letter provided assurance, giving untold boost to inner strength as he coped with attitude adjustment within prison. He read and reread her letter often.

Dearest Will,

Thought of your wound and capture devastated me for days. I could not find a way to tell our boys. I simply could not function. Then through help of Ezra and Nettie, and many prayers to keep faith in

God, I regained my resolution and strength to carry forward.

I realized that you and our children need my strength, all a greater concern than for self. I now know that the children and I will find a way to make it through calamity. You must feel isolated and alone, but please know that we are here for you always. Will, I have great confidence that you have faith and inner strength to survive your ordeal. We need you home . . . our prayers are always with you.

Our boys are doing well . . . they seem to understand. Please do not worry. I enclose an ambrotype of me, as I hope my likeness can remain close to your heart. I love you, always,

Maria

Will cherished Maria's letter keeping it close to heart, folded secure within cover of journal, along with her ambrotype. When ordeal grew most difficult, he relied upon both for added strength and resolve.

After six-week recovery and recuperation mostly complete, Will assumed assigned duties within the prison . . . working in the kitchen, going outside with squads to search for firewood, serving as nurse disposing of bed pans and cleaning squalor from bowel and stomach sickness, as well as assisting on burial detail. Burial detail comprised a most horrific experience. Will carried bodies to a 'dead house' outback, where corpses were stacked grotesquely without dignity to await burial. He dug graves for mass burial ...no coffins, dead being buried with nothing but canvas wrapped about them. Death consumed minds ...prisoners unable to sleep, prowled wards at night to see if anyone died through night. Ghoulish aura pervaded prison life. Will witnessed humanity reduced to abject animal instinct for survival ...strong coped, weak succumbed.

Gruesome day-to-day existence ...but, Will learned through guards and prison grapevine, far better than fate of fellow enlisted prisoners across the James River in stockades of Belle Isle Prison, or increasing number being transferred daily to newly opened Andersonville Prison in Georgia. From makeshift enclosures and squalid depravity of outdoor camps within these facilities, few survived their ordeal. Incarceration proved deadly as battle. Will used this information to advantage ...playing mind games to stay mentally tough ...staying positive by counting meager blessings and reliving memories. No one could take memories away. Will called upon memories to sustain him ..."*memories are fuel stoking my fire of desire to get back home,*" he repeated silently over and over again. It did not always work.

In late December, Will moved from first floor hospital ward to a third floor room measuring forty feet wide by one hundred feet long ...room shared by one hundred-fifty captured Union officers. This would be 'home' for months to come. Officers knew Will to be an enlisted man, so most officers remained aloof and showed little camaraderie. Fortune smiled when Will met a vivacious character who hobbled up on crutches displaying coy boyish smile. "My name's Ike Duffie," he said extending a hand to Will, while leaning stiffly and trying awkwardly to balance on one crutch. "Gents around here call me 'Daffie' ...Daffie Duffy."

"I'm Will Hodkins."

"Folks around here call me 'Daffie' ...cause they thinks me a little tetched ...little looney, light in the brain, ya' know. I do nothing to change minds ...keeps em' away from me, ya' know."

"You know, I think of myself as a little looney at times ...more so everyday ...this place makes keep-in' sanity darn near impossible," Will answered.

"Ya' don't say. Mind if we talk a bit?"

Daffie leaned knotted knurly hand-fashioned crutches at end of Will's cot, swinging a stiff right leg around by his hands, before plopping down aside Will on the cot. Will and Daffie talked for some time. Daffie was a Staff Sergeant with an Indiana regiment before being wounded and captured six months earlier. Daffie stood short of stature, rather scrawny ...cheeks chiseled, sunken and ashen. Pointy nose held rimless spectacles perched precariously on the bridge ..."*spectacles much like Papa's,*" Will observed silently. Above hollow dark forlorn eyes, bushy brown eyebrows sprawled. Hair long and unkempt, dirty and snarled, ends pointed wildly in all directions ..."*possible bird nest for a starling,*" Will thought. When Daffie spoke, head sporadically tilted sideways and downward toward left shoulder, like someone with affliction ...nervous jerking reaction accompanied by glassy far-off look to dark eyes. All of this added to Daffie's mystique of madness. Will speculated whether 'wackiness' was Daffie before severe wound that left right leg paralyzed and immobile ...certainly six month incarceration at Libby did no good. Evidently fellow captive officers derided and avoided Daffie ...so Will and Daffie found themselves unlikely cellmates in isolation. They bonded instantly, friendship grew.

One day as outcast twosome sat talking, Daffie said, "Will, I cannot leave this floor with ma' peg leg ...could ya' describe everything ya' see concern-in' this hell hole ...would appreciate know-in.'"

"Ike, I sure enough will do just that," Will responded.

"Ya' don't say."

Will returned after an eight-hour shift of duties and sat with Daffie to describe Libby Prison. "I paced our building, being about one hundred-thirty feet long and one hundred feet wide, I reckon …built of brick mostly, three story to its front, four story to the rear."

"Ya' don't say."

"Within are six rooms, each about forty feet by one hundred feet, separated by two-foot thick brick walls. A flight of stairs leads from each room to floor above, but at night stairs leading to ground floor are taken down, and sentinels stationed to prevent escape. Lower west room is partitioned off and used for prison offices. Lower east room is prison hospital, where I stayed for first ten weeks. Lower middle room is equipped with stoves and used as kitchen."

"Ya' don't say …wish we had us a stove up here."

"Ike, you've got that right," Will agreed.

Day-to-day inconvenience of last winter's army camp life paled in comparison to squalor of prison life. No where could Will find bunk, table, blankets, or simple utensils for eating …anything previously considered 'necessity'. In want of tin cups, knives and forks, prisoners often ate with their hands …hands none too clean. Bare walls and wet damp floors existed everywhere. No cleanliness practiced ...dust and dirt and voided excrement, all left untouched. A hydrant in each room supplied dirty water from the river, and a single pathetically filthy putrid smelly 'bathtub' was shared by prisoners. Once a month, Will assisted Daffie with bath …an event held in mutual distaste during their timeless sojourn in 'hotel Libby'. At one such encounter, Will peered at a countenance staring back in a mirror …not a man he knew, condition horrific …loss of weight, sallow sunken cheeks below dark hollow empty eyes, gray ashen complexion ...unkempt beard, dirty course and unruly. Hair long, matted and filthy, touched skinny arms and shoulders. He was despondent. Sensing friend's low regard, Daffie tried to make light of their dire situation, saying, "Ya' begin-in' to look like me, ma' friend …we best eat some more and put some meat around our bones."

"It's been a long time since we've been offered some meat."

"Ya' don't say."

Coincident with Will's arrival at Libby, rations were cut to half portions due to shortages …last two months, reduced to quarter portions. Prisoners survived hungry all the time. Will and Daffie most often took meals together, providing companionship where food was lacking. Rations consisted of cornbread, beans or cow peas …sometimes a half-pint of rice soup, and occasionally a portion of foul rancid bacon. Bread was un-sifted cornmeal mixed with water and without salt, baked in cards of twelve loaves …each loaf being two and one-half inch square by two inch thick, a single loaf constituting a ration. "Course sour and rusty …would make poor feed for swine at home," Will observed to Daffie.

Beans were small, somewhat larger than a pea, red or black with tough skin and strong bitter taste. Black bugs generally inhabited beans …having eaten inside kernels before dying. Will found it almost impossible to eat beans at first, but ravishing hunger soon made it possible. "I much prefer red beans," Daffie said, parsing his dirty finger through beans searching for red ones as if on fishing expedition.

Shaking head in mock indignation, smiling at friend's fantasy, Will said, "Not a one of them is any good."

"Ya' don't say …black critters are my favorite …I save 'em for last." When bacon was available, two ounces a day were rationed …strong, rancid and full of maggots. Soup at Libby came served in a pail, its top surface commonly spotted with floating carcass of numerous black creatures. "Ya' see there …black ones are best," Daffie volunteered, skimming top of soup.

Will befriended Daffie, and Daffie returned the favor …a special relationship developed and strengthened. Officers on their third floor mostly ignored Will, treating him with cold aloof deference, politely ignoring him …not inviting him into their restricted circle. Daffie found no one else willing to take interest either …mostly he was chided and used as butt of crude joke. In unusual sense, both Will and Daffie needed each other.

"You know, Ike, we are outcasts," Will said. "No one wants anything to do with us."

"Ya' see, I kinda' likes it that way, Will," Daffie answered. "Yer' friendship is all that matters to me."

"We are treated better by Rebs than by our own folks …somehow doesn't seem right."

"She's sum-thin' we must accept, ya' know," Daffie offered.

"I guess you are right, Ike," Will continued. "I feel like staying away from the officers anyway ...not bothering them ...don't want them making a fuss with Rebs about how I'm being treated."

"See, my friend ...you and I're meant to be together."

"All I know is without you, Ike ...I would be all alone ...don't think I could get by all alone," Will added. "Talking with you helps keep my mind together."

"Helps pass time too, ya' know."

"Yes, but it's more than passing time ...you're a smart man ...our talking reinforces my desire to continue ...to survive our ordeal at Libby."

"Me too, ya' know."

Time passed somehow. Eight months lapsed since that late September day when private Will Hodkins, captured Federal officers, and other prisoners and wounded Union soldiers were loaded onto rail cars in Ringgold for their journey to Richmond. It was now first day of May, 1864 ...long awful months into captivity at Libby Prison. Will leaned back propping himself against cold damp wall outside in prison courtyard, seated with legs crossed, contemplating what transpired. Time moved so slowly in Libby. Memories sustained him. He squirmed against the wall rubbing his back for circulation ...muscles and bones aching, particularly his left side which constantly gave reminder of past wounds.

Thoughts were drifting crazy for some time ...he lost track of just how long. Gathering consciousness, he reached into breast pocket and removed the journal ...now becoming well worn and tattered from heavy use, especially since capture. Torn pages removed from its binding reminded Will of many letters written to Maria. Over and over again he replayed life with Maria and courtship in Penn Yan, moving to parent's Oxford farm he held dear, and then children adding such pleasure and deeper meaning. "Within Libby this trusty book is my life-saver," he voiced aloud. "Entering thoughts and records of events helps pass time ...it buoys my sanity." Opening its cover tenderly, he removed ambrotype of Maria, sadness growing …her likeness held his glassy gaze for long moments. Then he kissed her likeness lightly, before returning precious picture to its secure location at journal's front.

He pulled dull nub of pencil from trouser pocket, and scratched out an entry.

May 1st, 1864
Libby Prison

Rebel politicians came today to see us Yanks …broad brimmed hats, gold-headed canes, they stared at us with aristocratic toss of head. Band accompanied them playing "Bonnie Blue Flag", which drew hisses and groans from prisoners. Prisoners answered with a chorus of "Yankee Doodle", much to Reb's displeasure.

More prisoners being moved each day to Andersonville… Rumors abound that Yank officers will be sent to Charleston to be placed under fire of Federal guns shelling besieged city.

Will began thumbing through tattered pages, reading past writings, reliving dreadful experiences of the last eight months …becoming lost in thought.

267

...prisoners, ragged and dirty, very thinly clad. Huddled together, forming motley crew that imagination scarce depicts.

...prisoners roll in dirt as hog wallows in mire.

...dream at night of something good to eat ...hungry always.

...guards steal clothing that arrives. Most guards dressed in parts of Yankee uniforms.

Will glanced upward, concentration broken, startled by commotion from a small crowd of prisoner's bartering for trade ...tobacco for hardtack, hardtack for tobacco. He surveyed others nearby gambling at cards, keno, sweat cloth and other games ...gambling for money or food. Two men in one corner engaged in an intense game of checkers. Makeup game of foot ball was underway in the small fenced exercise area at rear of prison yard. Some walked perimeter walls of prison enclosure. Will confirmed all routine, another day at Libby ...lowered head and returned to reading. Weeks earlier, he ran out of pages in the journal but obtained additional paper from a Sutler visiting prison. He used money received hidden in care packages mailed from Maria ...money concealed ingeniously by Maria, sewn into linings of articles of clothing. Now, he read from loose pages wedged between journal's cover.

...very cold, and men suffer terribly. Generally one blanket shared by three men, great many entirely without ...officers have it better. Not issued any wood, but allowed to go out in squads to gather scrap wood, but none cut down.

...drink no water until boiled, exercise as best I can, trying to keep clean and free of vermin but without luck.

...received a spoonful of salt today—first time!

...work outside from 9:00 AM, and return at 4:00 PM. Stood up today in drizzling rain.

Will looked away, brushing back tears welling ...choking with emotion ...personal plight poor, feeling sorry for himself but agonizing for Maria and children, alone without his help. From around corner appeared Daffie, awkwardly shuffling with crutches. "Will, you're look-in' like world's not treat-in' you right."

Will stammered, embarrassed by lack of composure, "Guess I'm feeling bad for myself ...thinking about home ...feel helpless, I reckon."

"Mind if I sit down with ya' ...ya'll have to help me get back up, I'm suppose-in'," Daffie said while smiling at his own immobile predicament.

"Sure enough, Ike." Will hoisted himself up to assist Daffie. With both down and leaning against the wall, Will continued. "I daydreamed about home, and what I missed."

"Go ahead, partner …talk to me, ya' know."

"I remembered lying on hospital cot October 23rd, knowing it was Will, Jr.'s fourth birthday …Walter nearly 2 ½ years old …boys too young to understand why Father is not home with them," Will confided to Daffie.

"They must be changing so much," Daffie interjected.

"Yes, and baby Minnetta is eleven months old now …I spend so much time picturing how she might look."

"…important for us to make it out of this here 'hell-hole' and get back home."

"Ike, tell me more about your life back home," Will said. At Will's urging, Daffie talked at length about his life back in Indiana. Talking together helped both men regain balance.

"Ike, I miss my friends," Will continued after Daffie completed his story.

"I never had friends …friends are good," Daffie answered, tilting head sideways as it bobbed up and down nervously.

"Friends are good, but losing friends is awful," Will replied. "I have lost seven friends …I feel so alone …you are my only friend, Ike."

"Ya' don't say!" That said, Daffie moved to get back up and Will rose to assist. Daffie regained control of crutches and ambled away, leaving Will alone with thoughts. Will settled back down against the wall, journal reopened. He regained composure and continued reading.

…Rebels say it has never been so cold. James River nearly frozen. Men limping with frozen feet, crying like children in the night. Suffering terrible!

...*received letter from home today!*

...*rations getting smaller. Rebels say it is either exchange prisoners, or starve with us, as they have no food for us. With scarcity of food, rats and mice have mostly disappeared.*

...*read "Richmond Enquirer" newspaper which spoke of bread riots in city, women yelling 'Peace or bread!"*

...*sick with scurvy and diarrhea* ...*troubled with the itch spreading through Libby.*

Turning pages, Will read further.

...*Rebels all drunk. Received extra wood today. Great cheering, yelling, and shaking hands, congratulating one another, as rumor spreads that prisoner exchange is about to happen. Five hundred taken out!*

...*prisoner buys a dozen apples, and all are treated. New prisoner*

271

captured in Tennessee tells us War news.

War enters its fourth year with no end insight. Eastern armies are lying quiet in Virginia ...one starving, other dormant. In the West, Ulysses S. Grant replaces Rosecrans in Chattanooga. Meanwhile, political battles over exchange of prisoners continue. But, in Richmond's Libby Prison, Will writes:

...raw rice and corn bread issued today. "Richmond Enquirer" says 500 left Belle Isle Prison yesterday and arrived Washington (others think to Georgia Andersonville).

Will paused, brushed at long shaggy unruly hair, stroking rough stubble of beard ...he shaved two days ago, but dull 'community' razor left beard coarse scraggy and unnatural. He could not get used to being dirty and unshaven. Grunting disapproval, he turned attention back to the journal and skimmed entries.

...some ladies visited to see us 'Blue Coats' ...laughed at our condition, thinking it comical how prisoners crowded together, compared us to wild men and dirty hungry dogs.

...large shell fired over prison which scared us today.

...all troubled with heartburn and sour stomach today. Drink weak lye made from ashes for it.

...lice getting upper hand ...ground covered with them.

...Holy Sabbath Day ...church bells ringing in city for morning service. Don't think we'll attend this morning! It is such a long walk, and we look so bad!!

Will chuckled reading last entry ..."*truly amazing how human spirit musters humor under bleak conditions ...all history now ...eight months passed in Libby Prison.*"

As May 1864 lapsed, War resumed on several fronts. Grant and Lee faced off at Spotsylvania Court House in Virginia. It was Grant's move. Lee could not afford to attack a larger Union Army and hope to survive. In Georgia, Sherman was trying to find a way around Johnston.

In Charleston, South Carolina, Federal Major General Gillmore bombarded the city daily, trying to force Confederate General Beauregard's surrender of Morris Island and Fort Sumter. Shells were lobbed into heart of city over nine months, all hours day and night, causing widespread panic and devastation. Confederate Major General Samuel Jones, in command of prisoners at Charleston, requested six hundred Union prisoners and fifty Federal officers of rank relocated to Charleston to be placed under fire of Federal guns ...an effort to shield and discourage Federal bombardment.

Will was not privy to any of this. It appeared just an ordinary day at Libby when prisoners on the third floor were ordered to fall into line. Will moved to a rearmost spot in lines of assembling captured Union officers. Daffie shuffled forward, swinging and dragging stiff right leg, wood crutches thumping on heart pine floor, as he moved toward a spot aside Will. Will turned to see Daffie laboring toward him, and made room in line for his friend. Will anticipated nothing out of ordinary, probably routine announcement from hulking Confederate officer poised and waiting before their gaunt and haggard band of captives. Will and Daffie stood casual and unassuming, thinking nothing of gathering's importance. Sun streaked through iron-grated window this Sunday morning, glass imperfection splitting sun's rays into vast dispersion of color …like spectacular rainbow after fierce storm …its brilliance causing Will to squint eyeing the stoic Reb officer.

Confederate officer began to speak in droning monotone, "…a handful of officers will be leaving Libby for transfer to Charleston." Will listened intently, interested but not as someone directly affected …he was not an officer. Names were called …one by one, tension and excitement building among prisoners. Out of the blue …"William Hodkins" was called. Will stood stunned, frozen …as if sound of name echoed surreally from faraway canyon walls, far removed from reality. Yet, it was real …Confederates were continuing to honor the 'gentleman's agreement' struck by Colonel Le Favour. Daffie dropped crutches instinctively, hobbling on one leg, arms outstretched to embrace Will in celebration of friend's good fortune …sound of crutches crashing loudly on wood floor jarring Will's thought, causing all heads to turn their way. Will put hands to face, instantly sobbing and shaking beyond control …steadied only by Daffie's bear hug, both breathless and overcome by emotion. "I am so happy for you, my friend," Daffie gushed.

Catching semblance of control, Will answered, "I am happy to leave Libby …not happy to leave Ike."

"Ya' don't say."

Chapter 27

Late morning Friday July 29th, a train carrying Will and fellow prisoners from Libby pulled into rail station in Charleston, South Carolina. Fourteen years passed since Will's last visit to Charleston as a young boy of twelve years, wide-eyed and awestruck by the city's charms ...so much now changed. Will 'celebrated' a 26th birthday in February, a prisoner in Libby ...beaten and worn, feeling much older than his years. Euphoria and hopefulness upon news of leaving Libby were dashed abruptly by hours of agony in overloaded rail car ...hapless men crushed together as animals, panting for air like dogs after the chase. Hours upon hours passed grudgingly with little movement among men, each sweating profusely from heat and humidity as their train inched its way south through parched Carolina midlands heading toward lowcountry.

Their train ground to a halt at the depot, huge iron wheels screeching as brakes grabbed ...locomotive's shrill wailing whistle signaling arrival. Will and others were ordered out of smelly, filthy rail boxcars ...men clamoring for open door, desperately seeking breath of fresh air. Will jumped out landing on ground harshly, muscles less than limber ...huge oversized Libby-issued shoes plopping awkwardly, causing a lurch off-balance sideway before regaining balance ...sharp twinge of pain in left side incessant reminder of past injuries. Stifling July mid-day heat and clammy dank humid air hit face like a hot sponge.

Local men and women crowded about the train station to catch glimpse of 'Yankee prisoners' ...many colored folk with heads bowed, hesitant to look directly upon the Yankees.

Charleston society women and men also gathered in groups, dressed in once elegant attire though now disheveled, showing unkempt wrinkles and tatters. They looked askance upon haggard prisoners, displaying countenance of arrogant disdain. Will made mental note, "...*their comeuppance will be well deserved.*" He looked upward across a street to an elegant mansion where a handsomely dressed lady threw open a third floor window and unfurled the hated Rebel flag. She waved the flag energetically in figure eights, a mocking gesture toward gaze of despondent prisoners from the North ...the flag a detestable emblem of Confederacy adding insult to their misery. Will reacted without thinking, thrusting right clenched fist into air in haughty defiance of her gesture. In a split second, Will felt a Reb's rifle butt crashing into his right shoulder, causing him to spin about and grimace from pain. "We'll have none of that, Yank."

Recovering, Will answered, "Yes, sir." Reb nodded and turned away, Will thinking, "...*that was not very smart ...I will not do that again.*"

Prisoners were ordered to form a line. Confusion and delay took time. Meanwhile they stood unsheltered under sun's intense heat, sweat streaked dirty grimy faces of distressed uncomfortable prisoners awaiting destiny with parched mouths and throats. "Could we have some water?" Will implored a Reb officer.

"If ya' keep flap-in' yer' mouth, Yank, ya'all be swallow-in' a heap of no-see-ums ...lot's of sand gnats in these parts, ya' know ...shut-er' up now!"

"Yes, sir," Will answered, learning acquiescence from prior incident.

Their march began about noon. Will and other captives began walking down dusty cobblestone street under escort of a company of Rebels from the City Battalion. A few Negro vendors sat street side with meager few vegetables to sell. Will caught the eye of one gray-haired old man, and nodded 'good day' ...the Negro looked kindly upon Will and returned a guarded smile. A smattering of Irish and German women looked with pity upon gaunt forlorn straggling prisoners, overheated and trudging with shoulders slumped and faces distraught. As beleaguered marching contingent turned onto Coming Street, heading south and east, scorching afternoon sun and sickening humidity caused legs to wobble. Will tripped over upstanding edge of cobblestone, large shoes betraying him once again. He regained footing as head danced and eyes blurred. Nearly feinting from heat exhaustion, he swiped burning salty sweat from eyes. As heat-struck stumbling procession made its way deeper into once thriving heart of city, Will witnessed a city now in ruin. Storefronts were mostly boarded and closed ...rubble everywhere. Grass stood rank, weeds growing haphazardly in streets, food for a few unfettered cows grazing untended, even a loathsome roaming pig. Few non-uniformed men could be seen, save for an old man here or there ...others were Rebel soldiers conversing in groups of small number. A few Rebel officers gallivanted on street corner with several southern ladies dressed with broad-brimmed straw hats and once elegant colorful satin full-length dresses, though now appearing stained and unkempt. Society ladies peered from under parasols partially shielding pale white faces from scorching sun ...gazing upon passing Yankee prisoners with defiant taunting stare, transfixed as if children looking upon captive animals in Barnum's Circus.

Will heard distant fire from Union guns. At one point a shell whistled past and exploded in air just overhead, so close that Will and others ducked instinctively. For nearly two miles, the lethargic contingent walked, past Boundary Street, toward City Jail located near the corner of Broad Street. Here a handful of captive Union officers, including Colonel Le Favour, were singled out and herded off toward a residence house on Broad Street which would serve for their confinement. Will and remainder of fellow captives were not so fortunate. At the corner of Magazine and Franklin Streets, they arrived at confines of City Jail yard, grand receptacle and 'holding area' for most Federal prisoners arriving in Charleston. Will stared upward at an ominous four-story structure, peering out and over high clay-colored stucco walls. As weary group waited for entry, a Rebel guard from the City Battalion boasted of City Jail's checkered past. Will and others within earshot listened as he jabbered like a tour guide. "She was built in early 1800's, atop ground once a potter's field before Revolutionary War," the guard said. "She was community cemetery for city's indigents and criminals." He droned on, "After powder magazine replaced cemetery, British Redcoats forced captured Continental soldiers to toss muskets inside, and a musket discharged causing horrific explosion that blew body parts into sky, raining down five blocks away onto steeple of St. Philip's Church." Will cringed at blabbering story pouring from mouth of talkative Reb. "This here jail housed some of city's most notorious villains ...yes sir, last of Charleston's pirates stayed here, before they met the hangman. Why, some folks are even now see-in' ghosts ...but she'll be your home for awhile now, Yanks."

Goose bumps coursed up Will's neck as he stared upward at worn brick walls, peering from beneath areas of decayed and chipped stucco, as if partially revealing structure's sinister heart and dark secrets. Iron-barred windows, decaying parapets and yawning archways with massive locked wrought iron gates all added to chilling aura of hulking structure. Once inside imposing walls, its jail yard appeared the nastiest, filthiest, dirtiest place Will ever 'visited' ..."*perhaps worse than Libby*," he thought. Jail yard embraced about an acre, enclosed by twelve-foot high stucco walls. A tower about forty feet high rose from center of building's octagon-shaped area where worst criminals were confined in cells. Will's despondency grew. From elation at leaving Libby, emotion crashed. Instead of relocation to Charleston generating hope, he now felt hopeless ...beaten, ready to succumb. He slumped to ground, propping against exterior stucco wall. Exhaustion and despair consumed every fiber of body and mind. "I am alone again ...no friend, no Ike to support me." Sleep overtook exhaustion.

He awoke at sunrise next morning to discover ground of jail yard covered with lice. Head slumped forward against drawn-up knees, despondency all consuming. Minutes passed. Then head rose slowly, Will gathering thought. He spit on fingers to rub some grime away, before wiping saliva onto a filthy shirt. With large sigh, he pulled journal from breast pocket and removed the ambrotype, studying Maria's image longingly. He stroked Maria's image ever so gently ...slowly, with two fingers ...as if she were there and he could touch her skin. Her image rejuvenated him. He kissed the image lightly before carefully replacing it within cover of journal. Will made a pledge aloud, "*I may be treated like an animal ...but I will not become an animal."* Momentarily reinvigorated and recommitted, he could turn to task at hand. One-by-one, Will spotted and killed, then removed lice from his shirt. He spent an hour removing dastardly vile creatures from clothing ...clothing reeking and so offensive that Will flinched and gagged from its putrid smell. Counting out loud as each critter met its fate, zany undertaking becoming a game. "Forty-eight ...another dead bugger," he said, chuckling at small pleasure ...killing creatures, killing time. "Forty-nine ...Fifty," he counted.

Second night it rained. Will located a board from a junk pile of debris within the yard. Scrap board proved handy, propping it up ingeniously so he could sleep above puddles of rainwater. A majority of fellow captives were less fortunate, men trying to find sleep amid slush and mud ...most without shelter. Next morning, Rebel guards brought 'A' tents, issuing sixteen tents for ninety-six men. Tents were arranged in rows, after first cutting them open so they could be spread wider and cover up to six men. No food was provided their first forty-eight hours. When rations were finally issued, they were meant to last for ten days, but sufficient only for five days. Will inspected their allotment of cornmeal, rice, and black beans or 'cow peas', none edible except to starving disconsolate prisoners ...food no better than Libby. Each squad of one hundred men was issued a single large sixteen gallon iron pot for washing purposes, a few tin twelve quart kettles or pails for cooking, small iron skillets for baking bread, several six quart tin pans for mixing meal, and four wood buckets for drinking water ...all shared by their hundred-man 'community'.

Two weeks passed as Will endured life outdoors in miserable jail yard. Rebels 'softened' arriving prisoners in the jail yard 'holding area' ...several weeks in this hell-hole softened the most diehard. After several week vile ordeal, Rebels offered better quarters to any who would take 'parole', pledging not to escape or hold communication with anyone outside of guarded location. Will's stellar record of service within hospital quarters at Libby qualified him as candidate for similar duties at Roper Hospital. When offered, Will contemplated opportunity to get out of the filthy overcrowded jail yard. "...signing Reb pledge goes against honor and duty, I reckon ...but, need to survive ...hospital duty not so bad, at least I can help other prisoners," he pondered. Reb officer pushed papers toward Will. Will paused, then signed parole paperwork joining fifty others ordered to Roper Hospital.

Charleston, SC – Meeting Street in Ruin

(Library of Congress)

Charleston, SC – Rubble everywhere

(Library of Congress)

Charleston, SC – Debris and
Devastation

(Library of Congress)

Charleston, SC – St. Michael's Church
Meeting Street

(Library of Congress)

Charleston, SC – Exchange Building
East Bay Street

(Library of Congress)

Charleston, SC – Mills House Hotel
Meeting Street

(Library of Congress)

Charleston, SC – Broad Street Officer's House

(Library of Congress)

Colonel Le Favour and captured Union Officers

(Library of Congress)

Chapter 28

Will marched away from City Jail amid a contingent of prisoners, along Coming Street heading north for four or five blocks on same route walked upon arrival in Charleston two weeks earlier. At Boundary Street, paroled prisoners turned left and headed west several blocks. Roper Hospital stood obliquely before them ...looming structure framed as backdrop against tree-lined street of blooming pink and violet crepe myrtle and majestic magnolia with remnants of spent huge white blossoms still clinging from massive tree branches. A grand building located at street corner rose in imposing fashion from behind low thinly-picketed black wrought iron fence.

Charleston, SC – Roper Hospital

Captive group waited street side. Will marveled at a magnificent edifice, strength and beauty of architectural detail ...structure untouched by Union shelling of the city. Built of brick, plastered over and marked with etchings, it gave appearance of elegant old brown stone. Size massive, it covered a city block. Will guessed the main building to be eighty feet at its front by sixty feet deep, rising four stories. Long building wings to east and west reached three stories high. On corners and at its center, towers extended fifteen to twenty feet above roof line ...six decorative arches extending as cover for porticos running between each rising tower. Grounds at front of building were laid out tastefully and filled with a myriad of colorful flowers and finely pruned shrubbery. No one could help but stand in awe of Roper's grandeur.

Will and other prisoners followed their guards to a huge trough out back, filled with water. Guards forced prisoners one by one to strip clothing and bathe in water which soon became filthy. "We want ya'all 'clean' now, boys ...no body lice in the facility ...ya'all understand," one guard kept shouting. But, naked bathers redressed in their same dirty creature-infested clothing. 'Bathing' embarrassment over, guards herded Will and other prisoners inside. A guard announced, "Ya'all will be working, attending patients, cleaning and doing whatever odd jobs assigned."

Inside Roper, within each wing and on each floor, three large rooms or wards contained long rows of hospital beds filled with patients. Main part of building had smaller rooms for dispensary, staff offices, living rooms, storage areas and support functions. Entire building was lighted by a central system of piped gas-burning fixtures, something revolutionary and never experienced by Will before. Though lighting appeared dim and of poor quality, Will marveled at such a new-fangled system. Lead guard explained proudly, "Ya'all be permitted to use lamps till nine o'clock each evening ...then lights out, ya' he're."

Will settled quickly into work routine within confines and grounds of Roper Hospital, changing bedpans, dispensing soiled bed linens and bandages, mopping floors, fetching brackish water drawn from three old cisterns out back, or going under guard to draw water from a street pump. Within a few days of arrival and while working, Will thought he recognized an old Irishman ...a neighbor of Will's from down the road in Oxford, who moved away several years ago to live in Pontiac. Will ambled up behind a rosy cheeked, well-built fellow prisoner with muscles rippling as he worked with a shovel, and asked, "What regiment, friend?"

A reticent man answered curtly, brogue dialect resonating, "23rd Indiana, mate." With indifference, he cast casual glance over a shoulder in direction of Will's questioning voice but turned away abruptly to continue digging. Will shrugged, turning back to work cleaning debris from rear yard, thinking he made a mistake. Moments passed, when brusque Irishman called over toward Will, "Ay', ain't you Will Hodkins?"

"Yes ...that you, Clancy?"

"Lad, ya' got that right," ...turned out to be Clancy Durnin. Clancy walked hurriedly toward Will toting shovel in hand. Will smiled and extended a hand to Clancy. They shook hands firmly, then bear-hugged, both happy to find someone known. They began talking. Five years passed since last seeing each other. Clancy was fifteen or more years older than Will, being one of the older prisoners. Hair sprawled long and unkempt ...snarled, knotted and dirty, like most prisoners. Will noticed salt and pepper graying to once jet black locks. Bushy eyebrows graying also, full mustache accentuated sharply chiseled high cheek bones and strong protruding jaw. Dark hazel eyes glistened as the two reminisced.

"You have taken good care of yourself, Clancy ...still strong as a bull, despite being guest of the Rebs," Will observed.

"Aye', back must slave to feed the belly, lad." Will and Clancy were never close friends ...mere friendly acquaintances in Oxford who spent time together on occasion at Paddy's pub over a pint or two of beer ...sometimes Irish whiskey for Clancy. Never married, Clancy remained outgoing, at times rambunctious ...a tough and hardy character, lean and lithe, muscular and strong ...carrying broad shoulders proudly on tall six-foot frame. He tired of farming and moved to city-life of Pontiac some five years earlier, but maintained a finely tuned physique by working as blacksmith in a livery in the city. He enlisted with an Indiana regiment after War broke out ...captured 1st day of July at

Gettysburg over a year ago. "Now I'm older, thinner, tired and drawn ...like most 'guests' of the Confederacy, ma' friend," Clancy added.

"You look fit and relatively healthy, I reckon," Will responded. Will was elated to find a past acquaintance from Oxford ...linkage to home. "But, looks like we could both use an hour or two at Paddy's pub."

"Aye', mate ...I'd step over ten naked women to get a pint right now," Clancy answered with wink and nod.

"I watched you down quite a few."

"That's no blarney ...whiskey was invented so Irish would not rule the world, ya' know," Clancy replied. From that day, Will developed a growing friendship with Clancy, spending idle time together ...reminiscing about their past in Oxford and soldiering experience that reunited them at Roper ...each man desperately longing to get back home.

Prisoners were permitted freedom of the yard, but Will found Roper's backyard filthy and unhealthy ...policing neglected, filth piling up two to three days at a time until stench overwhelmed. But more unpleasant was their latrine sink ...allowed to fill up and run over, pools of polluted sewer water standing in their backyard ...making matters worse, a backyard where prisoners did their cooking. Utensils for cooking were scarce, whatever Will and fellow prisoners could find around the building, or buy or steal from Rebel guards. Prisoners were fortunate to have service of one fellow, coppersmith by trade and formerly from Rochester, before joining the Union Army as a Lieutenant in the 49th New York Volunteers. He succeeded in obtaining a few old tools, some discarded stove pipe, and pieces of scrap iron. Clancy volunteered to assist by using blacksmith skill. Plying their craft and ingenuity, two men fashioned several kettles, frying pans, and dishes from castaway material. Pieces of iron served as griddles to fry pancakes. "Boys, a handful of skill ...she's better than a bagful of gold," Clancy quipped to fellow prisoners. Others pitched in to build several crude brick ovens to bake bread.

Rations were in small quantity and poor quality. Every ten days, each prisoner was issued three pints of flour, two quarts of cornmeal, two quarts of rice, three pints of black beans, and two ounces of rancid bacon ...black bugs inhabiting most portions, dead or alive. To supplement scanty rations, authorities allowed prisoners to purchase vegetables and fruits from local market women who conducted transactions through wrought iron fencing at sidewalk. Will and Clancy partnered to cook and take meals together. Daily conversation around meals strengthened their growing bond. "Did you know Johnny Predmore and Junior Webb ...both boys from Oxford?" Will asked Clancy.

"Can't say as I did, laddie."

"We joined the army together. Johnny died of fever in winter camp in Kentucky. Junior was captured with me on the 'Horseshoe' ...Junior is a little older, with a bit of 'devil' in him ...spoiled a tad because he lived on his mother and father's farm, youngest of six children. Haven't heard anything about him," Will rambled, as dinner of cornmeal cakes fried over fire.

"May the wind be at his back," Clancy offered.

"Cakes smell good ...you're a good cook, Clancy ...reminds me of Papa ...Papa and I did most cooking for all our boys."

"Lad, sounds like you're a-miss-in' em' a good deal."

"That I am. Feel empty without them ...can't get over feeling responsible ...should be with them to help," Will continued.

"Come now, lad ...time to eat ...ya' say little, but say it well, my friend."

Meanwhile, long days wore on. Will spent non-working leisure hours reading **Charleston Mercury** or **New York Herald** newspapers ...Rebel authorities allowed Will and other prisoners working in Roper as many papers as chosen by paying 25¢ each. Maria sent editions of **Atlantic Monthly** magazine in regular 'care' packages. Will enjoyed the best of mail facilities ...it helped pass time. Will wrote often to Maria, and received Maria's regular letters informing of happenings back home. He smiled broadly ...proudly ...reading of baby Minnetta:

...Will, I must describe a dear scene for you. I was holding Minnetta by outstretched arms, steadying her standing. Ezra reached arms toward Minnetta, coaxing her to come to him. Minnetta took two steps toward Ezra ...her first steps! Nettie, Ezra, and I were so amazed and happy ...Minnetta beamed with pride in her accomplishment. I do not know what I would do without Ezra and Nettie to share these moments. I feel so badly for you ...missing this time with our children.

Now, Minnetta is sixteen months ...she is toddling about all over. I cannot keep up with her ...she gets into such mischief...

How he wished he could see Minnetta. He shared the letter with Clancy. "Aye', distant hills look green, lad," Clancy offered.

"Clancy, I feel both happy and sad ...happy my family is doing alright, but sad I am not a part of it."

"Irish have a saying, my boy ...bricks and mortar make a house, but children's laughter makes a home," Clancy quipped.

"Sounds like Irish have that right," Will answered.

"If you're lucky enough to be Irish ...you're lucky enough."

In one letter, Will wrote to Maria of life in Roper:

September 18th 1864
Sunday Evening

My dearest Maria:

Another lead pencil worn down to less than one inch ...I skirmished around for another, and trust this legible. I enjoyed a chance to bathe in a public bathhouse near Roper, with real soap, definite improvement on a 'sand' bath. Seems boarding with the Confederacy does not agree with me!

I received the new white cotton shirt sent in your package, and it pleases me no end. I used the 'Yankee script' you sent to purchase sweet potatoes, tomatoes, and rice from ever present Negro ladies ...they are always kind, and help us live in some little comfort. Three or four times Negro servants have come from houses nearby with water, milk, and food.

I realized last week that end-August I passed my second year anniversary since enlistment in Pontiac, but 'celebrated' in captivity. This evening I am listening to the bells of St. Michael's Church ringing, and I imagined being in Penn Yan during our courtship, gazing with you in my arms on spires of the old church in center of town. I miss you so much!!!

Rumors abound, and we watch, wait, and hope for prisoner exchange, but nothing happens. Shelling of the city makes it impossible to sleep. I lie awake thinking of you. Kiss and hug our children for me, until I get home.

With all my love,
Will

Will thought of little but getting back to Maria and family …thoughts all consuming …"*if only a prisoner exchange, or better yet an end to this God-awful War.*" And, he thought often about his 'family' of soldier-buddies, "*What happened to Junior and Jeremiah? And Papa? ...did Nathan get him medical attention? Are Lucius and Jeptha still alive?*" He left them that hellish afternoon on the 'Horseshoe' …not knowing causing anguish tearing inside, needing to know they were alright.

He spoke often to Clancy about Libby friend, Ike Duffie. "They called him 'Daffie' …he always said he was a little looney, light in the brain …but did nothing to change anyone's mind," Will recalled for Clancy. "He and I were exiled alone together …only had each other …we helped each other endure."

"It was difficult leaving Daffie?"

"Yes, very difficult …I fear for his safety …but I had no choice but to leave," Will continued. "I guess I am a lucky one …to be here at Roper …away from Libby."

From a remote window in attic of Roper, Will spent many idle hours whiling away time. It served as getaway spot unknown by others, a solitary place to escape reality …inconspicuous hideaway, safe harbor for Will. Hours passed in this perch, alone in introspection with self. Now he sat legs crossed, gazing longingly down the Ashley River toward Charleston bay and Morris Island …he could see flash of Federal guns on clear evenings. He sat mesmerized in tower perch tracing course of a shell as it burst from gun's mouth, climbing higher and higher until reaching its zenith in night's sky. Then, instants after sighting, thunderous report of huge cannon rumbled, before stark shrill shriek of shell cutting through night air. He watched fascinated, tracing shell's glow, gradually and majestically descending on its arc. Nearer, and still nearer it came …until seemingly right over head, giving out its lightning flash, signaling danger past. Crushing report soon followed. Will listened intently for rattle among brick walls and wood tenements nearby, as its 'greeting' from Union General Gilmore wreaked devastation upon the Holy City.

Weeks passed for Will and Clancy …consumed by ten-hour days of routine work at cleanup duties within confines and grounds of Roper Hospital …endless changing of bedpans, dispensing of soiled bed linens and bandages, and fetching brackish water from cisterns out back. Will worked hard and developed a reputation for diligence among Rebel staff at Roper. One day, Reb Captain Mobly approached Will …Captain Mobly was top officer in charge at Roper. He walked toward Will carrying a pair of black ankle-top boots. "Thought these boots might fit a wee-bit better than those 'boats' ya'all are wear-in'," Captain Mobly said. "Ya' all bin' do-in' a good job here." Friendly Reb extended an arm toward Will, handing over slightly worn boots of smaller size.

"Thank you, Sir," Will answered. "Much obliged, Sir."

"Try 'em on, now."

Will discarded huge worn and dilapidated gunboats worn since issue at Libby. "Much better fit, Sir," Will offered. "My toes no longer feel lonely. Thank you, Sir."

"Ya' betcha." Captain turned and walked away. Will went back to cleanup duties.

On another occasion in early evening, Will was alone, busy mopping wood floor of dimly lit hospital ward ...lost in thought, mind drifting aimlessly, consumed by repetitive tedious task. Arms pushed and sloshed wet mop back and forth across grooves worn deep from years of traffic on soft heart pine flooring. Suddenly, a surreal sense struck Will that someone was watching ...he could feel eyes upon him. Will looked up, eyes fanning across long expanse of room. A uniformed figure lurked far off in dark shadow, partially concealed by one huge round wood column that supported part of the building. Mysterious figure did not move, giving appearance of apparition. Will felt certain phantom figure was watching intently, but he could make out little in way of detail or catch a look at facial features. "...*must be a guard on duty*," Will reasoned, lowering head and returning to mopping chore. Moments later, Will stole a glance up, but mysterious illusive figure vanished.

Upon return to quarters, he spoke with Clancy. "Clancy, what do you make of this?"

"Must've been a guard watching ...wouldn't give it a worry, lad."

"I reckon, but it was dream-like ...almost ghost-like ...think I was hallucinating?"

"Aye', maybe ...I think not ...she was probably real, alright ...must've been a guard watching, alright."

Over next days, concern passed from mind. Will thought no more about the unusual incident until a second occurrence happened in similar manner ten days later. Again, Will was working alone at night in far corner of dimly lit ward, when premonition struck ...someone eavesdropping, set of eyes fixed upon him. Ice cold shiver shot up spine, hair standing on arms. He felt instant clammy coldness, like triggered by ghostly presence near. Will looked up to see once again a phantom figure hidden in shadow ...lurking, face indiscernible ...wearing uniform and mysteriously looking Will's way. Instinctively, feeling self-conscious, Will lowered his glance and resumed task at hand. Once more, illusive ethereal presence disappeared when Will next looked ...vanishing surreptitious like a ghost. Reoccurrence of similar incident haunted Will over the next several days. "Clancy, I cannot put my finger upon what it all means."

Clancy could only shrug. "Aye', mate, a silent mouth is sweet to hear," he muttered, turned and walked away. Will's conundrum went unanswered.

Days later, from high atop Roper's attic window observation perch, Will looked upon 'burnt district' of city ...desolation everywhere. Broken walls of barren ruined mansions and public buildings stood eerie, mere reminder of where prosperity once thrived ...streets and thoroughfares deserted, replaced by tall rank weeds dancing lifeless in faint wind. Little evidence existed of improvements since the 'Great Fire' of 1861, when high winds of a December evening fanned flames that left more than one-third of Charleston in smoking ruin. Making matters worse, pestilence reared an ugly head. Yellow fever broke out in epidemic proportion. Negro ladies selling vegetables at improvised sidewalk market told Will of cases of fever in houses just down block from Roper. Fear of yellow fever plagued Roper through late September. War, storm, and disease punished once proud Charleston with vengeance untold, city's situation deteriorating rapidly. "...seems a curse of God is resting upon Charleston since firing on Fort Sumter," Will murmured softly.

More recent Federal firing upon hapless city continued daily, except when a flag-of-truce boat came into Charleston's harbor. Shells were usually launched in intervals of thirty minute duration. One Saturday afternoon, Will watched from Roper perch as fire broke out in buildings opposite the city workhouse. Union gunners commenced additional firing, shells twice bursting into middle of burning buildings. City's punishment continued unabated, no end in sight.

Then at sunrise Wednesday morning October 5th, 1864, able bodied prisoners were assembled, Will and Clancy among them. Rebel Captain Mobly called out an order. "Be ready to move to Columbia ...the capital ...in an hour, no time to waste," he barked to prisoners. "Ya'all will be better off in Columbia." Will and Clancy eyed each other skeptically and shrugged, questioning looks on both faces ...more likely, Reb's same old story ...offer of improvement often told, seldom realized. Both men stood frozen, caught off-guard, partially stunned by sudden unexpected order. "...perhaps yellow fever?" Will speculated to Clancy.

"Aye', laddie ...or, remove everyone from fire of guns?" Clancy responded. "Better yet, maybe Rebs fear city is about to fall to Union forces ...what's ya' think, mate?"

"...maybe prisoner exchange?" Will ventured hopeful. No one knew, so both moved away to prepare for departure and await fate. Will and Clancy finished breakfast, packed scant belongings, and by 8:00 AM moved down to gather in Roper's front yard with fellow prisoners. Will toted blanket and overcoat, few articles of clothing, and several cooking utensils. He checked to be sure journal safely secure. In courtyard, he purchased a small loaf of bread and some salt from a woman selling street side. Clancy purchased a roasted sweet potato. Amid mayhem, Irish and Negro washerwomen came flocking hurriedly aside wrought iron fence carrying bundles of inmate clothing given to wash only night before ...articles of clothing hastily retrieved from washtubs, wrung out quickly, and now being returned haphazardly. Prisoners jostled to retrieve clothes handed over fence, still wet and unfolded. Will and Clancy hassled among fellow prisoners to reclaim their belongings, when it became clear to Will that his cherished new white cotton shirt sent by Maria was missing ...yet another crushing disappointment.

A rag-tag motley looking group of prisoners crowded together in the courtyard of Roper. Rags containing bundles of belongings were tied at top with scrap pieces of old rope, bundles tied onto stick poles to be borne on men's shoulders. Assorted belongings cluttered ground about men milling, anxiously waiting. Clancy quipped, "Tis' a wonder how she'll all be moved ...need pack mules to get this job done, I reckon."

"Look at all different colors ...blues, grays, reds, whites ...every mixture," Will answered. "...dressed as we are, we look more like inmates of some county poorhouse or insane asylum …certainly not Union soldiers and officers."

"I'll drink to that, my boy," Clancy replied. "On second thought …good as drink is, it ends in thirst."

"Irish sure enough have a way with words," Will chuckled. "…guess we should be happy we're moving out of here."

"Irishman has abiding sense of tragedy, it sustains him through temporary periods of joy." Will could only smile and shake head in amusement at Clancy's undying wit.

Then, gates thrust open and prisoners began their march east along Boundary Street, armed Rebel guards moving along both sides. As they passed Marine Hospital, another one hundred or more prisoners joined their march. After a few blocks, a disparate entourage turned left and north onto King Street, previous bustling high-end trophy street of Charleston mercantile activity. But now streets and shops loomed deserted, tall grass and random weed growing haphazard from crevice of once posh bluestone walks and dusty dirt of seldom-used roadway. Block after block, Will observed closed shops, sometimes abandoned with doors left ajar, revealing scantily filled shelves and empty meager showcases. All serve as pathetic reminder of fruits of secession, city of past grandeur now laid waste by over four hundred days of Federal siege and bombardment. "Not a look I remember from my last visit to Charleston …some fourteen years ago, I reckon," Will muttered under breath to Clancy.

"Aye', looks worse than an Irish pub after a long party," Clancy agreed. Not much more could be said. Will and Clancy lowered heads and kept legs walking.

By ten o'clock, nearly exhausted, four to five hundred marchers reached train depot of the Charleston & Branchville RR, tired and sweat-stained from trudging, shoulders stooped and drooping from toting cumbersome load and weight of belongings in intensely hot morning sun. At depot, Will and Clancy found a train of freight cars waiting. Captives rested through an hour's delay, but not without incident …General Gilmore sent 'greetings' in form of a thirty-pound shell, which struck and burst in explosion in untended field nearby. Spontaneously, Will and Clancy joined fellow Union prisoners in three rounds of hearty cheers. "Here!

Here!" "Here! Here!" "Here! Here!" came cries, Will and Clancy joining throngs thrusting fist-clenched right arms skyward in defiance ...all giving great displeasure to Rebel guards.

Eventually, order came to board boxcars. Cars were old and filthy, used previous to transport coal ...floors covered with coal dust.

Dusty, Dirty Railroad Cars

(Library of Congress)

Rebel guards herded less than eager prisoners toward cars. With pushing and prodding, guards urged reluctant inmates up and into dingy cars. Will and Clancy drifted rearward, lingering, wanting to avoid loading as long as possible. After each of ten boxcars filled to over-capacity with forty to fifty men, seventy-five to one hundred prisoners remained standing rail side ...Will and Clancy among them. Stragglers were ordered to get on top of boxcars, so Will and Clancy climbed rungs of steel ladder on side of boxcar, upward atop last car of the train. Other prisoners distributed themselves in small clusters among cars upfront. Guards positioned themselves mostly inside cars ...very few climbing atop cars.

About noon, train whistle sounded its shrill wailing cry, huge iron wheels groaning and creaking, grabbing for traction on smooth glistening surface of track's rails. Train load of pathetic prisoners rolled out, leaving desolate city behind and heading northwest toward Columbia, soon entering a poor section of desolate South Carolina countryside. Will and Clancy reclined and rested on boxcar's roof, watching scrub palmetto palm and southern pine foliage pass along flat lowcountry terrain, silhouetted against vivid Carolina blue sky and lazy drifting banks of white cumulus clouds. Train's movement gave some relief to sun's rays beating down onto boxcar roof. "Air is fresh, breeze cool," Will offered. "We're lucky to be here, and not inside coal cars."

"That's no blarney, my boy ...like I say, lucky enough to be Irish ...you're lucky enough."

Chapter 29

A string of dingy boxcars inched west toward Branchville, SC, traveling no more than ten miles per hour to avoid derailment. Will and Clancy dozed, relaxed and made small talk, while perched as solitary prisoners atop last rail boxcar just ahead of caboose. A Rebel guarded car's front end, near steps and ladder leading up onto their car. Will and Clancy languished at rearmost end, far removed as possible from their guard. They stayed prone, lulled by rhythmic swaying motion of car rolling on rail as their train weaved its way across low wood trestles made of cypress, traversing a plethora of lowcountry swamps, across silt-choked rivers and canals. It crossed crude dirt roads wending ribbon-like among swamps ...roadways often underwater and inaccessible. At small town stops along the way, small groups of curious local folk gathered to see a trainload of captive 'Yanks'.

Will and Clancy watched mesmerized as sun began to set ...its ball of red and orange fire diving ever faster toward horizon, sky turning vivid casts of pinks and blues accented by massive banks of lazily drifting white cumulus clouds ...good weather omen for their day to follow. Train reached Branchville station where tracks split, left section headed toward Aiken and Augusta on Savannah River, while other track veered right and north toward Orangeburg, St. Matthews, and Columbia.

About 10 o'clock, train crossed blackness of Congaree River ...no stars lighting their way ...no sound, except for repetitive droning 'chug-chug' of thirsty locomotive, rhythmic rocking of boxcars and metallic grinding of iron wheels on rail. One half hour later, their train came to screeching halt at rail side water tank, pitch black night nearly concealing dense woods on either side of roadbed. As locomotive took on water, an exchange of guards took place. Will and Clancy watched …half asleep, heads bobbing and nodding …both men only half aware, as relieved guard moved down ladder and off car's roof. Within moments, replacement guard climbed up ladder, brim of floppy hat appearing first above roofline at car's far end, full image blurred by darkness. He climbed atop boxcar, remaining in shadowy crouch, calling in muffled tone and gesturing wildly with both arms for Will and Clancy to come forward. Will and Clancy could not mistake the drift of his rapid gestures, though it seemed odd. Eyeballing each other with unknowing shrugs, they hoisted themselves up, complying by crawling on all-fours some thirty feet forward. Will led the way. As Will drew within a few paces of their new guard, he reacted instinctively with shock, calling out, "My God, is that you? …my God!"

Guard waved frantically, placing hand and finger to mouth, saying, "Quiet! Quiet!" Clancy stopped motionless, bewildered by rapid unexpected events unfolding.

Lowering voice, regaining a degree of composure, Will blurted softly, "Robert …cousin Robert …is that really you?"

"It is."

And surely it was. Two men crouched together, embracing …as emotional and unexpected a reunion as could be imagined …a uniformed and armed Rebel soldier, arm and arm and bear hugging fiercely a long estranged cousin …a captured Union prisoner. "I am so happy to see you …to find you are alright …Maria and I have been so worried," Will said.

"And you too, cousin Will," Robert replied in hushed voice. "I wish we could take time to catch up on everything ...but time is of the essence, and I have a plan." Robert explained that he watched Will from afar for sometime, since learning of Will's being held in Charleston. "I received a letter from Maria informing me of your capture and movement to Charleston and Roper Hospital."

"Now it all makes sense …the lurking figure, I saw twice peering at me from shadows at Roper." Robert was there, waiting

301

and biding time, hoping for an opportunity to help his cousin. "It was you, Robert ...at Roper ...why didn't you let me know?"

"Everything required that we not be seen together," Robert answered. Robert, a loyal adopted 'Southerner', loved his city of Charleston. An agonizing decision ensued for Robert. He did not want to betray the Confederate cause held dear, but Will was 'family' and Will's safety and wellbeing trumped all other consideration. "Will, you and your friend must leave this train now ...while I can help."

Will crouched breathless alongside Clancy, heart pounding, pulse soaring. He could utter not a word. Dumbfounded and queasy, he looked questioningly at Clancy ...both feeling panic, adrenaline surging, downright fear overtaking them. They listened astonished as Robert explained quickly, in hushed tone, his 'plan for their escape'. Will and Clancy eyed each other skeptically, eyes popping from sockets in awe and utter disbelief. "You will have to move quickly ...before train starts rolling again, in blackness of night ...climb down from this car, lay prone along rail bed," Robert explained. "When I verify all clear, you both dart into woods to conceal escape."

Will reacted spontaneously, "Not without you accompanying us, cousin." He was emphatic. "I'm not going without you, Robert."

Robert did not hesitate. "No. I cannot join you ...my heart is with our cause, though all is going badly."

"...but ...but ...what about your safety, Robert?" Will stammered. "If they learn you aided our escape, you will be hung as traitor!"

"Maybe ...but, it is a risk I must take," Robert replied. "I've given it much thought." Will tried with last passionate plea to change Robert's mind, but to no avail.

Reluctantly accepting that Robert would not budge, Will acquiesced. Everything became a blur, no time for deep thinking, "...*my opportunity for freedom ...perhaps only way to get back home.*" Will needed no further thought. He looked questioningly at Clancy ...each man nodded affirmatively. It was agreed.

Robert called them into action, "Quick, let's get moving." Sensing train mere minutes from rolling, three men scrambled hurriedly down boxcar's ladder ...Robert first, to be sure their way was clear, followed by Will and then Clancy. Sweaty clammy hands grasping slippery rungs of ladder tightly, groping in utter darkness, each man climbed down until one foot reached coupling, before stepping quietly down onto soil. Will sensed a chest about to explode with fear ...cold sweating, he swiped perspiration dripping from forehead. Hunched over, he and Clancy in unison lunged for ground. Noses nearly touching track, two men spread eagled face down horrified with fear, sprawled with half body exposed over end of rail ties, clawing ground from tension. Panic and fear gripped both as never before, knowing that if discovered, other guards would fire ...killing one or both instantly, exposing Robert as accomplice.

Robert moved away to last car, a caboose with rear door and platform, lighted lantern mounted to door's side. Robert climbed onto rear platform, posing as if assuming position of guard, poised with musket at ready. He peered around corner of caboose, looking up the line. Then he called softly to Will and Clancy, lying prone and motionless facedown on rail bed below, "Go. Go now!"

At once, train's whistle blew and iron wheels began to move slowly, while Clancy hoisted himself up, and began scurrying toward dense cover of woods bordering track. Will followed, hunched over, scrambling away. He reached first cover of woods, but hesitated and turned, glancing back. As amber light from train's lantern receded with caboose's movement down rail track, muted image of cousin Robert in uniform, standing on platform musket in hand, etched indelibly in Will's mind. "*...I may never see Robert again.*" Then, Robert waved meekly, bittersweet 'last goodbye'. Will turned to resume fearful flight for cover. He ran and ran ...chest heaving, breathless and panting, pain shooting through injured left leg and left side. In absolute darkness, snarly vine and weed undergrowth combined with uneven terrain made running more difficult. Bobbing and weaving without good vision, stumbling over stumps and downed branches, Will struggled in panic to keep balance. He followed the thrashing sound of Clancy running ahead. Low tree branches and young saplings wacked Will's face and arms, only fear and adrenaline driving him onward. Farther into even denser darker woods, Will called ahead to fugitive companion, "I'm just behind you ...wait, Clancy." Clancy stopped until Will caught him. Both men doubled over with exhaustion, on the verge of vomiting ...needing to pause, regaining breath proved impossible for long minutes. "I could never imagine doing this," Will sputtered, gasping and choking. "We must be crazy."

"Aye', not crazy ...courage is what we need, laddie," Clancy said, choking and coughing, trying to utter words. "...and maybe a little good 'ol Irish luck to boot, I reckon." Will nodded 'yes', and they resumed running.

Two fugitives continued to make their way farther from train roadbed ...deeper into unknown woods, panic their driving force. Two escapees in country unknown, they possessed nothing more than meager general knowledge of its geography ...knowing nothing of woods, swamps, or streams. They simply skedaddled away. After an hour of running pell-mell in absolute fear, sheer exhaustion caused them to pull up winded and cramping. "My eyes are blurrin' and my head is whirlin' ...don't think I can go any further," Will coughed and stammered. No choice existed but to stop, rest, and reason which direction to take. Upon a fallen log, two drained souls sat down to recover energy and gather thought, assess their situation and forge a plan. "Coast is probably little more than one hundred miles east," Will offered.

"...but mate, where do we go from there? ...she's staunch Rebel country."

"I agree, going east or north does not seem a good choice," Will answered. "...on other hand, walking northwest through South Carolina, mountains of North Carolina make a long hard route into Tennessee."

"Aye', ...don't know if we can git' across 'em mountains, alright," Clancy questioned.

"Maybe we can get help along our way," Will offered. "...have to avoid Rebs scouting for runaways."

"Rebs probably know we're missing already ...probably after us now, I reckon."

"Best chance is northwest, across mountains ...find a way back to Union lines in Tennessee," Will suggested.

"Choices not good …but I think I agree with ya' laddie."
After further debate, both agreed, heading northwest their best
chance for survival.

"It will be a long walk home."

"Irish have a saying, lad …two shorten the road."

"Happy we have each other, my friend," Will replied.
"…we cannot wait …have to keep moving."

"Aye', mate …but public roadways or following railroad
tracks is too dangerous," Clancy added. Will nodded agreement.
So next three or four hours they wandered through woods, farm
field and boggy swamp, trudging and sloshing through night's
darkness. Then weather changed, clouds masking any stars to
guide their way. It became clear all sense of direction was lost
…unfit and unprepared for such undertaking, without water or
food, fatigue soon overtook them. Both men abandoned all
belongings while fleeing the boxcar, with no time for thought of
what they would need or could carry …they left with nothing to
sustain them.

"What have we done to each other?" Will sighed dispirited.
"Did we make a mistake?"

"No mistake, mate …we had no choice given opportunity
to flee …our lease on life is short, and that's no blarney."

"I reckon, Clancy," Will agreed. "…we'll just have to trust
our instincts, and follow God's plan, alright?"

"God's help is nearer than the door …Irish say."

They decided to lie down, gather wits with rest, and wait
for daybreak to regain bearings.

Chapter 30

At daybreak Thursday, October 6th, two beleaguered fugitives awoke at sun's first rays. Eyes surveyed to confirm safety and assess surroundings, bodies struggled to crawl out from under low hanging pine bough branches that provided cover last few hours of rest. Bodies rebelled, stiff aching muscles from over exertion during panicked running flight, compounded by dampness from night on ground in sweaty clothing. "We've got to find out where we are," Will said. "Let's get moving." They started early but without success, searching in vain for a road with signage to guide their direction ...greater fatigue a result. Dense virgin woods thick with understory of prickly bramble thicket and briar, coupled with soggy ground and wet footing, caused the duo to slog and trudge tediously step-by-step.

"My feet are so wet ...they feel like lead weights are strapped to my ankles," Clancy blurted.

"Yeah, my legs are aching ...don't think I can move my left leg one more step," Will added. "We should stop now, rest and stay hidden for daylight hours ...we can travel in darkness, it will be safer."

"Ya' got that right, mate," Clancy readily agreed. Two escapees collapsed under large oak tree at edge of swamp ...slumping bodies shutting down, unable to go further. Will's face turned ashen, distress showing clearly. Noticing, Clancy voiced concern, "What's wrong, lad?"

Will touched at breast pocket, much relieved to find beloved journal safely ensconced. "Oh my! ...had not given it a thought until now ...my journal's more important than all lost belongings, Clancy …guess being alongside an Irishman gives me luck too."

"That's no blarney."

"Ya' know, I'm worried, Clancy," Will confessed. "…if cousin Robert writes to Maria, she'll be sick with worry …should've told him not to let her know."

"I reckon she'll do just fine, she knows yer' a strong man, Will Hodkins …besides, you've got much more to worry about here, alright?"

Time passed as both men lounged and recovered. "Remember Lieutenant Parker," Clancy offered, breaking the long silence. "…escaped from prisoner train bound from Savannah to Charleston …recaptured by blood hounds."

Will nodded and grimaced, "Parker, badly torn by dogs …so weak he could scarcely stand from blood loss when he entered Roper Hospital."

"Aye' …died next day from wounds …sacrifice to Southern hospitality, I reckon."

"Hunting parties, and vicious blood hounds, are after us too ...we can be sure of that," Will opined. Nonetheless, they were simply too exhausted to move, and decided to spend remainder of day and night where they were. First day of 'freedom' came to a close.

Friday broke cloudy, and by afternoon rain started making existence miserable, getting steadily heavier as nightfall approached. Will and Clancy moved for shelter under dense cover of wisteria thicket, growing bunched underneath thick cypress stand. Storm turned violent …lightening flashed, thunder cracked. "God snapping a dry stick," Will mused aloud to Clancy. "…that was Mother's explanation of thunder, when I was very young." "*Mother, I miss you,*" Will mumbled under breath.

"She's a fine day for young ducks," Clancy gushed, wide grin lighting face dripping with raindrops. Both men laughed, finding modicum of humor in their dismal plight.

"Listen, Clancy …hear sound of passing train?" Will asked. "We're still near railroad."

"Let's stay under cover of woods, but follow railroad track until a wagon road appears," Clancy suggested. Will agreed. "When storm passes, we can move," Clancy added.

They waited until darkness when rainfall eased, before heading off again in what they judged a northwesterly direction toward Columbia. Moving cautious, creeping hunched over and lurking hidden by cover of woods, rail bed appeared. Following railroad track about five miles, they found a promising dirt wagon road that seemed to run in track's same general direction. "...road will be easier walking ...rutty, muddy road not traveled much ...should be safe in darkness," Will suggested.

"Aye', lad."

Roadway served as pathway, walking on grassy shoulder to avoid muddy center and wagon ruts, following it through night until near morning. A turn of roadway left found an abandoned field roadside, just beyond heavily weed grown timber fence row. "Wait a minute, mate," Clancy said. He spotted a deserted scarecrow standing reluctant sentry on abandoned farm field. Will waited while Clancy hurried off toward forlorn scarecrow. Clancy greeted scarecrow, "Aye', bub ...have-in' a good evening? ...ya' got a hat I'd kinda like to have there." Clancy snatched a floppy brown wide brimmed hat off scarecrow's straw head, and unbuttoned and removed a checked flannel shirt. He returned with bounty to Will, "Scarecrow said she'll not be a problem ...hat'll do a better job of keep-in' rain off my noggin ...we can use an extra shirt when we wash one of ours." Will smiled.

Passing through grassy field, drenched travelers came upon a narrow ledge covered with gravel ...nary a spear of grass penetrating its surface. Clancy suggested, "We should follow this gravel pathway ...still's raining ...leaves less scent than if we stay in grass, should blood hounds be tracking."

"You bet-cha' ...good idea." A rivulet of rainwater percolated through roadside ditch. Sprawling prone on belly, both boys scooped water for desperately needed drink. "Rain has value after all," Will observed after satisfying thirst.

At daylight their trek ended, both thoroughly soaked and chilled from steady rain ...teeth chattering, bodies quivering ...nothing but wet clinging clothing. "I'll try to get a fire going,"

Will suggested. "You find some dry firewood, if you can ...and possibly something to eat."

"...sounds good, my friend." Clancy ventured away.

Will wandered to find two dead sticks, kept dry on pine straw needle bed under cover of briar bush. He peeled dead bark away from the sticks to expose smooth wood. With a large rock placed on ground, he cupped dry pine needles and handful of yellowed dead leaves to form a nest on top of rock. Crouching low, Will placed sticks in palms of hand and started rubbing sticks together furiously to generate friction on bare wood surfaces. Minutes of futile effort left Will exhausted and defeated ...no sparks to light the nest of dry needles and leaves. He tried again ...then again without success. About to give up, one more try resulted in glowing sparks. Excited, Will bent low, cupped hands around miniscule sparks, and blew gently to fan smallest of fire. It worked. A campfire cracked and snapped as Clancy returned toting a few pieces of firewood and armful of ripe ears of corn. Clancy beamed, "My friend, looks like yer' an expert at mak-in' fire."

"I reckon it's my first ever ...she's a miracle alright," Will answered with sheepish smile. Will's honesty brought laughter to both men.

For shelter, they constructed a cover of pine boughs over their heads, before sitting around welcome warmth of campfire. Boots and shoes were removed and placed near campfire to dry. Raw corn was devoured hastily, being so famished ...they attempted to roast and dry a few ears of corn over fire, but with little success. After eating, Will suggested, "How about one of us lay down at a time and get some sleep, while other keeps watch and tends to fire ...we can change after two-hour shifts."

"...good by me, laddie." Here they rested, before rain subsided.

Mid-afternoon Saturday, baying sounds of distant hounds startled Will. It certainly sounded like blood hounds ...too many dogs yelping to suit a Yankee runaway. Will poked Clancy from slumber. "Clancy ...Clancy ...wake up ...a pack of dogs coming our way." Both men scrambled up, agitated and panicked, alarmed and convinced dogs were tracking road they traveled. "Pick a tree to climb in case they come near. We cannot make fresh tracks," Will blurted to Clancy. Simultaneously, Will moved to snuff out campfire, burying last embers with mud scraped with hands, while Clancy clumsily gathered shoes and boots and loose articles of clothing drying near campfire. Two fugitives scurried up crotches of two nearby live oaks, climbing faster than either thought possible. Concealed by dense green foliage and perched precarious on huge overhanging limb, Will spotted a far distant posse barely visible through tree boughs. He signaled to Clancy by pointing furiously ...not uttering a word. Clancy acknowledged sighting with shake of head. Fear gripped Will like a vise ...he could not breathe. Staring bug-eyed and anxious, he watched thinking their end near.

Fortunately, it soon became apparent that agitated dogs lost their scent at the very place where he and Clancy entered gravel path. Yelping dogs circled crazily ...ferocious, frantic, and frenzied ...trying to regain scent. Muted voices of men on horseback could be heard, sound carried by a fortuitous wind blowing away from posse toward Will and Clancy. Horses snorting prancing and circling, men could be seen growing perturbed and impatient with their dogs. After spending minutes in futile frenetic effort, an impatient search party gave up and withdrew, meek and submissive ...much relief to two terrified escapees. "I was about to wet my britches," Clancy reported, after both men climbed down from hiding spot aloft.

"You got that right, my friend ...much too close."

After such near miss, Clancy said, "...can't risk campfire ...reckon we can't reenter wagon road at same point." Will agreed. Getting a head start just before dark, two traveled cautious via brisk walk through woods to bypass road, before returning to roadway. After no more than one half mile walk along road's grassy shoulder, bay of a hound a mere five to six rods to their rear startled them anew. Fear crippled them again, first thought being of returning search party. But looking around, only one dog could be seen, standing off, yelping and barking. Will grabbed a piece of downed pine limb from shoulder roadside and threw it at the dog, causing him to bolt sheepishly back into woods. "Every dog is bold on its own doorstep," Clancy blurted. Looking back further, a few men could be seen bearing lighted pine torch. Breathing deep sighs, Will and Clancy relaxed, satisfied only hunters out with their hunting dog.

Nonetheless, nerves ran ragged. Moving further down road, they came to a lane planted many years previous with now huge live oaks precisely aligned to provide magnificent canopy and accent to entryway, apparently leading into a large plantation. They stood motionless, eyes locked in admiration at entry's grandeur, when startled again by a man's unexpected address. "Good ev'nin', ge'men," a voice said in slow melodic drawl. Looking right off road and down ditch below road's crown, they discovered a colored man standing in murky darkness, eyes transfixed upon them, presence mostly concealed by leafy umbrella of weeping willow tree. He took several steps out from under cover of foliage and stopped.

They responded in unison, "Good evening, Sir." Both started walking on impulse, eyes focused straight ahead, back and shoulders rigid. He did not follow.

Traveling briskly, they walked on adrenaline for several miles without discussion. A fork in roadway presented itself. Will grew edgy, "...I reckon we are getting too close to Columbia."

"Let's go left and west ...away from Columbia," Clancy offered. Will nodded. Not going far, they spotted a campfire burning not far off road. Approaching closer and cautiously, they could distinguish several colored men seated in circle, silhouetted by fire's dancing flames, made vivid by night's utter darkness. Anxious and fearing discovery, Will and Clancy passed quietly, unnoticed ...fear driving them.

"We should avoid Negroes," Will said. "I read almost daily ...Charleston newspapers, boasting of faithfulness of servants to the 'Southern cause' ...reporting frequent capture of 'Yankee prisoners' by servants."

"...that's no blarney ...think yer' right, mate."

A few more miles and nearly daybreak of Sunday morning, they found hiding place for daytime in woods near another large plantation. "Think we should attend Sunday church service today?" Will questioned, chuckling.

"No way, partner …I'm too hungry to make much effort at attend-in' …could eat anything, I reckon." Will went on foray searching for food, but returned empty handed, except for an armful of all too ripe ears of field corn. Famished, both men grimaced as they devoured three or four ears of foul tasting corn. "…she does little to satisfy hunger," Clancy remarked discarding the last ear.

"I'm choking down last kernels …not fit for pigs, and I vowed not to become an animal …but getting desperately close, we are my friend," Will added.

While lying in hiding, in refuge concealed by bramble and thicket, a large flock of wild turkey came along outskirt of woods, pecking ground for food …clumsy fowl waddling and squawking tantalizing closer. Will and Clancy eyed one another silently. Wild, delicious thoughts raced through Will's mind as he pictured scrumptious turkey roasting over spit of fire. He was certain Clancy shared his vision …but, no means to kill even one plump bird. Dream-like vision proved fantasy, a mere fleeting thought …one bird sounded abrupt alarm, sensing boys in hiding. Flock shuffled off quickly, squawking violently in retreat, disappearing deep into woods. Only hunger pang remained.

That evening famished fugitives took bearings by North Star, visible in clear starlit sky. "…are you sure she's North Star?" Will questioned.

"Aye', mate …but would know better, alright …if I knew which way's north," Clancy answered with a smirk. Both men laughed at Clancy's truthful assessment …plight desperate, direction unknown. Leaving road for shortcut across untended field, weary travelers tramped through wet grass and waist high weed, briar and swamp, finally reaching a main road. A roadside directional fingerboard announced eight miles to Columbia …marsh and lowland signaling Congaree River nearby. Further up road and within three miles of Columbia, they sought hiding place and built yet another successful small fire.

Monday morning arrived, October 10th, fifth day of 'freedom' …still nothing eaten except overripe corn. Efforts to secure food failed without success. Number of dogs around each plantation discouraged thorough search and forage about buildings.

Then, stomachs revolted. Will spent most of morning hours doubled over in sheer agony, making unsightly mess at base of an unsuspecting grand oak tree. No way to move away, he gagged, choked and grunted in isolated misery …vomit accompanying severe diarrhea, in unending waves. Dangling tentacles of Spanish moss became handy to wipe away nasty oral and fecal untidiness. During brief moment of relief, Will called to Clancy, "Between vomit and loose bowels …I cannot decide which to attend to first …don't believe I can ever look at a kernel of corn again."

"Stay away, my friend …yer' mak-in' awful mess there, ya' hear …foul-in' air bad, laddie." Clancy kept a distance, but not much better off ...spending hours dealing with severe stomach cramps, unable to move. Strength was giving way for both men. No longer able to tolerate ripe corn because of nausea, crisis loomed.

Mid-day, Will recovered enough to shuffle weak-kneed back to Clancy. "I'm getting closer and closer to acting like an animal …weak one at that …how you do-in', partner?"

"Not so good …my stomach's tight as a knot …doubled over, can't stand up."

"…need to do something different," Will said.

"…cannot go further without something better to eat ...bodies are revolt-in' …we'll be too weak to walk," Clancy concluded.

"We need to take a chance …we need help …I think we must trust the slaves," Will proposed. "It is our only recourse, and last best hope."

"Couldn't agree more …need to put our trust in the big Irishman in the sky," Clancy quipped, trying to laugh despite still wrenching cramps.

Several hours passed with neither man moving. Late afternoon, having recovered partially from ghastly ordeal, Will volunteered to reconnoiter the area surrounding a nearby plantation. He ventured off while Clancy rested. Will spent two hours lying in wait, recuperating and regaining strength, concealed by tall grass along fence row surrounding plantation …building up nerve, hoping for opportunity to approach one of the slaves. It was evidently a large plantation, as he could see thirty or forty shanties that housed field hands, one-room white-washed wood structures aligned in three rows, all neat and clean. Off in distance, Will could see master's residence, red brick imposing structure standing proud in grandeur against horizon, made beautiful by muted rays of last sunshine. With dusk approaching, magnificent live oak trees cast long shadows. In adjacent field of tobacco, a score or more slaves toiled relentless through last hours of daylight. Will took careful note of lay of buildings and best path of approach to slaves' cabins. He gave up and retreated back to Clancy's hiding spot, to await safety of complete darkness before approaching cabins. "Lad, I was worry-in' mighty, alright …you were gone so long," Clancy said upon Will's return.

"…gathering strength lying in weeds, watching …forming a plan …you feeling better, Clancy?"

"Aye', mate."

"You stay behind, Clancy …only one of us in danger that way …besides, two men approaching would be more threatening to slaves," Will suggested. Clancy nodded.

In total darkness, except for light of splendid moon, Will started toward the cabins. Crossing over split rail wood fence, he approached slowly with great caution, inching forward, crouched low and almost crawling …still harboring deep misgivings about wisdom of approaching servants. In moonlight, with campfires lighting background, he saw several slaves sitting on a fence busily engaged in idle conversation. He closed within eight or ten rods, so close as to hear conversation, shielded somewhat by nearest cabin where freshly washed clothing still hung from line stretched between two cabins. Moving stealthily, Will noticed an old white-haired man sitting nearer and apart from others, smoke rising lazily from pipe, attentively listening to group's conversation from afar. Will crept near the man from behind. Laying a hand softly on his shoulder, Will whispered, "Please Sir, come down to the lane, so we can talk." Startled, the wiry old man showed fear, momentarily stunned by unexpected intruder. Will retreated …backpedaling slowly, arms extended outward with open hands and palms up to demonstrate he meant no harm. Obligingly, the man hopped off fence and walked down lane several rods and stopped. Will walked toward him slowly, extending a hand in greeting, "Can I trust you as a friend, Sir?"

Old man paused, full crop of tightly curled snow white hair jutting from under beaten broad-brimmed floppy tattered straw hat, long flowing pure white beard contrasting sharply against dark skin. He withdrew well-worn hand-fashioned corncob pipe from mouth slowly, nodding head he replied, "Yes, sah, I 'spect ya' can."

"Are you friend of Yankees?" Will asked.

Cautiously, old man replied, "Well, sah, I 'spect I'se a friend to most everbody's."

"I trust you will not expose me, Sir?" Will questioned.

"Yes, sah, ya'all 'ken do 'dat," old man answered.

"I am an escaped Yankee prisoner …my friend is hiding in woods a short distance away …we are both very hungry, Sir."

Old man brightened. "I'se a friend of de' Yankees!" He went on, "I's got nuth-in' to eat, but I'se go and brings de' oberseer down …I 'spect he's can give ya'all sum-thin' to eat."

Will blurted excitedly, "Ah, but he's a white man, isn't he?"

"No, sah, we's got a cullud oberseer here, and sah, he's all right."

Will said he would wait there, and the old man turned and shuffled away. Within ten minutes, old man ambled back accompanied by overseer. "My name is Will …my friend Clancy and I …we're both from Michigan."

"Yes, Sir …pleased to meet your acquaintance, Sir …my name is Wade …this here's Otis," the overseer answered.

"We have been five days without food," Will said.

"Yes, Sir, we'se yer' friends," Otis said. "We'se wants to help ya'all."

"We can supply your wants," Wade added. "Meet us again at head of lane …within one hour."

"Yes, Sir. Thank you, gentlemen …God bless you, Sirs," Will responded doffing cap and retreating hastily …anxious to tell Clancy of success.

Will returned to Clancy with new bounce to the step, broad smile lighting face. "Clancy, I met two slaves …but." Will paused without completing the thought. He summarized for Clancy all that transpired. "But ...but, I am still fearful whether or not to risk everything."

"Aye', we should be happy, lad ...I reckon it's our only opportunity," Clancy said.

An hour of waiting passed so slowly, both men silent, lost in contemplation. Two fugitives waited with renewed hope, energized, but mixed with fear and misgivings that all could end badly. "We've no choice, Will ...we must trust 'em."

"I will go."

Agonizing tormented wait over, Will went off alone to designated spot of rendezvous ...reached end of lane and waited with trepidation ...hunched over, hidden in long grass, trembling with fear. Soon, he spotted Otis and Wade heading toward him, toting baskets on arms. Will's spirit soared ...relieved, he breathed a deep sigh, tension suddenly disappearing. "Please come and meet my friend," Will called out, motioning and inviting two new friends to follow. In minutes they reached their hiding place, Clancy springing to feet seeing Will leading and two old Negroes following paces behind. Will stood beside Clancy, while the two slaves kept a distance. "Gentlemen, I want you to meet my friend, Clancy," Will said. "Clancy, this is Wade and Otis, two new friends of mine."

"Pleased to meet new friends ...my name is Clancy."

Otis and Wade acknowledged Clancy's gesture with cautious nod of heads, then both stepped forward. They extended arms outward, each offering a basket to Will and Clancy who stood with buoyant smiles. "Your kindness is much appreciated, kind Sirs," Will responded.

Two escapees voraciously explored content of each artistically woven sweet grass basket, while their two hosts watched, each with broad smile of kindness and look of utter satisfaction. Will removed a gallon ceramic crock from one basket ...filled with boiled rice and fat slices of smoked bacon. Other basket contained bountiful supply of cornbread. Famished fugitives wasted no time. "Please excuse us, gentlemen ...your kindness is overwhelming, but our manners may not be so good," Will said. Supplied with spoons, Will and Clancy attacked their crock of rice and bacon with ravenous abandon ...bacon, smoky old and strong smelling, but to starving men ...delicious. In very short time, crock emptied. Next, they turned to cornbread, devouring each piece with insatiable ferocity. They could have finished it off, but chose wisely to save some for next day. With food, Will could feel new blood course through veins, wasted strength returning with each bite.

Clancy felt the same. "Men are like bagpipes ...not a sound comes to 'em 'til they're full." Clancy opined. Otis and Wade lost some of phrase's meaning, but laughed just the same, though faces looked quizzical. "Sorry, lads ...just an old Irish saying ...reckon you don't know about bagpipes ...sure enough thank you for saving two starv-in' boys."

Meal complete, Will asked Wade for information. Wade was happy to help ...quite intelligent and conversant. Raised near Knoxville, Tennessee, he crossed over the mountains several times, so he could describe the route to Will and Clancy. "Will we find slaves friendly along the way, Sir?" Will questioned.

Wade answered, "You should be safe with field hands, but avoid house servants ...generally sympathetic with their masters." Wade went on to explain that Will and Clancy were five miles from Columbia, but on the wrong road headed north toward Charlotte, NC. He would send one young field hand to guide them back to the right road.

"Gentlemen, your generosity is beyond words ...we cannot thank you enough," Will offered in closing.

"Aye', much obliged, lads," Clancy echoed. Two hospitable hosts waved adieu and headed off to fetch the young guide.

Shortly, the boys spotted a youngster bounding through brush, eager and with no apparent fear. "Ma' name's Sam ...I ain't never met a 'Yankee' ...I considers it a pleasure," Sam said. Beaming, he extended a hand to Will and Clancy.

Will and Clancy shook hands with Sam. "My name is Will ...this is Clancy." Will and Clancy eyed each other. They guessed their 'guide' to be only twelve to fourteen years of age, a good looking young Negro. Tall and lanky, with thin chiseled face and features, Sam walked with energetic bouncy gait. He seemed genuinely pleased and proud to be 'guiding' them. Sam toted a multi-colored clay pitcher with whittled wood stopper sealing contents.

Extending clay pitcher with outstretched arm toward Will, Sam said, "Ain't yah boys thirsty?"

Will eagerly grabbed the vessel and removed its stopper, "We certainly are, young man." He gulped fresh cold spring water so hurriedly that he began to choke.

"Easy ...easy does it, lad," Clancy cautioned, before taking a turn to quench thirst. Clancy emptied the vessel and reached out to return it to Sam.

"Nah, Sir ...ma' gran-poppie Otis says yuz' should keeps it."

"Your grandfather is a kind man," Will responded. "It will be of great value to us."

"I hav's sum-thin' else for ya'all." Sam withdrew two gifts from pockets of britches, extending open hands toward Will and Clancy ...package of wood matches and gleaming bone-handle pocket knife. Sam simply glowed, so gratified to offer such gifts.

"You could not bring us better gifts, Sam ...thank you," Will said.

"Aye', ya' can't know how important for our survival," Clancy seconded.

"I'se show yuz' da' way now." Sam bounded off down road, Will and Clancy scrambling to catch up to their energetic and youthful guide.

A short distance down road, Clancy asked Sam, "Son, any chance to get sweet potatoes?"

"Oh, yes Sir," Sam answered enthusiastically. "Thar's a nice patch jest ahead. When we'se comes to it, I'd be pleased to gets ya' some, Sir." He did just that. Rounding a bend in road, Sam pointed toward field just beyond. "Sweet taters," he exclaimed. He departed roadway, crossing gulley in dead barefoot run, vaulting over split rail fence.

Two smiling escapees took off in cheerful pursuit, though not able to keep pace with Sam. "Yo! Gracious, gracious me!" Clancy whooped. The three dug as many sweet potatoes as could be carried, clawing ground with intensity. First filling a basket given by Wade, next they filled handkerchiefs after removing cornbread which they stuffed into pockets. Spirit soared, buoyed by prospect for success brightening.

After guiding them to correct road for travel, Sam bid fond goodbye, wishing good fortune. Clancy and Will hugged Sam, Will saying, "We will never forget you, Sam ...God be with you, young man ...please give thanks to Wade and Otis." Sam went on his way.

Chapter 31

Will and Clancy now had bounce to their step. Despite bodies and legs aching, renewed energy and focus kept legs moving, step-by-step trudging forward. They trusted in new friends, and new friends rewarded them with undue kindness. "I nearly gave up hope ...before we met Otis, Wade, and Sam," Will said. "...I questioned our decision to leave the train, lost confidence ...allowed weakness of mind."

"Aye', mate," Clancy answered. "Laddie, we've got to stay strong ...it's a long road that has no turns." Will nodded, enjoying Clancy's turn of a phrase.

Finding friends they could trust, they could proceed without loss of time, confident of heading in the right direction. Rejuvenated upbeat travelers put fifteen miles behind them, most ever in one night ...before they stopped at daybreak to hide in woods off roadway, build a small fire and roast sweet potatoes. They rested for an hour or more before hearing tramp of horses approaching. Sound grew louder and louder. Startled, Will and Clancy eyed each other. Anxiety took over, where confidence last resided. ...pulses beating faster and faster ...again fearing search party with hounds. Will signaled, arms motioning, no sound uttered ...Clancy to smother the fire and gather loose articles, while Will moved off toward public road to reconnoiter. Will found protective swale not more than five rods off roadway, its visibility shielded by dense cluster of rhododendron bushes. He sprawled prone face down just below crest of swale, perfectly still in cold sweat ...abject fear causing spit to stick in throat, unable to swallow, almost gagging with stomach threatening vomit.

320

Moments later, gathering courage, he raised head slowly to peer over swale, gazing through rhododendron leaves, underbrush and woods. Will watched a company of Rebel cavalry approaching ...enemy soldiers on horseback, now walking horses slowly. Imbedded face down in dirt, maintaining lowest profile, Will lay motionless, simply quivering. Rebels passed so near he could make out faces and hear muffled casual conversation. But, Rebel riders passed without casting a look in direction of hiding fugitive. With Rebel contingent safely down road, Will scurried back to Clancy. "...yet another close call, Clancy," Will reported.

"Ya' got that right, partner."

As Tuesday evening approached, the fugitive duo resumed a westerly trek, across rolling rural countryside of northern South Carolina. Over their next two days, supply of sweet potatoes dwindled. They stopped at several plantations to bolster provisions ...but found nothing to eat. At the last plantation, one slave directed Will and Clancy to a Colonel Fenner's plantation about five miles up road. Friendly slave told them no white folk were living on plantation now, Colonel and family having fled for safety. A colored overseer would see they had plenty to eat. With good directions, they reached outlying woods of Fenner plantation after midnight. Much fatigued, they decided to rest in hiding until daybreak. About sunrise, Will spotted two slaves coming through woods and walked out to greet them. "I am a friend ...my name is Will ...I am a Yankee ...my friend and I are hungry and ask for something to eat," Will said.

One slave replied, "We's has nuth-in' ...jest go-in' to da' cornfield over yonder ...ober-seer takes wagons thar' ...we's tells ober-seer yuz' hy-ar' now."

Half an hour later, a fine looking colored man of fifty or sixty years of age approached through woods. Will and Clancy sprang up to attract his attention, and he walked forward calling to them, "De' boys done tole me 'dar wuz' some Yankees up hy-ar' ...now, is ya'all Yankees?"

"We are the genuine article, good Sir ...Yankees, thru and thru," Will answered. "My name is Will ...my friend here is Clancy."

"God bless ya'all ...never see'd no Yankees 'fore now ...bless de' Lord," he said. "Folks hy-ar' calls me Mosey ...I's de' ober-seer hy-ar', ya' know." Mosey bubbled with joy and excitement with his good fortune. He asked many questions about progress of the War, prospects for freeing his slaves, and all about 'Mas'ser Lincum'. Mosey heard rumor that Lincoln ordered freedom for all slaves, but he doubted it would ever come to pass. More than an hour passed in questions and answers from Will and Clancy, when sudden thought struck Mosey, "Bless de' Lord ...I's forgots to axe' ya'all if yuz' hads any breakfuss?"

Will explained they had not eaten, eaten little yesterday except for sweet potatoes. "It is nearly forenoon ...we can wait for dinner," Will answered with coy smile. "We have become accustomed to fasting." Will looked toward Clancy for reaction.

Clancy rolled eyes, mocking disbelief, "You can believe that, good Sir!"

Mosey bowed head, nodding to accept Will's request. He replied, "I's go-in' now and brings Uncle Friday up, and den' I's see to yer' dinner. I's got plenty. I's runs dis' plantation, ya' know." Kindly old Mosey left, but returned shortly with another colored man of about same age. He introduced him to Will and Clancy as 'Uncle Friday', assistant overseer. He, like Mosey, expressed unlimited interest and questions regarding the War ...and their chance of securing freedom.

Will and Clancy assured the two old men the Confederacy is wearing down. As conversation drew to a close, Clancy said, "I reckon within a year or two you will be free men."

Hearing this, two slaves went into spontaneous celebration with sheer ecstasy. Will and Clancy stood awestruck as two old men danced a jig, arm-in-arm, whirling each other around. Uncle Friday leaped into air, clicking heels together, exclaiming, "I's an ol' man, but if dis' here war'll give me freedom, I's can s'port me and de' ole' woman yet ...God bless ya'all!"

They talked past noon. Among things discussed, Mosey asked if it were true that "Mas'ser Lincum is a nigger?" When told he is a white man, Mosey said, "Our folks all says dat' he be's a nigger."

"Just a minute," Clancy said. Pulling a lonely crumpled Yankee greenback from pocket, Clancy showed Lincoln's picture to the old men. They studied it for some time, shaking heads in disbelief. Finally, Mosey said, "He's da' looks of's ah' mighty good man."

Then, two slaves turned to leave Will and Clancy, with Uncle Friday saying, "We's git' ya'all some good dinner, ya' know."

Not long passed before the two returned, each bearing a basket. Setting baskets down, they spread a clean tablecloth of homespun cloth upon ground, removed plates from a basket, and meticulously arranged knives, forks, and spoons in orderly arrangement about two settings. Mosey and Uncle Friday beamed, twinkle in their eyes, so pleased and self-satisfied with their gift to Will and Clancy. "Lay ya'all a plate an' set up …I's lets folks he'p thersevs," Mosey urged. Will and Clancy wasted no time, or required further urging. Dinner consisted of a large clay dish of chicken potpie, basket of hot biscuits, butter, syrup, and milk. It was a feast.

Will was fond of chicken potpie. "It's best ever tasted," he exclaimed between voracious gulps.

"Aye', he got that right," Clancy chimed. And, how delicious buttery biscuits topped with maple syrup tasted …their first real meal in seven days. They ate until fully satisfied for the first time since escape. After dinner, many Negro men came from fields to see 'Yankees', and spend remainder of afternoon talking. A number of colored women also came to see the strangers, but would come no closer than four or five rods, despite being assured they would not be harmed. Women brought two clean shirts for Will and Clancy, and took grimy soiled shirts back to be laundered. Before donning fresh shirts, the boys were led to a nearby creek where they bathed in cool clean flowing water, and lathered thoroughly with a bar of soap provided by Uncle Friday. Uncle Friday and Mosey and others stood on creek's bank laughing and slapping knees …thoroughly amused, enjoying a show as Will and Clancy frolicked …splashing each other, pushing and shoving, like youngsters at play in favorite swimming hole.

Slaves urged Will and Clancy to stay a few days, but two grateful men were anxious to push on, wanting to get through mountains before winter's arrival. That evening, Mosey furnished a fresh supply of biscuits and corn bread, and he and Uncle Friday accompanied the boys for two or three miles to start their journey. After giving directions and advice on avoiding danger, two slaves bid good-bye. "God bless ya'all!" "God bless ya'all!"

"Thanks to you kind gentlemen," Clancy called back.

"We will always remember your kindness ...thank you to everyone ...Godspeed," Will shouted, turning back to wave a last 'good-bye'.

Several days passed without further incident. Will and Clancy were becoming anxious to cross the Broad River. They trudged along following river's east bank, but it was getting them too far north ...they needed to move directly west, and soon. Mosey advised not to attempt a river crossing until they reached a point forty-five miles upriver from Columbia, where the Columbia & Spartanburg RR crossed river. Will and Clancy followed Mosey's advice ...he warned, "*...railroad bridge is guarded by Rebels, though a ferry is near the bridge and run by a slave ...perhaps you can take ferry across river at night.*"

An additional night of travel brought them within a mile or so of the bridge ...they guessed. Both suffered greatly from sore feet ...feet blistered and raw from very first night's walking ...suffering constant, adding to fatigue, with appetites proving insatiable. Now thirteen days into their trek, they enjoyed only two substantial meals ...no choice but to make due with corn bread and sweet potatoes, even another attempt at ripe field corn. Thursday evening, October 20th, heading out just after dark as usual, they decided to split forces. Clancy headed off toward nearby plantations in search of food, while Will tried to secure information about a slave in charge of the ferry. As Will approached a road that led in general direction of the bridge, he heard a man singing a rhythmic religious spiritual song, sound growing louder as he moved slowly down road. Scurrying behind a massive magnolia tree, Will waited as a colored man walked closer, shuffling along with no hurry to gait. Boldly stepping out from behind tree's concealment, Will startled the man by saying,

"Good evening, good Sir. Will you step to side of road so we can talk?"

Alarmed, the man began to back peddle, saying, "Well sah, if you's gots sum-thin' ta' say, say it hy-ar', sah."

Seeing fright, Will said, "I am a Yankee."

"Is you?" Without hesitation, the man ducked into shrouded darkness of woods roadside.

Will followed. "I am an escaped Yankee prisoner ...a friend and I want to cross the river ...do you know the man that attends the ferry?"

"Well, sah ...I's de' nigger dat' runs de' ferry."

Will inquired whether he could take them across the river now. "We hear the bridge is guarded," Will said.

The man answered, "Can't takes ya'all ...hav's to meets 'Ol Marse' at once." He went on to tell Will that bridge is guarded by only one man who lives in a house at far end of bridge ...goes to bed about ten o'clock each evening ...perhaps sneak across while guard sleeps.

"I trust you will not expose me?" Will questioned.

"I's see's nuthin' ...hears nuthin', I's reckon." Will thanked the man and departed to rejoin Clancy.

After ten o'clock next evening, Will and Clancy advanced to within rods of the bridge, where they stopped and made careful reconnoiter of their situation. "We must cross the bridge," Will suggested.

"I agree, laddie ...let's see if our Irish luck is still hold-in' true." Both men nodded.

With coast clear, both shrugged ...Clancy whispered, "Let's go." Will led the way, beginning a precarious climb up several wood timber crossbars of bridge trestle work ...arm-over-arm, straining muscles to pull weary body upward and mount the trestle. Up and over, he succeeded in gaining a teetering unsteady position atop rail ties. Regaining balance, he looked back over shoulder, extending an arm to assist Clancy up and over. Each man sighed audible in relief, attempting to catch breath, knees wobbly, hunched in precarious position high above river ...night pitch black, nary a star in sky to light their way. They paused trying to build courage. "I reckon big Irishman in the sky can see us, mate ...let's go, lad." Blindly stepping timidly from tie to tie, awkwardly balancing high above Broad River, Will heard water lapping shore far below. "Feet ...do not fail me now ...sore feet at that," Clancy whispered as he followed Will, both crouched over, at times crawling, inching across trestle. Nerve-wracking time unending, they completed their quarter-mile traverse ...much relieved at being safely across, undetected.

Next several days fugitives continued on course toward Spartanburg, traveling by night until daybreak, finding hiding place for daytime and building fire, eating what they could garner and resting, before resuming travel in darkness. It became routine ...weariness, aches and pains, sore blistered feet and hunger their constant companion. One evening, they encountered a bright campfire burning roadside before them. Cautiously advancing through an edge of woods to within three or four rods of campfire, they spotted a cavalryman with saber resting at his side ...its shiny blade glistening in glow of campfire's dancing flames. Sitting before campfire, a Reb soldier peered ahead, motionless ...mesmerized by rhythmic repetition of lapping flames consuming tender pine branches, embers sputtering and cracking, breaking night's silence. Soldier's horse grazed nearby, tethered to timber fence extending roadside. Heavy timber and cedar thicket made it impractical to enter woods and bypass the soldier, without undue risk of spooking soldier or horse. They waited and watched ...patiently, concealed by thicket in low lying ditch roadside. An hour later, cavalryman stirred glowing last embers of fire, unfolded blanket and lay down. Waiting until campfire burned down, Will and Clancy inched close enough to hear soldier's snoring. Convinced he was sound asleep, they advanced on tiptoe, noiseless ...passing within a rod of the unsuspecting slumbering Rebel soldier ...still another close call.

Next day, a Saturday, drizzling rain set in ...constant chilling rain compounding misery. Obliged to lay low, cold and damp, they constructed partial shelter from pine boughs placed overhead, on top of bushy thicket serving as hideaway. They hunched together side-by-side, sharing body heat ...arms wrapped around legs drawn upward against chests ...trying to reduce exposure to increasingly heavy driving rain and penetrating cold.

"Rain drops keep drop-in' off pine needles ...run-in' down my neck ...makes me shiver," Clancy said. "My body is ach-in' ...we're like two animals holed up, but they have it drier."

"You got that right ...my joints are 'disagree-in' with this weather ...only good thing about bad weather is nobody will be out chasing us."

"Aye', well now ...there's something positive, partner," Clancy replied.

"We best stay here until rain stops ...do not think I could get up to move anyway."

"Ya' got that right, my friend," Clancy agreed.

Time passed hunkered down, pelted by constant heavy rain. "I'm constantly thinking of Maria ...and my children ...I miss them so much. Wanting to get home keeps me going, otherwise body would just give up." Will's words triggered deep emotion, then gentle sobs of anguish ...tears running down cheek ...tears mixing with dripping raindrops.

Clancy hugged Will, reassuring a friend in torment, "You're a good man, Will Hodkins ...and that's no blarney."

"I'm sorry to get so emotional ...not very strong of me," Will confessed. "I just couldn't do this without you, Clancy."

"Aye', laddie."

Will pulled journal from pocket, hands cupping to protect it from raindrops. With nub of pencil, he marked off another day ...using journal to keep track of time lapsed. He gazed forlornly at Maria's likeness. "Clancy, it is three weeks since my last letter to Maria ...she will worry ...no way to let her know of our escape ...mailing a letter could reveal our position."

"Aye', laddie." Clancy could offer no further help. Reluctant, Will closed journal's cover and returned it to secure pocket. Despondent, he moved away from Clancy ...sulking, needing to gather himself.

By Sunday morning, rain subsided ...it became foggy, lending eerie gossamer feel to densely foliaged forest. Filmy cobwebs of vapor hung low enveloping forest, like surreal cotton balls drifting suspended. Wet grasses and bushes glistened, dew forming prisms of light as sun's scant rays fought to displace dense cloud cover. "...feels like we're two moths in cocoon," Will observed.

"Hope we come out of our cocoon soon ...two healthy butterflies," Clancy added, expanding on Will's metaphor. "...butterflies need to get home."

"Reckon that sums it all up, my friend."

That evening two exhausted fugitives resumed their trek, advancing within about two miles of Unionville. Feet causing great suffering, inflamed and blistered, they could scarcely keep shoes on feet. Blood and puss-caked socks wore thin ...at creeks and ponds, they washed filthy socks and dangled blistered feet in soothing water ...replacing wet socks on aching feet, easing feet back into worn thin-soled shoes. Will stuffed wet moss into shoe sides to cushion blisters ...it helped but little. Despite rebelling feet, two escapees slogged onward calling upon sheer inner tenacity to continue walking.

Will was doing guard duty during daylight hours, apart from Clancy, lying behind a log with shoes off. He heard children's voices talking and laughing, skipping and playfully jostling each other as they came down road. Suddenly a little dog came around the log surprising Will, barking in Will's face with all miniscule menace it could muster. Fearing it would divulge his hiding spot, Will grabbed a stick and threw it, causing a less than tenacious dog to yelp and beat a hasty cowardly retreat. He chuckled recalling Clancy's saying, "Every dog is bold on its own doorstep." Not long after children passed unsuspecting, a young colored field hand of about twenty years of age came along in two-wheel horse drawn cart. Will stepped out of brush in bare feet and hailed him, waving arms to stop, "Good Sir, I am a friend ...where do you live?"

"On's de' Foster plantation ...'bout two to three miles up yonder," the young man answered, somewhat startled and unsure of how to respond to sudden inquisition.

"Could you get my friend and me something to eat?" Will asked. "I'm a Yankee," he continued, catching himself off guard by sudden trust in man and demeanor. The young man proved lithe and limber as he leaped down from cart, broad smile lighting face. He walked toward Will with buoyant nimble bounce, reins in hand moving horse and cart alongside ...nearly as tall as Will, with curly black hair close-cropped, except for braided ponytail. He wore no hat ...white muslin shirt clean neat and tidy.

"My name's Isaiah ...folks here calls me Izzie ...pleased to meets ya', sah." He was handsome with chiseled features and unusually fair complexion. An infectious smile revealed beautiful pearly white teeth ...brown eyes sparkled, as he extended a hand in friendship, apparently fully trusting Will.

"Izzie, pleased to meet you," Will answered, shaking the young Negro's hand vigorously. "My name is Will."

"Yez', sah ...reckon I's kin' find some eats," Izzie answered. "Now minds 'dat none of 'de white folks sees ya'all ...especially Mas'ser Jack ...'dey calls him Squire Jack ...we calls him 'Ole Jack' ...has ah' mighty hate fer' Yankees, he do."

With that caution, Izzie directed Will to meet again within fifteen minutes ...across the far field, near the stable. No time for Will to rejoin Clancy with opportunity at hand. After waiting minutes in hiding, Will started cautiously across a field of cotton, crossed over split rail fence and up a sharp ravine. Short distance further he heard Negroes singing. Inching forward, he could make out several robust Negro women in long drab color dresses, heads wrapped in brightly colored handkerchiefs, sitting in semi circle. They were singing hymns while husking corn from a large pile of ears in front of them. Then Will heard a man's shrill whistle, and turned to see Izzie motioning him to come forward. Will raised himself cautiously and started slowly walking forward around gathered women. As he passed gingerly, one woman said, "Now, ya' minds 'dat Ole Jack don't see ya'all."

Will nodded assent, "I will be careful ...thank you, mam."

Izzie offered Will a handkerchief holding cornbread and course muslin sack containing corn meal, salt and tin plate. "Thank you so much, Izzie ...you are a kind man ...I am a lucky man to meet you." After thanking other slaves for their generosity, Will left to reunite with Clancy at their designated spot of hiding ...ecstatic once again, he knew Clancy would be as well.

"Where have you been, lad ...worried when you didn't return," Clancy called out, spotting Will's approach. Will beamed, holding muslin sack aloft in triumph and carrying handkerchief containing cornbread. "Yo', mate …you're amaz-in' …good job, my friend," Clancy exclaimed. Clancy slapped Will's shoulder in congratulation, excited to see sack's contents. "Let's get started, lad."

They built campfire and waited for a good bed of coals. Meanwhile, Will went off in search of cold spring water from small bubbling creek noticed in travel to Foster plantation. He filled their clay jug with fresh water, and lay down prone to drink from cool rushing brook. Enthralled as he cupped cold clear spring water to mouth, he looked up in fright …peering most unexpected into a pair of eyes …terrified, eyeball-to-eyeball, eyes popping. A horrifying moment later, he realized it was a herd of nosy curious goats, one watching him drink while standing nose-to-nose. He chuckled at the humor. "Goats, you should not scare me so," he voiced aloud, directing comment to the goat eyeing him.

Brazen goat answered, "Baaaah. Baaaah. Baaaah."

"Well thank you very much," Will answered, laughing heartily …goats ambling away harmlessly. Will returned to Clancy with filled jug of water. He shared goat story with Clancy, explaining his difficulty in conversing with an audacious goat.

Clancy said, "Aye', what would you expect out of a pig but a grunt." They laughed.

Clancy was already organized and started …he directed Will, two men working well together. They mixed precious corn meal with salt and water from their jug. On tin plate, they formed the mixture into three to four inch diameter cakes three quarters of an inch thick. Clancy gathered lush leaves from a small low hanging chestnut tree. Wrapping cakes in fresh green chestnut leaves, they laid leafy packages among campfire's coals. Leaves protected corn mixture from ashes as their concoction baked. Removing packages from fire, both were ecstatic to find corn bread good as any eaten …leaves apparently acting to seal flavor inside tasty cakes.

"Reminds me of Papa's cooking …you are really a good cook, Clancy," Will said. After stuffing stomachs with hot corn bread, they continued baking until late afternoon, converting all corn meal into corn bread for travel. Instead of travelling that evening, they decided to spend another night resting ...stomachs too full to move.

Next afternoon, Tuesday, October 25th, Will went to scout roadway, leaving Clancy behind to soothe swollen aching feet. From thick clump of young chestnut bushes growing around a stump two rods from road's edge, he waited and watched. He began to squirm from long wait when he heard horse drawn wheeled vehicle approaching. Soon, open carriage came into view ...occupied by aristocratic old gentleman dressed in fine grey suit and black top hat, accompanied by a lady in refined long flowing yellow silk dress with straw bonnet perched jaunty on rich coiffure. Carriage driver sat erect, shoulders squared, a slightly-built Negro man wearing uniformed black suit and sporting tall black stovepipe silk hat. From opposite direction came open two-wheel buggy with two ladies ...both dressed to the hilt, each peering from under perky wide-brimmed straw bonnet shielding intense afternoon sun, true 'Southern' ladies. Will became alarmed when both horse-drawn vehicles stopped in roadway just opposite his hiding place ...vehicles side-by-side so occupants could engage in conversation.

Two ladies in buggy inquired about condition of road ahead, after which both couples conversed about health of families, and seemingly endless other subjects ...all consumed by small talk. Meanwhile, Will feared the pompous neatly uniformed Negro carriage driver would look his way, possibly spotting Will from elevated carriage bench above roadway. Will's mind raced with thought of dramatic irony ...high-toned Southern ladies and gentleman chatting casually, while hated 'Yank' lay low concealed just steps away. But, both carriage and buggy resumed their journeys with no harm done. Will returned safely to campsite rejoining Clancy.

Early evening, boys feasted ravenous on fresh cornbread ...stomachs becoming bloated and aching from overeating. Later, as dusk replaced daylight, Will returned from squatting in woods to relieve gaseous indigestion. Dozing in campsite clearing, Clancy sat propped at base of huge live oak ...head bowed, hat pulled down over eyes and forehead. Without warning Will screamed, "Clancy! Clancy!" Clancy's eyes flashed open to spot a small black bear approaching …young bear cub apparently unable to resist scent of freshly baked cornbread. Clancy hesitated, before reaching into pocket for Sam's pocketknife. He opened knife's blade, while slowly rising to standing position …bear still advancing, now within a rod's distance of Clancy. Will watched in shock and awe as Clancy charged the bear, brandishing open knife's shiny blade, flailing arms wildly as he charged, whooping at top of lungs. Bear cub, unwilling to challenge commotion of a mad man, retreated …trundling down hillside awkwardly, moving away into forest's depth. Clancy looked back toward Will standing aghast.

Panting, out of breath from confrontation with unexpected intruder, Clancy said, "Wipe your bottom, laddie …cub's momma or papa may be com-in' back …we best be mov-in' out of here quickly."

They left in haste. After three or four miles walking brisk, they met an old slave on the road. "Sir, is there any other plantation along our way?" Will asked softly.

"Dis' is de' las' plantation on dis' road."

"Sir, we need help …we are Yankees," Will replied.

"I's 'kin sees 'dat you is."

Will asked if other colored folk lived further up road. He answered that a fine colored man …named Henry Martin …lives some five or six miles ahead, a little distance off main road. Directions were given to follow public road until a second stream crosses roadway, then go about one quarter mile further …they would see path off to their left, leading to Henry Martin's house.

"Tell'm Joshua sent ya'all," he said. They thanked Joshua and trooped off to follow directions. They were now in foothills of Blue Ridge mountains ...nearly three weeks since escape …October 25th, when they reached Henry Martin's cabin at about 11 o'clock in the evening and rapped on his door. Will and Clancy were about one hundred sixty miles north and west of where they escaped their prisoner train …getting here, they walked a circuitous route of nearly two hundred miles.

Chapter 32

Kerosene lamp still burned in Henry Martin's small log cabin, smoke rising from field stone chimney. Will and Clancy stood back apprehensive, waiting under cabin's shed roof porch, after Will rapped several times on cabin door. Will and Clancy hoped Mr. Martin had not retired for evening, though hour late. Within moments Henry Martin opened a massive rough sewn split plank front door, its crudely forged iron hinges groaning under heavy load. He saw standing before him two forlorn men with look of itinerant vagabonds ...filthy, dirty and smelly vagrants, tired and beaten. "My name is Will ...this is Clancy ...we are Yankees very much in need of help ...a good man, name of Joshua, suggested we see you and gave us directions."

"Aye', Mr. Martin, we're sorry to call upon ya' so late at night," Clancy added.

"I was just about to retire ...my wife and sister-in-law are sleeping ...but please come inside," Henry Martin offered graciously, knowing Joshua and apparently judging these two could be trusted.

"Thank you, good Sir ...we're much obliged," Clancy said.

Will guessed Henry Martin to be in his fifties ...fair-skinned Negro of medium stature, closely cropped curly black hair showing specks of salt and pepper gray. He looked thin and wiry, but with strength of body. Carriage erect, he squared shoulders like a manual laborer. Clean and tidy white muslin shirt with bright red bandana tied about the neck suggested orderliness and refinement. From choice of words and speech, he appeared an educated man.

Henry Martin moseyed with confident gait toward huge river rock fireplace topped by crude timber mantle, where last embers glowed deep orange. He reached for a new log, tossed it onto remnants of fire, and stoked coals with iron rod causing fresh pine to sputter and hiss. In friendly manner he motioned for Will and Clancy to be seated at kitchen table, one of few furnishings in frugal chink-log cabin of modest size. Mr. Martin joined them at table. "Sir, we are Yanks, fugitives …escaped a prisoner train outside Charleston," Will offered.

"…have been runn-in' for bout' three weeks, I reckon," Clancy added.

"We want to cross mountains …get back to Union lines …we need help," Will said.

"I want to help you boys, if I can," Henry Martin volunteered.

"Who is it, Henry?" a woman's husky voice called from one of two rear bedrooms.

"It is alright, Sarah," Henry Martin answered. "Two young Yankees need our help." Henry then turned to Will and Clancy, "That's my wife, Sarah."

Henry Martin brought leftover cold baked sweet potatoes and tin cups of water to Will and Clancy. "Sir, you are so kind …Clancy and I have not eaten much but cornbread for several days." Conversation continued. Henry Martin explained he was a former slave as a youth, growing up on plantation …self-educated, and granted freedom when plantation's owner died.

"I've found safety and 'freedom' by living in foothills of these mountains," he said. "I believe in Union's cause if fellow Negroes can gain freedom like mine." Will and Clancy listened as Mr. Martin explained surreptitious help was all he could do, without undue risk to family. "I support Sarah and her sister by farming shares of land for others …we grow about everything we need here …it is a good life." Will sat enchanted by Henry's story …refinement admired, coupled with gracious friendly personality and love of family.

"Mr. Martin, you make the most of hard won freedom," Will concluded. Conversation turned as Will and Clancy inquired about public roads through imposing mountains.

"Mountain passes are all well guarded ...roads cannot be followed ...you need to traverse mountains cross country," Mr. Martin advised. Will and Clancy eyed each other with skeptical look ...drastic change in plan ...doubt and loss of confidence struck like bolt of lightning.

"Mr. Martin, can you guide us across these mountains, so we can reach Union lines?" Will asked.

Henry answered quickly and with firmness, "I cannot ...I am farming shares of land for a Rebel ...if I leave home it will surely raise suspicions." Will and Clancy's countenance sagged, chagrin painting faces. Mr. Martin immediately sensed a visage of disappointment, even rejection. He countered with a suggestion, "Why, you boys should spend a few days resting here, while I try to arrange a guide." This idea appealed to two weary men, faces brightening ...rest most welcome, and feet could recover for impending arduous trip over mountains.

"Mr. Martin, your generosity is warmth in a storm for two tired souls, I reckon," Clancy responded.

"Ya' got that right, my friend," Will agreed. "Thank you kindly, Mr. Martin."

With that agreement, Henry Martin gathered provisions for their comfort, including ground cloth and two quilts. Henry took two Yanks to a thick stand of forest about one half mile up hillside from the cabin. "I think you will be safe here, while I try to secure a guide ...can make a campfire, and rest."

"Thank you again, Mr. Martin."

"I will return in the morning with breakfast," he said. Henry Martin departed, while Will and Clancy began tasks now routine ...constructing pine bough shelter and gathering firewood for campfire. They pondered emotion over their journey that ebbed and flowed like a raging river ...pockets of calm tranquil water in spots, followed by segments of perilous cascading rapids swirling. For now, they were buoyed by sudden change in events.

"Mr. Martin ...mighty fine feller, ah' laddie?"

"I reckon Irish eyes are shin-in' on us," Will said. "Do you think we can make it across these mountains, friend?"

"Not by our lonesome, mate ...maybe with a guide," Clancy answered. "Irish have a fine say-in' ...man with boots does not mind where he places his foot." Will could only smile.

"We need to trust Mr. Martin can find us that guide ...let's get some rest."

Next morning Henry Martin brought breakfast of smoked ham and sweet potatoes. "I know a Rebel deserter from a South Carolina regiment, named Ray ...he lives a few miles away with family and can possibly be secured to pilot you across these mountains." Boys nodded, and Henry Martin left to make arrangements.

At noon Henry's wife, Sarah, appeared with dinner ...accompanied by another woman of about seventy years of age, a Mrs. Jones. Will and Clancy eyed each other quizzically as two portly older women emerged carefully picking their way knowingly through dense foliage and thick woods ...both women were white. "I'm Sarah ...this is my sister, Mrs. Jones ...we've brought you something to eat."

"Please to meet ya' ladies ...very kind of you ...maybe you would like to sit on that log and rest a bit," Clancy said, recovering quicker than Will from their initial shock. Sarah explained she met Henry soon after he came to the mountain ...she was ten years older than Henry ...a mountain preacher from up road married them nearly thirty years ago. "Henry is a good man ...takes good care of me and my sister ...all this time."

"Aye', a good man he is."

Then Mrs. Jones took over conversation. Sarah did little talking thereafter, content to let her sister speak. Mrs. Jones proved loquacious ...short and stout, with snow-white hair gathered in tight bun at the back ...wearing long red dress, homespun and dyed by berry juice. With plump rosy cheeks and twinkle in eye, she told the boys enthusiastically about her late husband, name of 'Hickcock' ...northerner from Connecticut. She stated proudly, "...was a heap smarter than other folks about here." She rambled on endlessly, citing avid support of the Union cause. Will listened politely and attentively, unable to get a word into her monologue.

Clancy lost patience with droning small talk ...it bothered concentration as he tore into dinner. With a mouthful, he said under breath to Will, "...woman can talk teeth out of a saw."

"Clancy, hold your tongue," Will whispered.

"She's a tongue that would clip a hedge," Clancy whispered again.

Mrs. Jones finally noticed the destitute condition of the two men ...dirty clothes and without overcoats, only two flimsy tattered quilts provided by Henry. She offered to go back home and return with things to aid their condition. Mrs. Jones and Sarah returned sometime later carrying a heavy hand sewn patchwork quilted bed comforter ...and two pair of home knit wool socks for Clancy, one pair for Will. She offered to take whatever clothing they wished to give her, as she and Sarah would launder the items. Will and Clancy gave her a sheepish look, trading questioning glances. Upon seeing hesitancy, Mrs. Jones chuckled, "Come on now, boys ...strip down, give me those britches ...noth-in' these 'ol eyes ain't seen before."

"Turn your eyes now ...don't want to embarrass you two ladies," Clancy answered.

"Embarrass ...noth-in' do-in' ...you boys er' seem-in' to be the embarrassed ones ...git' on with it ...what's ya' got to hide?"

Clancy was first to pull down trousers and remove shirt. Reluctant, Will followed. "Your kindness is very much appreciated ...Mrs. Jones ...Mrs. Martin," Will said stuttering, proceeding to undress, sacrificing all modesty for embarrassment. Ladies took clothing and departed. Will and Clancy huddled together sharing comforter, happy to be alone.

Toward Wednesday evening, Henry Martin came through woods riding bareback atop an old gray plough horse. He told the boys he went to Ray's house, "...wife was home, Ray was not ...I suspect he's hiding in woods." His wife expected Ray back in a few days because provisions would be running out. "We'll have to wait a few days before I return." Henry Martin brought a basket containing newly laundered shirts and trousers, and food prepared by Sarah. "Understand you boys were a little reluctant to give 'em up," he chuckled. Will and Clancy literally jumped into freshly laundered clothing, excited because smell of chicken and fresh baked biscuits beckoned. "Sarah killed a chicken and prepared a delicious supper, boys ...boiled chicken, plenty of biscuits, corn bread, jam and butter," Henry said while emptying the basket. "Hope you enjoy all." It was a feast. Henry Martin left early at dusk, so two fugitives could rest ...stomachs full, no longer famished.

Next afternoon, Will and Clancy lounged half-napping, slumped and hunched in shade at base of two oak trees. Neither man kept sentry, both presuming safety. Caught off guard, they scrambled awkwardly to their feet, completely surprised by two figures thrashing through brush and briar toward them. Rugged, stout, determined and fearless, two trudged closer partially concealed in shadow ...one toting a menacing rifle. Will and Clancy stood frozen, unable to move. Both intruders were white, but as they drew close, Will and Clancy grew bug-eyed ...they were women, both dressed more like men than ladies. True 'mountain women' stood before Will and Clancy, posing stark contrast to Mrs. Martin and Mrs. Jones. One with rifle wore rough-fashioned buckskin britches with tall hunting boots, and checkered shirt tails out ...other a man's hunting coat ...both sporting floppy brimmed felt hats, tugged down tightly fully concealing hair. "Easy fellers ...ya' looks like spooked coons up da' tree wit' dawgs a-bark-in' below ...Henry says yuz' two Yanks ...no fear-in' us, ma' name's Nell ...this here's ma' sister, Ruth ...I've come out-ta' da' plough to meets yuh," Nell said shouldering her rifle.

"I'm ...uh, I'm Will ...this is Clancy," Will replied. "We're Yanks alright."

"I knocked off plough-in' cuz' Ray ...uh, he lit out ...he's gone out to kill a squirrel."

"My friend and I need help getting across these mountains," Will continued. "We wanted to talk with Ray."

"Well now, he listens to me, an' I's listens to him," Nell said.

"Can Ray help us?"

"Ray ain't feared o' nuth-in', but I's don't hardly know," Nell answered. "When he comes out, ya' kin' ast' him right."

That said, Nell and Ruth turned abruptly and walked away. Will and Clancy stood awestruck. Will suspected their purpose in visiting ...they feared he and Clancy could be Rebels trying to entrap Ray ...a deserter on the run. With some assurance they were Yanks and not to be feared, two women departed, apparently satisfied everything could be alright. Another day passed.

Saturday morning arrived, fourth day waiting in camp, fugitives growing edgy. Mrs. Jones entered camp with breakfast. Will ate hurriedly, patience wearing thin. After eating, he stood, announcing abruptly, "Excuse me, but I need to get a little air and scout the area ...Clancy, know you'll enjoy talking with Mrs. Jones."

"But ...but ...wait, mate," Clancy stammered, standing with arms gesturing wildly, not wanting to be abandoned with talkative Mrs. Jones.

Ignoring Clancy's plea, Will headed off for stroll down hillside and through woods, keeping close to a rapid flowing stream so he would not lose his way. Will drew deeply, filling lungs with cool crisp morning mountain air ...so refreshing compared to heat and humidity of South Carolina's lowlands. Will wended down rocky outcropping of densely forested hillside, stepping gingerly, picking steps carefully. Fresh smell of forest rejuvenated him. He walked briskly where terrain permitted, amid plentiful lush growth of laurel, rhododendron, sourwood and dogwood ...sourwood and dogwood bursting with ruby red color. Underfoot, assorted variety of mushroom and lichen fought for precious turf, amid abundant patches of forest fern. Dense canopy of oak, birch and maple contrasted with an array of cedar, juniper and pine. He paused along segments of mountain stream where placid pools of clear cold water formed within random boulder crevice, before cascading down over groupings of rock and stone. He drank from an inviting pool, while noticing fresh animal tracks streamside, evidence of deer or elk sharing the watering hole. Nature's magnificence and solitude of forest refreshed the mind ...bringing momentary peaceful calm, where impatience troubled him from long uncertain wait in camp. Soon entrancing stream led to open meadow offering wide valley panorama. Late October and mountain foliage abloom, breathtaking vista of color appeared as far as eye could see. Will marveled at clear 'Carolina' blue sky with nary a cloud drifting, sky serving as backdrop for endless range of gorgeous mountain peaks, ridges, valleys and ravines …all cascading before him …imposing, even frightening, but magnificent in their raw beauty. He stopped for a moment, breathless. Dichotomy came to him upon reflection …sheer overwhelming beauty, but such intimidating challenge to setoff hiking across endless rugged range of mountain. Will shuddered, before voicing aloud for only bird and animal to hear, "…such daunting task, I wonder if I can make it …but, I must make it …have to dig deep to survive and get back home." Recommitment helped. He breathed a deep sigh, re-energized, and continued walking.

Sun played on leaves and trees, shadow creating depth …some distant valleys muted in shadow, blue haze blurring image of distant ranges …some still cloaked in trace of foggy lingering cloud cover hovering to mask valley below. Colors came from painter's palette …brilliant hue of red, orange, yellow and green …birch, beech, buckeye and tulip poplar in bright yellow …maple in red, orange, and yellow, while oak showed shades of orange and red. Will noted all texture of bush and brush, accented by flowering ground cover …lush green foliage from massive bank of rhododendron …a lone juniper rising tall, silhouetted against rolling range beyond …stands of pine, juniper and oak, with occasional sweetgum …deep crimson of Japanese maple, craggy bark of oak.

After fifteen minutes additional brisk walking, enjoying views and listening intently to chirping call of cardinals high in massive oak trees, Will looked up, startled. Adrenaline surged as if confronted suddenly by black bear or wild hog. A man sat casual upon downed log, not more than two or three rods away on the right, dressed in Rebel gray uniform with gun and full set of soldier's accoutrements. Will gave hurried glance, turning face away …first impulse, keep walking as if not seeing. After meager few paces, Will looked back over shoulder …man still sitting idle, simply watching Will intently. Will changed his mind, deciding instead to approach and see what action he intended. He sat rock still as Will approached, eyes frozen on Will, unflinching. Small of stature, perhaps he could be overpowered if needed. Within five paces of each other, he stood abruptly bringing gun to ready, calling out with shrill voice, "Halt, yuh' hy-ar." Will halted. "Yer' comin' a leetle close now …who are yuh?"

Will challenged right back, quickly asking, "Who are you?"

"Nuthin' doin' …I want yuh' ta' answer me first, yuh' hy-ar," the man said sharply, showing agitation at Will's challenge.

Will refused to knuckle, "What's your name, friend?"

"Ma' name's Ray," he replied. "Ain't yuh' one of da' Yanks?"

"I am looking to meet you, Ray," Will answered. "I'm a Yankee …name's Will."

Will took a step toward Ray. "Halt, yuh' hy-ar …jest keep yer' distance now," Ray shouted. Will complied finding persuasive a loaded musket pointed directly in the face. Ray seemed to be in his forties, short of stature, thin wiry physique …apparently strong for his size. Chin jutted strong, cheeks bony, sunken dark eyes. From under cocked brown felt hat with duck feather wedged in leather band, sandy hair snarled, dirty, disheveled and unkempt. Several days' whisker growth and bushy eyebrows added to 'rough' persona …uniform tattered, not laundered in some time. He took several steps menacingly toward Will, walking with bowed legs and stooped shoulder. Chewing tobacco, he spit a mouthful of brown nasty juice onto ground in haughty challenging manner, as if marking turf. "Where's dat' friend o' yorn?" Ray asked.

Will pointed upstream. "Will you go with me to my friend?"

"Well, I reckon I will," Ray answered. "So long as ya' don't make trouble fer' anybody." They moved off in direction of Clancy. Will stood six inches taller than Ray with larger frame walking erect and square-shouldered, while Ray shuffled behind bow-legged and slumped …a most unsightly unusual twosome.

Two men approached campsite …Will leading, Ray trailing a few paces, gun still pointed at ready. "Clancy, I want you to meet my friend, Ray."

"Aye', pleased to meet you, Sir," Clancy responded, extending a hand in friendship.

Ray seemed to relax. He lowered his musket and extended a cautious hand to Clancy.

"Sir, you can put that gun away, we're friends," Clancy said.

"Nah, I shore won't," Ray said, still uneasy. "Look yonder." Ray's wife Nell and her sister Ruth came through woods into camp ...Ray's wife still toting trusty rifle.

"See hy-ar, I'd told ya', when he comes out, ya' kin ast' him right yerselves," Nell called. It became clear Ray was home when Henry Martin called several days ago ...afterward three mountain folk hatched a plan to meet the escaped Yankees.

"I'm hearin' yer' powerful set on crossin' these hy-ar hills," Ray offered.

"Aye', mate ...can you guide us up and into the mountains to Union lines?" Clancy responded.

"I kin' do it, I reckon ...if I has a mind to."

"Ray ain't feared o' nuthin', like I'd told ya' fellers," Nell added.

Ray boasted of being well acquainted with country within fifty miles in that direction. "I'll do it ...provided ya' pay me fer' ma' trouble."

Ray could not be further from the guide they envisioned when Henry Martin suggested an arrangement. Clancy and Will eyed each other with questioning looks. But no real choice existed except to trust in Ray's ability. Both men nodded assent. They had no money, except for Clancy's lone Union greenback. But, Clancy had a silver cased pocket watch worth about twenty or twenty-five dollars 'Union' ...reluctantly, he pulled it from pocket and offered it to Ray. Ray studied the pocket watch closely, rolling it over, up and down in his hands ...before eyeing Nell who winked agreement. "We's got us a deal hy-ar, fellers ...yup, by golly," Ray said, extending a hand to Clancy, spitting a wad of tobacco and juice onto ground for emphasis.

Financial arrangement made, Will asked, "Can we start this evening ...both Clancy and I are well rested and anxious to get going?"

"Nah, we shore kan't," Ray answered. "I must git' ma' family thar' supply o' winter meat 'fore I go ...nuthin' laid out fer' winter …ain't comin' back fer' some time …five child-in' ta' home, ya' know …plus da' Mrs. and hern sister."

Will suggested that Ray make arrangements that afternoon for a supply of meat. "Nah, I kan't git' er' daytime ...must go at night ...take's me two nights, I reckon." Will's curiosity caused him to ask what kind of meat he was getting. Ray replied sheepishly, "I know's whar' thar's em' nice fat lamb …but kan't get'em daytime." Will and Clancy nodded, realizing Ray's plan for getting a 'supply of winter meat' …he employed the old fashioned method, stealing it. Nothing more said.

Three men decided to start out on Monday evening. Ray's wife urged him to go all the way to Knoxville, to remain until War's end for safety, because of daily danger of being captured or killed by Home Guard if he returned home. But, Ray proved stubborn, having none of that …"too many mouths ta' feed ta' home," he said.

Fifth day in camp, Sunday, October 30th, and Will grew increasingly pensive …he moved off by himself, sulking …creeping thoughts of home, sad and melancholy. He realized one week ago, last Sunday, Will, Jr. celebrated a fifth birthday …he missed it, too busy trudging about in search of food to recognize and give proper attention. Clancy sensed his friend's low spirit and walked over to Will. Crouched against a tree with journal in hand, Will stared ahead dazed. "Aye' now, what's got you down, laddie?"

"…my son's birthday …five years old …a week ago today, and I let the day slip by without giving it proper recognition."

"Aye', I see mate …tell your ol' buddy more …let's imagine you're home," Clancy said.

"What do you mean?"

"Let's have a party …you and I …right here and now," Clancy offered. "…better late than never, I always say."

"…don't know 'bout that …but I reckon I can," Will replied, choking back emotion.

"Go on, Will …describe what's happenin' at your party."

"Maria is baking a birthday cake, with five candles …proper celebration is important."

"I'll wager you like parties too ...go on now, tell me more, lad."

"Ezra and Nettie are surely at our party ...Will, Jr. will get presents, a drum or a kite ...I vowed to make a kite with my son ...maybe Ezra made one."

"You're doin' fine ...it's a good party," Clancy prodded. "...keep goin' my friend."

"Walter is already three years old ...old enough to know about birthdays ...excited about flying Will, Jr.'s kite with Ezra. Minnetta is nearly eighteen months old ...a toddler now ...I missed her being a baby, and her first steps," Will continued. He was down, but talking about it with Clancy helped. "...good idea, Clancy ...I reckon Irish have good hearts, my friend."

"Ya' know, mate ...we have us a guide to help ...things are looking up ...maybe Ray falls a little short of our hopes, but he can help us find our way home," Clancy added.

"Thanks, partner ...I know we can make it ...you and me working together."

That forenoon Ray returned to campsite with cooked mutton for dinner ...certainly not lamb. "Reckon yuh' boys know what I done," Ray said. "...kilt me a sheep up yonder, sky's goin' to miss her ...thar' ya' kin' see top ridge o' da' cove 'tween them two peaks."

"Successful hunt, eh' Ray?"

"I ain't got no heart fer' it ...wa'n't no glory in what I done, as I see it ...I wudn't tech it, but family needs ta' eat."

Will and Clancy worked hard to get every bit of flavor out of unrelenting morsels of meat, chewing endlessly on each bite. "Tough as horsemeat," Will whispered to Clancy.

"I wouldn't know, son," Clancy answered coyly. Clancy glanced toward Will, removing a badly chewed piece of meat from mouth when Ray wasn't looking, tossing it away disgustingly into brush.

"We thank you for bringing dinner, Ray," Will offered.

"I wern't meanin' to stop," Ray said. "...it'll take o' nuther night to git enough, I reckon."

On Monday morning Ray informed the boys of good success again last night ...he will be ready to start at dark

...provisions gathered last two days and preparation for their trek complete. That evening, Ray brought more provisions to camp and another piece of roast mutton. He dressed in 'civilian' clothing, discarding Rebel uniform ...he looked like a grizzly tough mountain man, toting trusty musket. Wife Nell and her sister Ruth joined men for supper, leaving their five children to fend for themselves. "...an' we kan't eat biscuits 'thout salt in 'em," Ray complained during supper.

"Tain't no use complain-in' ...a woman kinder puts up with what she's got," Nell answered quickly.

"Nature was agin' you, woman," Ray retorted. Looking toward Will and Clancy, Ray continued, "...ain't high-stocked with brains, but she's got a' 'nuff fer' a woman."

"Don't ya' believe any o' them things, boys," Nell chided, getting in a last word.

After eating, Ray asked that Clancy's pocket watch be left with Nell. Clancy reached into pocket, slowly, reluctantly ...eyed his watch a last time, sighed deeply and handed it to her. Later, Nell pulled Will aside while Ray and Clancy prepared to depart, renewing her plea. "I won't keep back a dad-blessed thing ...I'm plumb worried ...he's as tender as butterweed, ya' know," Nell lamented softly to Will.

"I'll take your word for that, Nell."

"I'd miss 'em poorly if sum-thin' happened," she continued.

"I know you would."

"He'd stay out all night huntin', but never jower-in' me when he come in. An' he's stout enough to wear out a hoe handle, when he's fixed to it."

"We'll take good care of each other," Will assured Nell.

"Please, Mr. Will, you and yorn needs to git' 'em to stay wit' ya's ...all da' way to Tennessee ...stay thar' til War's over, safe I reckon."

"Please tell Henry Martin, Mrs. Martin and Mrs. Jones that we appreciate everything ...thank them for generosity."

"We'll tell 'em ya'all think on 'em kindly, now."

Soon the two women departed. Three men began their nighttime journey, first fifteen miles trooping cross country among foothills of the Blue Ridge. Ray took the lead, musket resting on shoulder. "I always take da' gait I kin' keep," Ray said. Will followed Ray. Clancy walked last. Not much conversation occurred, they just kept walking. Will lost himself, listening to sound of birds and tree frogs, even a whining howl of coyote. By daylight, they halted just over a crest of Blue Ridge, having traveled about twenty-five miles over hills and up mountain. Yet, Will and Clancy felt scarcely fatigued. They began to realize how much they benefited from several days rest. After resting until about four o'clock Tuesday afternoon, they started again ...leaving public roads for a route through woods and byroads until after dark ...then taking main roads, traveling steadily until after daylight. Ray led them onward to woods surrounding a small mountain farm owned by a Mr. Bishop ...he knew Mr. Bishop and sought assistance.

Chapter 33

Ray knocked at cabin door just as it began to rain heavily. Mr. Bishop recognized Ray and invited the three men inside. "Come in …too rainy to stand outside," Mr. Bishop said gruffly.

"Well, I reckon ya' know me …name's Ray."

"We met in the woods out hunting, I recall," Mr. Bishop replied.

"Yup, 'bout o' month ago …we went to ma' shack on northy land in da' holler, down yonder," Ray added.

"I remember well …your hunting dog got lost."

"Ma' dawg got onter a fox trail, an' coon wasn't nuthin' to him after that …so I let him goon by hisself …bin' wantin' to git' rid o' him from way back …I was aggervatin' him, he was aggervatin' me."

"Your wife …name is Nell, I recall …was very kind," Mr. Bishop offered. "It rained that day, and you gave me shelter."

"Ah, ya' got that right …she baked some loaf bread, an' put lasses on it, an' some butter …an' we 'et it."

It took little time for Will to assess Mr. Bishop …an old codger in his seventies …short and pudgy, balding with double chin and puffy beet red cheeks. Long bushy white sideburns, white snarly eyebrows and rimless spectacles distinguished the look. A crotchety old man, he spoke with brusque delivery in short phrases. But kindness became apparent …kindness a trait he tried to conceal via cantankerous demeanor.

"Boys 'er Yanks …need our help," Ray explained. "This here's Will …Irishman name's Clancy."

"Pleased to meet you, Sir," Will said extending a hand to Mr. Bishop.

"That we are, Mr. Bishop …Yanks needing help to cross these mountains," Clancy added, shaking Mr. Bishop's hand with a strong grip.

"Glad to help you boys," Mr. Bishop said. "Have a chair." He stood before three seated men, lecturing as if to school boys. He placed both thumbs under red suspenders, pulling bracers out, letting them snap against a puffed out obese stomach …stomach overhanging and bulging over trousers. He boasted of being a soldier in the War of 1812, droning on for several minutes citing examples of personal exploits. "…now I'm zealous Union supporter," he concluded. "My farm is off beaten path, away from public highway …will be safe to stay until weather clears."

"I know it ta' hang wet fer' o' month, at times," Ray interjected.

"With rain continuing …night travel not desirable …you boys make bed in my stable," Mr. Bishop offered.

"Your offer is mighty kind, Mr. Bishop," Will said, with Clancy and Ray nodding agreement. The three retired to the stable to sleep the rest of Wednesday and into evening …their bed among corn fodder.

Next day rain stopped. Everyone assembled just before dawn to get an early start hunting deer. Mr. Bishop loaned Will an old rusty Austrian rifle so he and Ray could go into woods together. "…rifle not fired in years," Mr. Bishop commented. "but she'll work."

"We'll git' us o' deer …no fearin'," Ray boasted to Mr. Bishop. Will looked skeptical.

"Deer and elk are plentiful in these mountains," Mr. Bishop said.

Clancy stayed with Mr. Bishop as Will and Ray trooped off on hunting expedition. They deployed and traveled about three miles without seeing a deer. "Ya' kain't see 'em, lessen it's an awful fair day, an' yer' in da' big pasture top o' dis' hy-ar' mountain," Ray coached.

"Ray, I've hunted deer before," Will countered.

"I reckon ya' know then." Ray and Will continued their climb. Soon they reached a clearing, rolling meadow before them. "Sagebrush tis' high hy-ar', an' maybe they's rattlers under it," Ray cautioned. Will cringed. They wended through high grass, Will following Ray. "...whole passel I kain't see fer' weeds an' briars."

"Just following you, my friend," Ray answered.

Making their way through meadow, at its edge they reentered cover of woods. "...an' da' la'r'l's so blustery hy-ar', it'ud tangle a wild hog," Ray commented demonstrating prescience unexpected.

Mere moments passed when sound caused both men to freeze in their tracks. "Oinck ...oinck." "Did you hear that?" Will questioned in high voice. "Oinck ...oinck," sound again.

"Look yonder," Ray sputtered. At base of huge oak, in partial clearing four to five rods distant, two wild hog piglets feasted snout to ground, oblivious as they devoured a myriad of fallen acorn. "Let's shoot us o' hog," Ray said quietly, motioning for Will to move closer. "...be ready to skedaddle up o' tree o'er thar' ...they's lean an' mean ...one knocked me into briars when I follered him 'bout two months ago." Will grew excited, hunching over with gun at ready, inching slowly closer. "...aim fer' middle o' shoulder."

With little confidence in an old gun, Will took aim and fired. Gun belched smoke, its kick throwing Will off-balance ...smoke cleared and Will's ears rang ...relieved the gun did not explode in his face. Will and Ray danced a jig, whooped and cheered in amazement as one hog dropped ...other squealed and scurried away. "...tarnation, ya' got 'dat right ...we kain't wait fer' da' sow to come a-lookin' now ...let's move 'er away from hy-ar," Ray urged. Ray and Will each grabbed a leg, dragging their prey through woods and briar, frantic and fast, far away in case a sow came back for her lost piglet.

Reaching an area far enough to be safe, both men stood over their fallen beast, catching their breath and gloating. "I've never seen a wild hog," Will said. With brownish-black coloring, it had ears smaller than a pig, but longer snout, hind legs shorter than front legs, and straight tail with small tuft of hair at its end.

Judging by effort needed to drag its carcass, their piglet weighed about one hundred pounds.

Using a hunting knife given by Mr. Bishop and pocket knife from Sam, Ray and Will skinned and dressed their hog, before skewering the beast on a wooden pole fashioned from downed tree limb. With end of pole resting upon each man's shoulder, bearing hog between them, Will and Ray returned to Mr. Bishop's cabin with gushing smiles of accomplishment. They approached cabin ...smoke curling lazily upward from stone chimney ...a chinked log cabin with red metal roof and expansive full-length shed roof covering front porch. On its porch, Clancy occupied a single rocking chair, hand-fashioned from tree limbs. He rose abruptly, slapping knees, spotting two smug hunters returning. "Now look-ey' here, would ya' ...great white hunters return ...Irish eyes are shin-in' alright," Clancy called out.

"I hav'ta be whar' thar's sum-thin' happen-in' I reckon," Ray boasted.

"Good job, boys," Mr. Bishop added, coming out front door hearing commotion. "Come on ...let's get your hog a-cook-in' ...will taste mighty fine." While Ray butchered the meat into pieces, Mr. Bishop pulled out a large Dutch oven with cast iron lid. In this vessel, they baked pork and potatoes with a top layer of cornbread. While hunters were away, Clancy was directed to a small nearby orchard ...he returned with a good supply of red ripe apples. Apples were baked ...feast complete ...thoroughly enjoyed by all. With bellies full, content to rest a bit longer, three fugitives decided to stay with Mr. Bishop another couple days.

On Saturday evening, one month into Will and Clancy's journey, Mr. Bishop announced arrangement for a guide to lead them further back into mountains. Before daylight Sunday morning, November 6th, their guide arrived. "Name's Ethan ...he'll be your guide," Mr. Bishop said. "...reports a company of Rebels scouting this area, so he'll lead to 'Rock House'." Mr. Bishop explained a large overhanging rock cliff furnished shelter for up to twenty men. Local mountain men subject to Rebel conscription found numerous secluded hiding spots, shanties built deep in woods or natural spots like 'Rock House' ...hiding places to keep locals safe from military duty. "You'll be safe there ...until Rebs leave our area," he said.

After loading a stock of cornmeal, potatoes, pork and apples, Will, Clancy, and Ray started out following Ethan for six or seven miles before reaching 'Rock House'. In a remote isolated valley location, near its base stood precipitous mountain, narrow winding pathway up of loose rock and debris requiring great care not to lose footing. About four or five rods below, fast moving river flowed over succession of rocky beds and falls that kept constant deafening roar. On opposite side of river, mountain rose in spectacular perpendicular climb of several hundred feet. At 'Rock House' three men hid waiting for Ethan's return when area cleared of Rebels. They built campfire at outer edge of cliff, and spent most of next two days doing little, but eating and keeping fire going ...keeping watch for intruders.

On Tuesday morning, Ethan returned saying they should go at once to ex-Sheriff Hamilton's where he would provide further information and help on their journey. "It's about twenty miles cross-country through rugged mountain," Ethan said. They started immediately. By daylight next morning, it began raining heavily. Travelers traversed only twelve miles, going being extremely difficult and slow through heavily wooded and steep mountain terrain. Clothing soon became drenched from downpour, when Ethan said they should stop and seek shelter, while he made his way to a farmhouse nearby. An hour passed. Ethan returned accompanied by a middle-aged woman in rain slicker. "This is Mrs. Fisher ...she will take you to her farmhouse, get you something to eat, and guide you further." This said, he turned abruptly and started back, few words spoken.

"I am happy to help you gentlemen," Mrs. Fisher said. "Friends of Mr. Bishop are friends of mine."

"We are grateful to Mr. Bishop and Ethan for their help," Will offered. "We will be most appreciative of anything you can do for us, 'mam." Clancy and Ray nodded.

"Please follow me gentlemen."

Will, Clancy, and Ray followed Mrs. Fisher ...through driving rain she trudged, brushing back wet foliage and brush, picking her trail, keeping steady pace. Small of stature, grit and determination made strong early impression.

Within fifteen minutes their group approached the Fisher farm ...everything impressive, neat and tidy. In modest pasture running up hillside, four or five milk cows lay hunkered down in driving rain. A few goats grazed in pen just off small rough hewn barn. Chicken coop stood aside barn. A quaint two-story white clapboard farmhouse, with green shutters and green metal roof, looked so inviting to cold shivering travelers. Shaking rain from her slicker before entering, Mrs. Fisher said, "Gentlemen, please come inside ...take off wet clothes and get warm." Will and Clancy brushed water off clothing, and wiped feet on a mat before the door, before stepping inside. Ray stood back looking puzzled and uneasy. Once inside, a soaked threesome dried outer garments before a blazing fireplace, while Mrs. Fisher went off to prepare dinner. "You men make yourselves at home." Will gazed about the room as he warmed himself, rubbing hands vigorously before roaring fire ...modest accessories and furnishings, all arranged neat as a pin ...abundance of books filling shelves against one wall ...an open book lay ready at reading table beside large comfortable looking well worn chair ...fresh cut flowers arranged colorfully in porcelain glazed vase on cherry wood table. Mrs. Fisher entered the room calling men to dinner ...voice soft and gracious ...a petite woman with delicate features and pearly white skin. Shiny brown hair glistened in soft fire's light ...hair neatly arranged and held in-place by a pair of white bone combs at back. White blouse neat, freshly ironed, she changed into a long gray dress covered by red apron.

Will thought, "*...not a 'mountain woman' ...reminds me of Maria ...educated and cultured.*"

Clancy whispered to Will, "...handsome woman is easily dressed, lad."

"No question," Will agreed. Obviously nervous and uneasy in Mrs. Fisher's presence, Ray said little. In contrast, Will relished moments and conversation with Mrs. Fisher.

Conversation during dinner turned to Mrs. Fisher's story. "I grew up in northern Virginia, not far from Washington ...moved to North Carolina and these mountains years ago with my husband who wanted to leave city and 'pioneer' a small farm."

"My wife's name is Maria ...I moved Maria from a nice life in New York state to life on a small farm in Michigan," Will related.

"My husband is deceased ...died far too early in life ...blood poisoning from a wound suffered when kicked by a mule."

"I am so sorry, Mrs. Fisher."

"My husband poured heart and soul into building this farm ...his dream, our livelihood," she continued. "We managed to persevere over last several years ...with my daughter ...keeping his dream alive, though very difficult."

"Must be very difficult alone ...but it appears you have done well," Will added.

"Perhaps some day we will make it back North," she said wistfully. "I am a fighter, you know ...I am determined to aid the Union cause, and see this awful War end ...I do not believe in wars, but freeing slaves is a good thing."

"Mrs. Fisher ...my wife, Maria, is a fighter too," Will continued. "Your story is so similar to our family's ...you, left alone to tend to your family on a small farm ...I left Maria and our children ...all alone to tend our farm ...I have been away for over two years ...I feel badly for leaving them with such burden."

"You say she is a fighter ...she will survive ...perhaps some day I can meet your Maria."

"God willing, you can."

"Yes, soldier ...God willing."

Following dinner, Mrs. Fisher informed them her daughter was upstairs suffering from an attack of diphtheria. "She is quite anxious to see a Yankee." Mrs. Fisher asked whether someone would take risk of going to visit her.

Concerned glances passed among three men, but Will could not refuse after Mrs. Fisher's kindness. "Mrs. Fisher, I would be pleased to see your daughter."

On entering her second floor room, Will found a young lady of obvious culture and refinement, sitting before open fire

...face white as the neat white wrapper she wore. "My name is Mary ...thank you for coming to see me."

"It is my pleasure, young lady."

She informed Will that her older brother was forced into joining the Rebel army ...now he is a prisoner of the Union at Camp Douglas in Chicago. "Please inquire of him should you reach Union lines safely." Will told her he would. After short conversation, Will offered a cordial 'goodbye'. "Please get feeling better, Mary," he said softly. He turned and left down stairway, heartbroken.

At darkness, the group started on their way, Mrs. Fisher as guide ...night complete darkness, no stars to light their way. Rain ceased, at least temporarily. Mrs. Fisher led the foursome ...Will and Clancy following, Ray bringing up the rear. First thirty minutes of utter pitch black night, Will stumbled awkwardly over uneven terrain, low hanging limbs, leaves and brush whacking face and body. While he and Clancy labored clumsily, he marveled at effortless ease expended by Mrs. Fisher and Ray as they traversed dense rugged forest ...demonstrating years of familiarity in the mountains. Hike grew easier for Will and Clancy as eyes adjusted to darkness, and they fell into steadier walking rhythm and cadence. After traveling between four or five miles, they reached a point of ferry over the French Broad River. Mrs. Fisher pulled up, saying, "I will leave you here ...Mr. Orr will come to ferry you across river and be your guide."

"Mrs. Fisher ...we cannot thank you enough ...you have been so kind," Will said in parting. "We wish the best for you and your family ...my prayers are with Mary."

"Here. Here. Yes, 'mam ...we wish you the best," Clancy added. Ray merely shook head in agreement.

"I shall look forward to meeting your Maria some day," Mrs. Fisher reminded Will. Will nodded. Mrs. Fisher left the three men and turned toward home. Clancy, Ray, and Will plopped down along river's bank to rest and await Mr. Orr. Will eyed the French Broad River ...a wide river, maybe fifteen to twenty rods across. It appeared shallow in most places and rock filled, with many large boulders. But he guessed swirling deep pockets and strong undercurrent existed. Will's nerves tingled contemplating an impending dangerous crossing. Roaring sound of water moving swiftly, dashing and glancing off rocks intimidated the mind ...rapidly rushing white-capped water and swirling currents making crossing hazardous, especially in darkness. Anxiety heightened when Mr. Orr appeared ...a quaint old and somewhat dapper 'gentleman' dressed as if going to Sunday supper ...white-skinned, thin and frail ...hardly inspiring confidence. He shuffled to river bank and pointed toward a crude hand-tooled dugout wood canoe concealed in river reeds. "...a vessel to take us across," he said.

Will glanced with questioning look to Clancy. "A man not afraid of the sea will be drowned," Clancy whispered cavalierly, shrugging with a grin.

"Must be another old Irish saying, my friend?" Will said, big smile lighting face. Both men laughed, resigned to fate. Four men climbed teetering into wobbly small canoe, Mr. Orr pushing off bank. It did not take long for Will and Clancy to change opinion ...Mr. Orr demonstrated adeptness and skill maneuvering his craft through currents and around dangerous rocks.

"Looks like he's done this before, mate," Clancy quipped. After successfully crossing river and tying crude canoe on opposite bank of the French Broad, Mr. Orr led them through forest until they came in sight of ex-Sheriff Hamilton's house. Saying 'goodbye', he turned back toward home. Too late that evening to approach the house, three boys waited. Weather began to change. Breeze picked up, trees rustling, storm approaching. Ray quipped, "It's goin' ta' rain, an' I laid out to wash to-morrah."

"Didn't know your sense of humor, Ray," Will observed.

"Well, I reckon ya' know now," Ray answered.

"Ah, she'll take some humor to get through this night alright," Clancy added. Almost coincident with Clancy's remark, lightning cracked and thunder roared.

During night, rain resumed ...becoming downpour once again. Huddled together in misery, a hapless threesome waited as nighttime mountain temperature plummeted ...soon soaked to bone, freezing cold, they waited.

Chapter 34

Night passed so slowly. Three fugitives sat elbow-to-elbow, sharing what little body heat mustered. Rain continued, trees providing little cover. Will pulled knees to chest, arms clutching legs, hat pulled low on forehead, trying to dodge heavy steady rain. He glanced toward Ray. "Ray, rain seems to jump right off you ...doesn't it bother you?" Will asked.

"Ya' kain't stay hy-ar' all da' time, no more'n I kin."

"Ray's like a duck ...water just runs off his back, lad," Clancy moaned.

"I's as slippery as da' beak of o' blackbird," Ray added. Conversation ended. Soon Ray fell asleep, serenading Clancy and Will with his snoring. Clancy followed, soon dozing, leaving Will alone.

Will found little sleep, unable to keep warm, torn by conflicting thought. Cold, shivering wet agony opened a door for recurring thought of 'giving up' ...too cold, too tired to go forward. He fought to slam down negative thinking ...success so much closer. "...*I can persevere a little longer ...Maria and our children are waiting, counting on me coming home ...I cannot disappoint.*" Night did end.

Daylight began to replace darkness. Boys eyed Sheriff Hamilton's large log house, standing ominous some distance off public road ...image blurred in a mysterious way by foggy smoky mountain haze, steady downpour continuing. Smoke began curling skyward from stone chimney, indicating someone awake within. Concealed in bordering thicket of woods, three men hunched over for shelter, rain running off hat brim and down neck, teeth chattering from piercing cold. "Aye', men ...I think we need to be cautious," Clancy suggested. Both Will and Ray agreed.

"I will go alone," Will offered. "Clancy ...you and Ray watch from here ...Ray can cover me with musket." Clancy and Ray nodded agreement. Will moved forward, reaching forest clearing bent low in crouch ...shoulders stooped and head down keeping low profile against pelting rain. Will placed a first step gingerly onto porch, approaching rough hewn log plank door apprehensive. He rapped. Instantly, he heard scurrying persons within, but only for a brief moment ...then all became deadly quiet. Several minutes passed as Will lingered and paced, sheltered by overhanging roof of home's wraparound front porch, but shivering uncontrollably ...chilly mountain breeze penetrating drenched clothing. Finally, he heard footsteps ...door opened slightly, a young girl peering through crack with visible fright. "Is Sheriff Hamilton at home?" Will inquired in friendly voice.

"Just a moment," she replied timidly, so soft as to be barely heard. She turned and walked away, front door standing ajar, Will remaining outside.

After more minutes waiting anxious, door reopened fully, this time by a stout middle-aged woman ...apron soiled, hair disheveled, face etched with deep furrows indicating tough life. "What do you want?" she said brusquely. "I am Mrs. Hamilton."

"Mrs. Fisher and Mr. Orr sent me ...and my two friends waiting out there," he answered pointing toward woods. "...my name is Will." Will removed his hat, flicking water away. In now friendly but cautious manner, she motioned for Will to come inside. He did. Before him stood a large open fireplace made of field stone, a robust fire burning ...glowing red and orange embers and fluttering flame casting shadows of dancing light throughout otherwise dark room. At her urging, Will stepped eagerly toward its hearth ...fire's warmth pouring forth. Will extended hands toward fire, rubbing them together vigorously to savor warmth ...soaked clothing dripping from drenching rain, droplets pooling onto rough hewn plank flooring at his feet. "I apologize for making a mess," he said, looking down. She shrugged acquiescence. "Mrs. Hamilton ...I am a Yankee escaped from

357

Rebel prison trying to make my way back to Union lines. Sheriff has been recommended to me and my two friends."

Mrs. Hamilton scrutinized Will from head to toe as he spoke. As he finished, she turned and shuffled out of the room without making reply, closing a door to the room behind her. Again minutes passed, Will waiting before warmth of fire, uncertain. Then, door opened. In walked a portly man in his middle fifties ...maybe older, Will guessed. Red suspenders strained to hoist soiled gray trousers about massive girth of stomach ...stomach protruding boldly, pressing against tobacco-stained homespun checkered muslin shirt. Full growth of matted salt and pepper beard partially concealed plump rosy cheeks, cheeks already bulging from wad of tobacco. Rimless spectacles perched low on fleshy red nose ...he drew deeply from corncob pipe clenched tight in snarly tobacco-stained teeth. Never had Will watched a man chew tobacco and smoke pipe simultaneous ...a true mountain man. "Ma' name's Roy Hamilton ...folks 'round 'bout call me 'Sheriff Hamilton' ...used ta' be one."

"Mrs. Fisher and Mr. Orr sent me ...my name is Will." Will extended a hand to the Sheriff. After guarded exchange, Sheriff Hamilton asked Will if anybody else was with him. Will answered, "Yes, Sir ...I have two friends waiting outside in the woods."

"Then, bring 'em in, ma' boy ...imagine she's pretty wet out yonder," Sheriff urged, chortling ...then breaking into full gutsy laughter, belly rolling in self-indulgent enjoyment. "Guess yer' alright, my boy." Going to the door, Will signaled Clancy and Ray, beckoning them to come.

That afternoon and into early evening three men sat about fire warming frigid bodies, talking with Sheriff Hamilton. Boys clothes removed and drying before fire, Mrs. Hamilton stayed away while men talked. Will found Sheriff Hamilton to be an earnest Union man more than willing to assist the Union cause in any way he could. He explained, "I'm like most o' ma' neighbors ...too old fer' soldier-in' ...compelled to serve da' Rebs in 'Home Guard' whenever called upon." Principal duty of Home Guard is to hunt deserters, but Sheriff said he always tried to send word ahead warning anyone in hiding ...though duplicity placed him at dire risk of facing firing squad if detected. Ray cringed upon hearing talk of hunting deserters.

After supper offered from leftovers, Sheriff Hamilton donned rubber rain slick, slung over hefty shoulders. "I'm goin' 'bout two miles up road ...to ma' neighbor's ...need ta' see if danger from Reb's in neighborhood." Returning, he said all is safe but still raining heavily. "Well, I reckon ya' boys 'kin sleep on da' floor 'fore da' fire." No one objected.

Next morning early, Sheriff Hamilton awoke three reluctant men. "This here's Bobby Joe ...he'll guide ya' ...follow him."

"Why it's 'fore sun struck it 'dis mornin' ...'dat freeze'll sting yer' eyeballs out yonder," Ray objected half-heartedly, as they scrambled to gather clothing and dress. Friday, November 11th ...they were to wait until Monday to begin their trek into Tennessee.

"Meantime, I'll git' supplies ...five days o' rations ...unable to git' any 'long da' way," Sheriff explained.

Bobby Joe directed the boys to a nearby isolated mountain cabin furnished by the Sheriff. They gathered corn fodder that stood in nearby field, using it for bedding and comfort. During ensuing three days, they were given a supply of cornbread and meat for a five-day journey. Will, Clancy, and Ray became acquainted with several local rugged stalwart mountaineers ...folk determined to aid the Union cause, willing to die rather than serve a Rebel army ...young men liable for military duty and conscription, but spending most of their time hiding in woods. One young man boasted, "Reb posse hunt's us ...but 'dey meet's defeat ...we ban's ta'-getter an' ambush's 'em." When Rebel sympathizing 'Home Guard' come with bloodhounds, he went on to say, "...not ah' blood dawg git's out ah-live."

They spent much of Friday and Saturday resting, getting ready for arduous trek ...plenty time for talking, getting to know Ray better. "Tell us about your family and upbringing, Ray," Will probed.

"Well, I reckon I kain ...ma' muther and daddy ...they're reg'lar 'jump up' farmers, raisin' corn in 'jump up' country ...an' their cribs ain't bin' empty in twenty years."

"What about your mother?" Ray questioned.

"Folks ast' me, how's yore mother gittin' along," Ray continued. "I'd say, she's always fill-in' 'er ears with other folk's complaints, but she's secretly 'bout what's hern ...she don't hardly know me ...sometimes I'm 'most a-feared of her ...she might turn an' claw me with 'dem hands, like chicken feet."

"My mother died when I was young ...my father taught me farming," Will said.

"Ma' daddy'd say, I kain't wait 'round fer' her ta' make up 'er mind ...ya' kain't stay 'hy-ar all da' time, no more'n I kin, he'd say," Ray rambled. "...he lit out huntin' ...he'd leave me in dat' black holler by myself an' stay out all night huntin' ...in da' holler, so dark ya' kin' see lightn'in' bugs in thar by daylight."

"You get along fine with your father?"

"Shore, he's fine ...we've swapped idey's lots o' times ...he's always got duck oil on his tongue ...does his loafer-in' on da' kitchen porch ...didn't miss a word dat' feller says."

"I learned a lot from my father too," Will added.

"Well, da' whipper will ain't much a smart bird, and I reckon I ain't much a smart bird 'tither," Ray answered.

"Do you see your father often?" Will asked.

"They took 'em red-handed, stirr-in' da' mash." Conversation ended on that note. Clancy shook head side-to-side, walking away muttering in disbelief.

On Saturday evening, Sheriff Hamilton returned and spent the evening. Sunday morning all awoke to find an inch of snow on ground, but soon it melted away with morning sun.

Four-man group headed out on Monday toward a destination some twelve or fifteen miles away. Reaching this place, they found seclusion in a narrow valley, little more than precipitous ravine bounded on sides by high steep hills. Here they paused to rest, unload gear and build campfire. After mere hour and one half rest, sudden volley of musketry startled them, apparently from less than one half mile down ravine and below. "Crack. Crack. Crack-crack," came sound of explosion resounding off mountain wall. More gunfire, then blood curdling scream echoed through mountain pass ...frightening in its horror, scream of a wounded man. Apparently, marauding group of Home Guard found an ill-fated target.

Four men hastily grabbed gear and supplies, stomping out campfire, covering it with dirt to prevent further smoke revealing their position. Keeping hunched over close together, they scurried away quietly to a safer point higher up mountain. Falling to ground, they hid unwilling to make sound or move limb, hearts pounding and nerves frayed from fear. They waited anxious, adrenaline pumping …each man straining to hear any telltale sound of imminent threat. It was too close a call.

When danger passed near sunset, their group faced back deeper into mountains. Traveling slowly, cautiously about four or five miles, it became quite dark descending a steep mountain. At its base rapid clear and churning mountain stream cascaded over rock and boulder. Pulling off shoes and socks, pulling up trousers, all four men waded into stream, Ray and Sheriff holding musket above head. On opposite bank, they found a level place several rods wide, covered by abundant growth of rhododendron shrubs …thicket dense with branches and foliage five to six feet above ground forming canopy overhead. Here frightened men lay down for the night believing no human could find them. Will reached to snare a lush green leaf from rhododendron overhead …he placed a single leaf carefully in front fold of journal, closed and kissed its leather cover. He returned journal to breast pocket, thinking …*"God willing I will see this flower gets home."*

Next three days it rained torrents …cold drenching mountain rain of November. But, four men traveled undaunted though thoroughly soaked. Through dense forest, up and down steep rugged mountain, they pressed onward relentlessly avoiding all settlements. "Mate, if we'd had more time off our train, we could've packed a rain slicker," Clancy quipped to Will.

"Don't think we prepared for all of this," Will answered. Both men chuckled.

By late Thursday, four weary travelers reached a choice in their route …cross valley which lay in front of them, a valley extending about fifteen miles to mountain on opposite side …or, opt to circle around the mountain an extra distance of twenty-five miles. "Boys, we've got us ah' choice …shortcut, down and up that mountain stands before ya' …or easier walk 'round er', longer though she be," Sheriff said.

"Lookie hy-ar', fellers, say-in' goes …if yer' late, go straight …reckon we go straight over yonder," Ray offered, looking quizzical toward Sheriff for a fellow mountain man's affirmation.

"Aye', halfway down this mountain …halfway up that mountain …sounds like it's a wash to me," Clancy chimed.

"Sounds like 'straight over yonder' is right," Will agreed, smiling at semblance of weird logic exhibited by Ray and Clancy.

"That settles 'er …we go straight 'cross dis' here valley," Sheriff concluded.

They crossed valley that night, despite continuing heavy rain, reaching opposite mountain's summit near daybreak. Exhausted, at sunrise they rested upon a bald replete with huge boulder outcropping at its ridge and grassy surrounding meadow, allowing marvelous panorama of forest clad mountain peaks cloaked in mist. Mystical mist hung suspended like wispy cotton balls, floating magically among peaks and shrouded valleys. Remnants of breathtaking fall color lay muted but not totally diminished by rain and early snowfall. Majestic heart of beautiful rugged gateway to the Blue Ridge stood before them. "We're at 'bout 5,000 foot elevation here," Sheriff observed. "…high mountain in da' distance, she's Mt. Pisgah." They traveled further during daylight, and camped Friday night at the base of Mt. Pisgah, one of North Carolina's highest mountain peaks.

Chapter 35

Saturday morning sun came out bright as rain ceased overnight. Ray's eyelid twitched open from flashing ray of sunlight darting through tree's leafy canopy overhead. Ray awakened while three others slept soundly alongside. He prodded Clancy, "I shore the-nck she's time to git' up now ...come-on now." Clancy's eyes opened reluctant, grunting and rolling on his side. "Well, I reckon sun's as soft as ol' blanket, I always say."

"Well mate, blanket must be very soggy ...last four days steady rain, not a stitch on me is dry," Clancy mumbled.

"Nature was 'agin ya' ...ain't got no heart fer' it nither."

With commotion about him, Sheriff's huge paunch convulsed and he awakened. Clancy jostled Will awake. Four weary traveler's hiked mountainous terrain since Monday, now muscles ached and stomachs churned ...provisions nearly exhausted. "Yer' o'leetle short on some of 'em, ain't ya?" Ray confirmed with Sheriff, who nodded agreement. "...well, tain't no use to moan, o'course we're smack out o' stuff," Ray scolded Clancy and Will. With little to eat, they resumed their trek.

"Boys, we've got 'bout eight hundred foot climb up yonder," Sheriff said pointing toward Mt. Pisgah. Near eastern base of Smoky Mountains, they came upon a small ramshackle farm, apparently abandoned for years. Near remnant of dilapidated house stood a couple large apple trees ...on ground lay several bushels of good ripe apples. They stopped to eat all they could before filling pockets. Apples provided needed energy to keep them walking for remainder of Saturday. Sheriff Hamilton led their foursome trudging single file, Ray bringing up rearmost position in line. Both men carried muskets at ready, eyes surveying countryside intently for any intruder. Will and Clancy maintained middle of a snaking line tramping through rugged brush, briar and steep terrain. "...them morning glories keep me fluttery, lookin' at me all da' time," Ray offered in jest.

Sheriff walked erect, red suspenders tugging to keep trousers upright and circumvent plentiful girth, teeth clenching corncob pipe. "...truly amazing how he keeps pace," Will commented under breath to Clancy.

"Ya' got that right, partner," Clancy added in whisper.

But Sheriff overheard their comments. Turning back over shoulder while continuing his gait, he removed corn cob pipe and spit tobacco juice for emphasis, "Well, I reckon I keep ma' pace ...waste leetle energy wit' idle talkin', ya' hy-ar." He peered at Will over top of spectacles, eyes glowering, puffy cheeks growing rosier.

"No offense intended ...my apology, Sir," Will answered. They kept walking.

They made their way in northerly direction, generally following the Pigeon River. More fast flowing shallow creek than river in this location, it wended serpentine-like among variety of gulley, ravine and meadowland within deep valley, mountains rising on its sides ...chilling water coursing with gurgling rumble and frothy foam over abundance of slippery rock and random boulder. Then they veered northwest skirting around base of Cold Mountain, wanting to avoid a settlement in Waynesville some fifteen miles further northwest.

About sunset, Sheriff Hamilton stopped abruptly, raising right arm into air to signal halt, coming upon a tumbledown farmhouse in disrepair. "I wasn't meanin' to stop," Ray said.

Sheriff Hamilton said, "...Davis' live hy-ar' ...good spot ta' spend o'r night ...maybe git' restocked."

"I reckon ya' know," Ray consented. "...maybe kain' borrow me a smooch o' coffee."

As they approached an isolated house tucked remote, a man fled from rear of house, hastily running into woods. Approaching rundown whitewashed picket fence in front yard, a yelping shaggy dog came bounding toward them. Barking viciously, it circled menacing Sheriff and group who pulled up cautious. A mountain 'lady' emerged from house onto front porch stacked and crowded with assorted debris. Torn screen door slammed as she stood angrily facing intruders …red babushka about her head, stained white apron tied over tattered ankle-length gray dress, bearing a musket aimed directly at four strangers. "Don'cha' come in here …jest clear out, wud'cha …we'se don't want no Rebs o' hy-ar."

"Aye', madam, we're not Rebels!" Clancy stuttered in fright. "We're all Union men …well mostly Union men …part of us escaped prisoners of Rebs."

"Mrs. Davis …it's Roy Hamilton hy-ar' …ma' boys 'er alright …we mean no harm," Sheriff said.

After momentary delay and hesitancy, she became convinced they were all right …she lowered her musket slowly and invited them to come inside. "Mam, this hy-ar' two 'er Yanks …now Ray hy-ar', he's 'ah Reb runaway …try-'in to git' 'em ta' Union lines," Sheriff explained.

After getting acquainted, she told them her husband fled first thing when she saw them coming. Then she summoned a couple of older children to go fetch 'Daddy' …"tell 'em it's safe …skedaddle back home …hurry on now, young-'ins." Two children scampered outside.

Just then another figure entered dimly lit room from a small bedroom rear of house. Will stood back turned to doorway, but he noticed as Clancy, Ray, and Sheriff looked sideways to eye a man now standing in doorway. Instinctively, Will turned to see. Will's chin dropped to chest mouth agape, arms thrusting into air uncontrolled, standing awestruck before nearly screaming, "My God! Is it you? Is it you?"

He could not be mistaken. Before Will stood a man short of stature, dirty worn clothing hanging loose from undernourished body …face thin, sallow features concealed by unruly unkempt growth of beard from many days …but ample crop of helter-skelter red hair and freckled face unmistakable. Boyish grin lit the man's face. "It'll be me alright! …ya' can't git' rid of me easily, ya' know," Junior exclaimed excitedly, hurrying toward a stunned Will. He threw arms around his mentor and friend in bear hug. "…I'm a com-in' at ya' like a coon dawg' chas-in' a squirrel!"

"Junior ...Junior ...you're a sight ...never thought I'd see you again."

Two dumbfounded men nearly knocked each other off their feet, embracing wildly, beginning to spin themselves around the room in a jig of frenzy. Mrs. Davis and three men watched bewildered. "Friend o'yorn?" Ray remarked.

"Yer' ah' smil-in' like a butcher's dog," Junior observed of Will.

After some emotion ebbed, Will regained a degree of composure, "This is my friend, Junior. Last time I saw him being led away, captured with me ...that evening on the Horseshoe in Chattanooga ...I cannot believe you're here, my friend."

It quickly became unexpected celebration. Junior told a story of escape from Rebels while being transferred from Andersonville Prison in Georgia to Savannah. He made his way north, being directed to Davis' cabin as safe haven ...he too trying to return to Union lines. In remarkable coincidence, both men shared stories of irony that now reunited them.

"What about Jeremiah?" Will asked.

Junior said both he and Jeremiah were sent to Andersonville upon capture, but separated soon thereafter. "Rumor's that he died at Andersonville," Junior said sadly.

Will's shoulders slumped. "Oh, no! Oh, no!" he lamented, lowering head, disconsolate. "What about other boys? ...Lucius and Jeptha ...Papa and Nathan?"

"No news on any of 'em," Junior answered. "But we're safe ...back together, Will."

"You're right, my friend ...we can be thankful we're both alive ...and celebrate good fortune," Will remarked.

Now five men banded together, all bent on getting to safety. Stories and backslapping good times continued into night. Mrs. Davis offered something to eat and a frightened Mr. Davis rejoined his family. She had little to give hungry travelers but cornbread, but it was enough. Beside, they were pumped high with adrenalin surging, buoyed by thought of imminent success ...journey's end now within sight. A good amount of Mr. Davis' corn whiskey did not hurt their celebration one bit either ...whiskey fresh from Mr. Davis' still tucked away in remote area nearby.

"This here whiskey ...makes ma' hairs stand on end ...puts fire in the belly, now," Junior observed, filling tin cup numerous times.

"Go easy, Junior," Will cautioned. "We've got to walk out of here tomorrow."

"Aye', lads ...she compares mighty favorable to good Irish whiskey ...ma' head's a danc-in' ...knockin' cobwebs away, she does," Clancy added. Ray and Sheriff Hamilton were accustomed to potent mountain brew ...they kept steady pace and watched as young Yanks made merry.

"So ye're enjoyin' yerself to-night," Ray observed.

Clancy answered raising tin cup in toast, "Aye', what whiskey does not cure, cannot be cured, mate."

"Well, I reckon ...hearin' yer' powerful set agin' waistin' stuff, Mr. Davis ...I'll have ah' nuther cup."

That night they slept on Davis' kitchen floor, bare dirt though it was ...whirring heads and queasy stomachs from too much corn whiskey. Sunday morning at daylight, men bid Mr. and Mrs. Davis and children goodbye with many thanks, and resumed their trek. It can now be said they are between Union and Rebel lines ...mostly out of danger. During day's walk, however, while crossing fields they came upon two men digging, while two others stood guard with muskets at ready. As five travelers approached, they observed four country farmers digging a grave. Sheriff Hamilton went to the grave diggers alone ...others waiting at a distance. Sheriff returned, saying, "...old man cruelly murdered jest' yesterday by Rebel cavalry ...we'd best stay alert."

Toward early evening, they passed an old mill where a rather fine looking old gentleman sat jaunty astride a gray mule while talking to the miller. As five hikers approached, the old man scrutinized their group closely. They closed to within several rods, when he greeted them with tip of hat, calling out, "I'm for Lincoln ...don't know who you are for." He apparently convinced himself they were not Rebels.

Will answered, "We most heartily agree with your sentiment, good Sir."

He seemed congenial enough, dressed in black head-to-toe, crisp starched and fresh ironed white shirt flashing from under long-tailed formal jacket ...black stove-pipe top hat sitting squarely on large head of flowing shoulder length white hair. Will guessed him to be a traveling preacher. He motioned for the boys to come over. "I am a practicing physician travelling countryside administering to those in need ...a stout Union man, I'm proud to say," he said. Sheriff asked where they could find a safe stopping place for night. "Go to Jones Cove ...about three miles up road ...four or five families there ...all good Union families." He paused and spit tobacco juice. "Call on Zachary Long," he went on. "Zach'll take care of you." That said, he turned away abruptly, back to ongoing conversation with the miller. Five mismatched compatriots continued walking down roadway.

They walked until sun began to set over Balsam and Cataloochee mountain ranges. Will pointed toward brilliant sunset painting western horizon, vivid orange and red coloration reflecting spectacular on sporadic white cumulus clouds drifting ...all framed by imposing mountain peaks rising from cascade of mountain ranges superimposed one against another. "...it's awe inspiring, my friend," Will remarked to Clancy. "...man upstairs is a good artist."

"Aye', laddie ...and red sky at night makes for a good 'morrow."

As sun began last descent over mountain peak, five men entered Jones Cove through a gap in mountains. Narrow cove extended before them ...small in area, cleared from one end to the other, abutting heavily wooded steep bluff at its far end and pinched at sides by mountains. The group walking into the cove represented an unlikely amalgam of contrary characters ...looking like motley crew of nomads. Sheriff Hamilton led their way and set pace, toting musket lowered at his side ...middle-aged portly man, girth of stomach protruding, rimless spectacles perched low on fleshy red nose, smoke rising from corncob pipe. Beside him marched Clancy ...in his early forties but well-built and muscular, bushy graying eyebrows with rippling full mustache, unshaven, dirty and unkempt. Behind them came Junior and Will ...Junior short of stature and young, with flowing red hair and unruly red beard, thin and emaciated from prison confinement at Andersonville. In contrast, Will walked erect, tall and strong despite ordeal of incarceration, broad shoulders and confident gait, though dirty and unshaven. Ray followed at group's rear …in his forties, short of stature, thin and wiry 'mountain man' walking with bowed legs and stooped shoulder, musket carried menacingly at ready as if on sentry duty.

Within minutes of their approach into Jones Cove, an alarm bell rang out, "Clang-clang-clang." Armed men poured from each door of a cluster of cabins situated in the tiny cove. Women folk pushed faded yellowed muslin curtains aside to peer from cabin windows. Fear spread quickly …everyone uncertain of intention of five men approaching, two carrying musket. Will and others kept moving forward, slowing their pace, raising arms above heads to indicate they meant no harm and were friendly. With that gesture, tension eased noticeably.

Sheriff called out, "We've bin' sent ta' see Mr. Zachary Long ...we're friendly …no harm intended."

One citizen waved, signaling the group to come toward him. "What's your purpose?" he shouted, musket now half-lowered to his side but finger on trigger and pointed toward the boys.

Sheriff answered, "I'm take-in' 'em ta' Union lines …most of 'em 'er Yanks."

The man lowered musket fully, relaxed and smiled, "You're welcome here, boys."

Will and others showed immediate relief. After brief introductions and small talk, they received directions on a route to Zach Long's secluded cabin deep into woods. In going to Long's place, they followed wooded trail for some distance, back and away from main road. Pathway led them through a large thicket of huge rhododendrons which concealed Long's cabin. Ducking while passing under dense thicket of branches, Will looked upon a small, crude rough hewn log cabin, showing open space between logs with no chinking. Mr. Long met them, coming out onto a small front porch, as their ragtag group approached and pulled up short. "Ma' name's Roy Hamilton …we've bin' sent ta' Zachary Long fer' assistance … I'm take-in' 'em ta' Union lines …most of 'em 'er Yanks."

"I'd be Zach Long ...come forward ...believe we can help." Hearing this, his wife emerged cautiously from inside, arms draped around two small children who looked frightened. Sheriff introduced each of the four men. Mr. Long introduced his wife and two small children. "Ya'all be most welcome at our home," he said with warm smile. He explained he built this cabin tucked away, so conscripting officers could not find him. "I'm a Union man ...not much for Rebs."

He instructed his wife to get corn whiskey, while he went to nearby pen to make preparations to butcher his lone hog. Will protested, "You are so kind, Sir ...but you will need that hog with winter fast approaching."

"No ...all folks in this here cove help each other ...they'll be com-in' with some fix-ins for ya'all." He would have none of Will's objection and hurried off. All five men congregated and milled about outside, resting from day's long hike. Meanwhile, Mrs. Long began making cornbread, as boys eagerly sampled stiff mountain whiskey, fresh from nearby still ...apparently learning little from prior evening's overindulgence at Davis' cabin.

Within the hour townsfolk began arriving, bearing cornbread, jams, butter, potatoes, and hard cider. Will concluded citizens of Jones Cove were used to such impromptu gatherings with Yankees ...village being a known stopping-off point for Union sympathizers. This occasion prompted improvised late-night celebration. Soon a large pot boiled with enough pork and potatoes to satisfy a growing party ...men and women coming from Jones Cove, children left at home. Everyone gathered casual outdoors, lingering about large bonfire, enjoying spontaneous community feast as if on 4th of July celebration ...trading stories until well after midnight. As last party stragglers departed, five vagabond travelers curled up on ground around last embers of campfire and fell fast asleep.

After daybreak they awoke ...groggy, eyes squinting against bright sunshine, heads spinning and stomachs churning from aftereffect of excess corn whiskey and hard cider. They thanked Zach and his wife for being gracious hosts, received directions and resumed their journey ...five diverse characters trudging forward, shoulders and heads stooped, feeling less than energetic after partying late into night …saying almost nothing as they walked.

Will's thoughts drifted to Maria. He replayed the last night with Maria before leaving home …more than two years ago, but still so vivid in memory. They stood facing each other, tears welling, choked with emotion …he gave her a cameo brooch …she said, "*I will wear it always while you are away.*" Neither imagined he would be away this long.

"I hope she is wearing my brooch now," he whispered to himself. He reached for beloved journal, removing her ambrotype, studying her image as he walked. Her infectious bright smile and piercing dark brown eyes stared back at him …so strong, resolute and determined. He loved her so much.

Memory of their last evening grew intense. She stood barefoot on tiptoe, kissing him …he could feel her lips, warmth of breath. They embraced, holding each other tightly for a longest time. They nestled in bed, unable to get close enough …talking long into night, neither wanting night to end. He pictured stroking long and flowing dark brown hair, caressing each other's body …passion surging, blood rushing …bodies entangled as one. Will relived the intensity of their rhythmic dance, before he possessed her.

He tried to concentrate on morning's walk, but found it difficult …too excited now, end of journey so near …stomach churning, energy surging. "Clancy, we are almost there, my friend," Will said. "Butterflies are dancing in my belly."

"Aye', mine too, laddie …mine too," Clancy answered. "…must confess …doubted we could make it this far, my friend."

"We helped each other …couldn't do this alone."

"…fine people who helped along our way," Clancy agreed.

"They treated us like family," Will added. "…you're a good man, Clancy."

"Aye' …you too, my friend," Clancy replied. "…and that's no blarney."

Will regained presence of moment, lowered head, and continued walking. Two days passed, strenuous hiking through rugged terrain as they headed northwest across isolated section of Smoky Mountains, crossing into Tennessee at some point. Group

371

picked up pace the third day ...all energized by prospect of reaching destination ...like a racer sprinting harder near finish line, surging with last burst of power.   A little before noon on Wednesday, they emerged from mountains into beautiful fertile valley of the Little Pigeon River. Late afternoon they found a mill near a small village of Sevierville, needing to make arrangement to cross the river. A large dugout canoe was available, and the miller agreed to assist them in crossing the Little Pigeon River. "Where ya' headed?" miller asked.

"Knoxville," Sheriff answered.

"Strawberry Plains better ...closer ...only sixteen miles on Holston River, nearer than Knoxville ...it's occupied by Union troops," miller explained. "Go to Mrs. Smith's home ...she'll take ya' in." They decided to change course, pushing onward until dusk in a new northerly direction following eastern side of Little Pigeon River.

Thursday, five eager nomads rose early, midday crossing French Broad River where Little Pigeon joined the larger river, traversing over twenty miles by late afternoon. Another mile or two up road they reached home of widow Smith, a staunch Union supporter. She offered them privilege of sleeping before fire in her sitting room, but boys declined wanting instead to reach Union picket lines that evening if possible. She gave directions, saying just outside picket lines they would come to the farm of Mr. Thompson ...a Union man who would offer lodging, or tell them if they could get through picket lines.

Evening grew cold and frosty, so they traveled briskly, reaching Thompson's farmhouse about half past eleven o'clock. Sheriff knocked on the door and awoke Mr. Thompson. "Well now, Sir ...'kain we git' ta' picket lines ta-night?" Sheriff asked.

"Best stay here tonight ...ya'all kin' sleep on ma' floor til' mornin'," Mr. Thompson answered. "I'll builds ya' a fire in ma' fireplace o' yonder." They could not refuse, being fatigued from covering a lot of ground that day. Mr. Thompson proved to be quite a character, 'entertaining' guests with constant chatter well past midnight. They sat before raging fire enjoying its warmth, listening politely to endless recital of Mr. Thompson's adventures during the War ...even back to recollections of War of 1812 when he was a youngster. Then he reached for a well-worn banjo leaning against wall adjacent to fireplace, and started singing ...'singing' being a kind stretch of term. Little 'music' came from voice. Discordant and off-key, he launched into strains of song, plucking banjo's strings awkwardly with gnarled meaty fingers.

When Johnny comes marching home again,

Quality of music unimportant, they were having a good time. Everyone joined Mr. Thompson in song, thrusting clenched fists into air with each chorus.

Hurrah! Hurrah!
We'll give him a hearty welcome then,
Hurrah! Hurrah!
The men will cheer and the boys will shout,
The ladies they will all turn out,
And we'll all feel gay,
When Johnny comes marching home.

"Aye', mates ...just thought, today is Thanksgiving Day ...good time to give our 'thanks' lads," Clancy toasted.

"...could not be more appropriate," Will added.

Raucous singing continued despite lack of musical proficiency. Fortuitously, evening eventually ended at nearly three o'clock in the morning. Mr. Thompson brought out several army blankets, confiscated from Rebel cavalrymen ...five exhausted men lay down before last glowing embers of fire. Mr. Thompson stoked fire and put on a last log ...they slept until daylight.

Next morning at sunrise, after mere three hours sleep, they arose eager to resume their trek. They thanked their kind host and departed. After short distance, they passed through a last expanse of timberland, abruptly emerging into vast lush open valley of the Holston River. Each man stopped instinctively. Will, Clancy and Junior stood awestruck. Breathless, three escapees gazed into distance, beyond river and onto a gentle rise of ground beyond.

Pure emotion surged through veins. Will shivered with goose bumps, hair standing on end …sight overwhelming, especially for captured soldiers. Contrasted against clear blue cloudless horizon, row after row of precisely ordered white canvas tents glistened in bright morning sunlight …hundreds of tents, and myriad of soldiers going about their business. Smoke curled lazily skyward from countless morning campfires …a scene beyond imagination, its aura of strength and power magical. From moist eyes a tear welled, then meandered slowly down Will's cheek. He swiped away a lonely tear with back of hand. Teary eyes glistened in early morning sun, broad smile lighting face, countenance displaying both relief and joy. "My knees are wobbly, Clancy," Will said softly.

"Aye', mine too …mine too, lad."

Pride and reverence coursed through Will's inner being. Most moving, Will eyed 'Stars and Stripes' flag rustling, glorious in gentle breeze. Will, Junior, and Clancy's first sighting in so long of their revered old flag …never more powerful. "Lads, never thought I'd live to see that flag flyin' again, that's for sure," Clancy exclaimed.

"It could not be more beautiful," Will added.

After identifying themselves upon reaching Union pickets, the five men were ushered through Union lines and directed to the tent of Major Newell of the 10th Michigan Cavalry, commandant of the post. Major Newell was awakened from routine morning nap, and informed by staff that captured Union soldiers were returning. He scrambled out of tent, set out applejack and ordered breakfast for hungry men.

Will and boys were now within Union lines, having reached this outpost on Friday morning, November 25th, 1864, the 52nd day since Will and Clancy's escape. Will was safe behind Union lines, though more than two hundred miles by rail from his beloved 22nd Michigan regiment …and five hundred miles from Oxford, Michigan. Will felt after a long walk he was almost home.

Epilogue

Will Hodkins and Maria are a young loving couple, simple rural folk striving to make ends meet on a small farm in Oxford, Michigan. Events of Civil War tear apart their lives. He responds reluctantly to peer pressure and patriotic zeal, 'volunteering' to become a foot-slogging down and dirty infantry private in Union army's '22nd Michigan Volunteer Infantry' regiment. He leaves young family behind to struggle …he and Maria willing to accept hardship and sacrifice for cause held higher than their own. Through his journal, and tender exchange of letters between two lovers, their story of sacrifice, hardship and emotion evolves. Will is torn constantly by sense of 'duty' to Union cause and fellow soldiers who bond like family, while feeling sense of betrayal of Maria and young family left behind.

Both Will and Maria utilize personal core values and strength of character, determination and tenacity, allowing them to succeed against great turmoil …values still relevant today. Theirs is a simple story comprising a single thread among many, all weaving a tapestry of great national sacrifice. Stories like Will and Maria's enthrall nearly one hundred fifty years after events happened.

Will Hodkins and Junior reached Union lines, and shipped back to rejoin their 22nd Michigan regiment, assisting General William Tecumseh Sherman in his drive to Atlanta and the sea. Rendezvousing with remnants of a decimated regiment, Will reunited with Papa and Nathan …Nathan successfully moved Papa from rear of Horseshoe Ridge where medical personnel tended Papa's wounds. Will learned that Lucius and Jeptha were not so fortunate, both sacrificing their lives in heroic charge down Horseshoe Ridge's slope.

Clancy returned eventually to blacksmith work in Pontiac.

Cousin Robert's role in Will and Clancy's escape went undetected. He helped rebuild his beloved city of Charleston. Over time, he built a successful mercantile business, only to see it destroyed by devastating earthquake of 1886 that shook the city ...Charleston lay in ruin once more.

In June 1865, Will and other soldiers of the 22nd Michigan mustered out of Federal army service. Will returned home to Michigan, finally reuniting with Maria and family ...nearly three years after leaving. Will and Maria went about putting lives back together. They resumed farming, eventually relocating to a small farm in northern Michigan, Isabella County, near rural town of Clare. Family grew to include seven children. After some years, Will could no longer perform farming chores, body finally giving out ...result of a foot soldier's life sleeping on ground with endless long marches, undernourishment, recuperation from two wounds, incarceration as prisoner of war, and escape before a long walk home through countryside and Blue Ridge mountains.

Will applied for Federal invalid's government pension as compensation for service and sacrifice. It took several years of petitioning and appeals before pension was granted ...eventually, Will received stipend of $8 per month for his troubles.

Maria Hodkins died in 1904. Heartbroken without her, Will died a year and one-half later on October 5th, 1905, at age 67 years.

Will and Maria Hodkins were among countless patriots serving our Republic ...men and women from both North and South. Great conflict 'fired' our country, like blacksmith's 'fire and anvil' ...forging a Republic much stronger ...one nation, indivisible ...a country Lincoln proclaimed "the last great hope of earth."

"Mine eyes have seen the glory of the coming of the Lord;
He is trampling out the vintage where the grapes of wrath
are stored;

Long Walk Home/James Funk

He hath loosed the fateful lightening of His terrible swift sword;
His truth is marching on.
Glory! Glory! Hallelujah! Glory! Glory! Hallelujah!
Glory! Glory! Hallelujah! His truth is marching on..."

§§§§§§§§§

Will ...in later years.

www.ingramcontent.com/pod-product-compliance
Lightning Source LLC
Chambersburg PA
CBHW020258030726
47499CB00001B/255